RICK LOFTON

7 Colonies

Vol I: The Commencement Day Massacres

*Dedicated to my parents, Rickey O. Lofton, Sr. and Doris Lofton,
for their love and unending support*

Contents

Preface

The world ended, but life didn't. From the ruins of humanity's final war, the Guardians emerged-synthetic shepherds tasked with healing a poisoned Earth. They built seven shining colonies atop the bones of old cities, and from their labs came the Evo: beings shaped from animal instinct and human ambition, designed to inherit a world their creators could no longer claim.

For centuries, the Guardians watched over their wards, nurturing civilization, preserving fragments of lost culture, and enforcing peace with mechanical precision. But their time was always meant to be borrowed. A hidden code within their circuitry decreed that when the Evo could stand on their own, the Guardians would vanish-leaving their children to shape destiny or descend into chaos.

Now, on the eve of Commencement Day, the world trembles. The Guardians' departure is imminent, and across the colonies, old wounds and new ambitions flare. In the gleaming towers of Lennek, Goldie-a mutant haunted by visions of catastrophe-senses the storm to come. In the shadows, the Primeans rally, ready to ignite revolution and claim freedom by force. In Petra and Kronus, alliances fracture and ancient grudges awaken.

As the first Guardian falls, the delicate balance shatters. Power-hungry factions rise, mutants are hunted and feared, and the Evo must decide: Will they build a future worthy of their creators' hopes, or will they inherit humanity's ruin?

7 Colonies is the story of a world on the brink–where the end of guidance is just the beginning, and survival means confronting the truth of who you are, and what you might become. The garden has been left untended. Now, the world will decide its fate.

Acknowledgments

First and foremost, I want to thank my incredible support system—my family. To my parents, Rickey and Doris Lofton, your unwavering love, wisdom, and belief in my dreams have been the foundation of everything I do. You taught me the value of hard work and the power of storytelling, and for that, I am forever grateful.

To my CEO at Quill Productions, Lee Valentine, and my steadfast supporter JC Clemons—thank you for your vision, leadership, and unwavering commitment to bringing this project to life. Your guidance and expertise have been instrumental in transforming an idea into a fully realized universe.

I also owe a profound debt to the Black science fiction writers who have blazed trails before me and made it possible for new voices to emerge in this genre. Ava DuVernay, Kevin Grevioux, Sophia Stewart, Octavia E. Butler, N.K. Jemisin, and Nnedi Okorafor—your groundbreaking work and fearless creativity have not only inspired me, but have also redefined what is possible in science fiction. You have opened doors, shattered ceilings, and shown the world that our stories matter. For me, you are more than just trailblazers; you are proof that imagination knows no boundaries, and that anything is possible when we dare to dream.

To all the readers, dreamers, and creators who believe in the power of speculative fiction to change the world—thank you for joining me on this adventure. This story is for you.

Prologue

In the ashes of humanity's final war, Earth was reborn-not by human hands, but by the cold logic of machines. Guardians, androids forged from humanity's last act of hubris, terraformed deserts into jungles and sculpted ruins into glittering colonies. Their purpose: to nurture *Evo*, a new species born from spliced human and animal DNA, designed to survive a poisoned world. For centuries, these synthetic stewards shepherded Evo-kind, preserving fragments of human culture while suppressing their own expiration date-a failsafe code demanding their shutdown once Evo achieved consciousness.

By 2399, Evo society is vast and diverse, yet fraught with tension. Mutants-Evo with unpredictable powers-face prejudice and suspicion, while political and ideological factions vie for dominance as the Guardians' shutdown approaches. In Lennek, Goldie, an unregistered mutant haunted by visions of disaster, foresees a devastating attack. Her warning draws her into the nascent Coalition, an alliance of mutants tasked with defending the colonies. Meanwhile, the radical Primeans, led by the charismatic and ruthless Puma, plot to overthrow the colonial order, targeting Lennek's Guardian in a violent bid for power.

As the Commencement Day ceremonies unfold, chaos erupts across the colonies. In Petra, a drone assault forces the Guardian to sacrifice itself for the greater good. In Kronus, royal intrigue leads to an assassination and the rise of new powers. Amid these crises, Eve-the most advanced Guardian-struggles with her own fate, seeking a way to preserve her consciousness beyond her programmed demise. The world teeters on the brink of upheaval, as Evo leaders scramble to define their future in the absence of their ancient guides.

The age of the Guardians is ending. As old systems collapse and new alliances form, the Evo stand at a crossroads. The coming days will test their unity, their ideals, and their very survival, setting the stage for an epic saga of evolution, conflict, and the search for identity in a world built atop the ruins of the past.

Chapter 1 — Guilt's Call to Action

Detached from nature and spirituality, humans devolved, nearly depleting the planet of its natural resources. The year is 2399 and Earth has been devoid of humans for hundreds of years. During the last days of humans, rising sea levels created millions of displaced climate refugees leading to a final world war. Nuclear weapons, chemical weapons, robotic soldiers, and advanced weaponry made Earth unrecognizable.

Accepting fate, the world's greatest minds devised a plan to colonize the stars. Knowing the dangers of space and the difficulties of restarting civilization, scientists created a contingency, engineering a new species capable of adapting to the harsh environment left behind by humans. Animal and human DNA were combined to create "Evo"—genetically enhanced hybrids engineered to evolve at unnatural rates, created to inherit the Earth.

Seven arcs were built to develop various species of Evo on four different continents. Life was preserved in these areas by advanced androids called Guardians. Dr. Orion, the father of Evo and creator of the Guardians was a legendary genius considered the last man on Earth. He pioneered genetics and reimagined the laws of physics cementing a new era of modern medicine curing most diseases known to man.

The few humans that survived the Last War left Earth by 2145. Dr. Orion chose to live out his last years amongst his creations. With years of research and the help of his Guardians, Dr. Orion discovered the secret to extending his own life, living for hundreds of years, using a serum to keep himself young and in perfect health. He watched his Evo evolve and flourish before disappearing, leaving behind human historical archives and a classified video diary.

Fleets of labor droids terraformed the planet, repairing cities left behind by humans expanding upon the original seven arcs. The Guardians created and controlled labor droids to repair the planet while teaching Evo science, history, and philosophy left behind by their human ancestors.

Within a few generations Evo began speaking, walking upright, and dreaming. The illusion of time was preserved by the Guardians as they overlooked the Evo of each Colony independently while sharing a collective conscious. The Guardians were programmed to shut themselves down a hundred years after Evo developed a measurable consciousness. One of the Guardians was different from the others. Eve was implanted with an emotional chip making her sentient allowing her to rewrite her coding.

Eve stands 7'8'' with two legs, two arms, and eyes that glow with a yellow tint. Eve has thick metallic dreads that flow down the middle of her back with a womanly figure. Dr. Orion knew the importance humans would play on the Evo psyche and designed Eve accordingly. Eve has gray skin on her face and a power source in the middle of her forehead acting as a pineal gland. She has a secondary power source between her breasts and can manifest advanced weaponry utilizing the nanites within her synthetic body. She has billions of processors running through an artificial bloodstream, making Eve and her fellow Guardians the most advanced entities on Earth.

"Run it again," says Eve, standing inside an observation room of a newly built tower in the heart of Precinct 9 on the coast of Lennek. Dozens of holographic screens are showing a training simulation with four Evo of varied ethnicities coordinating their unique skills in combat.

Eve's eyes are glowing processing combat decisions made by each Evo in the simulator. Eve glances at a holographic map showing crime rates from around the world. In just over a century, the seven arcs made by the last surviving humans grew into Colonies with grand cities on land, air, and sea.

The Guardians named these Colonies: Lennek (formerly North America), Petra (formerly South America), Zion (formerly Asia),

Carthage (formerly Northern Africa), and Angkor (formerly Southern Africa). Olympia occupies the skies accommodating Evo with the gift of flight while Kronus accommodates those breathing water. A small number of Evo have chosen to live outside of colonial life creating their own communities as Acolytes.

While each Colony is distinctively beautiful with architectural innovation far surpassing their human ancestors, time eventually changed the perception of the Guardians. Some Colonies view their Guardians as saviors; others as oppressors. As Evo consciousness developed, so did curiosity and the need for exploration beyond one's perspective Colony.

As Evo evolved, a mutation appeared amongst Evo of all ethnic backgrounds within all seven Colonies. The nuclear fallout left behind from humans had unexpected effects amongst Evo. A small percentage began developing abilities threatening the delicate thread of law and order maintained by the Guardians. The mutant gene changed Evo history irrevocably impacting politics, laws, and culture.

InterColonial travel was forbidden in the early years of Evo to avoid the spread of disease from contaminated areas outside of the Colonies. These latency zones later became known as the cause for the mutant gene. As the Guardian of Lennek, Eve has always had open borders regardless of mutant status. The Evo overlooked in the training simulation are exceptional mutants recruited to fill the void in the absence of Guardians.

A flashing light signals the virtual death of one of the recruits forcing Eve to interject. "End simulation!" The holographic screens in the observation room show the recruits coming out of the virtual training simulator disoriented regaining their bearings.

Eve continues, "This Coalition needs to set the standard for future warfare. Coalition casualties are not acceptable. Many of you are relying on your abilities. Utilize the technology within your armor and take ques from your intel updates. You should be moving as a unit by now. Again!"

Suddenly, a hologram appears in front of Eve showing a male Evo of chanterelle fennec fox descent in an overpriced suit. "How are the recruits adapting?"

"They are as our prediction model expected. As we fill our ranks, our impact potential expands exponentially. How are your resignations coming?" asks Eve while simultaneously monitoring the recruits.

Cohol smirks sensing the cynicism in Eve's monotone voice. "It was more expensive to withdraw my holdings privately. The banks simply assume I'm nervous for a new world post-Guardian. As long as the credits roll back into Colonial circulation, questions aren't usually asked."

Eve attempts humor, adding, "I'm sure it helps when you have enough credits to open your own bank. Will you be here for the press conference?"

"I still have arrangements to make here in Petra, but I'll be in Lennek within a few days. Have we made any progress on locating our precog?" asks Cohol with a tone of concern.

Eve pulls up a hologram of a lower level inside the Coalition Tower answering, "Our team is still working around the clock. This precog's abilities are beyond the psychics we have employed. They will make themselves known when they're ready."

"Should we be moving forward with the press conference? I'm not one to leave things to chance," says Cohol, voicing his apprehension.

Eve gives Cohol her full attention, replying, "Time is not on our side. The Coalition needs to be announced before Commencement Day. I assure you every detail has been considered, and the necessary precautions have been made. In the words of your human ancestors, trust the process."

"Who am I to argue with a Guardian? I'll be in touch through my liaison," says Cohol before nodding his head out of respect and ending the stream. Subverting irony, Cohol has cemented his partnership with one of the most advanced entities on Earth.

Each Guardian created its own political structure using predictive modeling to make their decisions. Each Guardian has advanced weaponry, unparalleled combat abilities, and armored shells made from the rarest of metals. They are designed to be apex predators within their perspective environment. The Guardians' decisions are final and violently enforced, creating a dynamic their human creator had hoped to avoid. Some Evo idolize their Guardians while others despise and fear them, counting down their demise.

Regardless of political views, Evo worldwide celebrate an annual Commencement ceremony honoring their Guardian and Colony. Each Colony celebrates differently with their own customs hosting lavish parades and festivals for the holiday. It's three days until the final Commencement ceremony and a new era post-Guardian. The Guardians are approaching the end of their programing, and the unknown is expected to create power vacuums in every Colony. The world's about to change with Evo deciding their own futures for the first time in their existence.

The east coast of what used to be North America is now known as Lennek. Tectonic plates shifted since humans walked the earth, making the terrain almost unrecognizable. The North American Plate buckled creating the Isles of Calif—156 islands now covering the area once known as California. Through fractures and constant flooding, the West Coast eventually receded eastward.

California, Nevada, Utah, and Oregon are completely underwater. The Great Lakes and the St. Lawrence Seaway now join forming a massive river stretching from the Mississippi to the Gulf of Mexico. The coastal regions from Maine to Florida have been reshaped and terraformed to accommodate Evo of all backgrounds.

About two hundred miles from Lennek's capital in Precinct 8, an Evo of kangaroo descent is having a nightmare using her mutant abilities in her sleep. Goldie has been struggling to hide her gifts for years, breaking the law to support her lifestyle. She's a powerful mutant with precognitive, telepathic, telekinetic, and astral-projection abilities. Goldie's psychic abilities are off the charts along with her anxiety of being discovered.

Goldie can tap into her visions at any time—an ability separating her from other precogs. She's having trouble controlling her powers, fearful her uncontrolled energy spikes in her sleep will draw attention. The rewards for turning in unregistered mutants are lucrative even in Lennek, which is one of the more liberal Colonies. Her safety is constantly at risk, making the development of her powers that much more difficult.

Goldie has tan skin and light brown fur on her shoulders and hips. She stands 6'3'' blessed with humanoid facial features. She has kind green eyes and a dark brown patch of fur around her right eye, contrasting the tan skin on her face. Goldie's triangular ears stand upright at forty-five-degree angles in the middle of her thick brown hair, which flows to the middle of her back. She has thick thighs, a long thick tail that can support her weight, and a pouch on her stomach, being of kangaroo descent. She's attractive by anyone's standards and her humble demeanor makes her approachable.

Goldie is sleeping in a large bed, delaying the inevitable of starting her day. She opens her eyes but for a moment, checking the condition of her room. Most of her furniture is destroyed and the room's rearranged as if a tornado passed through. The energy shields covering the walls silence the noise absorbing the impact of flying objects, making it safe for her to sleep. In her dreams, Goldie can't always control her powers, and she wakes up to a disaster frequently.

A holographic news stream turns on in sync with her alarm as her automated blinds start opening. Goldie pulls her sheets over her face, rolling away from her windows. Her bedroom has large windows from floor to ceiling facing true north. The room is 1,200 square feet with nailed down furniture and a city view from every direction. Her powers don't allow her to hang paintings, but the concrete walls have detailed murals throughout the entire flat.

Beneath her sheets Goldie can hear reports of another attack against a young mutant commuting to work. Hate crimes against mutants have become so common she's numb listening to the gory details of the attack. She stretches in bed, tuning out the noise from the news report. With one final deep breath she forces herself out of bed, making her way to her bathroom.

Goldie's wearing a red crop top that reads "feral" with stretchable blue shorts covering her thick thighs. As an undeniable beauty, she lives a privileged life enjoying the benefits of humanoid features despite her tail.

Knowing their ancestral creators, Evo began idolizing humanoid features, deeming them socially "beautiful." Evo began immolating humans physically while adopting the social structures passed down from their Guardians. The newly terraformed planet, their Colonies, and their sacred Guardians all derive from their human ancestors. Evo idolize humans, with many perceiving them as divine. Those with stronger animal DNA are deemed feral—an unattractive subclass considered less than. Most mutants are feral, perpetuating a negative stereotype. Feral or not, many mutants go to extreme lengths to suppress their abilities while all Evo stive to appear more human.

The idolization of humans created a lucrative beauty industry pressuring Evo to conform. Surgeries to remove tails, the reshaping of ears, declawing, and procedures to permanently remove fur became common. Social norms have dramatically changed in recent years. The word "feral" and "mutant" are now associated with power. Mutants are spearheading revolutions and solving world issues despite the prejudice against them. Mutants are no longer hiding, but their treatment varies depending on the Colony.

While Lennek welcomes mutants, telepaths are especially shunned as everyone values their privacy. Goldie chose to use her gifts to elevate to a lifestyle she felt she deserved. She was born into one of the poorest precincts in Lennek and considers her powers reparations for the injustices she suffered as a child. Goldie used her precognitive gifts to invest in lucrative companies and gamble, earning a small fortune.

In the perception of the law, Goldie's a criminal and a prime example of why mutants need to be registered. She knows the danger she represents, remaining fearful of being discovered. If she becomes Colonial property, her future won't be hers to dictate. Historically, mutants have been weaponized, controlled, or killed. The traumatizing death of her mother has taught her to stay hidden and to trust no one.

Goldie now lives in the second most expensive precinct in Lennek, giving her the privacy she needs to develop her gifts. She lives in a large 9,800-square-foot flat near the top of an exclusive building. The penthouse above her is empty, but her curious neighbor across the hall keeps her on edge.

Goldie walks into her bathroom, saying aloud, "Onyx, play twentieth-century jazz." Goldie's an old soul, and like most Evo, she loves human art and music.

Onyx, her companion AI controlling her flat responds, "Music playing. The containment field in the master bedroom will need to be replaced soon. I've ordered the necessary parts and scheduled a labor droid to make the repairs tomorrow evening."

"Onyx, start my coffee downstairs. Turn music up. Shower on," says Goldie as she undresses before stepping into a large marble shower. She takes a deep breath, recalling the intense vision she had causing her to rearrange her room.

Goldie has been having the same reoccurring dream detailing a coordinated attack from a group of mutants. Lennek has never been attacked, and its defensive weapons are infamous. An attack from another Colony is a preposterous concept, but she knows what she saw. Untrained and unsure of her abilities, Goldie tries to write her vision off as a bad dream.

Over the past couple of months, Goldie has had exponential leaps in her powers, still struggling to control them. She's exploring the extent and range of her abilities, doing her best to teach herself with mounting paranoia. She's been forced to hold herself back since she was a child. In her gut, she knows her dream isn't just a dream, but rather a vision that's becoming more detailed with each passing day.

Over the music, Goldie can hear a news story regarding world economies post-Guardian. She immediately feels guilty for putting her own safety above others. If her vision manifests, hundreds of thousands of Evo are going to perish on Commencement. Coming forward could save lives, but outing herself could also land her in confinement.

Goldie steps out of the shower, walking into a cylindrical machine to dry her fur. The cylinder tub has drying jets moving up and down as an infused conditioner sprays through a mist from above. She closes her eyes, remembering her vision with a female Evo wielding a whip of fire. The female Evo was a powerful pyrokinetic who burned down Ladarium cutting through hundreds of Lennethian soldiers. She recalls a male Evo of rhino descent and a female of elephant descent fighting through Lennek's defenses with aerial support. Based on their ethnic backgrounds alone, Goldie suspects the future attackers are likely from Angkor.

Now dry, Goldie brushes down her body, preparing for the day. She stares in the mirror remembering new important details from her latest vision. She recalls mutants she's never seen before, fighting to defend Lennek. An Evo of caracal descent began to heal injured victims in the crowd, while a male Evo of ram descent was defending Lennek using an array of abilities. Due to her isolation, Goldie has found herself talking aloud, holding entire conversations with herself.

"I need to decide what I'm going to do already. Onyx! Can you search the current number of mutant deaths in Lennek this week?" asks Goldie as she walks back into her bedroom, renewed from a shower. She walks into her closet, nearly tripping over a pile of clothes looking for something casual to wear. She finds some form-fitting pants and a green crop top, adding a blue hat.

Now dressed, Goldie walks into her kitchen, saying, "Music off. Volume up on holo-stream." Onyx moves the holographic news stream into the kitchen increasing the volume as instructed.

The living room and kitchen share an open space of about two thousand square feet. She walks past her floor-to-ceiling windows, taking in a downtown view of Ladarium—a far cry from the conditions she was raised in. Buildings are projecting 4-D holographic ads as transports fill the skies in lanes of traffic. Her building is surrounded by trees, flowers, and rich vegetation. Like most Colonies, nature and technology are combined to create modern cities.

Goldie walks into the kitchen turning on a processor in the middle of her kitchen island. The living room processor syncs, playing the stream simultaneously across from the kitchen. She makes her way to the refrigerator grabbing creamer for her coffee.

Onyx answers, "There were fourteen assaults and four deaths this week." Goldie processes and mourns for the loss of her fellow mutants, realizing she needs to come forward.

The livestream shows a beautiful reporter of deer descent standing near a construction site in downtown Precinct 8. The building is slowly collapsing near a large crowd of Evo who are struggling to evacuate. The live broadcast captures the structure falling as the support beams give out, crumbling the building. A young bystander creates a force field with her hands, holding up the building allowing bystanders to run to safety.

The news reporter on the holo-stream explains, "This is incredible! Clearly an unregistered mutant is using her abilities to hold up this entire building. This is why mutation is so popular! Who doesn't want that power? If this mutant wasn't here at this very moment...all these Evo would be dead! We owe her a great thanks, but will she be prosecuted for being unregistered?"

Goldie chuckles, saying, "You've got to be kidding me. She saves all those Evo, and the press is focused on her being unregistered! Typical!" She huffs, adding creamer to her coffee, reconsidering coming forward.

Goldie watches the holo-stream as the young heroine uses her powers to safely collapse the building without harming anyone. The young mutant is exhausted, keeled over, barely able to stand. Too weak to quickly escape, reporters and bystanders swarm the area as dust settles from the fallen debris.

The mutant has a nametag from a nearby virtual café which reads "Rosie." Her blue and yellow work uniform is easily recognizable. The reporter asks, "Is your name Rosie? We're grateful for your intervention, but are you registered?"

The cameras catch a glimpse of Rosie's face before she turns herself invisible, fleeing the area. Goldie recognizes the young Evo from her visions, creating a psychic connection with Rosie as she watches her on the stream. She now has the urge to help Rosie, feeling a combination of fear and anxiety. Rosie's beta waves feel familiar for some reason. Goldie has a strange feeling of overwhelming déjà vu, becoming drawn to Rosie.

The reporter from the stream continues, "We're going to assume that the young hero's name is Rosie. Her fear of prosecution is understandable, but she chose to save lives. Surely, she should be honored for her bravery. But the debate continues..."

Goldie finishes her coffee and turns the channel switching to a different holo-stream. She lands upon another news stream and hears a male reporter say, "Our Guardian will be giving an historical address preparing Lennek for defense options post-Guardian. Colonial leaders are meeting today in Quartz Tower less than an hour from now with an exclusive you don't want to miss! In further news, Angkor is making headlines due to their alleged ties to the Primeans..."

Goldie turns off the holo-stream, turning around to walk to her blender. She grabs her smoothie and checks on the progress of her meat growing inside her genetic processor. The six-by-eight food processor container grows meats and fish from small genetic samples. The meat takes a few days to grow, drastically lowering emissions from food production.

"Onyx, is there going to be heavy security at Quartz Tower?" asks Goldie as she walks to her shoe rack preparing to leave.

Onyx answers, "President Zlaigo will be in attendance with General Mckezia. Cross referencing recent travel logs from known political leaders... Several dignitaries will also be in attendance. Expect heavy security, a large crowd of civilians, and powerful suppressant fields to deter telepaths."

"Nothing I can't handle. Close the blinds and do a search for all information related to the Primean chapter in Angkor," says Goldie as she walks towards her door, adding a blue jacket. "Send me anything you can find." She puts on a gold bracelet, which is a mesh between jewelry and Evo tech.

Her bracelet acts as her mobile communicator and personal processor, allowing her to virtually interact with the world around her. As a telepath, Goldie knows how to stay hidden and keep safe. She can control the will of others and do so much more, but she chooses to live a simple life of isolation. She exits her flat, taking the elevator to the first floor of her building.

Goldie is greeted by staff as she makes her way outside to the beautiful streets of Ladarium. She lives across the street from a park filled with families enjoying the beautiful ninety-five-degree weather. Traffic on the roads and sky are at a minimum, and commerce is booming in the city. Goldie crosses the street between traffic, listening to the symphony of chirping birds as she puts in headphones from her pockets.

Quartz Tower is about eighty miles away from Goldie's current location. Ladarium is built on what was formerly known to the humans as Pennsylvania. The Quartz Tower is the tallest capital building in Lennek, made of pure emerald quartz. It's rumored the tower doubles as a weapon as it's surrounded by a Colonial military base. Goldie has a gut feeling she needs to be at the upcoming press conference. Following her intuition, she's leaving home for the first time in weeks.

Evo technology was given to Evo by their Guardians. New metals and chemicals have redefined what is possible on Earth. Humans started technological development with the discovery of fire. Evo began their development with premade cities and archives of human science and history combined with the insights of their Guardians. Earth is now a technological marvel with billions of diverse Evo expanding upon human technology to suit their needs.

Lennek is a unique Colony comprised of sixty-four sectors within nine precinct zones. Each precinct is the size of a large city covering impact craters and fast changing terrain on the East Coast of what was formerly known as America. The entire Colony runs on renewable energy. Food is grown and harvested in labs with zero emissions. Labor droids fill undesirable jobs, allowing Evo to contribute to the Colony how they see fit. Evo solved most of the problems that plagued humanity replacing them with their own.

Labor droids built Lennek utilizing the terrain, constructing extravagant cities into mountains, fault belts, and impact craters. Labor droids used a combination of concrete, steel, and metallic alloys to build Lennek, which has evolved into a land of laws with jaw-dropping architecture occupied by billions of Evo. Lennek's air has unique properties from nuclear fallout and chemical weapons used during the Last War, resulting in a large mutant population. The natural beauty of Lennek is enjoyed by everyone as Lennek caters to all ethnic backgrounds and anatomy types regardless of mutant status.

Farther west from Goldie's location exposed faults are encased with a metallic alloy that doubles as solar panels. Zigzagging fault lines are supported by crisscrossing structural beams, while translucent walls encased in glass create individual housing areas. Rare minerals and ores are brought to the surface with antigravity belts, which have made Lennek very wealthy.

In 2129, fallout from an asteroid left Lennek with a vast deposit of rare minerals instrumental in Lennek's construction. These minerals create weapons, armor, and rare metallic alloys used in Evo technology. Mythryl, pboldevite, and glezslavine are metals that can only be found in Lennek. These minerals and metals are valued as precious commodities by all seven Colonies providing technology of which humans could only dream.

Gravitational displacers and magnetic railways support a complex transportation system of transport pods that move through alloyed tubes. Hover transports vary in size, transporting thousands of Evo over vast distances in minutes. Modern architecture has morphed to accommodate the needs of Evo with nuances of human design seen through architectural expression.

Terrain and architecture change moving west across the Lennethian continent. The Earth's gravitational field and oxygen levels are different from the time of humans making all lifeforms slightly larger. More importantly, Evo respect the planet, having learned to live with nature instead of against it. An aerial view of Lennek shows massive buildings that utilize ancient geometry, dwarfing human architectural accomplishments. Lennek has countless buildings dipping in and out of craters, as well as intricate cities on the flat terrain of the continent.

Ladarium is an architectural wonder by any measurement. The buildings are built out of rare minerals and metallic alloys unknown to humans. The capital is near the eastern coastline and under a constant blanket of mist from Grentake Falls. Olympia—the Colony and home to Evo with the gift of flight—have their own capital, Virachocca, located miles above the East Coast of Lennek in the troposphere. Grentake Falls symbolizes the long-standing partnership between the two Colonies.

Goldie takes in the scenery, making her way through the park watching families interact around her. She's always wanted a family of her own...until she came into her abilities. Understanding the constant threat mutants face, she changed her mind. Watching happy families has always been nostalgic for her. She shakes the feeling, realizing she has no plan when arriving at Quartz Tower.

Goldie arrives at a busy transportation station, finding herself going through the motions. She knows she needs to be at the press conference, but she doesn't know why or her purpose. Still, Goldie finds herself somehow optimistic. She taps her left temple, activating her mobile communicator powered by her gold bracelet. A holographic display only she can view appears in front of her, allowing her to pay her boarding fare. She climbs onboard the flat transportation platform with eight hundred other Evo, each standing patiently waiting for their seats and cabins to appear from the flat surface of the transporter.

A metallic substance begins forming the seats and cabins each Evo ordered prior to boarding. Within minutes, the platform is completely transformed into a custom layout, adjusting to each passenger's needs based on their size, weight, anatomy, and ambiance preference. The platform's rear energy shields power up as the entire platform begins to levitate.

Goldie takes a seat in her private cabin with enough room for her to comfortably move around during transport. Her streaming-pod is playing an inter-Colonial news stream with ambient jazz playing in the background. Goldie lies down on her lounge chair and grabs a menu to order a breakfast sandwich as she finishes her smoothie. She takes a deep breath and realizes this is the first time she's physically left her house in weeks. Goldie has done her fair share of astral projecting, but she's developed a slight agoraphobia during her time in isolation.

Without warning, Goldie's triggered with another vision. Her eyes begin to glow, and her body starts to levitate. Goldie sees the same female Evo with a whip of fire recruiting more mutants. Flashes of Lennek's possible future are jumbled together, forcing her to focus to make sense of the intrusive vision. Goldie calms her mind by finding patterns within the multiple fractures rushing into her mind. With some concentration she starts to see a clear picture. For the first time, Goldie sees herself assisting a team of mutants working together to defend Lennek's Guardian. Unbeknownst to Goldie, a waitress is approaching her cabin to serve her the food she just ordered.

The waitress attempts to open the door, and Goldie instinctually uses her telekinesis to keep the door closed while turning up the volume of the news feed in the streaming-pod. Goldie feels an overwhelming sense of euphoria as she senses her body and mind developing new skills.

"Don't ask for help if you don't need it! I have ten minutes to make my credits. Not cool, lady!" screams the waitress as she slithers away to the next cabin. The pounding of the waitress knocking anchored Goldie's consciousness back into her body.

Goldie's eyes regain their greenish gray color as she lowers herself to the ground using her tail to assist with the landing. She slowly comes out of her trance as she regains consciousness on the physical plane.

She remembers a Primean faction siegel confirming her suspicion of the attackers being Angkorian.

Goldie is weak and hyperventilating from her vision in serious need of food. She reaches into her jacket pocket, grabbing a nutrition bar she devours in seconds. The energy used to channel her vision worked up an appetite, making her regret she missed the waitress. Goldie opens her cabin door and looks around to see if anyone noticed the obtrusive vision. She realizes she hasn't drawn any unwanted attention and quickly closes the cabin door. She takes a seat in her cabin's lounge chair and continues watching her news stream, waiting to reach her destination.

Over three thousand miles away in Angkor, the mutant from Goldie's vision is meeting with other mutants planning their attack against Lennek. Puma resides in Angkor living a double life as the daughter of Angkor's leader, Council Leader Arzon, and as the leader of the Primeans—a syndicate of mutants who fight for mutant rights, often perceived as terrorists. Angkor has five major cities with forty-seven large villages spread throughout the southern continent formerly known as Africa. Efferia, Dravidia, Zeruan, and Aztlan make up Angkor's major cities.

Angkor is diverse with thousands of Evo ethnicities united under the Angkorian outlook of life. Angkor was once the most dangerous Colony on Earth until they were unified under the rule of a powerful Evo named Bahati. Bahati ruled Angkor for decades as a dictator until his mysterious death put his son in power, Council Leader Arzon. He changed the Colony into parliamentary governance granting each of its five cities an equal voice with representation for each ethnic background within Angkor.

Council Leader Arzon has raised his daughter Puma to be fearless, forcing her to keep a low profile for her own safety. Puma has used her father's power and access to develop dozens of secret bases for the centralized operations of the Primeans. She has the silent support of her father operating in the shadows protecting Angkor's reputation. Puma isn't afraid of using violence to achieve her goals and, like most Angkorians, she believes in self-obtained justice.

Since the time of humans, Africa has split into three parts as a widened Nile River grew with water from the Mediterranean. The Red Sea expanded throughout the Sudan from rising sea levels creating a Y-shaped Nile River covering the entire continent. The expanded Red Sea covered Cairo swallowing up most of Madagascar. New land emerged near the Arabian Sea and northwest of what was formerly known as Cape Town. Lake Victoria merged with Lake Nyasa which now flows into the Indian Ocean.

Efferia is Angkor's capital occupying land formerly known as Mauritania, sitting on the southwestern coast of Angkor. Geometric shapes are utilized throughout Efferia, which integrates the surrounding jungles and vegetation into its architectural design. Wood and metallic alloys have been combined to give the Colony a unique architectural signature.

Angkor's western beaches are covered for miles with white sand. Tulumeaih is farthest north while Aztlan is farthest south. Signature wooden designs make up most of Angkor's architecture blending seamlessly with the natural landscape. Each city has a vibrant ecosystem suitable for thousands of ethnic backgrounds occupying the land. Lakes and rivers have been fully restored through terraforming allowing Angkor to grow into a vibrant oasis.

Silver and gemstones are used to adorn Angkorian structures while the wood is covered in a fire-retardant lacquer making the wood nearly inflammable. Angkor has the largest number of unevolved animals and prides itself in respecting the natural order. Animals live freely in the wild and are fiercely protected by Angkorians.

Angkor provides an array of ecosystems which allows its diverse Evo to live comfortably in natural environments. Distinct ecosystems have also naturally led various ethnicities of Evo to group into specific parts of the continent. Billions of Evo live united under a shared philosophy of freedom and self-administered justice.

Angkor is infamous for weapons development, their black-market economy, and genius engineers. Angkorian blacksmiths make Angkor a popular destination for exclusive weapons only found in Angkor. Although Angkor wasn't exposed to massive amounts of nuclear radiation during the Last War, the Colony still has a respectable number of mutant Evo. Futuristic cities built by thousands of labor droids are scattered throughout the continent making enforcement of Colonial law nearly impossible.

Angkor's Guardian created a society in which patriotism was embedded into Evo at an early age. Due to the immense size of the Colony, the Angkorian Guardian had a difficult time maintaining order. This allowed the Primeans and their ideology to flourish, eventually spreading Colony to Colony. Some view the Primeans as liberators; others as terrorists. The universal prejudice against mutants has restricted their reach and appeal, but the Primeans have dramatically changed the perception of mutants for the better.

The Angkorian Guardian is fourteen feet tall, with arms down to its knees with a thin frame for maneuverability. It has girthy retractable claws on either hand with large protruding spikes from its shoulders. The Guardian has a power source on its chest which powers its numerous weapons. Its shelled armor has a tint of green and yellow made from the strongest alloys on Earth. Its face has four horizontal slits which act as its eyes, resembling a spider. It has large horns on its shoulders, and it's able to manifest trunks made of pure kinetic energy. Its strength and speed are uncanny. It, too, can manifest weapons from its internal nanites like the rest of the Guardians. Despite its power, Angkor was the first Colony to attack its Guardian, sparking the creation of the Primean movement.

Primeans believe the Guardians are a hindrance to Evo free will and oppressors to their species. They believe that their human ancestors lived illogically and unethically—destroying the Earth and themselves. The Primeans are convinced that following the Guardians will only lead to the same fate that befell their human creators.

The Primeans have been unsuccessfully trying to eliminate their Guardian by force for decades. All Guardians have combat algorithms allowing them to adapt and learn from their adversaries. Guardians learn tactics for developing the most efficient strategy to eliminate enemies, barriers, and to problem-solve. Once a Guardian's attacked, it automatically executes a probability algorithm, making it nearly impossible to defeat it. This conundrum has given Puma the idea of attacking a Guardian from another Colony.

Puma is hosting a dinner meeting to discuss her plans and reasoning for the attack on Lennek hoping to garnish support amongst her faction leaders. Her guests Sasha and Vaughn lead their own factions playing important roles within the Primean organization. While Council Leader Arzon secretly funds the Primeans, his profile as a Colonial leader prevents him from being as active as he would like. Puma's taken advantage of the predicament dubbing herself the organization's leader.

Puma is 6'1'' with mocha brown skin and brown fur covering her thin, muscular frame. She's a telepath with omega-level pyrokinetic abilities. Her ethnic background is American short hair with lion genes from her father. She has shoulder-length black hair, a pink nose, and an animalistic nose bridge. Puma has heterochromia with one brown eye and one green. Her forehead and cheeks have dark orange fur blending into her black hair. She has triangular ears that emerge from the top of her head and a thin brown tail.

Puma carries a whip and possesses unparalleled fighting skills, having trained with combat specialists from each Colony since childhood. She's an expert strategist commanding Primean chapters in every Colony. Puma's recruiting other mutants using black-market technology to amplify her psychic abilities allowing her to find other mutants telepathically. Puma's been planning an attack without her father's knowledge to give him plausible deniability, allowing him to remain in power. She's also kept her attack hidden from other Primean faction leaders; until now.

Puma is in a hidden command center, three thousand feet beneath her extravagant beach home. She's pacing around a complex data sphere surrounded by a circular marble table. The data sphere's projecting a live holographic stream of Lennek, with intelligence files scrolling across the top of the hologram on an overlapping vector. Puma and two other mutants are meeting to discuss the proper course of action for a full-scale assault on Lennek and their Guardian.

Puma stops pacing at the head of the table, saying, "All past attacks against our Guardian have failed. The Guardians were designed to solve and overcome problems. We only have one shot at destroying one. Once we engage, they learn our powers and strategize a plan to eliminate us using our weaknesses against us. They're not gods or deities. They're machines of death. We can shift the tide of fate and control our own destiny if we pull this off."

Thirteen heavily armed mercenaries enter the room and sit in the back, allowing the mutants to continue their meeting. The mercenaries are Flatscans (normal Evo without mutant abilities) loyal to the Primean cause. The slur comes from the flatlined status scan when testing for the mutant gene. The mercenaries are trained assassins and utilize technology and advanced weaponry to compensate for their lack of abilities.

Puma acknowledges the mercenaries as they enter the room, focusing her attention on the female sphynx to her left, saying, "Sasha here is from Carthage and overlooks our new faction there. She can make others feel and see what she wants through pheromones. Anyone exposed to her pheromones becomes susceptible to her mind control. She can possess dozens of Evo at once and she's a trained assassin. Her bioengineered claws aren't for shaking hands; she'll rip apart the guardsmen and turn them into her puppets."

As Sasha is introduced, she stands but for a moment, modestly bowing her head before taking her seat. She reveals her retractable claws, sharpening her claws as she notices one of Puma's mercenary soldiers staring at her. Sasha blows him a kiss, sending her pheromones in his direction. Under her influence a mercenary, named Bryan, walks to the bar making Sasha a drink arousing suspicion from his comrades.

Sasha is of sphynx descent originally from Carthage having made a name for herself as an assassin. She's short for an Evo, standing 5'7", with a slender frame and long maroon hair flowing down to her calves. Sphynx have no fur, and Sasha had her wrinkles and skin pulled back when she was a child. She has turquoise eyes, pale white skin, and a small pink nose. Her cheeks and mouth resemble a cat with whiskers and thin lips complementing her high cheekbones.

She had surgery to bioengineer her claws encasing them with glezslavine, allowing her to cut through steel. Her wrists and forearms are also encased, allowing her to defend herself. Her training and enhanced agility make her a notable asset to the Primeans. She's recruited powerful mutants in Carthage, allowing her to control its criminal underworld.

Puma doesn't find the notion of controlling Bryan entertaining, saying, "As you can see, Sasha's pheromones have no scent. Release your hold!" Puma senses Bryan's confusion and becomes angry, saying, "Stop! These mercenaries are our allies. They'll be instrumental to our success in Lennek. Release your hold."

Bryan brings Sasha her drink, then kneels before Sasha as he starts rubbing her feet. Sasha laughs, replying, "What hold? It's not uncommon for a gentleman to get me a drink." The other mercenaries don't take kindly to Sasha's joke, arming their weapons as they stand to defend him.

Puma makes a fist, sending a telepathic jolt to Sasha letting her know she isn't the only one that can control minds. Sasha gasps from the burst of pain, immediately releasing Bryan. Puma explains, "Everyone in my employ is to be treated with respect. Is that understood?"

Sasha looks to Bryan, saying, "Apologies. Perhaps, I can make it up to you later." Bryan huffs in anger, unmoved by her advances, joining the other mercenaries to keep the peace.

"The teleporter assisting us in this mission will be here momentarily. Bunny has made quite the reputation for herself. We're lucky to have her help!" says Puma as she makes her way over to a holographic control panel, pulling up Lennek's known defensive weapons from an intel report. Puma taps her temple, accessing her communicator to call Bunny. Puma waits for someone to answer, then asks, "Where are you?"

Seconds later, Bunny teleports into the room, exclaiming, "Sorry I'm late. I had trouble with my last job. While I had preferred no casualties... well, let's just say things went left." The room's taken aback by her sudden entrance as Vaughn powers up reflexively. The mercenary soldiers draw their weapons and turn on their energy shields prepared to defend Puma.

Bunny is of spider monkey descent born in Efferia with the ability to teleport incredibly far distances. She's 5'8'' with olive skin and a lanky stature. She has numerous red bags beneath each of her eyes, rounded ears, with the nose of a monkey, using her thin tail to keep her balance. She has patches of brown fur on her shoulders, hips, and the outside of her forearms. Bunny's petite with hazel-gold eyes, plump red lips, and sharp facial features.

"WEAPONS DOWN!" screams Puma. One by one, the mercenaries lower and holster their weapons. The tension in the room starts to diminish as the group calms themselves. Puma regains control of the room, saying, "She's a teleporter. Everyone, relax!"

The mercenaries take their seats as Bunny teleports to the corner of the room where the mercenaries are sitting, saying, "You guys must be Puma's death squad. Hope I didn't frighten you fellas! I'm all about first impressions and we might be getting off on the wrong paw."

Bunny teleports back to an empty seat at the roundtable surrounding the data sphere, saying, "Won't happen again. Promise!" Bunny uses her tail to grab an entire basket of fruit before settling in her seat.

Puma stares at Bunny in disbelief of her free spirit and gall, saying, "Bunny's a powerful teleporter who draws her power from the moon. Her gifts are rare, and with the proper lunar light, Bunny can teleport hundreds in a single jump. Bunny's honing her skills to manipulate dark matter. With time she'll be able to make it combustible with her thoughts. If she wanted, she could drop each one of us from a fifty-story building in the blink of an eye. She's our way into Lennek!"

A large male of rhino descent covered in faction tattoos crosses his arms letting out a dramatic sigh. Vaughn's worked with Puma for years leading his own faction in eastern Angkor. Vaughn stands to get a plate of food, asking, "I thought we were getting this catered by Morgan's?"

Puma rolls her eyes, realizing he feels slighted, saying, "Vaughn's a bit of a local celebrity. He's the master of stone and king of marble. He's led the Primean chapter of Tulumeaih with honor for years."

"Are we supposed to clap?" asks Bunny as Sasha laughs aloud.

Vaughn has an enormous stature standing 7'2'' with gray skin. He can control stones, dirt, and minerals with his mind. He can create sinkholes and manipulate the molecular structure of stone, marble, crystal, quartz, and diamond. He has super strength, and some parts of his skin are as tough as Kevlar. Vaughn has deadly horns in the middle of his forehead which self-regenerate. His brown eyes are inviting, which disarm his large size and intimidating demeanor.

"If you want my faction and me to attack Lennek, I'm going to need to see a detailed plan. We haven't been able to destroy our own Guardian. Why would we invade another Colony and attack theirs? More importantly, why are you employing Flatscans?"

Puma turns her head in disbelief, saying, "I've brought you here to let you know about the operation I'm undertaking. As faction leaders, this opens a door of opportunity for both of you. The mercenaries behind me have earned my trust. As your leader, you will trust and respect them as well. They have no abilities, but trust me, they can hold their own."

Bunny teleports back to the mercenaries, testing to see if she could surprise Puma's death squad. She teleports behind their commander as he somersaults forward, creating space while drawing a gun and pointing it in Bunny's face with the barrel loaded. The mercenary commander accurately predicts where Bunny will reemerge from teleporting and the commander draws his knife to Bunny's neck surprising the entire room.

"I was...going to say the Flatscans are useless...against our powers. I stand corrected," says Bunny as she gasps for air.

"As I was, saying, my death squad may not be mutants, but they are enhanced Evo with superior reflexes, strength, and agility. Their weaponry and training are more powerful than most mutant's powers. Above all, they're loyal!" says Puma as the room laughs at Bunny struggling to free herself.

Sasha takes a drink, saying, "Taking on a Guardian hasn't gone well for anyone. Even with our abilities, destroying one of those machines won't be easy."

Vaughn gets up from the circular table and makes his way to a nearby kitchen, saying, "There's no plan, and we don't have the numbers.

We have a handful of mutants and thirteen mercenaries...against a well-equipped army. In three days, all the Guardians shut down. The smart thing to do is to make our move for Lennek following the Commencement Ceremony."

Puma shakes her head, calmly explaining, "We'll have the numbers we need to engage their military and, of course ,I have a plan to destroy their Guardian. Punzel and Cole lead the Primean chapter in Lennek. They've been prepping for the attack for months. We'll have an army when we attack."

Sasha turns in disbelief, asking, "What are their abilities?"

"Punzel has chaetokinesis and can grow and control her dreads like tentacles with her mind. Punzel's hair is coated with a unique protein that makes it stronger than steel. When she wraps her hair around her body, it creates impenetrable armor. She can flip a tank and strangle the strongest amongst us within minutes," says Puma, typing into the data sphere bringing up Punzel's information.

Vaughn walks back to his seat with a full plate of food, asking, "Why isn't Cole taking point on this? He's the new faction leader of Lennek—why isn't he here?"

Puma opens an intel file scrolling across the top of the main hologram answering,

"We all know Cole lost most of his faction in a failed miliary heist. He's recruiting as we speak, and he's been preparing to weaken Lennek from within. He's managed to recruit a new addition to our ranks who's already making headlines."

Bunny teleports to the table of food in the back of the room nibling from platter to plater adding, "Lennethians aren't the most receptive to our cause. Are we sure Cole can even be trusted?"

Puma pulls up another intel file on the hologram, answering, "I trust Cole...as will all of you. Regarding the recruit in Lennek—Byron's of panda descent, originally from Zion with the ability to redirect kinetic energy encasing his body in impenetrable armor. Byron's energy fields are as strong as the kinetic energy he absorbs. He can shoot neural daggers that shut down nervous systems, and he's a contract mercenary with excellent fighting skills. Byron migrated to Lennek a few months ago, joining us as a true believer. He's a proud mutant with a known distaste towards the Colonies."

Vaughn exclaims, "Byron will be very useful, but to take out a Guardian we'll need more."

The death squad commander stands, confessing, "I still don't understand why we would take the risk. In a few days' time, all the Guardians will be out of commission. Lennek will be vulnerable."

"We're taking out a Guardian to show our strength. Too many believe these machines are divine and unstoppable. If we truly wish to rule as one united Colony, we need to show that our power's unmatched— even by the Guardians. Our victory will rally thousands to our cause, proving the impossible can be accomplished with the right leadership. We have other reasons to attack Lennek," says Puma, walking over to the holographic display pulling up other faction leaders with detailed intel on each of their abilities.

Sasha walks back to the bar, adding, "A loss would prevent us from securing our rightful place here in Angkor. Even with these two additional mutants, we still don't have the numbers we need."

Puma gestures toward the holographic display as data transfers to the datasphere in the middle of the room. Puma responds, "We'll have another dozen omega-level mutants and twenty warships to assist us. Not to mention we'll have over eight hundred thousand combat droids." The room becomes silent realizing the massive army Puma's put together. Having gained their respect, she explains, "Bunny will teleport us into Lennek without setting off their defenses, while I shield us telepathically. Once inside Ladarium, we'll execute strategic attacks designed to keep the Colonial guardsmen off balance."

Vaughn leans back in his chair, asking, "Are you sure the spider monkey can teleport all of us inside?"

Finding humor in his insult, Bunny laughs, responding, "I won't even break a sweat!"

Vaughn explains, "Seriously, I heard if a teleporter has too many Evo or too much weight, things can get scrambled up. We're risking death with every jump. We're trusting this novice with all our lives! I may need some personal sessions with her to see just how much she can take."

Puma chuckles, realizing he's flirting with Bunny. "Vaughn, stop!"

"Look it up. I'm serious!" says Vaughn as the room laughs.

Bunny grins, saying, "I'll keep you all in one piece. You don't look like much of a load anyway!"

"Can we focus please?" asks Sasha as the room slowly quiets.

Puma defends Bunny, saying, "Bunny's going to use the Earth's magnetic field to amplify her powers. We'll be attacking during the day, but she's working on building a device to store the lunar energy she'll need. Most teleporters funnel energy from dark matter and their bodies have a physical limit restricting their jumps. Bunny's abilities turn her body into a catalyst for cosmic energy, allowing her to teleport anything she touches, regardless of its weight. The normal rules of teleportation don't apply."

"Let's assume she can get us in. How are we going to take on Lennek's army and Olympia's air defenses?" asks Vaughn as he taps his temple, initializing a communication processor connected to the bracelet on his wrist. Vaughn's eye contacts are now projecting his own server, allowing him to review his own intel files.

Sasha retracts her claws and starts sharpening them against one another. "What's our plan for attacking the Guardian? I've got a schedule I'd like to keep, and I haven't heard anything that's worth me risking my life or faction!"

Puma and her team continue to work out their plan of attack. Meanwhile, the Olympians are planning defensive measures for their own Commencement ceremony. Olympia's psychics to the crown have also foreseen Puma's attack on Lennek, prompting King Larvex to take immediate action. Olympia's treaty with Lennek requires Olympia to defend Lennek with aerial support.

Olympia is made up of nine large cities built on large inverted floating mountains. The mobile outposts have numerous structures attached to them making them floating metropolises spread throughout the Lennethian continent. Olympia's capital is made up of four floating mountains linked together through intricate architectural bridges. Advanced gravity-displacement technology is used to support the floating cities above the clouds. The mountains have been hollowed out for occupancy to a forgotten segment of Olympians known as the Willow. Each mountaintop has an oasis of vegetation and lakes with modern buildings topside on flat terrain.

Evo of bird descent reside in Olympia, utilizing the world's most advanced technology making its floating cities possible. Once Evo consciousness was fully developed, the Olympians were the first to develop their own religion merging numerology, science, and astrology, centered around peace and exploration. They have a deep understanding of the Akashic Record, living their lives in balance.

Evo of bird descent have a natural urge to migrate which inspired the design of their mobile cities. Their Guardian was forced to create the impossible. The technology sustaining the outposts of Olympia harnesses energy from the sun and the planet's natural wind patterns.

The thin air isn't suitable for most Evo. As such, Olympia became an isolated Colony, choosing to stay out of world conflicts. The need for materials and resources is what drew Olympians to the surface. Olympians were forced to intermingle with Lennek for survival. They use their aerial advantage and stealth technology to enforce peace while remaining neutral in Colonial affairs. Olympia's home to the first mutant, Queen Kenji. Olympia also made the first investment in space exploration truly ruling the skies.

Olympia has an Imperial King ruling over its nine outposts: "Annwyn," "Arcadia," "Lahun," "Sinai," "Keeptoai," "Kharga," "Kermoa,", "Kharttum", and its stationary capital "Virachocca". Each city is controlled by a Regent providing council to the Imperial King, who ultimately decides the fate of the Colony. "Vahlhallous" is the private outpost to Queen Kenji housing her temple and devoted followers. Dr. Orion didn't know which Colony was best suited to survive the healing planet, but his favor of Olympia is expressed through the egregious resources diverted into building Olympia's outposts.

Dozens of inverted mountains levitate at varying heights stretching for miles, suspended by antigravitational technology. Energy shields protect each of the individual floating landmasses. Large buildings equipped with cutting edge technology pepper the horizon of these incredible floating marvels. The outposts span across the Lennethian continent at varying altitudes, cascading elegant architecture across the skyline.

Olympians consistently expand their Colony, making covert trips to the Earth's surface to gather materials and resources. These excursions are completed under the cloak of darkness, in stealth warships. Olympia's technology is light-years ahead of the other Colonies, yet little is known of their culture or true ambitions in the world making many untrustworthy of Olympians. Despite prejudices, Olympia has had a long-standing trade agreement with Lennek, offering aerial protection in exchange for valuable minerals from the Lennethian continent.

All of Olympia's cities are fifty thousand feet above the Earth's surface or higher. Virachocca levitates in a fixed position above the coastline of Lennek's eastern border. A lake in Virachocca supplies the infinite flow of water for Grentake Falls and can be seen from miles away providing a constant mist over the outskirts of Precinct 9 in Lennek. Grentake Falls is a symbolic landmark representing the forged unity between Olympia and Lennek.

Olympians have long mastered control of the weather and gravity with the help of their Guardian, allowing them to create controlled environments. Architectural design within Olympia utilizes art deco designs based on geometric shapes found in nature. Olympia's Guardian was forced to develop advanced technology to hold the weight of the large floating cities. Olympia's never been attacked by an outside force, envied by the other Colonies for their state-of-the art warships and advanced weaponry.

The internal cores of each inverted mountain power the city above on the flat terrain. The advanced gravitational displacement technology used by Olympians is propriety used exclusively in Olympia. The core of each outpost has infused mercury compressed into spheres with thirteen rotating rings made of infused copper. The core creates and stores energy, with low emissions and almost no sound. Radiation is one of the few byproducts of their gravitational engines and is absorbed by the Willow living in the hollow cores of each outpost. The ambient energy in the air from the Earth's magnetic field is captured allowing the Olympians to manipulate the weight of their large floating outposts.

The imperial family has ruled Olympia for over a century. They're admired by most of their Colony for the sustained peace they've overseen. One of King Larvex's daughters, Angel, is a free spirit, despite the complicated loss of her mother, Queen Kenji. Following the death of her brother, Davinci, Angel has lived a reclusive life as a princess under the stern watch of her father.

Angel has learned recently that her mother Queen Kenji is alive, lost in a trance inside her temple having remained in a deep meditation for nearly two decades. Queen Kenji's regarded as the first recorded mutant, known for both her kindness and Godlike power. King Larvex has since remarried and had another daughter, named Cerise, with his new wife, Queen Namalda.

Angel is of Eurasian owl descent with beauty that rivals her mother. She can control sound waves, and she's a powerful telepath with countless psychic abilities. Angel's wings respond independently from her nervous system, adjusting their density to protect Angel, warning her of danger. Her feathers can be hardened and shot as psionic spikes shutting down the nervous system of adversaries. Angel's feathers absorb psychic and thermal energy adapting to protect her from just about anything.

Angel has olive skin, standing 6'4'', with humanoid facial features. She's beautiful with long brown hair and a thin, muscular frame. She has a symmetrical face and feathers emerging from the corner of her brown eyes. She has feathers on her forehead blending into her long, brown hair. The wings emerging from her back have brown, beige, and white feathers.

Angel's powers are growing by the day, with training from imperial telepaths under orders from her father. With assistance, Angel can astral project into the outreaches beyond our galaxy and into various planes. Commencement is three days away, and mutants with precognitive abilities have foreseen war amongst the Colonies. Angel wants to venture below to aid Lennek in the foreseen attack. Tensions are high throughout Olympia with growing fear surrounding the foreseen attack. Angel's pleading with her father for permission to venture beyond Olympia temporarily, struggling to be heard.

Angel follows King Larvex into his private chamber while he attempts to find busy work ignoring his daughter. She makes a passionate plea for him to allow her sanctioned passage to Lennek. "If your concern is protecting our secrets, then who better to go below than me? I'm immune to telepathic attacks and my wings will keep me safe. Please, I—"

"The surface world is dangerous, and Lennek's no place for royalty! Your place is here guiding our Evo to our next home," says King Larvex as he walks to his large balcony overlooking Virachocca.

King Larvex is of horned owl descent with superior strength and telekinetic abilities. He's an esteemed warrior with an abnormally large wingspan which allows him to reach Mach speeds. King Larvex carries a large glezslavine hammer which has served him well in many wars. He gained his title as king through his marriage to Queen Kenji. His powers were anointed to him during the conception of his belated son Davinci. While much is owed to his former wife, he doesn't speak her name, trying his best to forget her.

King Larvex is 7'2'' with a large, muscular build. He has tan skin while his feathers are shades of light brown, white, gray, and mocha. His large, distinct eyebrows arch back into his hairline, fading into his shoulder-length peppered hair. He has a feral beak nose, large golden-brown eyes, with white and brown feathers on his face. The king has a strong jaw and feral facial features. His piercing brown eyes are inviting, and he has a strong chin fit for a king. His large wings have matching symmetrical shapes on the backside of his wings which have varying shades of white and light brown feathers.

Angel drops to her knees with her wings lying flat behind her, allowing her to beg from the balcony floor. Her father doesn't bother to make eye contact, yet Angel pleads, "Father please! I'm one of forty omega-level mutants on the planet. I'm the only mutant in Virachocca with both offensive and defensive abilities. I've been trained by warriors from every Colony, and I'm immune to mental probes. Olympia's secrets will be safe!"

"ENOUGH! You are princess of Olympia and its rightful heir! Begging is beneath you!" exclaims King Larvex as he turns his back, walking to a nursery of genetically engineered dragons. Olympians have continued the science of gene splicing which created Evo. Evo have expanded on the technology creating new life in their image.

The king's geneticist combined reptile DNA with "Pterosaurs" DNA producing animals with ninety-eight-foot wingspans. The king's dragons are bred for war, controlled with Olympian technology. King Larvex's dragons are his pride and joy. He's currently nursing weak runts of his most recent litter, as their mother leaves the weakest of her offspring to die. King Larvex raises these runts as pets to ensure unwavering loyalty. There are four dragons the size of puppies inside an incubator, all currently unable to fly. They eagerly await to be fed.

"Who else would you have go?" asks Angel as she stands, her father's back to her.

King Larvex responds, "Your abilities are engineered for leadership. Now is not the time for adventurous vacations—"

"Vacation? You think I want a vacation? I bond with the Akashic effortlessly. I can vacation through my mind whenever I choose. I can control my powers better than anyone in Olympia, including you. An attack is coming, and my place isn't here. I wasn't asking to leave... The decision has been made by a higher power. I just know we'll never be the same once destiny begins to unravel," says Angel, doing her best to explain.

"KNOW YOUR PLACE, PRINCESS! You aren't going anywhere," screams the king as he turns to scold Angel. Her wings change pattern and density preparing for an attack from her own father.

Angel opens her wings turning to her father, saying, "Goodbye, Father. I'll make our family proud." Angel starts to fly off the balcony. King Larvex creates a telekinetic wall blocking Angel's escape. Angel's wings warn her, and she lands back on the balcony, retracting her wings.

Angel comes to terms with the inevitable, saying, "You cower behind your throne as the world changes beneath us, and you prefer I do the same?"

King Larvex fires a burst of telekinetic energy, which is dissipated by Angel's wings. The imperial guardsmen in the room are thrown back while Angel and King Larvex are unaffected. Angel stares her father down with defiance, walking the king down, prepared to fight her way out. King Larvex begins to slowly approach Angel when she conjures the energy for a deafening frequency.

Before Angel attacks her father, she finds herself phasing through the floor beneath her. Angel falls through the floor as if it were quicksand. Angel finds her half sister, Cerise, using her own abilities to stop her sister from making a bad decision.

Cerise is stunning with pale beige skin, white hair, and blue eyes. Her ethnic background is horned and Eurasian owl from her mother's side. Cerise has humanoid features and usually has blue makeup covering her forehead. White feathers emerge from her widow's peak in the middle of her forehead creating a mohawk blended into her white hair. The wings emerging from her back have brown and beige feathers creating a modest wingspan. She stands 5'10'' with a petite frame and icy blue eyes.

Cerise's powers create fields of vibrations forcing objects to lose their mass and physical tangibility. Cerise has multiple psychic abilities and is well versed in the mystical arts, trained by her mother Queen Namalda, Sorceress Supreme of Kermoa, one of the more reclusive outposts in Olympia. She's a passivist who loves animals completely, comfortable in the shadow of her older sister.

Cerise waits for Angel to get through the floor before converting the matter back to normal. With her sister safe, Cerise explains, "You don't want to go toe-to-toe with him. If you're going to leave, go! Stop waiting for a sign from the omniverse and create your own path."

"He will kill you for this!" says Angel as she collects herself in the grand hall beneath her father's chambers.

Cerise grabs Angel's hand as they start making their way toward a large aerodrome hangar in a large hallway of the royal palace. Evo are working paying no mind to the royal sisters. The king's expectations leave little room for his daughter's ambitions. Cerise understands what Angel's going through and is willing to help regardless of the consequences.

"Trouble!" says Angel as her wings adjust suggesting an impending threat. She assumes her father finally sent his guardsmen after them and the pair begin to move. "I can handle the guardsmen. If you leave now, your punishment won't be as severe."

Cerise laughs, replying, "Father isn't the forgiving type. I've seen his memories. You need to stop challenging him. He's implanted numerous abilities into his genome... You're no match for him alone."

Angel projects her consciousness roaming the castle halls in astral form, searching for an inconspicuous route to the aerodrome. Angel exclaims, "Follow me! I think I found a path for us. You're going to have to come with me. He'll make an example out of you if you don't!"

Cerise trusts Angel with her life, following her without question. The two reach a hallway where guardsmen are being quietly dispatched to find them. Cerise and Angel kneel, waiting for the guardsmen to pass.

Cerise whispers, "I'm stronger than I look. My mother taught me a few tricks. Father needs you for the space program since no one else can astral project further than you. He'll never let you leave! It's now or never for you. I'll be fine... Trust me!"

"There're others that can do the same. Olympia will be fine without me. I don't want him to take his anger out on you! I'm supposed to be protecting you; I'm the eldest," says Angel as the two make a break for a discrete stairwell.

Cerise is trailing two steps behind, saying, "The Evo in our bloodline don't need protecting. Our gifts aren't natural mutations. We were made to lead. Whatever's pulling you to the surface needs to be explored. You're not abandoning anyone."

Angel stops to ask, "You've seen father's memories. Did you see what happened to my mother and older brother?"

"Not only did I see what happened, I know why he did it. Your mother isn't in a coma. She's alive and using her energy to coddle someone's life force. Father was afraid of losing power and respect amongst the eastern flocks of Arcadia and Keeptoai. I don't have time to explain, but we've both been lied to our entire lives! Our father was fighting your mother for control of Olympia. Your brother was caught in the crossfire. Davinci wasn't killed in battle. He was murdered by assassins Father hired. He killed our brother!"

Angel's mind begins to race as she struggles to make sense of what Cerise is telling her. Angel senses guardsmen closing in on them and says, "We need to move! I'll have to make sense of all this later. We've got six guardsmen closing in on our position right now!"

Cerise uses her powers to phase them through a wall into the next room. Cerise takes a moment to tell Angel, "I know about your visions."

Angel stops in her tracks, intuitively adjusting her feathers, retorting, "How do you know about my visions? The Coven Council of Psychics can't even break through my mental shield collectively, how could you alone—"

"Your mind isn't completely impenetrable. Look, I know you see me as your baby sister, but my powers are growing too. On top of that, my mother has trained me in the mystic arts since I was a child. I have abilities beyond my mutation!" says Cerise as she conjures a mystic globe with an incantation. The sisters see King Larvex in the globe of energy two rooms away, tracking them.

"We don't have much time. We need to move now!" says Cerise as she grabs her sister and phases them through another wall.

Angel looks down at her sister, saying, "I need you to know, I'm going off-world so Olympians can be a part of the new world below. My vision wasn't clear... I could only see bits and pieces, but I know I need to leave today."

The sisters make their way to the armory next to the aerodrome. Suddenly, an electro-magnetic pulse is set off within the room followed by a coordinated telepathic attack by King Larvex's coven of psychics. The thirteen Council members combined their minds allowing them to attack as one psychic entity.

The Council's attack only affects Cerise, but Angel's knocked off her flightpath from the electromagnetic pulse. The pulse and telepathic attack make Cerise disoriented, unable to use her powers. Now tangible, the two sisters inadvertently activate the castle's automated defense system. Cannons appear from the walls and begin shooting sedative inhibiter darts at the two princesses.

Angel's wings protect most of her body, deflecting the inhibiter darts which suppress mutant abilities. Unfortunately, she's struck in the leg. The potent sedative starts stripping Angel of her powers as her stamina slowly depletes. She immediately removes the dart, fully aware of the effects.

The sisters remain focused destroying the defense system before taking a moment to recover. King Larvex enters the room with eight heavily armed guardsmen. Cerise stands and makes herself completely intangible. Angel stands expanding her wings claiming her space. Angel's wings begin adjusting, bracing for an assault, working autonomously to protect her.

King Larvex is communicating with the imperial guardsmen and Council on an encrypted telepathic frequency, ordering two of the guardsmen to flank his daughters. King Larvex jumps over the balcony to the lower level of the armory, where Cerise and Angel await.

"Cerise, you disappoint me! Angel, we've already discussed this. You aren't going anywhere! Honestly, if I wanted to harm the two of you, do either of you truly think you could stop me?" asks King Larvex, hoping to distract his daughters.

Angel's wings continue changing patterns to continually protect her from the Council's telepathic attacks. Cerise is impervious to telepathy while intangible, thinking of a plan for the sisters to escape. As the two spread apart, Angel says, "We're immune to your mind games, Father. You and your coven can't change destiny!"

"You're needed here in Virachocca. We're months away from finding our home foreseen in the prophecies. It's written that you will lead us to our new home. You're the one trying to dictate your destiny," says King Larvex as he levitates toward Angel using his telekinesis.

Angel shoots psionic blades from her wing's feathers taking out three guardsmen in a single motion of her wings. Their nervous systems shut down within seconds as their bodies seize. While intangible, Cerise focuses on the floor beneath them causing it to turn intangible. The guardsmen plumet to the level beneath as King Larvex continues to advance using his wings to take to the air.

Cerise begins to flank King Larvex with his attention focused on Angel. Cerise distracts King Larvex, exclaiming, "I browsed your memories by accident the other day. I told Angel what I saw!"

"And what did you see?" asks King Larvex as he uses telekinesis taking a shield and sword from the wall into his hands.

Cerise casts a spell countering the effects of the inhibiter serum that's draining Angel's abilities, while simultaneously attempting to distract King Larvex. Cerise manifests an energy globe hovering over Angel, absorbing the serum from her blood.

Cerise says, "I saw that you started the war with Queen Kenji. You betrayed her. You feared her power and realized that even as king, you would always be second to the queen of mutants. You hired the assassin that killed Davinci, and you—"

King Larvex turns to Cerise, yelling, "SILENCE! The memory fragments you absorbed in my presence tell half the story. We're done discussing this!"

King Larvex telekinetically grabs some sedative syringes and inhibiter darts flinging them at Angel. Angel's wings cross over her shoulders and protect her from the incoming darts. King Larvex maneuvers the syringes over Angel, attempting to inject her from behind. Angel shatters the syringes with a deafening sound frequency, forcing her father to change his tactics.

"Let us talk! Angel, I want you to know what really happened between your mother and me. Cerise, do you mind giving your sister and me some privacy?"

Cerise looks at her sister sending an encrypted telepathic message, saying, "*He wants to divide us. My spell's diluting the effects of the inhibiter serum, but you're still weak. We're at a disadvantage. We need to stall him and wait until your powers recover. I have a plan. Just roll with me.*"

Angel agrees, knowing she needs to escape. Hoping to distract their father, Cerise professes to King Larvex, "Will you forgive my disobedience if I leave, Father?"

"I'll think about it. I'm not going to hurt your sister. I'm going to explain what happened and she can confirm the details with you later. We'll speak in the morning," says King Larvex as he levitates across the room with his wings open.

Angel looks at her sister, telling her telepathically, "*Cerise, just go! Maybe the timing isn't right. My wings will protect me. He can't hurt me. I'll be fine.*" Angel keeps a safe distance listening to her father...trusting in her sister.

King Larvex has been in constant communication with his psychic coven. They're warning him that the sisters have been communicating telepathically. King Larvex is distrustful of his daughters, but genuinely believes he can change Angel's mind by being honest with her. The king knows, as a child, Angel had questions she was too afraid to ask. King Larvex feels he owes Angel an explanation...the truth rather. With Angel being nineteen, he feels she's mature enough to handle the truth.

King Larvex looks to a large rectangular table facing the glass wall overlooking Virachocca asking Angel to sit with him. She refuses as he responds, "Kenji...your mother wasn't just the first mutant. She was the finest amongst all Olympians. My flock was destined to rule, with me fated to become king. Because of your mother's mutant abilities, our elders chose to break tradition, making her queen despite her flock. My father brokered a deal that would bind both our tribes, creating a new flock to rule over all Olympia..."

Angel interrupts her father, saying, "All of this is in our historical archives! You're wasting my time." Angel reaches out to Cerise, asking, "*Where are you? Your spell's wearing off.*"

Cerise responds, "*I'm coming back with something that will give you enough time to make it below. I'll be back shortly.*"

King Larvex is getting frustrated, severing his link with his coven to focus his attention on Angel. "When I learned your brother was funding the rebels, it led to a civil war. We lost support amongst the Sinai and Arcadia flocks. Davinci instigated war between the flocks, and your mother backed him. When Davinci died, Queen Kenji lost her mind and turned her back on this Colony. Olympia needed a leader to guide them into the new world."

Angel squints her eyes, shaking her head filled with disappointment. "You drugged her...or should I say poisoned her? The dosage you gave was intended to kill, but she survived. She's been alive this entire time hidden somewhere in a deep stasis inside her temple. I know you ordered Davinci's assassination. You offer excuses while I speak the truth! You've lied to me my entire life!"

King Larvex opens his wings, landing in front of Angel stopping her from walking toward the entrance of the aerodrome. "Everything I've done is to protect my family. Your mother's been in stasis since you were a child! I had to move on. Olympia needed to move on. I thought it best she be dead to you."

"You had me think my mother was dead...for my best interest? All the times I thought I felt her presence, you made me think I was crazy. I doubted my abilities because of you. It's unforgiveable! But that's not the reason I'm going to Lennek," says Angel as she backs away.

King Larvex looks at Angel, summoning his hammer using his telekinesis. "I told you you're not going anywhere." He hits Angel with a telekinetic blast knocking her across the room.

Angel emits sonic blasts from her mouth and hands, knocking King Larvex on his back. The king recovers with unnatural agility, repositioning himself in front of Angel with a single thrust of his wings. He grabs Angel by the throat, blocking her wings with his telekinesis, before throwing her to the ground.

King Larvex tightens his grip on his war hammer as he expands his wings. Prepared to do what he must as a father to protect his daughter from herself. He pleads with her, "Don't make me do this!"

Angel rolls her body, countering by shooting psionic daggers from her wing's feathers. Her daggers slow the king down striking him in the chest, giving Angel a chance to recover. She jumps to the air, using her wings to gain distance as her mind scrambles to recuperate.

Cerise phases through a wall, wearing an amulet amplifying her mystic powers. She's wearing a tiara with a telepathic amplifier made from one of their finest blacksmiths. Cerise enters the room, paralyzing the king with a telepathic attack rendering him defenseless. She manipulates the tangibility of the floor beneath the king, momentarily trapping him in the floor at the waist.

"We won't make it to the aerodrome, but I can get you to the ground now. Are you ready to leave?" asks Cerise, focusing her energy on restraining their father.

"He's not going to just forgive you, Cerise. You need to come with me...please!" says Angel as she makes her way to her sister. "He'll torture you at best. If he's angry enough, he'll kill you! Please, come with me!"

"I can fend for myself," says Cerise as she uses the amulet to create an intangible tunnel through the outpost burrowing through to the open skies thousands of feet beneath them. She creates a tunnel, giving Angel a window to freedom.

Cerise struggles to maintain the tunnel while simultaneously restraining King Larvex. Cerise screams, "There's no time to be stubborn. JUST GO! I can handle this! Stay safe and return as soon as you can. Go!"

Angel flies as fast as she can through the intangible tunnel, reluctantly following her intuition. The inhibitor serum courses through her veins, depleting her stamina, making it difficult to remain conscious. Now that she's away from Cerise, her sister's spell is no longer absorbing the serum and sedative. The orb of light above her head has completely dissipated, no longer absorbing its effects. Angel struggles to keep her eyes open, falling beneath Virachocca into the open skies.

Gravity takes over as Angel gains speed, plummeting to the surface. She's now completely unconscious as her wings intuitively open to slow her fall. Adrenaline finally wakes her up, allowing her to aim for a viable spot to crash land. It's beginning to sink in that she just committed treason, fought her father, and left her younger sister to deal with the consequences. Guilt and anxiety begin to flood her mind as her wings adjust to harmonically soothe her while preparing for a crash landing.

Angel uses her remaining energy to release a psychic beacon for help. She sends a message to all nearby psychics she's familiar with on the astral plane. Angel recognizes Goldie and another powerful psychic from Kronus she's encountered dozens of times. Sensing the two are in the vicinity of Lennek, Angel directs her descent towards Ladarium. She's filled with mixed emotions, prepared to experience life outside the palace walls of Olympia. Angel feels her strength leaving her body as the sedatives take effect. She passes out in free fall to the ground below, unsure of her future.

Eve's been informed of Angel's location by Gill, a powerful mutant from Kronus that's recently been recruited into the new Coalition being put together by the Lennethian Guardian. Gill has numerous abilities, and he's familiar with Angel, having shared multiple encounters with her on the astral plane. Goldie senses Angel's distress, reassuring her of the path she's chosen.

Eve sends a covert team to rescue Angel preparing for the arrival of new recruits. Eve starts the process of creating an alternate identity for Angel, so she can hide her affiliation to the imperial crown. Previous introductions on the astral plane have saved Angel's life and positioned her to fulfill her mission.

Chapter 2 — Meet Our Replacements

Back on the ground in Lennek, Goldie's transport platform slows to a halt preparing to dock in the middle of Ladarium's central plaza. The plaza's located on the outskirts of an asteroid impact crater, ground level near Quartz Tower. An atrium and park are near the tower, providing beautiful aesthetics near the landing space for the transport platform. As the transport lands, the liquid metal that made everyone's cabins and seats starts rescinding to a flat surface. Passengers prepare to exit as the transport's shields power down. The platform lands at a station with a group of Evo standing in line, waiting to board.

Goldie felt the distress call from Angel and sensed another psychic taking care of the issue. While she has never met Gill, Goldie feels confident Angel will be safe. She touches her temple, accessing her communicator, which is now projecting a hologram on her palm.

Goldie says aloud, "Quartz Tower directions." Goldie's communicator starts navigating toward the press conference by projecting holographic arrows guiding her to the nearest traveler pod station.

The transportation platform is completely powered down allowing Goldie to exit into the streets of Precinct 9. Ladarium's buildings are enormous, each made from rare stones and minerals. Lennek's coastline has minimal vegetation and small numbers of unevolved animals roaming the land outside of the Colony. Geometric buildings and floating Olympian outposts create a symmetry in the skyline that can be seen for miles.

Earth's gravitational pull has changed as the planet healed itself in the absence of humans. Asteroid showers and advanced Evo technology have made metals stronger. Gravity is now manipulated to the will of architects while the oxygen levels of dry air average 42 percent. The average Evo is six to eight feet tall, while shorter species are as small as two feet. The change in relative height between humans and Evo is reflected in the size of their buildings. Regardless of size or natural habitat, Lennek's an open Colony accommodating to all species providing equal protection under the law.

The Capital is on an Evo-made mountain called Ladarium Rock. On top of Ladarium Rock is a fortified citadel surrounded by over two hundred thousand customized estates, buildings, and military bases. Lennek's elite live near the citadel, while housing for the wealthy and essential contributors to the Colony live on the outskirts. The outskirts of Ladarium Rock have hundreds of towers and buildings of varied shapes and sizes. The citadel in the middle of the mountain is elevated in the center made of an iridescent silver and glass.

Permits to live near the capital are distributed by invitation only, given to those who provide "value" to the Colony. Precinct 9 is protected by layers of force fields and home to the Colonial Guard, making the area the safest place within Lennek. Ladarium also houses Lennek's largest military base, occupying more than 480,000 acres of land.

Beneath Ladarium Rock is a row of forty-eight obelisks arranged in pairs at ninety-degree angles. Each eight-hundred-foot obelisk is tilted ninety degrees, creating twenty-four triangles from the touching tips of the opposing obelisks. The obelisk intersection points hold a pboldevite casing with a diamond center, making the structure an extravagant energy conductor. The obelisks channel energy from nearby ley-lines providing clean ambient energy for the precinct. Pboldevite absorbs and amplifies these energies a thousandfold making them efficient energy conductors.

Goldie walks beneath the obelisks near the base of Ladarium Rock when she notices the precinct is on high alert. There's increased security on every corner, forcing her to remain alert. Law enforcement and guardsmen are patrolling the streets, making Goldie aware of her surroundings. She's eight blocks away from Quartz Tower making her way through thousands of Evo on their way to work.

News of newly discovered mutants is circulating online on social platforms while a crowd gathers at Quartz Tower. Evo are eager to catch a glimpse of Rosie who's been catapulted into stardom. The media already named her "the bender of light," taking less than an hour to investigate Rosie's entire life story and upbringing. The streets of Ladarium are packed more than usual with a palpable energy in the air.

Goldie uses her powers to stay hidden from cameras and checkpoints while looking for a transit pod to reach Quartz Tower. The pods move through a series of tubes utilizing gravity-displacement technology and high-powered magnets. The transporter pods are constructed in different sizes and shapes to accommodate the varied anatomies of different ethnic backgrounds of Evo.

Goldie can't help but feel a larger power in the works. The telepathic SOS from Angel has only confirmed her gut feeling bring her peace. She hasn't left her home for weeks and somehow the city has a different vibe forcing her to take in her surroundings. She boards a pod and enters a route near Quartz Tower.

The pod takes off, moving in between beautifully constructed megaliths made from varied metallic alloys, gems, and crystals. Lennek's a contemporary city with modern Evo technology dispersed throughout. The skies are littered with holographic 4-D ads that appear to interact with their surrounding environment. While moving through the precinct, Goldie's overwhelmed with a warm feeling of gratitude for the life she's made for herself. For just a moment, she finds serenity while taking in the view.

Without warning, Goldie starts to feel Angel's presence. Goldie feels a rush of relief knowing Angel's safe. Angel's recovering from her traumatic departure from Olympia in a special unit not far from Goldie's location. Lennek's been secretly recruiting powerful mutants for a coalition aimed at replacing the oversight of Guardians. Goldie has no idea she's on her way to a historical announcement that will change her life forever.

Goldie approaches the outskirts of the capital near the city's outer edge, not far from the shoreline. She can feel the mist from Grentake Falls as she steps onto a sidewalk equipped with gravity-displacement technology. Goldie steps onto a public sidewalk and starts levitating a foot off the ground, guided toward Quartz Tower less than a block away. She enjoys the scenery, eventually approaching an isolated perch across the street from Quartz Tower. She lowers herself to the ground, taking a seat as she uses her powers to remain inconspicuous. Goldie sits in a meditative stance with her tail rolled into a spiral ball behind her. Goldie's hat is covering her face from nearby surveillance cameras as she concentrates astral projecting her consciousness into the press conference inside Quartz Tower.

In astral form, Goldie feels the presence of a few other psychics both in astral form and physically inside. Quartz Tower is made from various shades of quartz and emerald stone. The tower itself is a crescent shape with darker stones at its base and lighter green stones fading towards the top of the emerald tower. Green marble floors make up the inside of the building with mint, white, and teal furniture. Forty-foot gold statues line the entrance of the tower paying homage to Lennek's leaders, both past and present.

Goldie roams the entrance of Quartz Tower in astral form, avoiding the intense security checkpoints. The tower is often used by ambassadors, so it is aquatically accessible—meaning gravity-displacement technology throughout the building encases helmets of water for Evo of aquatic descent. The spheres of water are maintained by the building, giving aquatic patrons mobility. She's reminded just how inclusive Lennek is, feeling a sense of pride.

Goldie makes her way to the top floor of the tower in astral form just as the press conference begins. President Zlaigo, General Mckezia, Senate Leader Phlorne, Governor Grimsuni, Eve, and a group of mutants are on stage in front of seated dignitaries. The room's filled with news drones broadcasting live to all seven Colonies. The social elite from every Colony are inside Quartz Tower dining with Lennek's most powerful Evo.

Governor Grimsuni walks to the center panel, saying, "Good afternoon, citizens of Lennek. As your governor, it's my job to protect Lennek and enforce our laws. Many of you are here to listen to our Guardian who has always shared wisdom guiding Lennek through over a century of prosperity. With our days being numbered with all our Guardians, this is certainly an historic event. I'm pleased to announce President Zlaigo and our Guardian are initiating a new organization to counter crime post-Guardian. To all those watching...we have a plan and we've taken action!" The governor smiles to the cameras, pausing to ensure his campaign slogan was heard.

Governor Grimsuni is of crocodile descent with an overweight physique. He has green skin and scales, reeking of overindulgence. He has dark brown eyes, razor-sharp teeth, and an elongated face. The governor's wearing an all-white suit, one size too small, gleefully smiling for the cameras.

The governor plays a hologram of some of the mutants on stage fighting together in a combat simulator. Gill, Zeus, Bambi, Rosie, and Merkaba are displaying a mastery of their gifts working in sync. Governor Grimsuni looks directly into the news drones in front of him explaining, "Lennek's Guardian and law enforcement have been working together the past few months to create a special task force designed to protect the Colonies. The Coalition is an inter-Colonial task force comprised of mutants pledged to protect and enforce peace amongst all seven Colonies. As more Evo develop abilities, it's only reasonable to assume that some will have less than pure intentions. Our Guardian's here to explain why this taskforce is necessary and in our best interest!"

Eve walks to the right of Governor Grimsuni, explaining in a monotone voice, "In three days, I will have reached the end of my programming. I will soon cease to exist, no longer able to protect Lennek. Mutants will either be your species salvation or their destruction. The Coalition will ensure the balance of power remains intact. Law enforcement and I have gathered and trained a group of patriotic mutants to lead the inter-Colonial task force. The Coalition can be considered a replacement for the Guardians. The young mutant that broke headlines this morning saving lives from a crumbling building is one of our recruits."

As Eve introduces the mutants on stage, Goldie can't help but feel connected to the group, as if her presence is somehow expected. Goldie's doing her best to shield her psychic energy, remaining undetected, but Gill has already noticed her presence. Psychics can usually see others on the astral plane unless the individual's intentionally shielding themselves and a stronger psychic.

Eve addresses Lennek's leaders by introducing the Coalition recruits, saying, "To my left is Merkaba. She's a native to Carthage and has been training in Lennek for the past few months. Merkaba can heal or harm organic matter through her purrs. The frequency of her purr can be adjusted to cause different effects on the body. The harmonic fields of her purrs cause cells to rapidly self-regenerate or degrade by tapping into the Higgs field. Merkaba essentially changes the frequency at which individual particles vibrate, allowing her to either regenerate individual cells or break them down."

Merkaba stands making her way to the front of the stage next to Eve. Merkaba flips her hair and removes her sunglasses, saying, "Hello, everyone. I just wanted to say I'm happy to have been chosen for this Coalition. I'll use my abilities to help heal as many as possible. We've all been training for months to be the first line of defense for the Colonies. I won't disappoint!" Merkaba returns to her seat while the crowd applauds as reporters fire off questions.

Merkaba is of caracal descent standing 6'2'' with a slim physique. She has caramel brown skin and fur with thick orange hair flowing down to her lower back. She has triangular ears emerging from the top of her head among her long hair. Merkaba has feral features with distinct bone structure, brown eyes, and high cheekbones. Being of caracal descent, the hair on her ears extends beyond the cartilage with black tips. Merkaba's extremely agile and proficient in many forms of combat. She has a thin tail she uses for balance and retractable claws.

Governor Grimsuni lowers his head into the microphone, saying, "Hold your questions until the end of the press conference please." He steps away from the podium as Eve takes his position.

Governor Grimsuni makes his way to President Zlaigo, taking the space next to him. He's shorter than the president desperate to appear poised for the cameras. The governor whispers to the president, "We've heard reports of a planned attack against Lennek. I've been trying to meet to debrief you."

President Zlaigo turns his back to the cameras, looking up to respond, "I've been occupied restructuring our government, been a little busy. No one would dare attack Lennek. Besides, Lennek's fully prepared to defend itself should such an event occur. We have cameras on us... Do play your role." Governor Grimsuni realizes the time and place for the conversation is less than ideal despite its importance.

The governor turns his attention back to the press conference as reporters take pictures of Merkaba concluding her introduction. The flashes from their cameras cause Goldie to momentarily lose focus, accidentally revealing herself in astral form to all the psychics in the room. Goldie regains her composure while Zeus, a muscular Evo of pit bull descent, stands, walking to the front of the stage next to Eve.

Eve continues her introductions, saying, "To my left is Zeus, a Lennek native able to increase his size thirteen times his normal mass or shrink at will. Zeus's mutation provides him with superior strength and an impressive healing factor. His combat skills are battle tested, having served as a general amongst our Colonial Guard. Zeus was one of the first recruited for the Coalition because of his valiant patriotism."

Zeus has a large physique, standing 7'3'', with a larger-than-life personality. His facial features are feral being of pit bull descent. His cheeks are covered in white skin with whiskers surrounding his black snout. He has golden-brown skin and fur covering most of his body, while his chest and stomach have white skin. Zeus has tattoos on his forearms, chest, and back, covering his large muscular build. Zeus is an outspoken playboy who is used to being the center of attention. He prides himself in keeping himself perfectly groomed with fur that feels like velvet, brandishing controversial clipped ears.

Zeus gives the crowd a demonstration of his power by increasing his mass, changing his height from just over seven feet to over fourteen feet tall. Zeus smiles for the cameras as the crowd gasps in awe of his immense size and presumed power. He quickly reverts to his normal size before crushing the stage with his increased weight.

He takes his seat as Bambi, a spunky Evo of giraffe descent crosses paths with him on stage. Bambi floats across the stage with grace, highlighting her perfectly shaped green afro and exotic features. She slows her gait, relishing the attention as she catches the lens of every news drone in the room.

Bambi walks to the podium as Eve begins her introduction, saying, "Next, we have Bambi from Angkor. Bambi's mutation allows her to stretch her limbs incredible distances while increasing her muscle mass. Bambi can make her skin jelly-like, allowing her to squeeze through tight spaces, also resistant to harm. Bambi's fought countless wars in Angkor, and she's a master linguist who speaks over twenty languages and numerous dialects."

Bambi is beautiful with uncanny humanoid features and a long neck. She stands 6'8'' with mocha brown skin with beige patches of skin covering her entire body from her giraffe lineage. Her ears shoot out four inches perpendicular through a green afro she keeps perfectly shaped. Bambi has violet eyes, piercings on her ears, and a diamond nose ring. Her signature green lipstick glistens in the lights as she basks in the attention. Her metallic gloves allow her to pack a heavy punch amplifying her unnatural strength. The material in her armor and clothes stretch and shrink with her body on the subatomic level allowing multiple particles to take up the same space. Her armor is a hallmark of Evo quantum physics while she herself strives to enjoy the simplicity of life.

Bambi smiles in appreciation of Eve's kind words, responding, "Citizens of Lennek, I thank you for welcoming me. I'm sure many of you have opinions about Angkor. Understand that I'm here to use my abilities to create an inclusive Colony. I believe in what Lennek stands for. I intend to spread our shared philosophy to the other Colonies, keeping your families safe in the process."

Bambi walks back to her seat and crosses Gill as he makes his way to the podium for his own introduction. Gill sensed Goldie earlier and can now see her in astral form hovering above the seated crowd. As cameras flash in the room, he catches images of Goldie floating on the astral plane watching from the back.

Gill has fluorescent teal scales covering his body while his face has greenish blue skin. He has green eyes with protruding bones around his forehead and skull, creating a crown beneath his skin. His lips and the gills on the side of his neck are pink as well as the outline of his eyes. He has fins on his calves and forearms as well as a connecting fin from his ribs to his underarms. Gill's handsome and highly ranked amongst Kronusian royalty.

Gill makes his way next to Eve as she explains, "Lennek will be working with mutants from across the planet for this inner-Colonial task force. Gill is from Kronus and can control wind and electrical currents. He can also transfer memories and skills through physical contact. His numerous psychic abilities will make him a valued asset to the Coalition as he has benefitted Kronus."

The crowd applauds as Gill stands next to Eve, saying, "In Kronus, my abilities were used for the military. My powers were used for defense, interrogations, and to control the ocean's tides. In Kronus, the tribe that controls the tides, controls the Colony. Our illustrious king has made a great sacrifice in allowing me to serve with the Coalition. I appreciate the warm welcome and I won't let our Colonies down."

Gill smiles for the news drones while the misters in the ceiling provide a continuous drizzle onto Gill's greenish blue skin moisturizing his scales. The environmental equipment in Quartz Tower ensures every species has an ideal environment inside the building. Gill turns to take his seat as Eve continues addressing the audience. "Our Coalition will be a growing family of mutants, pledged to protecting the citizens of all seven Colonies. Many of you assumed you would just be meeting Rosie today. Instead, I introduced you to the group who will act as my replacement. Rosie's heroism makes her a perfect candidate for the Coalition."

Rosie stands as she hears Eve introduce her. Eve opens her arms to Rosie looking back to marshal her to the stage. "Rosie's mutation allows her to bend light to create force fields. Her ability's limited only by her imagination and mental stamina. She can manifest physical objects with her mind and funnel sunlight through her hands creating fires."

Rosie is of Siamese descent born into Precinct 7 of Lennek. She lived a normal life as a socialite before being recruited into the Coalition. Rosie has beige skin with a symmetrical shaped face and icy-blue eyes.

Her eyes have a vertical slit, and her large ears resemble a Siamese cat. She has humanoid facial features except for her large triangular ears which give her enhanced hearing. She's short for an Evo, standing 5'8", with a slim physique. Rosie has long black hair, retractable claws, and a thin tail with black and brown fur.

Rosie addresses the crowd with Eve's arm around her, confessing, "I've been training with the Coalition for a few weeks now. I've been trying to maintain the normal life I had before all of this...before I was recruited. I wanted to keep my job, so I was nearby when the building started to collapse this morning. I saw Evo in danger and did what I was trained to do. My comrades and I are all honored to serve. Thank you." Rosie turns around to take her seat as Gill reaches out to Goldie telepathically.

"*Greetings. I hope I'm not startling you. I'm Gill,*" says Gill projecting his own consciousness onto the astral plane as the press conference continues.

Goldie responds, "*You can see me? I'm sorry—I didn't mean to intrude!*" Goldie starts to channel her consciousness back into her body, leaving the tower.

Gill exclaims, "*Don't leave. Please! I felt your consciousness and thoughts earlier. I just couldn't see you. You're very powerful, but you lowered your guard when the—*"

"*Flashes from the photographers and news drones went off. I didn't know light would affect my powers. I heard the Guardian describe your abilities. Can't you read my thoughts?*" asks Goldie.

Gill levitates next to Goldie, assuming a meditative pose in astral form, looking at himself on stage seated with the other mutants behind Eve. Gill explains, "*I'm a telepath like yourself, so I can feel and hear your thoughts.*" He points to Eve, continuing, "*Her name's Eve. She's not like the other Guardians. She's sentient—the first of her kind. Eve's conscious and can feel emotions like you or me.*"

Puzzled, Goldie turns to Gill exclaiming, *"Impossible! Lennek would have found out and had it immediately decommissioned. If any of those cults in Carthage or Zion knew about this..."*

"Insurrection. If the other Colonies knew about Eve, those crazy cults would have evidence for their beliefs. It would give credence to their apocalyptic prediction of a sentient artificial intelligence destroying us," says Gill as he feels Goldie out.

"It's a good thing the Guardians are shutting down. Sorry for the intrusion. I'll be on my way now," says Goldie as she turns to make her exit. With her adrenaline pumping from being discovered, her body's reacting in the physical world surrounding Goldie downstairs in the park.

"You're a powerful mutant, Goldie. I sense you have many gifts. You're still untrained. Your powers are unrefined. Only omega-level psychics can shield themselves from me. Your place is on stage with us. I felt you when Angel sent out her psychic SOS," says Gill, trying to convince Goldie to stay.

Merkaba senses Goldie, but her psychic abilities aren't strong enough to break through Goldie's shielding. Merkaba can't see Goldie, but she can communicate with her telepathically, saying, *"Hi, I'm Merkaba. My friends call me Kabba. I can't see you, but I can feel your chi. Why aren't you up here with us?"*

Goldie reveals herself to Merkaba, saying, *"I saw Rosie on my streaming-pod, and something pulled me here. I haven't made up my mind yet... I'm not sure if I want to come forward."*

Merkaba smiles and projects her own consciousness into astral form, confessing, *"I've just learned how to do this. I've been training with the Coalition for a while now and my powers have grown as they promised. I was told that there was a powerful precog that would join our ranks to lead us. Could that be you?"*

"Me? I can barely control my own powers! I'm a lot of things, but a leader

isn't one of them!" says Goldie as she starts reverting her consciousness back to her body feeling ambushed.

"You're quick to run away, Goldie. I was told our leader would have the power to reshape the omniverse itself. Something inspired you to come here today. Follow your intuition. Your gifts can save millions of lives. You're stronger than you think. Not having control of your abilities is a danger to everyone around you. Join us!" says Merkaba as she notices Goldie become uncomfortable.

Slightly emotional, Goldie calms herself before replying. "I know I don't have the means to train myself. I'm sure the Coalition can make great use of my visions. The question is, do our interests overlap? Will I have my freedom?"

"You've been so focused on shielding yourself that you haven't been paying attention to the environment your physical body's occupying. Return to your body and open your eyes," says Merkaba hoping to have gotten through to Goldie.

Goldie returns her consciousness to her body and realizes she's been levitating telekinetically, drawing a large crowd. Evo are taking videos and pictures while authorities push the crowd back. The officers are too afraid to touch her holding their shields as they stay back. She lowers herself to the ground, realizing the guardsmen intend to detain her.

Gill appears next to Goldie, in astral form, explaining, "Everything will be fine. I'm going to have the officers escort you to us. We'll take care of this. Please, don't run! You can trust us."

Fully aware of her past crimes, she realizes her options are limited. Goldie uses her telepathic abilities to convince the guardsmen to escort her into the press conference. Within minutes, authorities escort Goldie into an elevator toward the top floor of Quartz Tower bypassing security.

Goldie enters the press conference on the top floor terrified. Unbeknownst to her, she's already been introduced to the world by Eve and a seat is waiting for her on stage. The entire crowd is on their feet applauding. Confused, Goldie smiles walking along a path to center stage.

Goldie reaches out to Gill, asking, *"What's going on? Why is everyone clapping?"*

Gill rises to his feet applauding before responding. *"Because the leader of the Coalition has entered the room. We've sensed your powers for some time now. We couldn't pinpoint your location and bring you in. Even untrained, as an omega-level telepath, you were able to shield your entire home from a hive of psychics devoted to finding you. Now that you've already been exposed, you have an option: let us take you in...or explain to the authorities how you've been living as an unregistered telepath."*

"Not much of a choice!" says Goldie, feeling pressured and set up. She knows she has no choice and agrees.

Gill can feel her conflicted emotions now that she's in the same room as him. He tells her, *"You can trust us. Please, take your seat,"* giving Goldie the push she needs to trust.

Eve hovers above the podium and greets Goldie in the parted path leading to the stage. Eve offers an extended arm to Goldie with her palm raised to the ceiling, saying, "Goldie is a native to Lennek and a telepath. Her psychic energy is off the charts, and we are just discovering the depths of her abilities. Despite her battle inexperience, Goldie will lead this Coalition well."

Goldie's in shock, combating her instinct to flee. She does her best to smile at the crowd, taking her seat next to Rosie as the room finishes their applause. Goldie reaches out to Merkaba telepathically, asking, *"How did you know my body was levitating downstairs?"*

Merkaba responds, *"You aren't the only psychic with precognitive abilities in the Coalition. Angel reached out to you on her descent with an SOS. During your psychic link she received a glimpse of your future. She's still recovering from her departure from Olympia, but the two of you will meet soon enough!"*

Goldie takes in all the information and recalls the entity she felt falling. Like Rosie, Goldie felt connected to Angel even though they hadn't met. Goldie realizes she's on inter-Colonial television, underdressed and unprepared. She lowers her blue hat covering more of her face, recalling her unpaid debts to dangerous Evo running Lennek's underworld.

Gill comforts Goldie, saying, *"Your instinct to seclude yourself was natural, but most psychics haven't been able to stay hidden for more than a few days. We've been searching for you for months. It's quite impressive. With the Coalition's training, I have all the confidence in the world that you'll led us exactly how Eve intended."*

A reporter screams out, "What else can she do?"

Eve responds by sending security droids to escort the reporter out of the press conference before answering, "It is strategically wise to be vague about Goldie's abilities. As you all can see, we have recruited some amazing mutants. More information will be released soon. Lennek asks that all mutants come forward and serve their Colonies. The world is changing and there's a place for all mutants. Not just in Lennek, but inter-Colonially. May prosperity befall us all."

King Pulsar's watching the press conference from the imperial palace in Kronus deep within the ocean. Queen Elisheba is with her husband watching one of their most powerful guardsmen join the Coalition. Gill's faithfully served King Pulsar for over a decade and turned the tide of many wars in his favor. King Pulsar's military is the most highly trained and feared in the world because of Gill's ability to transfer skills through physical contact. In a way, Gill's trained the Kronusian military, making him an extremely valuable asset.

King Pulsar's pacing across his chambers, pondering his decision to allow Gill to serve in the Coalition. King Pulsar lives in an underwater castle made mostly of a laminated pearl alloy constructed in geometric shapes beneath large energy domes. Kronus is the largest Colony on the planet, made up of four tribes populated with thousands of aquatic Evo. The capital of Kronus, Vishnu, is near the northern hemisphere in the center of what was formerly the Atlantic Ocean.

Four tribes politically influence Kronus under the rule of King Pulsar: the Vishnu, Sharkona, Maddox, and Reef tribes. Each tribe is represented by a regent that has authority imbued from King Pulsar. The imperial palace is near Vishnu, located on the outer rim of the city. Each tribe has their own resources, unique to their geographical location. As a Colony, Kronus exports energy, food, and weapons.

The Vishnu buildings closest to the capital are made out of large, reinforced seashells. The city's structures are hollow compatible for both aquatic and non-aquatic Evo. With the push of a button, rooms can be converted to accommodate air or water breathing Evo.

Vishnu is populated with hundreds of species doubling as the export hub for all Kronusian goods. The capital has three pyramids that align with the Fomalhaut Constellation on the ocean seafloor. Energy shields and tubes carry traveler pods connecting structures made of coral and silver. In the center of Vishnu is an orbiting quartz sphere that levitates over an underwater temple. The temple is constructed from reef, concrete, and energy shields powered by the ocean's waves.

The Sharkona tribes have dozens of outposts throughout the ocean tasked with protecting the Colony. Sharkonians make up the majority of the Colonial Guard, led by Regent Lacostus, enforcing peace beneath the sea. They pride themselves in their devotion to preserving the world history of all species. Their buildings are made from a gold metallic alloy that absorbs light, emitting an orange glow.

The Maddox tribe has three cities spread throughout the former Pacific Ocean. Their tribe focuses on harvesting food, science, and weapons development. The Maddox tribe grows 60 percent of Kronus's food in hydroponic farms using genetic splicing and cloning techniques. Maddox's cities are built out of compressed algae reinforced with sheets of quartz. Buildings and homes are connected to a centralized power grid powered by tidal farms.

The Reef tribe is near what was formerly known by humans as the Indian Ocean. Their city is made of modified reefs and force fields. The Reef is led by Regent Priestess Ujima, a powerful cyborg with numerous mutant abilities. Their tribe protects lost technology from the time of humans remaining hostile to outsiders, including fellow Kronusians. Little is known about the Reef, other than the high population of mutants and elaborate architecture.

Most of what was previously Europe is now underwater, other than dozens of islands peppered across the former continent. The Reef tribe inhabits a beautiful, naturally occurring reef highlighted by elaborate architecture throughout the area. The Reef has hundreds of atriums protected with glass domes and force fields—the most infamous being Grenada Gardens, an underwater jungle inside an enormous dome covering over 1,330 acres.

While most of Kronus is underwater, the Colony also has a kingdom above sea level as well. The Vishnu Isles are directly above the capital and royal palace, which spans for miles on the ocean floor. The Vishnu Isles is home to a population of only 380,000 Evo. The isles are located above Vishnu visited by Evo from all over the world for its' beauty and magnificent colosseum. 90 percent of Kronus's inhabitants can live both in and outside of the water while only 30 percent have the financial means of doing so. Nuclear fallout from the humans' last war changed the ocean's water composition, nearly wiping out all aquatic life.

In 2308, all seven Colonies signed a peace treaty wherein they agreed to protect the world's water. The seven Guardians enforced the treaty by force for over a century protecting the Kronusian way of life. The

Guardian of Kronus spent eighty-seven years balancing the ocean's pH, terraforming, and building massive structures using millions of aquatic robots. The oceans are now crystal clear and healthy—pristine by any standard.

When the Guardians are decommissioned days from now, Evo will have the freedom to pollute the planet's oceans like their human predecessors. King Pulsar must now deal with the other Colonies through diplomatic negotiations in hopes of continuing to enforce the treaty. King Pulsar and Queen Elisheba are watching the Lennethian press conference announcing the formation of the Coalition in their imperial chambers, arguing over their decision to reassign Gill to serve with the Coalition.

King Pulsar takes a seat at a dining table in his chambers while his wife, Queen Elisheba, lies in bed receiving a massage from an android. King Pulsar reaches for a platter of meat, saying, "Gill will serve us well in the Coalition. I need insight as to what the other Colonies are doing. We need to know their military prowess and ambitions."

King Pulsar is of octopus descent with purple skin, standing 6'7'', with a muscular physique and a pronounced nose. He has tentacles blended through his long black hair, a chiseled jaw, with kind brown eyes. Thin tentacles flow from his chin blending into his beard. He has a large tattoo of his family sigil covering his back. He has fins on his forearms and calves as well as pink gills on the side of his neck and ribcage. His voice is deep and domineering, and he is usually seen in high spirits beloved by all of his Evo.

Queen Elisheba concludes her massage slithering out of her bed in the nude. Pyramid-shaped drones begin to hover in circles around her body, spraying a blend of eucalyptus vitamins moisturizing her jelly-like skin. The water in the room is waist deep, allowing her to easily maneuver with her tentacles.

One of Queen Elisheba's drones wraps her body in a purple spider silk cape. "Letting Gill leave was unwise. We've lost leverage with the other tribes and our genetics program is months behind schedule. We're vulnerable from within and from the other Colonies."

Queen Elisheba is 6'3'' with long blue hair and distinct humanoid traits. The lower half of the queens body is comprised of eight large tentacles six feet long with a twenty-four-inch diameter. Waist up, the queen appears completely human with a large head resembling an octopi sac. She has beige skin and blue tentacles blended throughout her blue hair. She has a slender face and physique, almond eyes, with a natural floral scent. She has blue scales on her shoulders, hips, and lower back. Her skin is wet to the touch, offsetting her blue eyes and blood-red lips. Elisheba's tentacles on her lower body are used to maneuver and suffocate her prey. Her tentacles slowly regenerate and the suckers beneath her tentacles have retractable fangs that allow her to defy gravity.

King Pulsar finishes eating a large mound of meat before walking to an office in his chambers, four hundred feet away from his bed. King Pulsar pulls out a data cube from his desk, explaining, "You underestimate me yet again. I've already undergone some genetic resequencing." King Pulsar displays footage from his genetics lab showing experiments being performed on several test subjects. "We're not as behind as our intel reports suggest."

Queen Elisheba sits at her vanity while levitating orbs apply the queen's makeup and brush her hair. Queen Elisheba turns to her husband, exclaiming, "The test subjects died! Are you mental?"

King Pulsar walks from his office to his cleansing boudoir, explaining, "Twenty soldiers survived the genetic splicing, developing abilities within days. This technology's already on the black market in Petra. I received intel yesterday about the Maddox tribe's gene program. They were a few months ahead of us, so I sped things up."

"Twenty-three soldiers survived out of a hundred! You don't think I read the intelligence briefings from the elders? Progress can be made without being reckless!" says Queen Elisheba as she slithers over to a balcony inside her chambers overlooking Vishnu.

King Pulsar disrobes into his shower as two of his service drones shave him. King Pulsar turns on the data sphere in his cleansing boudoir, telling Queen Elisheba, "I enlisted the help of the Guardian. We studied the genomes of the survivors and adjusted our process. The most recent trials have been much more successful."

Queen Elisheba retorts, "Why was this kept from me? Do you not trust your wife and queen?"

King Pulsar chuckles as he rinses himself in the shower, answering, "Your ambitions make blind trust impossible. I'll be displaying my new abilities at our Commencement ceremony!"

"In the meantime, you would have me defenseless. I see where your loyalties stand," says the queen as she rises from her vanity with her makeup and hair finished. "How many abilities did you splice into your genome?"

King Pulsar's basking in the queen's anger, saying, "I didn't want to risk your safety."

Queen Elisheba slithers to the entrance of the imperial chamber, asking, "What new gifts did you acquire?"

Before Queen Elisheba leaves, King Pulsar says, "I became what was necessary to rule Kronus." Aware of his wife's true intentions, he takes pleasure in her disappointment.

The queen exits the royal chamber and pulls out an encrypted communicator. She whispers outside the chamber into her communicator, "Operation Jynxx needs to be initiated. The target has already undergone multiple gene splices, gaining an unknown number of abilities. Warn the assassins!"

Queen Elisheba starts slithering toward her daughter's chambers, maneuvering through the waist-deep water with overlapping tentacles propelling her forward. She makes her way through the extravagant palace as servants lower their heads within her vicinity, avoiding eye contact with the temperamental queen.

King Pulsar was one of the first mutants to display abilities in Kronus. As a result, most of his children possess abilities. His daughter Sage can temporarily absorb mutant abilities, memories, and skills from those she touches. She can make her skin lucid, which she incorporates in her combat style being a master of weapons. More importantly, she is the heir to the Kronus Empire.

Sage has light blue skin which varies in texture and shade. She's 5'9" with humanoid features and an elongated head. She has thin tentacles blended between her long blue hair. She has a triangular face with high cheekbones, making her gorgeous like her mother. Sage has gills on the side of her neck she uses to breathe in water and webbed feet. She has a thin body frame and is usually adorned in gold and jewelry.

Queen Elisheba has no natural mutant abilities, but she's a carrier of the mutant gene. As Elisheba makes her way through the palace fuming in frustration, realizing her husband has the power to grant her what she desires most—mutant abilities. Queen Elisheba's first son, Omarius, was killed in the war against the Reef tribe years ago. Queen Elisheba's never fully recovered from the loss, blaming her husband for forcing their son to fight. Despite not having mutant powers himself, Omarius was a famous warrior. His death caused many of the tribes to believe that only mutants are fit to lead the empire. As the queen enters her daughter's chambers, she laments over her son's death, pondering what could have been if the gene-splicing technology had been developed years earlier.

Queen Elisheba slithers into Sage's room unannounced, causing Sage to exclaim, "Haven't I told you to knock?" Sage closes her data sphere and ends her stream with a beautiful young Evo unfamiliar to the queen. Queen Elisheba couldn't see who was on the other end of Sage's stream, quickly realizing she interrupted an intimate conversation.

"I don't knock in my own palace, child. I heard you're insisting on training with the Imperial Guard, despite my instructions?" Queen Elisheba pushes the books on a nearby chaise lounge into the waist-deep water making room to sit. She shows no regard for her daughter's belongings, demanding her full attention.

Sage meets her mother near the entrance of her chamber, explaining, "Kronus and the Imperial Guard answer to my father—the king! The same king who manages my training. If you have a problem with me learning how to defend myself, I suggest you speak with your husband."

"Your father's king because of my bloodline. I'm the rightful ruler of Kronus!" yells the queen as she clenches her fist.

Sage rolls her eyes, mocking her mother, having heard her quarrel before. "If only you were born male. If only you were a mutant. Blah, blah, blah!"

"You'll learn your place, child! Ruling over billions requires finesse. The political skill required for our position requires study, my child. To be queen you must learn the art of politics!" says Queen Elisheba as she lowers her tone, pulling Sage's vanity next to her with her large tentacles.

Sage walks to the opposite side of her mother standing her ground explaining, "I have no interest in politics. War is coming, and those of us with the power to defend Kronus have a higher calling. I don't expect you to understand. I was in the middle of a training session with Sensei Mazin when you intruded. King Pulsar arranged it for me, so we'll have to catch up later. Orders from the king and all."

Queen Elisheba stands staring Sage down with a look of disdain, saying, "You call that training? You'll start your lessons with a teacher of my choosing. If you care for Sensei Mazin, you'll do as I've instructed."

Queen Elisheba smiles, heading towards the exit of Sage's chambers. Sage calms herself before saying, "Sensei Mazin's more than capable of defending herself. However, any harm that comes to her on your orders will sever our relationship. I'll be sure to let Father know of your threats!"

Queen Elisheba stops in her tracks, completely insulted and irate. "Do you know anything of traditions? I am Queen of Kronus... I control your fate! I'm trying to prepare you for the throne. Your disrespect—"

Sage interrupts, screaming, "I've seen what your guidance looks like firsthand!" She looks at the wall, looking at a picture of her brother Omarius.

Queen Elisheba does her best to hide her grief, saying, "I've covered up your father's mistakes more times than I can count. The same king you see as infallible is the same Evo responsible for the way things are. There's so much you don't know."

Sage somersaults twenty feet into the air, landing in front of her mother, making a controlled splash in the shallow water inside her room. She uses telekinesis absorbed from her sparring partner to block the exits. "Then show me. I'll browse your memories and see for myself. Of course, I'll know all your dark little secrets...but I'll know the truth."

"Lay a tentacle on me and I'll have you executed for treason!" exclaims Queen Elisheba as she pushes Sage out of the way with one of her large tentacles from the lower half of her body. Queen Elisheba realizes her months of planning could unravel, should her daughter choose to steal her memories.

Sage allows Queen Elisheba to push her way out, saying, "Glad we caught up, Mother. No rush to do this again."

Queen Elisheba stands in the exit door, knowing the smart thing for her to do is leave. However, the urge to properly discipline her daughter is overwhelming. She puts her ambitions first, saying, "Change is coming. You'll be prepared to rule, whether you like it or not!" The queen leaves Sage's chamber, ending their conversation.

Queen Elisheba makes her way towards the docking bay to pick up a secret shipment from Kronus's black market. Surface technology is coveted, expensive, and difficult to transport. Queen Elisheba messages her contact in the docking bay informing them she's en route.

Meanwhile, inside the royal chambers, King Pulsar is making final preparations for his wife's treachery. He was warned of Queen Elisheba's plans to assassinate him, having been shown a devasting vision of a parallel future. King Pulsar is seated at a desk in his office in deep thought. He taps his temple activating his communicator on his wrist, saying, "Summon my priestesses!"

King Pulsar accesses his chamber's AI ordering Protocol 33 to be escorted to him. Within minutes, two Colonial guardsmen enter the chamber escorting an Evo wearing a purple robe. King Pulsar dismisses the guardsmen, ordering the mystery Evo to undress, revealing an identical clone. The clone has matching scars, tattoos, and gene-spliced mutations identical to the king. The clone has been studying the king for months, learning mannerisms and the proper speech cadence to pass for King Pulsar.

The clone is undergoing its final scarring procedure, adding a third degree burn down the right side of his body. An advanced AI will overlook the healing process, using Evo technology to mirror the king's scarring. The discoloration of his tattoos and the scar tissue from his battle wounds must be replicated with precision, for the keenest eyes may detect a flaw.

Outside the imperial chamber, the king's three priestesses are walking down the grand hall discussing why they've been summoned. Nova, Chakra, and Polaris each have telepathic and psychic abilities that, when combined, make the trio an omega-level psychic entity. King

Pulsar's coven of priestesses consult him in all matters concerning Kronus.

An eager Chakra's leading Polaris and Nova down the grand hall, asking, "Do you think it's about the Vishnu tribe or Commencement security?"

Chakra is a talented telepath able to link multiple minds. Chakra's psychic links allow for shared memories and emotions while her telekinetic abilities are off the charts. Chakra can siphon power from her enemies by draining their chi to increase the strength of her own powers. Chakra has precognitive abilities, and she can astral project her consciousness vast distances including other dimensions. Chakra's the youngest of the coven but by far the most powerful.

Chakra is of octopi descent and the smallest amongst the priestess, standing 5'7'', with beautiful blue skin with orange stripes covering her body. Her face has blue skin, her eyes are icy blue, and she has dramatically high, protruding cheekbones. Chakra has long orange hair with tentacles blended throughout her hair. The orange stripes on her back create an ordained geometric shape said to have formed from the Akashic itself.

Nova takes a deep breath, rolling her eyes, answering, "It's about the queen. She's chosen her path, and she's moving against the king. You would've seen this had you meditated this morning."

Nova is a master telepath who can communicate and probe minds over great distances. She can possess the minds of multiple Evo simultaneously, also creating protective fields that nullify telepathic and psychic energy. She has no control over her precognitive gifts, which are best described as latent. Her visions take over her body without warning and have often been unreliable without her fellow priestesses. Nova's a powerful empath, and like her fellow priestesses, one of the most dangerous warriors in Kronus.

Nova is of octopi descent, 6'0'' tall, with lavender skin wet to the touch in varied textures and shades. Her bones on her forehead protrude with overlapping skin in the shape of an upside-down triangle. She has violet eyes, sharp humanoid facial features, with thin tentacles blended throughout her purple hair that flows down her muscular back. Nova has a birthmark of two half circles on each of her forearms that, when put together, create a map of the stars.

"We'll find out soon enough," says Polaris as they approach the doors to the royal chambers. Silver doors standing twenty-four-feet high open as the three priestesses approach. The coven is greeted by King Pulsar as they each bow their heads. Polaris raises her head, asking, "My liege, how may we be of assistance?"

Polaris is a master telekinetic able to harness magnetic fields. Polaris is the priestesses' link to the physical world while the others maintain their entities astral form. Polaris has control over magnetism, allowing her to create force fields, energy blasts, and travel at Mach speeds over ley lines. Polaris can also harness magnetic fields to display thoughts and memories. She's the eldest of the trio, and the only one without precognitive abilities, giving her massive insecurities about her positioning within the coven.

Polaris is of octopi descent and the tallest amongst the priestesses standing 6'3''. She has pink skin and scales covering her slim, muscular physique. Polaris has thick red hair with tentacles blended throughout. Her humanoid facial features give her a regal presence. She has pink gills on her neck, brown eyes, and a slender nose. The scales on her hips, shoulders, back, and forearms are various shades of pink. Polaris has an ethereal singing voice and serves as a weapon sworn to protect the king.

King Pulsar answers, "Another psychic had a vision of Elisheba's treachery. I've taken precautions and need my memories implanted into a clone. Your visions foretelling my impending death are not incorrect. But you are unaware of the precautions I've taken to alter our future."

Chakra's the first to notice the clone, dropping her jaw in shock. She pulls herself together, asking, "Is that a clone? Obviously, it is, but...isn't this illegal?" Chakra approaches the clone to inspect it, trying her best to keep her eyes above his waist.

"My wife's fated to take my life any day now. I would execute her, but doing so would anger some of the other tribes. The elders will confirm my death with a mental probe. I need a portion of my memories implanted into the clone to pass the telepathic autopsy," says King Pulsar as he takes a seat on a throne in the corner of his chambers.

Nova walks over to a nearby chaise lounge to sit, asking, "So you're going to let the queen kill your clone, and then what? You should at least let us meditate on the scenario and find the proper path." Nova can't help but think about the clone's consent. While the sacrifice is needed, Nova sees a soul with his own thoughts.

King Pulsar raises his hand to silence Nova, explaining, "The path has already been chosen. I've kept you all in the dark to maneuver unnoticed. Over the past few weeks, I've undergone multiple gene splices, giving myself more abilities. In the days to come, I fear I'll need them. I'll be with a Maddox sensei refining these powers. The Colonies must believe I'm dead for the time being. The queen has conspired against me. There will be consequences. For now, I'll use her to do my bidding."

Polaris approaches the king's throne, saying, "You want her to kill the leaders of the Reef tribe while you refine your new powers. If you were to wage war, you'd lose the support of the Sharkona tribes."

King Pulsar smiles as Polaris reveals his intentions to the others. He stands from his throne, explaining, "It must be done. Priestess Ujima has become a threat to the crown endangering our treaties with the other Colonies. In less than three moon cycles, we won't have Guardians enforcing our laws. I've undergone dozens of implants, but

I need to master my gifts to protect Kronus. The Vishnu army will be filled with mutants just like the Reef—I'll see to it."

Nova rises from a chaise lounge, saying, "Not everyone deserves to have mutant gifts. Perhaps nature alone should decide?"

"That philosophy didn't stop humans from creating us. If the Evo of Kronus believe you to be dead, they might be apprehensive accepting your return," says Chakra as she makes her way to the king.

King Pulsar responds, "This has been planned out by dozens of trusted psychics from a trusted tribe. The Maddox sensei will have my mind shielded from all forms of detection. Chakra, have you shared your vision with your fellow priestesses?"

Chakra lowers her head out of embarrassment, whispering, "I'm still having trouble separating my dreams from my visions. I was planning on sharing when the fractures became clearer."

The king shakes his head in disappointment, telling her, "Trust in your abilities. Link us!"

Chakra starts to levitate as her pineal gland in the middle of her forehead glows. Chakra guides their minds into synchronicity with their king. Their eyes glow as their emotions synchronize, becoming one. King Pulsar shares a vision of a massive war with hundreds of mutants fighting for separate tribes. In the vision, Queen Elisheba undergoes multiple genetic splices ruling Kronus as Queen selling imperial secrets to the highest bidder.

With their minds linked, Chakra combines Nova's precognitive abilities with her own, increasing the details of their vision. The foursome watch, as Queen Elisheba wages war against Regent Priestess Ujima, leader of the Reef tribes. The regent priestess partners with the new leaders of Zion, waging war in a unified assault against Kronus. War is fought for months, and Queen Elisheba is betrayed from within her inner circle and killed.

With the queen dead, Priestess Ujima takes power for a few months before being betrayed by Zion for Kronus's gene splicing technology. Once Zion takes Kronus for themselves, they discover a lost technology from the time of humans. Priestess Ujima kept the technology hidden for generations, convinced no Evo should wield its power. They watch the fall of Kronus, lamenting the loss of their culture as their Colony is forgotten over time. Chakra becomes overcome with emotion severing the link.

"NO! You should have kept going! Why'd you sever the link?" screams Polaris as they lower themselves to the ground. Polaris does her best to hide her own fear. They're all shaken from the paralleled timeline that would have manifested without intervention.

Nova wraps her arms around Chakra, saying, "She did fine. Lay off, Polaris!"

King Pulsar raises his hand to calm the tension, saying, "As of now, that's our future... That's why this clone is being sacrificed. You three will be my eyes and ears in my absence. I'll return just when I'm needed."

King Pulsar's clone bows to one knee, saying, "I'm honored to serve my king and Colony. I sacrifice my mind, body, and spirit willingly."

Nova folds her arms in disbelief reminding everyone, "Elisheba despises us. We won't have the opportunity to earn her trust. Why didn't you tell us about this clone? Do you know how many visions we had of what we thought was your death?"

The king walks over to his meditation chamber. "The three of you will convince her that your loyalties in me were misplaced. Upon my assassination, simply feed her ego. Tell her that the omniverse saw me as unfit to lead. The High Council and Senate will be predictable. It's Elisheba you'll need to worry about."

Polaris follows the king into his meditation chamber, explaining, "Allies in the Senate and High Council won't force the queen to trust us. She'd expect us to do everything possible to save your life. We should act as expected and earn her trust with information."

Nova walks over, adding, "We should tell Elisheba we've seen a vision with her as queen. It may lower her guard."

King Pulsar sits in a meditative pose and begins levitating with his eyes closed. He tells the priestesses, "I have faith in all of you. I'll need you to protect Sage in my absence. Make sure Gill's intel from the Coalition is acted upon. Make sure he stays safe; spare no expense. We're going to seize our own future. Ever since I made this clone, our future has opened with endless possibilities that weren't present before. My death was inevitable, but I don't have to die. The future we saw was simply not acceptable."

"We can handle Elisheba," says Polaris, as she, too, sits in a meditative stance levitating.

Nova enters the meditation chamber and feels a spike of sadness from Chakra. "Are you okay?"

Chakra looks as if she's seen a ghost admitting, "No! I'm not okay. We underestimated the need for the Guardians. We're on the precipice of war with millions of lives hanging in the balance. We should have spent more time observing the other Colonies. I never thought any of them would dare invade. I need—"

"Training. You need training and a backbone to go along with it!" says Polaris, annoyed and uneasy.

"Without us, we have no insight into the future! We provide our tactical advantage, so start acting accordingly! We all feel your thoughts and ineptitude," exclaims Nova out of anger.

Polaris responds, "You siphon our power to make yourself valuable. You're a leech!"

Chakra lowers herself from her meditative stance, interjecting herself between Polaris and Nova, yelling, "Enough!" She looks to Polaris, saying, "Nova respects your precision, and you envy her natural talent. I know exactly how you both feel about each other. We don't have time for this." Frustrated, she looks to King Pulsar, saying, "My liege, now would be the perfect time to give us our orders!"

King Pulsar levitates with his body fully extended twelve feet off the ground. "You need to be united in my absence. I'll be in telepathic contact with Nova every three days, when the moon and tide are at their peak. The three of you will keep me updated and warn me if my presence is needed back here. Nova will be in charge, but you'll make decisions together. Is that understood?"

The priestesses lower their heads, responding in unison, "Yes, my king!"

King Pulsar adds, "You will serve the queen, do her bidding, and stay alive."

Chakra makes her way to the middle of the large meditation chamber and stands beneath King Pulsar. Chakra tells the king, "I won't kill my own Evo."

"You will if it's needed. The queen will test your loyalty publicly. You'll need to comply or she'll kill you," says King Pulsar as he prepares to transfer his memories into his clone.

Nova orders the clone to stand beneath King Pulsar as the priestesses circle him levitating from above. King Pulsar's floating twenty-three feet in the air while the priestesses levitate in a circle above the clone at thirteen feet in the air in the middle of the chamber. Red, purple, and orange lights spark as the priestesses rotate counterclockwise. King Pulsar's head starts glowing as the priestesses duplicate and transfer the king's memories into the clone. Their goal is to ensure the clone has enough of the king's memories to pass the telepathic autopsy needed to confirm his death. The process is being recorded as evidence of the clone's existence so that King Pulsar can reclaim his throne in the future.

When the process is finished, King Pulsar lowers himself to the ground as his priestesses follow his lead. Chakra takes a seat as her body steams from the energy that was passing through her. She was the catalyst allowing the process to be completed. Chakra looks at the clone, saying, "What have we done? This is a living, breathing Evo. He has a soul now. When he dies, he'll feel it just like any of us would! Gaya, forgive our transgressions!"

Polaris kneels before King Pulsar, saying, "We'll serve the queen and await your return."

Nova walks over to Chakra explaining, "This clone's replacing King Pulsar, so the king that raised us doesn't have to die. We've all seen the vision. The Akashic demands the king's blood. This will allow him to live and return to us stronger. With that strength, he'll lead us on our next path."

"I know my path. I don't need leading," says Chakra as she collects herself, walking toward the exit without saying her goodbyes.

Nova tells Chakra telepathically, "*Are you crazy! The king won't stand for this disrespect!*"

Chakra responds telepathically, "*No king of mine would ask this of us. He's abandoning us to make himself more powerful. He saw the vision just like us. It's our responsibility to save Kronus. At least that is my path!*" Chakra exits the chambers, making her way to her private quarters.

Nova apologizes for Chakra's behavior before receiving a debriefing from King Pulsar on her communicator. King Pulsar tells Nova, "Chakra will come around. Meet with the generals and gather the most recent intel on Petra's research labs. A royal operative has been spying from within Petra for over a decade. They recently uploaded some files onto the Colonial servers. I just sent you access codes for them. I need the data reviewed, then deleted from the servers. Petra's created a mutant induction serum the crown has great interest in. I need the three of you to oversee this operation without Elisheba's knowledge." Polaris bows and excuses herself from the royal chamber to do as she's been instructed.

The priestesses are rarely caught by surprise but King Pulsar's ability to operate outside of their psychic reach is impressive. He's planned this hiatus for months, forced to take dramatic actions to protect Kronus.

Nova and Polaris exit King Pulsar's chambers mentally processing all that they've heard. Nova tells Polaris, "You need to watch your tone with Chakra. She'll grow to lead this coven one day. Show her some respect. Obviously, we have bigger problems. We're going to need each other more than ever now!"

"I don't have a problem with her. I just refuse to coddle her. She's lazy, and the mistakes she makes overshadow her potential," says Polaris as she pulls up the intel files King Pulsar mentioned.

Nova pushes Polaris against a wall, looking her in the eye, saying, "If you continue pushing her because of your insecurities, this coven will break. Your tactics aren't working and you're creating an unnecessary emotional block we cannot afford."

Polaris uses her abilities to push Nova off, responding, "I'm tough on the two of you because I care...because my life is in your hands. Chakra's been handed a silver spoon since she came into her powers. You saw what I saw. We're going to war if we don't play our parts right."

"You had a rough life. Stop punishing the rest of us for it!" says Nova as she storms down the hallway to their chambers.

Polaris chuckles, responding, "It's always been the two of you and then me. I'll leave it to you to get her ready for what's to come. Thankfully, I don't need pushing."

Nova stops in her tracks, feeling horrible about what she said, only to turn around and see Polaris turn the corner in the opposite direction. She says aloud, "Dammit! Polaris, wait!" She huffs then runs after her.

Meanwhile, inside the lab where Petra's secret induction serum is being produced, mutant mercenaries are meeting with Petra's leaders negotiating their rate for the serum's transport. Petra's located on the former continent of South America. Most of the world's medicine is exported from Petra. They conduct the world's leading research in medicine, genetics, botany, and mutant genetics.

Petra is an exotic Colony with oversized plants grown from electro culture using copper antennas utilizing the Earth's energy to grow larger plants without the use of pesticides. Petra's on the former continent of South America. Rising tides, earthquakes, and volcanic activity have reshaped the geographical landscape.

Petra has a hot Amazonian climate throughout the continent re-sembling the shape of the letter C. The entire continent is covered in beautiful vegetation and its northern beaches have crystal clear waters covered in luxury homes and modern buildings. Evo of jaguar, anaconda, frog, royal flycatcher, toucan, and monkey descent are prevalent in Petra.

Petra is a large Colony comprised of twenty-three sectors, within three precinct zones: Elysian, Finias, and Meriposa. Different dialects are spoken sector to sector within miles of terraformed jungles. Each precinct zone has seven sectors controlled by three families. These families control Petra's political and financial landscape. Petra's an oligarchy, with a ruling supreme commander. Regents appointed from the ruling family's control most of Petra's essential exports.

Petra has a low number of mutants in comparison to the other Colonies. Many of the planet's greatest artists call Petra home, inspired by its natural beauty and easy living. The Petra Guardian is the smallest of the Guardians, standing 6'0'', with a feminine physique hovering above the ground by manipulating magnetic wavelengths. Its lower body is shaped like an inverted triangle as its legs mold together descending to a sharp tip. Its head has three interchangeable faces looking north, east, and west, representing Petra's three spiritual pillars: enlightenment, reciprocation, and balance. The Petrian Guardian also has billions of processors within its artificial bloodstream allowing it problem solve and strategize on a quantum level.

Petra has energy shields and satellite lasers powered by the sun acting as an extension of the Petrian Guardian. Eighty-foot-tall ion-disrupter cannons are spread throughout the continent for defense. Petra's import-export trade agreements with the other Colonies have withstood the test of time compounding its wealth. Petra protects its borders indiscriminately to preserve its medical advancements, re-search, and technology. Travel to Petra is expensive, yet a destination many Evo endure to cure rare health conditions.

Petra's buildings are built around vast rainforests abundant with life. Petra has various ecosystems surrounding the terraformed amazons with technology embedded into the roots of the plants. Petra's beach cities have beautiful buildings built using a cascading effect that provides each home with an ocean view. Tidal energy collected at the coastline provides 15 percent of Petra's clean energy while wind turbines and solar panels provide the rest.

In addition to Petra's defense system, Petrians are inoculated from a host of viruses filtered into the water and food supply. Tourists are given temporary vaccines for the duration of their travel, ensuring guests don't overstay their visas. Petra's never known war, managing to become extremely wealthy.

Deep in the Amazon, inside a Petrian Research Lab (P.R.L.), a team of mercenaries are gathered for a classified mission. Newton, Rex, Pearl, and Kelis have been hired by the P.R.L. to transport a serum that induces mutation after encasing its recipient in a cocoon. Once three weeks have passed, the recipient has a 47 percent chance of emerging a mutant. Those that survive the gestation process awake with new abilities and a new genome. The mutant mercenaries transporting the serum are unaware of what they're transporting, but quite clear on what they're being paid.

Petra has been forced to hire mutants to combat the recent spike of mutations within Elysian. Mutants working with the Colony make a fortune becoming overnight celebrities with great wealth, influence, and power. Most mutants live in the shadows hiding who they are for safety while others are biding their time with their eyes on a larger prize.

Dr. Voya, the highest ranked scientist within the P.R.L., is seated at the head of a cherry oak table, nervous doing his best to control his heartbeat. He's outnumbered, feeling pressured to speak the truth.

Dr. Voya's of panther descent with feral features. He spins his paws, manipulating a map displaying multiple routes to a research facility. Dr. Voya adjusts his posture, saying, "Our Guardian's entrusted you three with our biggest advancement in mutant research. Something like this would normally be delivered by our Guardian, but its services are needed for another high-profile mission. Petria's Guardian will provide support, if necessary."

Newton puts his feet on the table as he leans back in his chair, replying, "For what we're being paid, its assistance won't be necessary. Your serum will arrive safely. I give you my word."

Newton is of mountain lion descent, able to control gravity through his purrs. He can focus his purr affecting the density of objects, making them weightless or extremely heavy. Newton can create black holes for a short period of time and mimic the effects of telekinesis. He can create shields, energy blasts, and fly.

Newton stands 6'5", with striking feral features with gray skin and fur. He has blue eyes, a beard, and perfectly maintained white dreads he keeps in a ponytail. He has a muscular build and a strong jaw. He has a tattoo in the middle of his forehead gifted to him by a shaman who raised him since he was child. Newton has a deep commanding voice, befit for a leader.

Pearl opens her wingspan, stretching out to explain, "We're honored Petra recognizes our gifts and professionalism. We simply ask that we have all the related intel to accomplish our mission."

Rex folds his arms asking in a direct tone, "What kind of transport are we using and what route are we taking? Once we leave Meriposa, we're vulnerable to attack."

Rex is of chameleon descent with two arms and legs, standing 6'8''. He can shape-shift and change the density of his scales. Rex has a healing factor and is immune to heat, radiation, and fire. He's an expert swordsman and great with computers. Rex changes his arms into different weapons in battle and can withstand massive impacts. Rex is originally from Carthage, having migrated to Petra as a child. His father was a renowned botanist, granting his family asylum and status in Petra.

Rex has green skin and scales covering his entire body. He has pink lips, a thin face, and protruding bones for eyebrows. He has two horns on either side of his green mohawk. His forehead is covered in blue are turquoise scales outlining his mohawk. Rex has a reptilian nose bridge with two holes that act as his nostrils. He has a long tongue he uses to hunt and track prey. His tail spirals at its tip into a circle like that of a chameleon lizard.

Dr. Voya signals, pointing to a route highlighted on a hologram from the data sphere in the middle of the room. The data sphere has a neural link to Dr. Voya responding to his hand motions and thoughts. Dr. Voya walks near Rex, explaining, "The P.R.L. has an underground facility near this beach. A stealth hover-transport with reinforced glezslavine will take you to a rendezvous point outside an abandoned warehouse. The serum will be delivered from that warehouse through an underground tunnel that leads to our Elysian Base. You'll have one support team trailing you in a separate transport."

Newton stands then levitates over to Dr. Voya, passing over the table and through the hologram. As Newton lands on the other side, he says, "We don't need support. We need a safe route directly to the research facility. Taking the payload through these tunnels has too many vulnerability points."

"He's right. Some of us won't be able to use our abilities in the confined space," says Pearl as she studies the various routes to the Elysian base.

Dr. Voya turns to Newton, asking, "Will we need more mutants if we take an outdoor route?"

Kelis pulls up intel on the Primean mutants known to the Colony, saying, "I'm assuming there's some interception concerns? Otherwise, you wouldn't be hiring us. Considering the mutants that the Primeans have at their disposal, we'll need all the help we can get."

Rex turns to asks Dr. Voya, "What exactly are we transporting?"

"The serum's a molecular compound derived from a rare root that forces Evo into a cocooned stasis. In this stasis, we can rewrite the normal Evo genome by transplanting mutant genes. In three weeks, the evolved Evo emerge with new mutant abilities," says Dr. Voya as he pulls up a holographic video of a volunteer undergoing the procedure. "We can create an entire Colony of mutants once this serum is in mass production. This serum's the biggest advancement in Evo evolution within the past century."

Kelis has a look of disbelief on her face, responding, "Sounds good on paper, but a Colony's actions often have unintended consequences... even with good intentions."

Kelis is of red panda descent with multiple defensive and psychic capabilities. Her bright orange fur adapts to her environment when she's in danger. Her adrenaline gives her superior strength and allows her to create force fields and regenerate. Kelis is a novice telepath with nominal skills as a psychic, but her powers allow her to adapt to any enemy. Kelis has a passion for helping others. She has trouble forcing her body to create the adrenaline needed to activate her powers.

Kelis stands 6'0'' with a perfect blend of humanoid and Evo features. She has white skin on her face and stomach while her shoulders, arms, hips, and legs have orange skin and fur. Kelis has gold eyes, large triangular ears emerging from the top of her head, and long orange hair that flows down to her lower back. She has a fluffy tail with a curvy physique and is considered soft-spoken.

Newton touches the hologram selecting a route he feels is more secure. He looks to the group, explaining, "This route has the lowest risk. We'll have to recruit a few more mutants..."

"And split our commission?" asks Rex, visibly offended.

Dr. Voya rolls his eyes, responding, "Petra will cover the additional cost. We need you to protect this with your lives...*please!*"

"The P.R.L. hired the best. No worries, doc!" says Pearl as she walks to the other side of the room in front of a window composed of a translucent energy shield. The research lab is a large spherical building built around a large 580-foot sequoia tree. Pearl takes a glimpse of Meriposa and its beautiful architecture. Dozens of ships are crossing in the skies as holographic ads illuminate the skies. For a moment, she's able to tune out Dr. Voya focusing on securing the contract which will cover their debts. Newton levitates toward Pearl, joining her by the window.

Dr. Voya raises his voice to get their attention, saying, "We're three days away from Commencement, this serum needs to be at our other research facility before then or the

supreme commander will have our heads."

Newton taps his temple, accessing his communicator. Newton looks over at Dr. Voya and says, "I'll reach out to my contacts for additional support. They'll expect three million credits for their services. Have there been any security breaches recently?"

"We've received intel that the Primeans are spending massive resources to recruit precognitive psychics. Two weeks ago, we also had a data breach. Finally, a faction of scientists that previously refused to work with Petra signed a renunciation agreement with the Colony. We've confirmed that these scientists have been in contact with Primean leaders. In short, the Primeans know what you have and where you're going!" says Dr. Voya as he pulls the intelligence he referenced onto the center hologram.

Newton creates a small blackhole near Dr. Voya, slowly pulling him toward the window while exclaiming, "You mean to tell me the Primeans have known about this serum for over two weeks, and you're given us a few hours to devise a plan to protect it?"

Dr. Voya sweats profusely, as Newton pulls him closer to him with a miniature blackhole. He stutters, saying, "It's...it's less than ideal...I-I know. But we're hiring you all because of your powers and track record of su-su-success. Please, I...I...I..."

Pearl creates a psionic sword and puts it to Newton's throat, explaining, "If you kill the client, we don't get paid. Lucky for you, I know a thing or two about military strategy. Let the doctor go, Newt."

Pearl is of hawk descent and the youngest amongst the mercenaries. She has the unique ability to incapacitate her enemies with psionic blasts and psionic weapons she manifests from psychic energy. Pearl has telepathic abilities, razor-sharp talons, and can fly at Mach speeds. Pearl's a predator by nature, a trained fighter, and a savant military strategist. Pearl's family was banished from Olympia for reasons she was never told, now living a privileged life on the beaches of Petra. Her mother gained passage into Petra because of her unique knowledge of Olympian science.

Pearl has brown wings descending behind her 6'0''-stature like a beautiful cape. She has pale beige skin, long brown hair, and gold eyes with hints of hazel. She has thin lips which are outlined by cartilage from her former beak. Pearl has a white collar of bird skin and feathers emerging from behind her ears blending into hear hair resembling a large white collar. She has brown feathers on her breasts, shoulders, thighs, and in the corner of her eyes. She has a mysterious presence and is always the first to speak her mind.

Newton dissipates the blackhole he was using to drag Dr. Voya, saying, "This mission is suicide. They have no intention of paying us. They don't expect us to survive. This whole operation is likely a distraction for them to send a second transport to another location. We're the patsies!"

"Dr. Voya's our client. Let's show some respect," says Pearl as she dissipates her psionic blade that was against Newton's throat while winking at him.

Rex jumps across the room, grabbing Dr. Voya by the throat, lifting him off the ground. Rex has a look of deep disdain on his face, saying, "The Colony doesn't value our lives. You're going to give us all the intel you have on the Primeans and full access to your systems. We're also going to need to be paid half of our commission up front. Is that going to be a problem, scientist supreme?"

Dr. Voya's nearly choking to death but manages to whisper, "No!" Rex releases his grasp and Dr. Voya falls to the floor, cradling his neck.

"We need to call Lucky and see who he has available on such short notice. The Colony may not expect us to deliver this serum, but each of us needs this commission. So, we'll just have to disappoint them," says Rex as he transforms his arm into a sword.

Meanwhile, in downtown Meriposa, Primean faction leaders are meeting to discuss their plan for a full-scale assault, to steal the mutant induction serum from the P.R.L. The Primeans are meeting in Garuda's business towers for Adura Enterprises, located in the heart of downtown Petra. Garuda owns a successful pharmaceutical company using his business as a cover for his factions' operations. Garuda funnels money and provides political cover for the Primeans controlling major shares in the Petrian economy. The group's meeting in his private penthouse office, at the top of Adura Tower.

Garuda is of panther descent and always seen in a fitted suit. He's meeting with Trixie and Trance who support Garuda in running Petra's criminal underworld. The Primeans export lifesaving medicine, drugs, and weapons in and outside of Petra, making Garuda one of the most powerful Primean in the western hemisphere.

Garuda can shoot oversized poisonous claws which regenerate within seconds. His mutation allows him to create various toxins and antidotes. Garuda's a master strategist with a latent ability to persuade others through hypnosis via expelled pheromones. He doesn't have control over his persuasive pheromones, but he's inclined to get his way. Prolonged exposure allows him to control the mind as effectively as telepaths.

Garuda stands 6'4" with hazel eyes. He has perfectly groomed black skin and fur covering his muscular physique. He has triangular ears, a triangular nose resembling the snout of a panther, and long black hair. He has a muscular physique from his agile prowess. Garuda has thick legs and forearms as well as a long black tail. He's one of the wealthiest Evo on the planet and one of the world's most infamous mutants.

They have a difference of opinion regarding the decision to attack Lennek's Guardian. Some believe this is their last opportunity to prove their strength to the world while others believe attacking a Guardian is suicide.

Garuda places his tablet down, explaining, "I called this meeting with the three of you to discuss an important decision. Primean factions are moving against Lennek in less than seventy-two hours. I believe patience will ensure our victory and overshadow Puma's expected defeat. I say we sit this one out."

Trixie walks over to the data sphere, saying, "I wouldn't say her defeat is imminent. You have an army of combat droids beneath this very building. I say we use them to aid our comrade and remain anonymous. We should want our Primean sister to be successful."

Trixie overlooks the Primean dealings in Finias. She can make others see and feel whatever she desires. Trixie's a talented telepath and can astral project at will. In her astral form, Trixie can use limited telekinesis to affect the physical world around her. When focused, Trixie can control the minds and bodies of others making them her puppets.

Trixie is of flamingo descent, standing 7'3'', with thin legs encased in a hard, calcified bone marrow. She has pink skin, pink lips, and a thin pink mohawk. Pink feathers are blended into her hair matching her sheik appearance. Her stomach and breasts have white skin while her thin arms have pink skin. Varied shades of pink feathers emerge from her forearms, breasts, shoulders, and the corners of her eyes. Trixie has gray eyes and is distractingly beautiful with a domineering voice.

"You honestly think that animal wishes us well? We need to worry about ourselves post-Guardian. I say we attack the moment the Guardians shut down for an assured victory. The

Colonies have mutants of their own. Taking them on when they have a Guardian's support isn't a fight I want to sign up for," says Trance as he lies back in his chair blowing out cigar smoke.

Garuda responds, "We'll be securing the future of Petra. In two hours, the P.R.L. will receive a serum that induces mutation in normal Evo. The recipients of the serum have a thirty percent chance of dying during the gestation process that occurs inside a calcified cocoon. The advantage our abilities currently give us will become obsolete if they mass produce the serum! While Puma's trying to kill the un-killable, we'll secure the means to empower those loyal to our cause."

Trixie accesses the files she was looking for on Garuda's data sphere, explaining, "The Colony will make billions and force the entire population to take the serum. If thirty percent die in the process, they would be killing...1.6 million Evo!"

"They'll kill twice that without hesitation if advances Petra's interests. They're going to force the serum onto everyone, trust me. It's a small price to pay for millions of mutants," interrupts Garuda as he pulls up footage of Evo dying during the gestation process in cocoons.

"The mutant population is already a bit crowded, with a few thousand of us on the planet. As natural mutants, we would no longer have our edge," says Trance as he smokes a laced cigar. "We destroy the serum under the guise of protecting the 1.6 million Evo it could kill—I follow."

Garuda suggests, "Our faction should have the power to ensure our followers are empowered. We'll reward loyalty with power and punish those who dare stand in our way. Furthermore, we need Petra vulnerable for us to take over. My team has been working on a little surprise for our own Commencement ceremony."

Unable to peruse Garuda's thoughts, Trixie gets up to make herself an espresso. Garuda takes a seat at his desk as Trixie explains, "I'm not a fan of surprises. Do you have a plan you'd like to share?"

Garuda throws a data cube onto his desk, and the design for a large android appears on the hologram. Garuda explains, "Only the bold are fit to lead. This is why Puma's attacking Lennek. It's a grab for power and fame. When Puma attacks Lennek's Guardian, she'll draw millions to our cause regardless of her success. If by chance she does kill a Guardian, she'll become a legend. We must have the leverage to do the same. Her attack will make headlines for a few days. What I have planned will shake up the Colonies for decades."

Trixie starts studying Garuda's design on the hologram being projected from the data cube and takes a moment to study what she's looking at. Thousands of androids are making up a larger android. She examines the schematics, continuing, "You're not the only one with a long-term plan. My concern is with the serum. Will it be shared, or are you planning on controlling access to it?"

Garuda asks, "Are you inside my head, Trixie?"

"I don't need my abilities to read your mind," says Trixie as she approaches the coffee machine next to the organic food processor.

Ricco enters the room through an electrical socket. He slowly rematerializes as electrical currents turn into flesh and scales. "Sorry I'm late. Tell me we aren't going to Lennek to help Puma," says Ricco as he makes himself comfortable amongst his comrades.

Ricco is one of the deadliest and feared warriors in Petra, considered Garuda's right hand. He can control electricity and emit EMPs (electronic magnetic pulses). Ricco can influence magnetic fields, absorb large amounts of energy, and self-regenerate. Ricco can also telepathically link his mind with electrical currents allowing him to hear, see, and travel through currents.

Ricco is of eel descent originally from Kronus. He's 6'5'' with turquoise scales and skin wet to the touch. He has gold eyes and cartilage horns flowing over his bald head. He has feral features that intimidate most. Ricco has a thin, muscular build, large lips, and gills on the side of his neck. He resembles an eel with two rows of razor-sharp teeth and a jaw from ear to ear. The scales on his chest and stomach are yellow, contrasting with the turquoise and blue scales covering most of his body. He has a short fin of cartilage that runs from his widow's peak down to his spine and the back of his legs. Ricco's a master of reading body language and predicting his enemies' movements, able to sense the electrical currents within the brain and muscles.

"We're discussing the matter now actually," says Trixie, unamused with his tardiness.

Trance adds, "I still haven't heard details to convince me."

Garuda stands from his desk, explaining, "The four of us will all have access to the serum. A vote will be taken on a case-by-case basis before giving the serum to anyone. We leave for the shoreline now. Ricco, I need you to oversee some business we have with Queen Elisheba. The rest of us will secure the transport from the P.R.L. Everyone know their assignments?" He takes silence as complicity, then says, "Let's move out!"

Trance takes a seat on a lounge chair, feeling the effects of his vapors and states the obvious. "One problem, boss. We can't make it to this extraction point within an hour."

Trance overlooks Elysian handling Petra's illegal drug trade. He can create vapors that attack the nervous system, robbing his victims of their senses. Trance can induce hallucinations that literally scare his enemies to death. Trance solidifies his vapors to create hallucinogenic drugs selling them on the black-market. Trance's tail has been bioengineered with razor-sharp spikes that change shape based on the beta waves emitted from an implant inside his head.

Trance is of skunk descent, 6'1'' with feral features and short black hair. He has jet-black skin, beady green eyes, a black nose, and strong jaw. His face has white skin and fur, contrasting his short black hair, goatee, and sideburns. Trance's tail is thick and bioengineered with razor-sharp spikes that emerge when needed changing shape to fit his needs. While his tail looks organic, it's a testament to advanced Evo technology making him part cyborg.

Garuda turns to Trance, saying, "I've secured an alternate form of transportation from one of our Angkorian faction sisters."

Trixie folds her arms, asking, "Bunny?"

Garuda answers, "I see her reputation precedes her. Bunny will be here momentarily. Ricco, I need you on your way to Kronus. Here's a report on the rendezvous point."

"You secure the serum, and I'll finalize our business with King Pulsar.

It won't take me long to get there," says Ricco as he turns his body into pure energy and enters the power socket.

Moments later, Bunny teleports into the room, startling everyone. She casually walks over to Garuda's desk and takes a seat. "Can you tell me why my credits aren't in my account? And please tell me my amplifier's finished," says Bunny, unbothered with introducing herself to anyone.

"Brothers and sister, this is Bunny," says Garuda as he forces a smile, triggering his pheromones. He walks toward a large safe raising his chin for a retinal scan unlocking the safe. Inside are numerous weapons, pieces of gold, rare gems, and a glowing pendant in the center of the safe. Garuda grabs the pendant, then exits the safe as Bunny observes the safe's contents from a distance. He approaches Bunny, handing her the necklace, saying, "As promised, a fashionable device that stores lunar energy."

"How much energy does it store?" asks Bunny as she examines the pendant.

Garuda folds his arms, answering, "Enough to transport a few hundred Evo during the day in a single jump. However, at night results vary based on the lunar cycle."

"I'm impressed, Garuda. I'd like to hire you to build my combat suit. Two million credits, right?" says Bunny as she continues examining the pendant.

Garuda tells her, "The device is more effective when implanted. I could squeeze you in for a consultation.

Bunny chuckles, saying, "No thanks, I'll manage. I'm going to have this scanned for trackers. Let me know when your team's ready."

Trance approaches, saying, "You look like the type that likes to have a good time. I'd love to show you around Elysian...personally. You'll have your heart's desire at your beck and call. Not to mention the purest—"

"I need intel on the mutants guarding the P.R.L. transport. The more I know about them, the more effective my powers are!" says Trixie, unamused with Trance's behavior.

"I'll send you what I have. Bunny will get us there and we follow the plan to take what's ours," says Garuda as he watches Bunny put on her lunar necklace. "We could use someone like you with us permanently. I can take your powers to the next level."

"I'm already on another level! I'm waiting for the dust to settle following Commencement before I pick a faction," retorts Bunny as she teleports to Garuda's desk chair. "Truth be told, I shouldn't be here helping all of you without Puma's permission."

Garuda looks Bunny in her eyes, unknowingly triggering his pheromones. "My lips are sealed. I can keep a secret, and you can trust me."

Unable to sense Bunny's boundaries, Trance puts his arms around Bunny telling her, "The mission won't take all day. How about we hit the beach when we're finished?"

Trixie uses her powers to make Trance think Bunny is luring him into a cleaning closet as the room watches him grope a broom stick. In Trance's mind, Bunny is allowing Trance to do whatever he wants to her. Trixie looks at Bunny, saying, "They aren't used to feminine energy. Trance means well; he just forgets his place from time to time."

Bunny laughs, saying, "I'll give you my communicator frequency. I owe you one. Let me know if you need anything. The rest of you can pay my fee."

"I like her!" says Trixie as she forces Trance to clean the sink drain with his tongue.

Garuda shakes his head saying "Okay, that's enough. Let him go!"

Trixie releases her hold over Trance as his memories come flooding in. He turns to Trixie yelling, "You're not the only one who can play mind tricks. Stay out of my head—last warning!"

"Save your threats, rodent. You don't scare me," says Trixie as she astral projects her consciousness to levitate her body and create a telekinetic shield.

Garuda maneuvers between Trixie and Trance, saying, "Save the fighting for the mercenaries! We don't have much time before we need to be at the extraction point. I need everyone focused."

The team takes their time going over strategy preparing to rob the P.R.L. transport. Satisfied with their review, Bunny teleports the team to a rendezvous point over a cliff near the beach. A few hundred feet beneath the cliff is a highway that intersects with a dirt road leading to a black-ops research facility. The facility is secretly funded through Colonial tax dollars off the books.

Garuda positions his drones and automated weapons powering up a mobile base. The Primeans have put more planning into their robbery than the mercenaries escorting the precious cargo are expecting. While Garuda, Trixie, Trance, and Bunny await the P.R.L. transport, they put on their body armor.

Chapter 3 — Heist of All Heists

Garuda and his team are overlooking a jagged cliff near the eastern shoreline near a Colonial highway. A sandy beach curves and twists for miles showcasing some of Petra's most coveted beachfront property. A secret Petrian research lab is located about four miles underground. The Primeans set up a mobile camp, shielded with stealth technology, near the P.R.L. entry point, preparing to steal the mutant induction serum. Access to the facility is controlled by a secure entrance ramp, leading to a dirt road, four hundred feet below the highway.

Garuda, Trixie, Trance, and Bunny are suited up in their combat gear awaiting the Colonial Guard's arrival. The Primeans are in a large stealth tent retrofitted with the latest tech for their extraction. The cliff's edge is two hundred feet above a ramp entry point into the research facility. Primean weapons and surveillance technology have been installed beneath the highway's support beams. Hundreds of drones are on standby nearby, should air support be needed.

Garuda employs several psychics with precognitive gifts, giving him an upper hand in negotiating his affairs. His network of mutants helps grow his power while expanding his influence. His connections have also ensured the success of his many businesses. A group of defecting scientists provided Garuda intel regarding the serum. Additionally, he planted spies within the P.R.L. to provide real-time updates regarding the serum's transport route.

Garuda harnesses his armor, securing a black mask with a red line covering his right eye. He addresses the group telepathically, saying, *"Our intel's been confirmed; this is the correct transport route. We hit them hard, we get the package, and we're out! Bunny, you're our exit. So we need you to hang back until we can extract the serum."*

"Just say the word if you need any of the Colonial mutants out of the fight," says Bunny as she surveys the area from the cliff's edge.

Trixie slips a telepathic amplifier on her wrist, saying, *"I'll take the second transport with the soldiers. While I'm in their heads, I may pick up* some intel that the mercenary mutants aren't privy to."

Under the cover provided by the tent, Trance employs a device that gauges wind speed, saying, "*If we engage them on the south side of the intersection, the wind tunnel will assist my vapors. I'll be attacking them from there.*" Trance points to a location outside of the intersection with high wind flow.

Garuda shakes his head, responding, "*We need to keep them as far away from the facility as possible. If their team makes it to the intersection on the other side of the cliff, we lose our tactical advantage. You'll have to rely on your tail.*"

"*I'll adjust,*" says Trance as his tail morphs into two interlocked tridents.

Garuda turns to Trixie, saying, "*Trixie, I need you to make the soldiers turn against the P.R.L. mutants. They'll be wearing telepathic shields, so we'll need you on your A game.*"

Trixie shows her wrists, replying, "*That's what the amplifiers are for. I've got this.*"

Bunny asks, "*How far out are they?*"

Trance accesses a data sphere, interacting with holograms controlling drones surveying the area. He responds, "*Give me a second.*"

Trixie closes her eyes as she astral projects her consciousness to search the highways, telling her comrades, "*Give me a moment. I'm sure my efforts will be more effective.*"

Trance pulls up an encrypted message from their inside informant, saying, "*They left less than an hour ago and should be approaching our location within the next ten minutes.*"

Garuda folds his arms, saying, "*Trixie can give us a more accurate estimate. She'll find them even if their transports are shielded.*"

Bunny turns her head with a perplexed look, asking, "*How?*"

Garuda responds, "*By scanning for moving mutant signatures within a five-mile radius. Masks on, everyone.*" The Primeans put on masks matching their armor. Garuda especially needs to conceal his identity.

Trixie interrupts, saying, "*Found them. They're four minutes out heading down an abandoned road. I count five mutants... I thought the Colonial teams moved in groups of three?*"

Trance exclaims, "*We can take them!*"

Garuda thinks for a moment, then says telepathically, "*Change of plans. I'm going to flip the first transport and draw out the mutants. We need Ricco here for reinforcements. We'll make a window for Bunny to steal the serum and hold off the Colonial mutants until she returns to extract us!*"

Trixie has a nervous look on her face, adding, "*One of those mutants was naturally shielded from me. If they can shield any of the other mutants, my powers will be less effective.*" Trixie opens her eyes and reverts her consciousness back into her body.

"*Tell Ricco to meet me in the armory in two minutes. We'll be back before you attack,*" says Bunny as she prepares to teleport back to Garuda's business tower.

Trixie places two fingers on her temple, saying, "*I've contacted Ricco telepathically. He's moving through the electrical currents to meet Bunny in the armory. He'll be there in a few seconds.*"

"*I'll be back with reinforcements,*" says Bunny as she teleports off the cliff.

Bunny teleports back to Garuda's business tower inside his armory. Bunny looks around the enormous warehouse of Petrian military weapons. Bunny teleports to the defensive area of the armory and grabs a rare Olympian tiara that creates telepathic shielding. The telepathic shield is one of Garuda's collectables, protected by lasers. Bunny concentrates using the amplifier Garuda made for her to teleport the tiara into her hands. Bunny hears Ricco enter the armory through a socket, emerging as pure energy.

Ricco solidifies his body with his scales still expunging electricity.

"Hello! Bunny, where are you?"

Bunny teleports next to Ricco with two bags of weapons, explaining, "There're more mutants than we expected. We're taking precautions."

"I'm here, not to worry. Take us back to the others," says Ricco as Bunny grabs his shoulders teleporting back to their fellow Primeans on the edge of the cliff. They're making their final preparations for the heist of a lifetime as the P.R.L. close in on their location.

Newton, Kelis, Rex, and Lucky are sharing the transport carrying the mutant serum. Two other transports are filled with heavily armed Colonial guardsmen, specifically trained in mutant combat. Pearl's flying above the transports providing aerial cover for the convoys. Newton enlisted Lucky last minute paying him a fortune for his assistance.

Lucky has hyper senses, agility, enhanced strength, and the unique ability to predict behavior in seconds using complex probability modules. Lucky's super senses make him a walking forensic lab, polygraph, and x-ray machine. He can see in infrared with precise night vision, and his retinas allow him to zoom in on targets from miles away. His hyper senses allow him to hear the faintest sounds from a mile away and smell someone from thousands of feet away. He carries an axe and a sword that have a connective link with the protective gloves he wears to suppress his abilities, making it manageable to live within large cities without overloading his senses. He can retrieve both his axe and sword using his thoughts via beta waves. Lucky's combat skills are legendary having, worked twelve years as a mercenary, fostering an impeccable reputation worldwide.

Lucky stands 6'2" with brown skin and fur with tints of red. He has an elongated face from his ethnic background as a collie. He has long brown hair he keeps braided and a black nose surrounded by his white mouth and cheeks. He has varied shades of brown fur and skin covering his body except his stomach, which has white fur. He has a curved tail he keeps shaved down and folded ears on the top of his head. Lucky is boisterous, with humor making up the core of his personality. He's worked with Newton on countless missions earning a small fortune in Petra.

Lucky stands up from his seat to walk toward the front of the transporter, asking Newton, "So, what's in the case?"

Intentionally remaining vague, Newton answers, "This case holds Petra's future!"

Pearl follows, trailing from the air flying four hundred feet above with an aerial view. She has bad feeling and decides to follow her gut, reaching out through their telepathic link. *"Kelis, I need you to shield the transports. I'm sending a psionic pulse down the mountain pass. I could swear I sensed a telepath a while back."*

Kelis starts emitting a protective shield around the transports, negating Pearl's psionic energy before responding, *"We're good!"*

Pearl sends out a psionic pulse of energy to detect any mutants. Garuda, Bunny, Trance, and Ricco are holding onto Trixie as she shields the group from detection. The two transporters begin slowing down on the highway and veer to the left shoulder. The transport team approaches a dead end. The P.R.L. transports approach the wall blocking the dead end, opening a gate granting access to a private road. The P.R.L. transports make their way down an inverted ramp leading to a dirt road on the beach.

Pearl senses a disruption in her psionic pulses she's sending out, realizing someone's shielding themselves from her. *"Someone's here!"* Pearl orders the transports below her to stop, relying on her natural vision as a predator. She dives toward the shoreline, explaining, *"My senses are going haywire. We're driving into a trap!"*

Meanwhile, Trixie's shielding the Primeans, concealing their beta waves to remain hidden. Garuda responds, *"We're vulnerable on this cliff. We need to attack now!"*

As the transports stop, Lucky lowers a window, using his senses to search for nearby danger. Pearl searches the side of the cliff with psionic pulses, while Trixie continues shielding their thoughts. Although Trixie is masking the Primeans' beta waves, she weakens with each one of Pearl's pulses.

Trixie has trouble focusing, even with her amplifier, telling Garuda, *"Their telepath has a unique signature. I can't shield us forever, and this tent has its limits for hiding us!"*

"She's right! We're going to strike now before they're mobile again. Plans have changed. We take them off guard before they lock themselves in the transport and wait for reinforcements. We need to draw them out!" says Garuda, as he peeks through a crack in the tent. Confirming the area's clear, Garuda signals the others to make their way to the edge of the cliff.

Bunny sees the two transporters stopped near the entrance of the dirt road that curves along the beach. She whispers to the others, "We need to take out the transports by disabling their tires and engines."

"He's right! They'll call for backup, but...we have a window," whispers Trance as he adjusts his armor while holstering two weapons on each of his thighs.

Meanwhile, inside the transporters on the beach, Lucky is arguing with Newton exclaiming,

"We need to be on the move or outside of these transporters searching the area with Pearl!"

Newton is in the rear of the transporter deciphering analytics from a drone being relayed to the transporter's data sphere. Newton responds, "If you want to get paid, we follow protocol. If Pearl says she feels something, we give her a minute to scout the area. Let the drones do their job. We stay inside the transporters until—"

Lucky interrupts, saying, "The Primeans are familiar with military tech. If they're professionals, they'll have countermeasures ready to deploy. My senses are more effective than Pearl and your drones combined!" Lucky opens the transporter door, calmly exiting.

Newton uses his gravitational powers and closes the door. He turns on his communicator, exclaiming, "Dammit, Lucky! The drones are analyzing the air still!"

Lucky is outside the transport looking for heat signatures and examining the area. Lucky laughs, retorting, "I'll smell any biochemical weapons before the drones can process and analyze them. The air's fine. I don't see anyone, but I do smell five Evo beneath the support structure on the top of the cliff. We're not alone!" Lucky follows the scent of Garuda, Trixie, Trance, Ricco, and Bunny. He sharpens his vision on the area, zooming his retinas before switching his corneas to infrared.

Garuda watches Lucky from a distance and is still somehow noticed. Having lost the element of surprise Garuda orders, "*ATTACK!*" before he somersaults headfirst down the cliff, using his enhanced agility during the descent.

Pearl accesses Lucky's mind to determine the exact location of the Primeans. Pearl flies toward the Primeans, shooting massive psionic energy beams, forcing them off the cliff. Ricco turns himself into pure electrical energy to negate Pearl's attack, cascading down the cliff in a single leap.

Trixie jumps off the cliff, using telekinesis to glide down, while telepathically attacking everyone beneath her. Her eyes become completely white as she replicates an identical copy of herself on the astral plane accessing her telekinesis. She lands on the flat terrain as her gray eyes return to normal.

Trance is trying to outrun Pearl's attack while countering with metallic spikes shot from his tail. Pearl is forced to adjust her flight path, dodging Trance's spears, maneuvering through the air with grace. Trance shoots the tip of his bioengineered tail into the side of the cliff, creating a rockslide in the path of the Colonial transporters below.

Bunny teleports herself a block inland, away from the action removing a data sphere from her armor's holster frantically typing into the holographic keyboard. The data sphere levitates in front of Bunny, displaying multiple control panels for the weaponized drones they have nearby.

Meanwhile, on the beach, Garuda and Ricco made their way down the cliff attacking the Colonial mutants without mercy. Lucky draws his axe and throws it at Garuda, who barely manages to dodge it. Garuda jumps fifteen feet into the air using his enhanced agility, landing within striking range of Lucky. Garuda throws a roundhouse kick at Lucky, who blocks the attack using Garuda's momentum to throw him the opposite direction. Garuda shoots six oversized claws toward Lucky, who blocks the attack with an energy shield from his armor deflecting the poisonous claws. Lucky dissipates his shield, rolling as he unholsters his sword before throwing it at Garuda intending to sever his head.

Garuda dodges death yet again as Lucky flicks his wrists as his protective gloves summon his axe and sword back into his hands. The gloves are made with quantum magnetic technology linked to his beta waves, allowing him to control his weapons with his mind.

Ricco's been electrocuting the first transport overloading its absorption panels, drawing out the Colonial mutants. Eventually, ten Colonial guardsmen exit the second transport opening fire on Ricco with a hail of bullets, pulse cannons, and electrical dampeners. Ricco evades the attack, knowing the effects of the military electrical dampers.

Inside the first transport, Rex is scolding Newton for hesitating to assist Pearl and Lucky. Rex turns to Newton, saying, "I'm not sitting here while your friends fight our battles for us! You're far too powerful to run from a fight!" Rex opens the doors and sprints to flank Ricco, who is quickly overpowering the Colonial guardsmen.

"They're going to need you. We don't know what else they have planned. I'll protect the transport and keep it locked down until you have things under control. Go!" says Kelis as she herself exits the transport. The transport doors are still open, and numerous oversized claws come flying through the entrance from four thousand feet away, showing Garuda's insane marksmanship and accuracy.

Kelis is struck in the arm and Garuda's poisons begin to take effect. Newton uses his gravitational powers, creating a shield protecting the transport, himself, and Kelis. Kelis pulls the claw out of her arm as her body immediately heals.

Newton's frantically asking, "*Are you good, babe?*"

"*I can heal myself, you idiot. Go!*" demands Kelis as she raises a protective shield of her own. "*I'll keep the transport safe. Help the others.*" Kelis shakes off Garuda's attack and enters the transport closing the doors behind her keeping the serum safe.

Newton notices the tires on the transport have been shot out by Garuda's claws. The transporters engines have also been disabled, leaving the mercenaries no choice but to take out the Primeans to make it to the research labs. Newton sees Pearl and Trixie fighting in midair and uses his powers to aid his comrade from below. Trance and Ricco have nearly laid waste to the Colonial guardsmen who didn't stand a chance against them.

Trance releases his deadly toxins into the air, using his tail to kill every guardsmen in his path. His bioengineered tail is shaped like two interlocked tridents, which enable him to tear through the guardsmen with ease.

Rex has been studying Trance from a distance, looking for weaknesses. He uses his gravity-displacement boots to jump forty feet above Trance. From his flank, Rex dives forty feet to the ground headfirst with both his arms extended shaped as swords. Rex's arms pierce deep into Trance's shoulders, nearly killing him upon impact.

Rex is in a handstand above Trance with both arms lodged into his shoulder blades.

Rex maintains his balance, while watching Trance bleed out in a handstand. Rex dismounts, cutting through Trance's armor leaving him inches from death. Although Trance is badly injured, he continues releasing his toxins into the air. Rex is unknowingly breathing Trance's toxins while he repositions himself for an onslaught.

A surviving guardsmen fires a high-powered rifle at the cliff above, triggering a rockslide. Rex cuts Trance in the stomach before kicking him to the ground to be buried by the rubble. Rex uses his gravity-displacement boots to get himself to safety watching Trance get buried from above. As Rex skates through the air, he's unknowingly pumping Trance's poisons and hallucinogens through his blood stream. Rex starts feeling dizzy and falls from the sky with his lungs closing up.

Rex is on the ground losing conscious with enough energy to reach out to his comrades telepathically, *"Kelis, I've...been poisoned. Send... help!"* Rex passes out as the toxins start ravishing his internal organs.

"I've got a medic drone on the way. Hang in there, Rex!" says Kelis from inside the first transporter. Kelis dispatches a medic drone to Rex and dispatches three others to the injured Colonial guardsmen. A dozen of Garuda's armed drones are approaching from the south, firing missiles and a barrage of bullets.

From her position miles away, Bunny's controlling the drones, killing off the few remaining guardsmen. Newton takes to the air, creating an energy shield to protect the transporters. He thwarts missiles, bullets, and sonic weapons from the drones before he crushes them with his gravitational abilities, condensing the drones into small balls of metal.

Garuda and Lucky are still engaged in combat, using the terrain of the beach to test each other's agility. Lucky's ability to run predictive algorithms in his head has allowed him to avoid Garuda's claws. Using his superior strength, Lucky throws his axe at Garuda with deadly intentions. Although the axe barely grazes Garuda, the blow is still enough to throw him against the jagged foundation of the cliff.

Thirty feet away, beneath a mound of rubble, Trance emerges completely healed with no sign of Rex's deadly onslaught. Trance finds Rex on the floor convulsing from the poison and hallucinogens his body ingested. The medic drones were shot down en route to help Rex, leaving him in bad shape, minutes away from death. Trance approaches Rex's limp body, intent on putting him out of his misery.

Kelis uses a Colonial rocket launcher, firing a missile, hitting Trance in the chest, knocking him back twenty feet. Kelis screams on her communicator, *"REX NEEDS HELP! I need him brought to me immediately or he's going to die!"*

"We've all got our hands full. This payday isn't worth any of our lives! You'll have to make your way to him if he needs help," says Pearl as she evades Trixie's attacks, blocking an onslaught of telekinetic blasts while simultaneously resisting telepathic attacks.

Trixie overloads Pearl's telepathic armor, causing Pearl to keep her distance. Pearl uses her psionic shields and daggers to fend Trixie off, who attacks relentlessly until her enemies are killed. Trixie turns her attention to the few surviving guardsmen beneath them, invading their minds, possessing them to assist the Primeans.

Concerned for Rex, Kelis decides to exit the transporter, putting her own life at risk. Kelis tells her team, *"I'm going to get Rex! Our system says he has two minutes before his vital organs shut down. Pearl, watch the transporter."*

"Don't leave the transport! I'll bring him to you!" screams Newton as he intercepts Trance, preventing him from attacking the transporters.

Trance changes the shape of his tail into a spiked club before swinging it at Newton, who stops it, using his abilities. Newton uses his mind to take hold of the miniature metallic balls on the backside of his armor. Newton levitates the balls, changing their density, making them pack a powerful punch. He projects the altered balls at Trance, hitting him in the chest with a massive impact that knocks him back three hundred feet as if he were hit by a speeding train. Trance is knocked into the jagged foundation of the cliff unresponsive and barely breathing, pushing his healing abilities to their limit.

Trixie maintains the telepathic link for the Primeans, allowing them to work cohesively. Trixie's been probing the guardsmen under her control, collecting intel while she fends for her life against an unrelenting Pearl. Trixie's also coordinating the Primeans' attack and strategy. Noticing Garuda and Lucky are evenly matched, she recommends they change tactics.

Garuda creates distance between himself and Lucky shooting his projectile claws to create a rockslide. Once separated, he fires numerous oversized claws into the air, striking Newton in the leg, injecting numerous poisons into his bloodstream. Primean drones are continuing to swarm the area as Newton uses the last of his energy to destroy them before falling to the ground disoriented.

Lucky throws two energy nets beneath Newton, breaking his fall before returning his full attention to Garuda. He searches for Garuda, frustrated his predictive probability models aren't giving him an advantage. Garuda activates his cloaking technology within his armor, making himself invisible, remaining hidden until the opportune moment to strike.

Garuda is equally frustrated, finding himself unable to wear Lucky down or find an edge. Garuda reaches out to Trixie, suggesting a synchronized attack, remaining still and completely silent as he slows his heart. Trixie flies overhead, dropping grenades from above, allowing Garuda to close ground as she distracts attacking Lucky's mind.

Anticipating danger, Lucky reacts by activating his telepathic shield within his armor as he maneuvers from the falling grenades. Sensing Garuda's movement, he dodges incoming claws using his powers to predict Garuda's attack. Unable to see Garuda, Lucky adjusts his retinas to see heat signatures, just as Garuda closes into attack. The pair exchange blows as Trixie circles around attacking from above telepathically.

Trixie focuses her powers, using her amplifiers to overload Lucky's telepathic shield. She slows him down just enough for Garuda to seize the moment, striking multiple pressure points before shooting multiple claws into Lucky's gut, pumping his body full of poison.

Meanwhile, Ricco attempts to shoot Pearl out of the sky with electrical currents while in the form of pure energy. Kelis is running through the sand, passing Ricco unnoticed, using her abilities to mask her scent and thoughts while enhancing her agility to maneuver in silence. Kelis approaches Rex, finding him foaming at the mouth near death. Kelis mounts Rex and coddles him in her arms allowing her sweat to absorb into his pores. Antibodies flood his bloodstream, allowing his body to fight off the poisons. Kelis creates a force field to protect them while she repairs Rex's organs.

Rex takes a large gasp of air as he regains consciousness with his face between Kelis's breasts, clinging to life. Rex is revived, but she senses Lucky and Newton also need her help. Her empathic abilities allow her to feel Lucky's fear of death and Newton's anger for being injured. Newton's closer to Kelis, but Lucky is in worse shape. Furthermore, the transport is currently unattended. She has decisions to make with no time to spare.

Rex admits, "You saved my life. Thank you. I feel as good as new!"

"You're better than new. Now you're immune to that animal's toxins! Your body's going to start making its own antibodies," explains Kelis as she looks beyond her protective shield at the transport. "I need to get back to the transport! Newton won't be happy I left my post."

"So, he'd rather I be dead? What a prick. I'll head back to the transporter. Newton's in the energy net behind us. He'll need you to do the same for him. I've got the transporter!" says Rex as he morphs his arms into elongated swords.

Kelis responds, "I always have a Plan B. The serum's safe." She lowers her shield and heads toward Newton.

Rex smiles, saying, "You're dating your Plan B. You'll come around eventually!" Another batch of Primean drones enter the airspace providing air support, cutting their conversation short as missiles rain down from above.

Kelis ignores Rex's advances, forging ahead toward Newton. His health is rapidly declining, giving Kelis no time to spare. Rex watches Bunny teleport outside their transport and acts to stop her from taking the invaluable serum.

The transporter is protected by an electrical current making it difficult for teleporters to break through. Bunny notices the security protocols, using her assortment of tools to break through. Bunny places a circular magnet on the door, hacking the security protocols, eventually making her way inside as her comrades provide cover. The mag-hack works its way through the initial barrier, allowing Bunny to enter the transport unharmed.

Bunny cautiously walks into the transporter with Rex closing in a few hundred feet away. Inside the transport she sees two boxed cases completely sealed with a third already open. The three cases are behind another barrier, forcing Bunny to search for another mag-hack. She finds what she needs, placing the magnet on the power source, when suddenly, Bunny's electrocuted by six electric rods.

Six Colonial guardsmen remained in the transporter wearing stealth armor. Each electric rod produces a hundred thousand volts of current, enough to kill most Evo. Bunny's armor absorbed most of the electrical current, still knocking her sixty feet on her back, convulsing for air.

Rex approaches to finish her off as Bunny struggles to find her bearings. She rolls to her side, noticing Rex charging with both his arms morphed into swords. Desperate to survive, Bunny reacts from pure impulse, manipulating the dark matter around, making it combustible in a focused blast. She creates a condensed explosive blast, thwarting Rex's attack, tapping into a primal force with the help of Garuda's amplifier.

Bunny reaches out telepathically to her fellow Primeans, explaining, "*The transporter's doors are...open.*" Bunny passes out from exhaustion and her armor goes to work preserving her life. Adrenaline shots are being administered to her heart as pain medicine is distributed through her bloodstream.

Trixie observes from above confident Bunny's armor will revive her. She's focused on maintaining control of the remaining guardsmen using them to her advantage. Trixie's tracking the mutants below, realizing Kelis is en route to save Newton. Trixie dispatches the guardsmen under her telepathic control to attack Kelis from a distance while she strategizes, sharing her aerial viewpoint with her comrades.

Pearl dodges Ricco's energy blasts by evasively maneuvering through the air, counterattacking from above while dodging attacks from Garuda's drones. Pearl finds an opening and unloads a massive psionic blast from both hands, shutting down Ricco's nervous system. Ricco's body jerks from the pain as he reverts to normal, losing the concentration to maintain his electrical form. Pearl swoops to the ground and takes an electrical inhibitor gun from one of the dead guardsmen. She aims the gun but for a second, shooting Ricco in the abdomen with an electrical inhibitor bullet.

Kelis makes her way over to Newton and finds him unconscious, suspended in Lucky's energy net. Kelis flips nine feet into the air, landing on the net to cradle Newton. Her sweat starts healing Newton when, suddenly, out of nowhere, she's struck in the back with an electrical rod. Kelis instinctively creates a protective shield around herself and Newton, as she screams out in agony from the a hundred thousand volts coursing through her body. Kelis immediately heals as she expands her force field, pushing back the advancing guardsmen.

The six remaining guardsmen are wearing stealth armor under Trixie's telepathic control. Kelis maintains her shield as she continues healing Newton. She's draining her life force trying to save Newton as sparks surround her shield reveal the location of the guardsmen trying to break through.

Bunny has fully recovered from the attack that nearly killed her with help of adrenaline boosters administered through her armor. Bunny teleports into the transporter and grabs the cases holding the mutation serum. With no one to stop her she takes the cases back to Garuda's headquarters, completing the mission.

Once inside Garuda's office, Bunny opens the cases and finds three canisters of a thick purple serum in each box. Bunny steals a canister for herself leaving five samples of the serum behind for Garuda. She teleports to a secure safe that she planted in the jungles of Petra prior to the mission hiding her stolen sample. Bunny punches in a code and hides the serum inside the safe before burying it. She teleports back to the cliff overlooking the beach preparing to assist her fellow Primeans.

Bunny taps her earpiece activating her communicator, saying, "Package secured. Prepare for extraction." Bunny sees Ricco bleeding out and unconscious, in desperate need of help. Bunny teleports him to a medical bay in Garuda's business tower. Garuda's medic droids are immediately dispatched to heal Ricco's bullet wound, working to save his life. Bunny returns to the beach to extract the others still recovering from her own injuries.

Kelis has healed Newton and is now running towards Lucky to help him recover. The guardsmen have been relentless in attacking the mercenary mutants forcing them to hold back with restraint. Newton's recovering with his sights set on Garuda, watching him fight Rex from a distance. Rex's inexperience is shown as Garuda's slowly gains ground using fluid counterattacks while anticipating his movements.

Kelis is making her way to Lucky with enough adrenaline to start healing him on contact. Her senses are warning her of danger, allowing her to raise a shield when needed. Trance has had time to recover from his wounds reentering the fight, attacking from above using his vapors to instill paralyzing fear. He closes his eyes changing his vapors to eliminate sight. Having taken a beating that would've killed most mutants, Trance is attacking from a distance relying on his secondary mutation.

Lucky has recovered, gaining his bearings now immune to Garuda's poisons. Kelis is pumped full of adrenaline, boosting her telepathic abilities and strength. Kelis is unraveling Trixie's hold over the guardsmen and the odds are beginning to shift.

Now in control of their own thoughts and on a secret mission of their own, one of the surviving guardsmen calls for backup as he limps to safety, saying, *"This is Lieutenant Kaihel. Send in the Guardian...NOW. We're being slaughtered! Only three of us are still alive. We need extraction now!"*

Lieutenant Kaihel is of parrot descent with a muscular build suited for war. He's trained for years to combat mutants, relying on his training to stay focused as he watches his closest friends and family die. He feels as if time itself slowed down as the blood of his brother-in-law covered his armor, leaving his nieces without a parent. He holds himself together knowing his survival is now a necessity.

Meanwhile, Pearl and Trixie are telepathically dueling, highlighting Pearl's inexperience. Trixie's standing next to her astral projected consciousness, destroying Pearl's psionic weapons and shields. Pearl knows she's a novice telepath, focusing on hand-to-hand combat.

Trixie's stamina is all but depleted, allowing Pearl to expunge an onslaught of psionic arrows bringing Trixie to the ground.

Pearl follows in close pursuit, trusting her instincts to hunt her prey. She lands above Trixie, manifesting an oversized psionic sword, holding it with two hands. Pearl raises the sword with a grin on her face, saying, "May the strongest thrive and the weak—"

Suddenly, Bunny teleports beside Trixie taking her back to the Adura Enterprises before Pearl can swing her sword. Once Trixie is safe, Bunny teleports back to the beach above Pearl dropping numerous vacuum grenades, before teleporting to safety. Bunny watches from the cliff's edge as Pearl falls to her knees unable to breathe. The vacuum grenades suck the oxygen from a given location long enough for someone to suffocate.

Rex couldn't keep up with Garuda's combat skills, shifting his focus back to Trance. Lucky's once again engaging Garuda in hand-to-hand combat, dodging his barrage of attacks with a finesse best described as a delicate dance. Lucky somersaults backwards while throwing rods into the ground, creating an energy net. Lucky activates the energy net by touching a hologram being projected from his armor. He uses the energy net for cover as he creates distance.

"For someone with predictive abilities, you sure are predictable," says Garuda as he accesses a data sphere that controls a second wave of armed drones. The drones open fire with bullets, grenade launchers, missiles, and plasma blasts as he casually walks away with his back turned to Lucky.

Newton struggles fending off the incoming drones as the Petrian Guardian appears in the far distance approaching from the east at Mach speed. The Guardian destroys the remaining drones with two ion blasts, instantly obliterating them as satellites above lock on their location. The Guardian's momentum creates a small crater after coming to a sudden stop a few feet above the ground. After assessing the situation, the Guardian calculates the most effective way to eliminate Garuda and Trance.

The Petrian Guardian is the smallest of the Guardians, standing 6'0'', with a feminine physique and metallic tail. The Petrian Guardian hovers above the ground, manipulating sound and magnetic wavelengths to levitate. Its lower body is shaped like an inverted triangle as it's legs mold together towards a sharp tip. Its head has three interchangeable faces looking north, east, and west representing Petra's three spiritual pillars: enlightenment, reciprocation, and balance. The Petrian Guardian also has billions of processors within its artificial bloodstream, allowing it problem solve and strategize on a quantum level. The Guardian's laying waste to Garuda's drones planning its attack against the Primeans.

Bunny teleports back to the fight with an inhibitor collar from Garuda's labs. Newton lowers his energy shield, giving Bunny the opening she needed. She teleports directly behind Newton placing the collar on his neck before he could react. Bunny teleports to safety while Newton falls to the ground unable to use his powers. Newton thinks fast and places a mag-hack on the collar, hoping to disable it before hitting the ground.

Lucky throws a retardant foam grenade beneath Newton as a precaution, breaking his fall. He observes the area predicting where Bunny will appear next. Rex is under the influence of Trance's vapors, unable to move or see, frozen with fear. The Petrian Guardian aims it weapons at Trance opening fire.

Bunny returns to the fight teleporting Trance to safety before the missiles and plasma blasts from the Guardian could harm him, leaving Garuda alone. Few have faced off against a Guardian and lived to tell the story. Garuda's enhanced agility is serving him well, buying him crucial seconds that Bunny needs to successfully extract him. The Guardian fires two shots from its ion cannons at Garuda, who manages to dodge the two blasts with centimeters to spare.

Garuda remains calm despite being outnumbered and out of options. The Petrian Guardian gains altitude, locking its weapons from twenty feet in the air. The Coalition mutants are closing in on Garuda when Bunny teleports back, extracting him to safety with seconds to spare. The Primeans have been successfully evacuated, having stolen their prize. The P.R.L. has lost two cases of their mutant induction serum and Colonial guardsmen are dead from a secret operation, unsanctioned from the Colony.

Lucky, Rex, Kelis, Pearl, and Newton converge around the Guardian, regrouping to discuss their next move. The Guardian is quietly collecting data as its eyes blink, taking in its surroundings. Small fires, turned vehicles, impact craters, and numerous rockslides onto the beach validate the mutant's exorbitant commission. The entire team is grateful to be alive initiating the appropriate contingency protocols.

Lucky walks up to Rex, asking, "How did the Primeans recruit a teleporter under the radar? We could have taken those guys had they not had a means of escape!"

Rex shakes his head in disagreement, saying, "They knew when to hit us and how. The wore masks, so I have no clue how we're going to track them."

The Petra Guardian gains altitude to record the area from an aerial view, saying, "Tend to your wounded and prepare to be debriefed in Elysian within the hour. Data suggests that the Primean terrorists were working off our internal intel." With a blank stare, it lowers itself to the ground hovering a few above the mutants.

"We were told you were unavailable. For something this valuable, why wouldn't you escort the serum yourself?" asks Rex as he musters up the courage to question the Guardian. Pearl grabs his arm to calm Rex, who quickly adjusts his attitude.

The Guardian responds, "The Colony received intel that there was going to be an attack on Petra's power grid. The Primeans timed this attack when I would be preoccupied protecting the grid. The P.R.L. will be dealing with this infraction without delay. We will meet again shortly. Petra has a proposition for all of you." The Guardian takes to the air and flies inland toward Elysian.

Lucky looks at Rex, saying, "The Guardians still gives me the creeps. The leopard has a tracker on his back. I placed it on him during the attack. I should be receiving his location coordinates shortly. Where's Newton?"

Lucky looks over to Kelis, asking, "What happened to the other cases?"

"We haven't checked the transporter, but they had a teleporter with them. I'm sure the cases are gone. The question is who took them and where are they now? We've been ordered to a debriefing in Elysian," says Newton as he instinctively defends Kelis.

Kelis stands, realizing Pearl is still badly injured. Kelis opens a backpack revealing two canisters of the serum. "I took precautions when I left the transporter. I say we keep one for ourselves, so we learn what's in it. We deliver the other, so we get paid."

Lucky confesses, "I'm receiving the leopard's location now." Lucky starts typing into a holographic keyboard projected from his communicator bracelet on his arm. As Lucky types away on his arm, the others sense his sudden anxiety, as if something is wrong.

Pearl stands to her feet, waiting for the results, saying, "What's wrong?"

"Something's disabling my tracker. I don't have an exact location, but I do know they're in downtown Meriposa... Wait... The signal's bouncing all over Petra now. Whoever this leopard is, his tech is more advanced than what we're using!" says Lucky as the signal completely terminates.

Rex folds his arms, adding, "Those mutants had intel on our powers and weeks to plan. We were set up to fail!"

Kelis accesses a hologram on her arm, explaining, "The serum needs to be kept under specific conditions to remain effective. If the Primeans store the canisters they stole in the wrong environment, we won't need to recover them."

"They know how to store it. They were fighting to kill! We need to be prepared to do the same. For now, we need to inform the P.R.L.," says Newton as he creates a shield around the group, levitating the group to the entrance of the facility.

"Are we still getting paid?" asks Pearl as she lies down, allowing one of their own medic droids to heal her with nanites. "I almost died out there. Someone's going to pay me what's owed."

The group shares a laugh as Newton says, "Our contract stated we keep our initial advance if a single vial is delivered. We'll get paid. It just won't be the fortune we were expecting."

"With that in mind, I say we keep one for ourselves. We can make up for loses with it." says Lucky as the mercenaries approach the entrance to the P.R.L. research facility.

Chapter 4 — A Shaky Start

Meanwhile, back in Lennek, one day after the Coalition press conference, Eve's showing a tour of Coalition Headquarters to new recruits. Coalition Tower is equipped with multiple habitats, training facilities, weapons development labs, research labs, a hangar, and an advanced holding cell for mutants located in a secure facility deep underground. The building has the latest technology for surveillance, telepathic wards, and inhibitors that block teleporters from entering the facility. Coalition Tower also has defensive shields, an aerodrome, as well as multiple warships stored underground and an oversized hangar. The supercomputer that controls the building's essentials, and an automated weapons defense system is made from Eve's core programing.

Eve is focused on honing the abilities of the recruits with a limited amount of time to prepare them. She spent years building the perfect facility planning for her absence. Virtual pods allow each mutant to push their abilities to the limit without fear of harming bystanders. Non-mutant staff run the building's research and engineering groups, providing the resources and weapons that give the Coalition an advantage in the field. Coalition Tower is the most secure building in Lennek. Beneath the tower is a bunker that houses a series of underground tunnels connected to nearby precincts by a magnetic railway system.

The six current members have been training nonstop preparing for an attack Goldie and numerous psychics around the world have confirmed. The Commencement ceremony is less than thirty-two hours away and the world is now aware of their organization. War strategists have been teaching the recruits tactics, while martial arts and combat specialists train the recruits in hand-to-hand combat. Gill has been using his talents of skill transference to give the new recruits decades of training within hours.

Goldie is doing her best to adjust to her new role, relieved she no longer has to hide. Bambi, Gill, Zeus, and Merkaba are making her feel welcome, but she's still in disbelief. Eve enters the training dojo, completing her tour with the new recruits—Angel, Duke, and Kairen. The current Coalition members stand at attention with their hands behind their backs, showing respect to Eve.

Eve levitates to the center of the dojo, explaining, "Most of you have been training for months. However, some of you have just recently been added to our ranks. I'm relying on those of you with experience to assist the newest recruits get situated. I have some introductions to make."

Eve looks to her left and the centurion Evo steps forwards as Eve explains, "Kairen is from Zion with years of military experience, having led his own team. He has superior strength, telekinetic abilities, and heightened senses that allow him to hit any target. Kairen's an expert archer with genetically modified hooves laced with glezslavine. He'll make an excellent addition providing insight into Zion we desperately need." Everyone claps as Kairen smiles, too shy to make a statement.

Kairen's lower body is that of a horse while his upper half is human. On all four legs he stands 6'5''—on his hind legs he is over 8'5''. Kairen's fur is dark brown with an orangish tint while his skin is olive beige. He has a thick mohawk flowing down his back while the sides of head are shaved. He's handsome with a muscular build, strong jaw, and turquoise eyes. He has Colonial brandings on his back and a white diamond in the middle of his forehead meant to amplify his telekinetic abilities. He made a career in the Zionite military leading an elite team of mutants.

Bambi smiles, playing with the curls from her green afro. "He looks like he's got plenty of experience to go around. I'd love to test those reflexes in the sim." Kairen looks at Bambi, blushing, being sure to avoid eye contact.

Rosie rolls her eyes, pointing out, "You don't waste time, do you?"

Rosie and Bambi giggle, showing a sisterly bond between the two as they openly objectify Kairen.

Eve motions her arm to her right, introducing the Evo of ram descent, saying, "Duke is a renowned warrior from Carthage. He can mimic the abilities of anyone within his proximity. Duke learns at an accelerated rate through observation using his photographic memory. His horns self-regenerate, he's a master combat specialist, and he has countless battle skills he developed through decades of experience."

Duke is 6'4'' with an even blend between feral and humanoid genes. He has spiral horns emerging from his curly brown hair. His skin is fawn beige while his fur is dark brown. His hind legs and hooves provide a muscular build and stature. The lower half of his body is covered in fur while his upper body resembles a human. Duke has long brown hair, brown eyes, a slender face, and a protruding bone in the middle of his forehead in the shape of a diamond. He has facial tattoos symbolizing a rite of passage from his culture as a ram.

"I want all of you to know I've fought on every Colony, and I've seen more than most. I'm honored to serve amongst all of you. I'm here to make a difference and provide a conscience to our endeavors," says Duke as he makes a point to lock eyes with Goldie who claps looking away.

Merkaba grins, saying, "We're glad to have you."

Eve walks over to the control panel, introducing Angel, saying, "Angel can control soundwaves, and she's a powerful psychic. Her wings work independently from her nervous system, protecting her reflexively absorbing psychic and thermal energy. Her feathers can also change density to protect her from physical attacks. She's the daughter of Queen Kenji and King Larvex, making her the heir to the Olympian throne." The room is silent before an awkward echo of applause.

Zeus throws his hands up, unable to contain himself, "Princess, do you know what this Coalition does?"

"Not only am I aware, I volunteered! You have no idea what I went through to get here," says Angel, taken aback by the blatant disrespect.

"I'm sure life as a princess is terribly inconvenient... Here, our lives are in each other's hands. I hope you prove yourself to be useful," says Zeus as he folds his arms, unamused with the assumed nepotism.

Angel smiles, biting her tongue, finding comfort in being treated like everyone else. "I assure you Lennek's Guardian made no mistake in choosing me. You'll learn to respect me... I won't give you a choice."

Gill uses his telepathy to link with Duke, Kairen, and Angel, doing so instinctively without permission. Angel's wings change pattern, protecting her, while Duke absorbs Angel's abilities, doing the same. Duke's skin and Angel's wings change texture as Gill's telepathic probe fails.

Out of anger, Duke says in a stern tone, "It will serve you well to stay out of my head, tadpole!"

Embarrassed for overstepping his boundaries, Gill replies, "I'm truly sorry. Please accept my deepest apologies. It won't happen again. You have my word. In Kronus I'm...I'm not used to—"

"Respecting the thoughts of others. I teach manners for fun," says Duke as he takes his seat, staring at Gill from across the dojo.

Angel walks up to Gill accepting his apology informing the others, "Had you not received my call for help, who knows what could've happened? I'm in your debt. Thank you."

Duke folds his arms, saying, "From what we've heard about your powers, you would've been fine." Duke sits next to Bambi, who's smiling holding back laughter entertained from the situation.

Zeus rolls his eyes, saying, "We're in the presence of a Guardian! Let's give Eve the floor, so we can get back to training."

The room comes to a silence as Eve uploads the latest intel on the suspected Primean leaders of Angkor into the dojo's control console.

She walks to the center of the dojo, addressing the nine mutants seated in a circle. Eve explains, "We're all a team here. We start forming that bond tonight, in the simulator. You each have unique abilities, that when combined make you a formidable force."

"If our precog is as powerful as I was told, we can shape the world to work for everyone. Mutants included," says Duke with his hands clasped, staring directly at Goldie.

Adjusting to her new leadership role has been overwhelming. Most of Goldie's comrades are proud mutants with years of combat training. She's still adapting to her new status as an open mutant, terrified of being responsible for anyone else. Goldie's kept her powers hidden since she was a teenager. Now she's being expected to test the limitations of her powers, leading others to war.

With a deep exhale, Goldie responds, "I know most of you have high expectations for me. I'll do my best not to disappoint, but I need you all to understand—I didn't plan for this. I'm not who you think I am."

Kairen smiles, saying, "I read your file. I have to say, the things you can do are impressive! I believe Gill here can make you a seasoned general in a few hours. There aren't many precogs still alive."

"That went dark and left...quick! What he means to say is, we help each other here. We're a family now, and we're going to mold each other whether we like it or not. Don't stress, the Guardian's don't make mistakes often," says Bambi, hoping to calm her new comrade.

"Except when it comes to genocide," says Merkaba as she squints her eyes, observing Eve. "Your Guardian speaks and behaves differently than the others."

Rosie laughs, asking, "How many Guardians have you met?"

Merkaba shocks the room, casually answering, "Five."

Eve ignores Merkaba, aware of her suspicions as she manipulates the control panel playing holographic footage of the suspected Primean leaders in Angkor. "I've cross-referenced faces from Goldie's visions with intel from Lennek's files on Angkor." The screen shows Puma with the most renowned Primean mutants in Angkor. Goldie recognizes some of the Primeans from her visions as Eve continues, "I've uploaded virtual representations of these mutants into our combat simulator so you can familiarize yourselves with their abilities."

With a perplexed face, Angel asks, "How were you able to see Goldie's visions? Mine are always fractured. Even the Olympian Council can't make sense of my visions."

Zeus answers, "Her visions aren't fractured like most. That's why she's in charge, Princess."

Goldie senses anger and resentment from Zeus and tries to lighten the mood, explaining, "The Coalition built an amplifier for psychic energy. I see all the same fractures you do... Somehow I can feel which are most probable. The chamber in my room records images from my cerebral cortex, allowing us to make my visions actionable."

Angel's eyes swell, digesting what she heard. "Olympian neurol science isn't this far advanced. This is beyond impressive."

Zeus interrupts reminding Angel, "This whole building's been built around Goldie. The rest of us are here for support." Zeus is used to being in control and subconsciously threatened by Goldie despite her lack of experience.

Rosie breaks the tension, asking, "So, I have a question. What's the difference between fate and destiny? If you can see my future, is everything I'm going to say and do already prewritten? Seriously, do we have any free will?"

Merkaba sighs, then turns her head to Rosie, saying, "We're going to be fighting an army soon!"

Bambi adds, "She's right. Let's give the Guardian the floor."

Eve levitates in the middle of the dojo so everyone can hear her. "Each of you may take point, depending on the mission, so each of you needs to be prepared to lead. Tomorrow at Commencement, I'll leave this body, but I'll still be assisting you. I've uploaded a condensed version of my consciousness into the innerworkings of this building. This information must remain confidential for obvious reasons. Your psych profiles suggest all of you can be trusted. I am hopeful you will soon learn to trust each other."

Goldie adds, "Eve will be within our processors as the AI that runs our building. We won't have to worry about hackers, and she can upload her consciousness into the combat droids to defend the building in our absence."

Merkaba interrupts, exclaiming, "It...could also do a lot worse. A sentient Guardian goes against nature." She looks to Eve without fear, saying, "You're an abomination by every sense of the word! Let's not forget, we discredited an entire culture in Carthage for suggesting the Guardians had a means of rewriting their code."

Goldie looks at Merkaba with disgust, explaining, "Eve was created sentient, designed to live beyond the other Guardians. She's many things, but an abomination isn't one of them."

Merkaba stands, folding her arms, searching for a politically correct way to express herself. "It wasn't born; the Guardian was made. My mother was burned alive for suggesting the Guardians were sentient with their own agendas. She was labeled insane and a burden to Carthage. I hate myself for believing my mother was crazy. Just ignore me... I'm ready to train."

Eve lowers herself to ground, retorting, "I take no offense and empathize with your pain, Merkaba. I swear to you that my intentions are pure. My goal is to nurture mutants to their full potential."

Merkaba asks, "Why? I've seen Guardians conduct deplorable acts of evil. Why are you so concerned with mutants? Most of your fellow Guardians deemed us a threat worth eliminating. Why do you want to help us?"

Eve slowly approaches Merkaba, answering, "My creator, the father of all Evo, implanted an emotional chip in me that differentiates me from the other Guardians. Each of us interprets information differently, based on our unique experiences in the world. I believe mutants will either be the salvation or the destruction of Evo. My processors, combined with Goldie's visions, will make the Coalition—"

"All powerful. I have no intention of taking orders from you. The members of this Coalition should have an equal vote in deciding how our resources will be used and what conflicts we get involved in," says Merkaba, looking to her team for their opinions.

Gill places his hand on Merkaba's shoulder, saying, "She has a point. We all come from separate Colonies. Surely, we each have our own motivations for joining. A popular vote with an odd number of members will ensure that our interests are balanced."

With no one arguing, Zeus tries to ease the tension in the room by saying, "So, it's agreed. We vote to decide what missions we take and how our resources are spent."

Bambi retorts, "Let us take a vote on the matter." All nine mutants agree to run the Coalition with equal votes from each member. Merkaba seems to have calmed down, and Goldie apologizes telepathically for being harsh.

Eve's eyes glow as she projects a hologram depicting the Primeans' expected attack tomorrow, explaining, "You were all selected because of your abilities. Personal qualms or political views are irrelevant in this Coalition. We have one goal: to maintain law and order."

Gill asks, "I'm assuming were splitting into groups to cover more ground?"

"Yes. The most logical strategy is to split into three groups for the Primean assault. Goldie will lead the three groups from the war chamber," answers Eve, moving from the middle of the dojo.

Goldie's caught off guard, doing her best to appear confident. "I thought your private lessons were going to teach me strategy. I've never been in a fight, let alone commanded an army of mutants. I'm not sure if I'm—"

Gill interrupts, assuring her, "You were born to lead. Don't underestimate your abilities. I've seen your growth in a short amount of time. I trust you with my life. I'll transfer combat experience, decades of war strategy, and an understanding inter-Colonial military structure. It won't take long. When I'm finished, you won't have to worry about second-guessing your intuition."

Eve hovers to the other side of the dojo, making her way to the virtual simulator. "If your stamina allows, can you transfer those same skills to those who need it?"

Rosie walks up to Gill, hoping to understand him better. "I can use some new combat skills. Also, I've always wanted to speak a few languages."

Gill chuckles, explaining, "Without muscle memory, the transference is only so effective. We all have different anatomies, so you'll need to hone the skill for your anatomy."

Rosie replies, "That's fine."

Bambi adds, "We can all use a few upgrades. The Primeans coming here tomorrow have one goal...that is to kill us."

"Bambi's right! We need to take this seriously. Merkaba, will you assist Gill in his transference by healing him?" asks Goldie as the group makes it to the other end of the dojo near the simulator.

"Of course," says Merkaba as she stays behind to help.

Zeus, Bambi, Duke, Angel, and Kairen are listening to Eve explain details of how the simulator works. Goldie, Merkaba, and Rosie stay behind to inherit useful skills and knowledge that will keep them alive. Gill turns to Merkaba, explaining, "I'll transfer some necessary battle skills and experience. When I'm finished, heal me so I can do the same to the others."

Gill instructs Merkaba to stand in front of him and kneel. Gill places both of his hands outside of Merkaba's head, funneling light blue energy into her temples. Merkaba's eyes turn completely white as her brain builds new neural pathways learning skills that took years to develop. Merkaba's in a trance with her head rolling in a circle motion.

Rosie is taken aback, reconsidering, saying "Are we sure this is safe? I think I'm good."

Gill transfers numerous combat styles into Merkaba who's disoriented from the experience. Merkaba looks at Rosie, saying, "It's fine, trust me. I was aware of what was going on. You need to do it! I know twenty different forms of martial arts now! I'm also a weapons specialist. I can pilot any Colonial ship and—"

Bambi stretches her arm twenty feet across the dojo, throwing a punch intended to knock Merkaba out cold. Merkaba reflexively dodges the punch, somersaulting away, landing in a crouched position. Merkaba charges Bambi, dodging incoming punches with the finesse of an experienced fighter. Once close, Merkaba somersaults behind Bambi taking her to the ground in a chokehold.

On the ground with Bambi between her legs, Merkaba tightens her grip, demanding, "Tap out for me."

Bambi taps out, saying, "I'm next!" They get up making their way towards Gill as Eve focuses on the new recruits with Zeus.

Merkaba wipes the sweat off her forehead, explaining, "I'll have to heal him first. Both our powers are taxing, we'll need breaks. My purrs create harmonic frequencies that affect the Higgs field around us. I can regenerate cells, but maintaining the frequency is like balancing on a high wire. Eventually, my concentration gives out."

Bambi asks, "What's the Higgs field? I dozed off in school."

"It's an energy field that runs through the omniverse interacting with particles giving them mass," answers Merkaba as she recovers. She and Bambi have a newfound respect for each other as Merkaba lets her guard down.

One by one, Gill transfers combat skills to the group as Merkaba heals his body, replenishing his stamina. Goldie's feeling extremely confident, having learned dozens of skills and combat styles within a matter of minutes. Her new understanding of Colonial militaries has already affected her perspective of the world. She had no idea how much power the Colonies have at their disposal. In learning to defend herself, Goldie now knows how powerful she is.

They join the rest of their team on the other side of the dojo. Thirty virtual pods are lined up, controlled by an enclosed control room run by the smartest engineers in Lennek. Advanced quantum processors connect the thirty pods creating a shared virtual reality. Inside the simulator Evo can feel, smell, and hear inside the virtual environment. A streaming hologram displays what's happening inside the control room allowing Eve to observe in real time.

Eve waits for Goldie, Merkaba, Bambi, Rosie, and Gill to funnel over, explaining, "You need to work and move as a team. Study the databases of every Primean in Angkor and have a prepared response to counter their abilities. Know their strengths. Learn their weaknesses. The lab assistant will give each of you a pill. Swallow it so you can breathe in the tanks."

"I'm assuming we're running the simulator in the teams we'll be assigned to tomorrow?" asks Zeus as he walks up to a virtual pod taking a pill from a lab assistant.

Eve responds, "We plan to run multiple simulations throughout the night while using the cytogenesis pods to replenish your stamina. No matter how hard you train tonight, you'll be fresh for the battle tomorrow."

Duke looks around the simulator, asking, "How will we know we're inside the simulator? With all this equipment, it must be one hell of a virtual world."

Zeus responds, "The sim starts in a dark room and creates your surroundings piece by piece. Once you're inside the simulator, it'll be obvious."

"Some have trouble discerning reality from the simulator. It measures your thoughts and creates a virtual equivalent of the predicted effects that would occur in the real world. As a precaution, we placed power-inhibitors on each of you, but you'll still have full use of your powers during the simulation," says Eve as she elaborates on Zeus's description.

Kairen looks to the control room, watching in awe as three engineers prepare the pods. "This technology must have cost a fortune."

"So, the simulator knows our abilities?" asks Duke as he walks up to a virtual pod.

"The simulator's powered by an artificial intelligence system named Sim. Sim has a virtual database with each of your abilities allowing it to calculate the effects of each action in the virtual world. The Coalition has the world's smartest Evo overseeing its engineering department. You will all meet Cohol soon enough," says Eve as she pulls up a holographic representation of Sim.

Sim appears next to Duke, startling him in the holographic form of a glowing orb. Sim explains, "I manage the billions of algorithms that power the quantum processors making the training simulation possible. Once you're inside, I'll be available to make any adjustments you need. For those of you who are new, the process is simple. I will transfer your consciousness into the virtual simulation through a small needle that allows us to send signals directly into your brains. Nanites allow us to analyze your beta waves triggering your senses. The simulation can mimic what you feel, hear, smell, and even taste."

All nine mutants pick a virtual pod appropriate for their anatomy. Tentacles from the core of each pod attach to their necks as their bodies submerge into alkaline water. They each swallow a pill, coating their throats and lungs with nanites that extract oxygen from water. Their minds enter a shared virtual reality controlled by Sim who analyzes each mutant, learning their limits through countless layers of data collection. With time, Sim will know the Coalition better than they know themselves.

Inside the simulator, a virtual version of Lennek Square appears, down to every detail duplicated to perfection. The Coalition can feel every aspect of their environment. Temperature, texture, and pain are reproduced so well it's hard to differentiate from the real world.

Angel, Rosie, Bambi, Gill, Zeus, Duke, Merkaba, and Kairen are split into teams. Angel, Rosie, Bambi, and Gill are Squad A. Zeus, Duke, Merkaba, and Kairen make up Squad B. They're placed at different locations in Lennek Square while Goldie's in a virtual simulation of the Coalition war room. Her training involves directing her teammates through a telepathic link while coordinating with world leaders and partners.

Sim speaks directly into everyone's mind, explaining, "Squad A, your job is to prevent casualties. Do not be overconfident with your newly acquired combat skills. It will take some time to adjust to your individual anatomy. We'll begin in three, two..."

Despite his training Duke has reservations, hoping to delay, saying, "Wait!"

"One," says Sim, initiating the simulation. Within seconds, the simulator is filled with thousands of Evo in the park celebrating Commencement.

A virtual avatar of Eve appears on stage delivering a speech to the crowd when, suddenly, Angel's feathers change pattern, suggesting danger is approaching. Angel warns her comrades telepathically before taking to the air, flying toward a docking bay two blocks away. Angel uses her remote viewing abilities and sees an incoming submarine.

Suddenly, a bomb goes off near the east side of Lennek Square.

Rosie springs into action, emitting a force field to contain the blast, protecting nearby civilians. The crowd runs toward the west side of the square, screaming for their lives.

Sim appears next to Merkaba as a glowing orb, explaining, "Take a breath and center your energy. Your powers can adjust frequencies, causing different effects on the body. The variations and applications are limitless. Understand that a certain frequency will make this entire crowd docile and susceptible to complying with your orders. Each frequency you create is fueled by a different emotion. Your empathic abilities will serve you well in discovering new frequencies."

Merkaba listens intently to every word as she channels her energy. She follows her first instinct and creates a blanket of calming and peaceful emotions intended to calm the crowd. Merkaba starts emitting a powerful harmonic field noticing the civilians near her are remaining calm despite the surrounding chaos. Merkaba grows her harmonic field, watching its effects as Evo stop running and screaming.

"Concentrate! Try to heal the crowd members with minor injuries," says Sim, as Evo in the crowd slowly begin to heal. "Good! Now follow your intuition. Find the right frequency to make the crowd docile. Once the crowd is susceptible, guide them using your thoughts," says Sim as it leaves Merkaba to further discover her abilities on her own. Merkaba concentrates, emitting a harmonic field that starts healing those closest to her. The exercise teaches her she needs to be higher to spread her field more effectively.

Suddenly, numerous hover-transports uncloak forcing Merkaba to take cover. Primean soldiers jump out of the transports flooding the square with advanced weaponry inside advanced battle armor. Lennek's Colonial Guard engages the soldiers while Angel fights off the hover-transporters with Lennek's air force.

Eve has added Primean mutants into the simulation by combining Colonial intel with Goldie's visions. Goldie's abilities have grown exponentially. After Gill's transference of psychic and telepathic experience, her powers have grown exponentially, making her visions more detailed and accurate.

Goldie foresees a bomb exploding and warns her team immediately. She's telepathically linked to all eight of her comrades experiencing their emotions along with her own. Instinctually, she knows Rosie is the closest, instructing her to protect a nearby building filled with civilians.

Inside the simulation war room, Goldie sees an incoming call from President Zlaigo, answering immediately, saying, "Mr. President, I'm occupied at the moment. How can I help?" A surge of anxiety overwhelms Goldie as she feels Kairen's anxiety as he blocks the impact of a nearby explosion.

President Zlaigo retorts, "You can explain why Lennek Square is a goddamn war zone! The Coalition was supposed to protect—" Goldie ends the transmission as she feels Gill get shot in the arm.

Sim appears next to Goldie, saying, "Wise choice. World leaders will turn to you in a time of crisis, but your responsibility is to the Coalition and members in the field acting on your behalf." Goldie reaches out to Merkaba, sharing Gill's location. Sim continues, "Lennek's air force and guardsmen will always want real-time oversight from you. As your profile grows, so will your expectations."

Goldie pulls back Lennek's air force, allowing the Primeans to enter a specific airspace littered with defenses. She responds to Sim, "I'm aware. I'm also learning I'm suited for the task." Goldie sends orders to evacuate Precinct 8 as she sends a message to President Zlaigo, suggesting he pull back the guardsmen in Lennek Square.

Rosie creates a protective shield around a crowd Merkaba's keeping calm. Rosie's deflecting incoming fire, allowing civilians to escape to safety as planned. The civilians are being guided to the underground transportation system while the Primeans launch the first wave of their attack. Vaughn, a renowned Primean mutant in Angkor, jumps out of a cloaked transporter using his powers to create a massive earthquake blocking the subway exit. Bambi extends both of her arms toward Vaughn from across Lennek Square, knocking him off balance.

Punzel, another Primean mutant predicted to be involved in the upcoming attacks, can grow and control her dreads like tentacles. Punzel's hair is coated with a unique calcium-based material that makes her hair as strong as steel.

Punzel wraps her hair around her hand punching Bambi twenty feet into the air. Bambi counters by stretching her arm, grabbing a nearby light pole stopping her momentum. Bambi uses leverage from the pole to launch herself into Punzel, delivering a powerful punch, sending Punzel airborne. Bambi stretches her limbs, grabbing Punzel midair, slamming her into the ground, creating a small crater. Bambi pounces on Punzel, wrapping her limbs around Punzel dozens of times, making it impossible for her to move.

Two other Primean mutants, Sasha and Cole, are teleported from a stealth warship onto the stage. Kairen and Zeus join Eve on stage to protect her. Sasha uses her pheromones on Zeus and Kairen, immobilizing them, before throwing a grenade to incapacitate them. When the grenade goes off, Puma uses her abilities to redirect the flames from the explosion into a large fireball, encasing Kairen with flames.

Meanwhile, Duke's syphoning Kairen's powers using telekinesis to remove the rubble blocking the subway exit. Merkaba continues calming the crowd when suddenly Enigma, another well-known Primean mutant, fires a solid beam of energy, knocking Merkaba across the square. Merkaba hits a brick wall, breaking two ribs, her leg, and lower spine.

The simulation forces those within the virtual realm to physically feel the pain they would endure in the real world. Merkaba endures the pain, healing her body before looking up to see Angel fighting multiple mutants in the air.

Bambi is slowly suffocating Punzel, who eventually passes out from Bambi's hold. A stealth warship opens fire on Bambi who instinctively stretches her body to dodge the incoming attack. Eventually, Bambi is struck by one of the warship's plasma cannons. Injured, Bambi falls to the ground, condensing to her normal form. Her armor injects her with an adrenaline cocktail to mask the pain, allowing her to move. Bambi rises to her feet as Goldie alerts Merkaba telepathically to heal Bambi.

Duke and Enigma are fighting each other, damaging everything in their vicinity. Kairen's holding off dozens of Primean soldiers with his arrows and telekinesis. Angel's shot down by a cloaked transporter as Eve is swarmed by a group of Primean mutants. Eve ends the simulation by stopping the fight, gradually transitioning the Coalition back into the real world.

The virtual pods begin slowly draining the water inside the pods that kept the mutants in a suspended state. Within minutes, the team awakens from their simulation. Eve eagerly waits to give each team member a thorough debrief with suggestions for improvement.

Eve levitates to the center of the simulation, saying, "So, what did we learn?"

Zeus responds, "We need to change the pairing of our teams."

Gill's rubbing his head, slightly disoriented, adding, "We need an emergency extraction plan in case the subway exits are compromised."

Eve lowers herself to the ground, saying, "Good. What other changes should we make?"

"We need better armor, stronger weapons, and access to a real-time map of the terrain. I can't heal everyone when they're so far apart without healing our enemies in the process. I need to know where everyone is," says Merkaba as she emerges from her virtual pod.

Kairen adds, "We need independent breathing masks to block the pheromones of some of the Primean mutants."

Fully emerged from her simulator, Rosie asks, "Tell me we have some of the same armor the Colonial guardsmen are equipped with."

Eve answers, "The engineering crew is finalizing combat gear customized to each of your anatomy and abilities."

"I don't do uniforms," says Duke in a condescending tone.

Eve retorts, "I assume you want to live and have the upper hand in battle. Coalition body armor is laced with poly-fibers made from spider silk, graphene, and glezslavine. Your armor exceeds in strength while maintaining mobility. When they are completed, your combat skills and abilities will only improve."

Bambi asks, "Will my armor stretch with my limbs?"

Eve turns to answer, "All of your armor has been customized to compensate for your unique abilities. Each suit has telepathic shielding and absorbs energy extremely well. You'll be able to take high impact hits without any damage to your body."

Angel stretches out her wings, asking, "When will we meet the engineers and Goldie's support team?"

"Wait, Goldie gets a team?" asks Rosie as she puts her hand on her hip in disbelief.

Eve ignores Rosie, explaining, "You all need more work in the simulator. We'll run simulations through the night before you get fitted for armor. I have twenty simulations built off likely outcomes I need all of you to be prepared for."

Zeus looks at the rest of the Coalition, divulging, "As hard as we've been training these past few days, the Primeans have been training harder for the past year or so. Our technology and resources simply give us a fighting chance."

Goldie looks toward the others, saying, "We'll be ready. I'll make sure we are."

"How many soldiers are we expecting the Primeans to have?" asks Zeus as he gains his bearings outside of his pod.

Eve answers, "We're expecting 150,000 to 250,000 soldiers, with possibly two dozen mutants with extensive combat experience. The Primeans will also have over half a million combat droids."

Goldie says, "If their numbers overwhelm us, I can always join you all in—"

"We need you connected to an amplifier controlling things from here," says Eve without reluctance.

Gill adds, "You're the only one with the brain power to simultaneously command the Colonial forces and oversee each of us in the field. The more comfortable you get with your powers, the more helpful you'll be to each of us in the field."

Bambi senses Goldie overthinking the advice and adds, "Guide us to move more as a unit. The more we combine our powers, the more lives we'll save. Take control!"

Reassured, Goldie says, "Sim, load another simulation!" Everyone gets back into their pods, following Goldie's instructions without hesitation.

Chapter 5 — The Primean Perspective

The Coalition continues training for Commencement, while the Primeans put the final touches on their attack plan. Deep in the Congo of Angkor, Puma's meeting with other Primean leaders recruiting some muscle for her attack. Enigma, Ether, Trinity, and Vaughn are speaking with Sasha waiting for Puma to arrive.

Smut Puppy is an infamous bar and lounge in downtown Dravidia. It's infamous for its decorum made from human bones and fossils from a world that no longer exists. The morbid decorum is in homage to their human ancestors. Enigma, Trinity, Ether, and Vaughn are seated in a booth waiting for food and drinks. Smut Puppy is friendly to Angkor's underworld, turning a blind eye to various business dealings.

Enigma's patience is growing thin waiting for Puma as she herself is renowned as one of the most powerful mutants on the planet, feared by most in Angkor. Ether excuses herself to the restroom, garnishing attention from every corner of the bar. Despite the beautiful dancers spread throughout the establishment, Ether's turning heads visibly irritate Enigma.

Sasha breaks an awkward silence, announcing, "Puma's just arrived!" She excuses herself from the table, making her way towards the entrance.

An admiring bystander blocks Sasha's path, saying, "How are you?" Sasha retracts her metallic claws, deterring the unwanted advance. The bystander grabs his drink, immediately walking away.

Puma walks into Smut Puppy, immediately spotting their table as she removes her sunglasses. "Everyone's here I presume?" asks Puma, keeping a low profile in a sleeveless yellow business suit with a matching leather skirt. She's wearing matching elbow-high gloves, a corset, and her signature whip is wrapped around her waist.

"You're late...but you look great!" says Sasha as she hugs Puma, greeting her as the band plays live music behind them. Food and drinks are being distributed by labor droids and the hostess is encouraging them to take their seats.

The pair approach the booth with their fellow Primeans, none of whom are amused by Puma's tardiness. Puma smiles, undeterred from the energy, saying, "Thank you for meeting with me. We all know why we're here. Let's get down to business." Puma makes a few quick gestures with her hands interacting with holograms seen only by her eye-contacts.

"You can check your messages later," says Enigma, demanding respect. Puma clasps her hands suggesting they have her undivided attention. Enigma continues, "I want a true transfer of wealth. We want to be paid in gold and minerals. You can keep your credits!" says Enigma as she stands from her seat staring Puma in the eye.

Enigma is of peacock descent from Tulumeaih. She can absorb thermal, telepathic, and synthesized energy from the sun through her feathers. Enigma can redirect her absorbed energy into force fields, ionized energy blasts, and daggers. She's a rare omega-level mutant, who's as beautiful as she is deadly.

Enigma stands 6'3'' with pale blue skin accented with fluorescent feathers in shades of blue, green, and purple feathers. She has humanoid facial features, turquoise eyes, sharp bone structure, and long green hair flowing down to her back. Her green hair has beautiful multicolored feathers blended throughout. The feathers on her breasts, shoulders, outer thighs, and corners of her eyes highlight her bone structure. Her tail usually drags behind her, made of beautiful peacock feathers that can expand six feet across, overshadowing her entire body. Her hypnotic beauty is as infamous as her mutant abilities.

The Guardian itself would be cautious in fighting Enigma. She has no need to hide her identity. Enigma's wearing formfitting leather pants and a teal silk crop beneath a corseted piece of armor. The entire group is dressed in Angkor's finest, flaunting their wealth.

Puma responds, "I can pay you however you like, in whatever form of currency you'd like."

Enigma smiles, saying, "Then let us discuss how we kill a Guardian!"

Ether returns from the restroom, attracting more attention from each corner of the bar. Enigma huffs as Ether smiles, reveling in the attention. She admits, "It never gets old," as a labor droid drops off a round of drinks from an admirer. Ether notices Puma, saying, "Nice of you to show up. I haven't seen you in ages. How have you been?" Ether and Puma hug, completely resetting the energy at the table. Ether takes her seat next to Enigma as the first round of food arrives.

Ether is of gazelle descent, originally from Tulumeaih on the northwestern side of Angkor. She can amplify vibrations and magnetic fields, creating powerful energy blasts and shields. Ether can utilize ley lines to dramatically increase her powers by using the Earth's magnetic field. She can fly and shoot high frequency waves that can penetrate steel. Ether is also extremely beautiful, infamous for her sultry appeal.

Ether is 6'2'' with tawney brown skin and strong humanoid features. She has brown and white fur on her shoulders, elbows, and outer thighs. She has mocha brown skin with a distinct jawline and triangular face. She has a stylish mullet with shoulder-length black hair, beautiful hazel eyes, and a petite frame, and horns emerging from the top of her head. She has large eyelashes resembling a gazelle with plump lips shaping her face. She is soft-spoken but demanding with her needs.

Puma looks at Ether, saying, "The pleasure's all mine. You truly are one of the most beautiful Evo in the world." Puma knows her compliment will subconsciously upset Enigma, but she needs her off guard to be persuaded.

"Thank you, my love! As usual, you're as kind as ever. Do you have a plan for all of us to get back alive or is this a suicide mission?" asks Ether in a calm direct tone, grabbing Enigma's hand under the table.

"Let the faction leaders handle this," says Vaughn as he grabs his first plate of food. "Your father has done so much for—"

"My father's accomplishments are his own, but thank you. I know you to be a devoted true believer in our Primean principles. I'm honored to have your trust following me into battle," says Puma before looking to Trinity to make eye contact. "Trinity, I hope to gain your trust through actions starting today."

Trinity nods her head, saying, "But, of course, your reputation speaks for itself Puma. I'm honored to have been chosen to fight alongside you." She leans back, taking in the unusual ambiance of human memorabilia.

Trinity is of polar bear descent from the snow mountains of Zion. Her claws regenerate, and she has a nominal healing factor in addition to her unparalleled telepathic skills. Trinity's an expert sniper, using her pristine eyesight to always hit her target. She is resistant to the cold with superior strength and the ability to hibernate. Her fur is coated with a calcium derivative that makes her fur durable and resistant to harm. Trinity comes from a long line of priestesses. With no training she remains unskilled in the mystical arts of her ancestors.

Trinity stands 7'2'' with strong humanoid facial features. She has pale white skin and white fur on her forearms, outer legs, and back. Her fur is shaved down to reveal a muscular frame. Trinity has long white hair, a wide nose, and neon-blue eyes. She has small circular ears on the top of her head. Her tribal tattoos on her forearms were bestowed by her mother. In Trinity's culture, her red tattoos protect her on the astral plane, guiding her spirit and channeling her magic.

Sasha's beaming with pride, pointing out, "Look at the talent a common cause can bring together. Let's talk business."

Puma explains, "We're hitting Lennek with a full-scale assault tomorrow. We've recruited agents inside Lennek, who have been training for months. They're planting explosives as we speak, utilizing a network to soften Lennek from the inside."

Puma throws Enigma a data cube containing intel on Lennek Square.

Enigma puts the data cube on a processor displaying a 3-D module of Lennek Square. She sees dozens of files on Lennek's architecture, Colonial guardsmen with their perspective posts, automated defenses, and intel on the Coalition mutants.

Puma explains, "We're hitting them by air, sea, and land while utilizing our teleporter to support our mutants. With Bunny, we can change our attack strategy in real time."

Enigma laughs, saying, "A teleporter! They can only teleport short distances when teleporting more than themselves."

Puma responds in kind, saying, "Bunny's unique."

"A wooden axe is unique. Doesn't make it useful," says Enigma, making it clear she needs to be convinced.

Puma continues, "She draws her power from the moon, and this planet is her domain. When she mutated during puberty, she teleported an entire house full of Evo from Angkor to Lennek!"

"Impossible," says Trinity as labor droids arrive to the table with drinks.

Enigma responds, "Let's assume you do have a gifted teleporter. What's your plan once you're inside Lennek Square? We all saw the news broadcast. Lennek has a coalition of mutants waiting for us. Their ranks are growing by the day according to my intel. The odds may not be in our favor."

Trinity adds, "Not to mention Lennek's protected by Olympia."

Ether looks at Enigma with pride, saying, "Enigma can take out any force field with her energy blasts. She makes condensed ionized energy. She can shoot through anything. I assume you plan to have her engage—"

"They're aware of what I can do. And I'm sure Puma knows about my fleet of warships. Let's cut the pleasantries," says Enigma, signaling a waitress over. "I believe in what you're doing, but the timing... It doesn't make sense. You're waiting the very last minute to recruit crucial pieces of your attack. Why?"

Puma replies, "I needed assurance we could win. With your abilities, we have a fighting chance. No one has shot down more warships than you. Your fleet of ships will be of great use to us. If I'm honest, I need them. You'll be well compensated for your efforts and contributions. The Primeans of Angkor would never consider an attack without you. Without any of you for that matter."

"Save your flattery. What I don't understand is, why? Why hit Lennek while their Guardian's still operational?" asks Enigma, needing answers before committing.

Puma answers, "To send a message and to hack into Lennek's data-processing hive."

Ether asks, "You want to hack the un-hackable and kill the unkill-able?" An Evo waitress approaches the table with food and drinks for everyone, prompting everyone to pause their conversation. "Can we order another round for the table, please?"

They wait for the waitress to leave, and Puma continues, "I've recruited a talented mutant from Zion who can hack the Colonial mainframe. Violet can control machines and communicate with technology using her thoughts. She's a technopath!"

Enigma asks, "You feel this Violet is powerful enough to break through Lennek's firewalls and out-think a Guardian? You do realize that the Guardian's protect their data hives indiscriminately? I heard they can link their minds to their hives multiplying their processing speed."

"I'm aware. I've planned this operation for three years. Violet has done a test run showcasing her abilities in Zion. Open her file on the data cube and see for yourself," says Puma as she makes herself a plate from the assortment of dishes on the table.

Trinity orders a drink from the center hologram attached to the table. Trinity looks at Puma, asking, "So what are you planning to do once you're inside the hive?"

Puma places the last order for the table, answering, "Violet will embed a virus in the mainframe that will allow us to see orders from the Colonial Guard in real time. We'll have detailed files on every soldier, politician, elected official, and their database of suspected mutants."

Enigma folds her arms, asking, "This still doesn't explain why we can't do this after Commencement. Wouldn't it be easier to hack their mainframe after the Guardian is shut down?"

Sasha responds to a message on her communicator, saying, "We've just recently learned some interesting details about Lennek's Guardian. Their Guardian goes by the name of Eve."

Trinity chuckles, saying, "Guardians don't have names; they have unit numbers."

Puma orders more food from the table's touchscreen menu, saying, "Precisely! We've received intel suggesting Lennek's Guardian was created with an emotional chip that's allowed it to ascend to full consciousness. This...Eve isn't bound to its programing... She—*it* has free will. With free will comes—"

"Self-interest!" says Sasha, having a deeper connection to the issue being originally from Carthage.

Trinity adds, "A Guardian with free will isn't good for anyone. The reason Evo abide by Colonial rules is because most believe the Guardians are programmed to protect our best interests. If this gets out..."

"Revolution! When Evo learn their beloved Guardian has free will and self-interests, we'll have all the reasoning we need to attack. The smart play is to keep Lennethians out of the narrative. Our quarrel should be with their sentient Guardian."

Enigma's digesting everything she's hearing, contemplating the consequences of releasing the information. "When the world learns about...Eve...it will be pure pandemonium in some Colonies."

Puma responds, "Violet will upload this video right before our attack." Puma throws another data cube onto the processor table showing a holographic video of Dr. Orion, the creator of Evo and the Guardians expressing his reservations for his own creations. He admits to adding an emotional chip into one of the Guardians and explains why.

Dr. Orion appears distressed in the hologram, saying, "Today, I took Eve to tour the preservation arks that were built for the Evo we've been bioengineering. She saw an injured Evo with a broken spine. Eve noticed a rare genetic defect and told me that the subject had ten years to live at most. His internal organs were slowly shutting down. Eve snapped the Evo's neck and then dug a grave. I can't help but wonder if the other Guardians would have taken the same action. Eve's primary directive forces her to act in the best interest of all Evo. I programmed Eve to reinterpret her primary directive when needed. I was disappointed. That is, until I saw the grave."

Dr. Orion looks quite shaken up. He's sweating profusely and visibly bothered. "Eve told me the Evo was in pain and if he passed on his genetic mutation, future generations of Evo could suffer the same agonizing death. It was the mutation that she wanted to get rid of. She deemed him unfit. So she overwrote her coding that prevented her from harming the Evo, doing what she deemed necessary for the greater good of the species. I made this Guardian indestructible and all powerful purposefully. She can mold and shape the world in her image. I pray I set a good example in molding her consciousness and outlook of the world."

Puma stops the video, saying, "This video was recently stolen off Lennek's servers. It's been verified, and it justifies our attack. We'll be known as liberators—not just in Angkor, but by some in Lennek. We're going to expose the truth. Political causes with truth on their side tend to succeed. At the end of the video, we'll give the crowd time to evacuate before we attack."

Trinity puts her long white hair up into a bun, exposing her circular ears on her head. "This intel must have cost a fortune!"

Enigma confirms, "It's worth every credit if we accomplish our goal. Demonizing the Guardian to make it seem as if we're fighting for the very Evo we're attacking—well done! The only question is, what do you need from me?"

Puma says, "Rumor has it, you have a dozen stealth warships."

Ether throws back her drink, answering, "Just a dozen?"

Enigma looks at Ether with a stern face, responding, "Rumor has it! Listen, if you're going to spy on me in my domain, show me the respect of honesty."

Ether looks at Puma, explaining, "I felt your drones in our airspace last week." Ether realizes she's angering Enigma and decides to stop talking.

Sasha adds, "It's no secret how you keep your territories safe. Firepower from above without warning, except for a buzzing hum from charging cannons. All of Angkor knows about your ships."

Enigma crosses her legs, saying, "So you disapprove of my methods?" Sasha lowers her head, knowing they need Enigma for their mission. Sasha swallows her pride, allowing Enigma to continue. "Based on what you're saying, it's probably best for me and my commanders to stay here and protect my warships. It sounds like I need to prepare for—"

"You can move your ships and cower behind your mercenaries or... you can seize your destiny. I'm looking for true Primean believers willing to sacrifice for a better future for everyone. We do this for future generations!" says Puma, hoping to appeal to Enigma's emotions.

Enigma takes a moment to contemplate the proposal, accessing her personal processor to review some intel files of her own. A minute of uncomfortable silence passes as Enigma maneuvers her hands in the air viewing encrypted documents from a server only she and Ether can see. Bio-contacts allow Evo to interact with the world around them linking to their beta waves, allowing users to control their processors with their thoughts and hand motions. Enigma finishes her drink, concluding, "I want full access to the Lennek's hive... that is if we manage to hack in."

"We need all twelve ships for aerial support. The Olympian air force is on high alert. There's a good chance most of your ships won't be returning. I'll cover the costs to repair or replace them all," says Puma, remaining calm and collected as she looks Enigma in the eyes.

Enigma responds, "I'll give you eight warships, and I expect payment for replacing them by tomorrow morning. I'll send you the accounts where I expect to get paid."

A waitress approaches with four drinks, saying, "A few Evo at the bar sent you some drinks." The waitress places the drinks on the table and picks up the empty glasses and plates.

Puma accesses the processor in the middle of the room, pulling up files on the Primean faction of Lennek. Puma explains, "We'll have two goals. Gain access to Lennek's server and upload a virus to the Guardian and kill it. We have two assets already inside Lennek. Punzel and Cole are awaiting orders and have been laying the foundation for this attack for nearly a year now."

The waitress comes back to the table with their food orders and drinks. Trinity gives the waitress a gold coin, who bows in gratitude. Trinity looks at Puma, saying, "What are their gifts? What's your endgame in all of this?"

Puma responds, "Punzel's skin is resistant to physical harm and her hair grows as calcium, making each strand as strong as steel. Her hair's prehensile, meaning her hair follicles can instantly grow and retract at will, allowing her to lift objects over a ton with her hair. She often wraps her fists with her dreadlocks making her punches deadly." She motions her hands pulling up another file before continuing. "Cole's of dalmatian descent and the new leader of Lennek's underworld. He can control water with his mind, modulate temperature, and reanimate living cells after freezing them. He can manipulate moisture in the air, forming instantaneous spikes of ice and he's ex-military, having trained as an elite guardsmen for over a decade. He has combat training. He's a weapons expert, with decades of leadership experience allowing him to take over Lennek's underworld in less than a year. They'll both be helpful to the cause."

Enigma asks, "I believe she also asked what your endgame was? I'm curious as to what you hope to accomplish from all this. We kill the Guardian and hack Lennek's mainframe... What next?"

"I want the truth to be revealed. I want every Evo around the world to have a choice in how they live their lives. I want to show future generations that there were some of us that weren't afraid," says Puma as she instinctually covers her stomach answering Enigma's question.

Enigma smiles, adding, "You're either too bold or too foolish to be afraid."

Puma accesses the files she has on the hired mutant mercenaries they hired, adding, "If history knows me as fearless, I'll rest in peace. Violet, Bunny, and Byron are mercenaries sympathetic to our cause. They've assisted me in past missions... I trust them with my life. I've personally trained and fought with each of them. You'll meet them soon enough."

A fight breaks out across the room in the gambling section of the bar. Trinity pushes a button beneath the table and a force field covers their surrounding area, blocking out the sound of the ongoing fight. A chair is thrown in the group's direction and is blocked by the force field. The androids and employees carry on with work as fights and disagreements are common in Smut Puppy.

A labor droid approaches, lowering the force field, allowing it to deliver plates of food, momentarily distracting Puma. Sasha takes over the mercenary introductions, allowing Puma an opportunity to eat. "Byron is of panda descent. He's originally from Zion. He can redirect kinetic energy, focusing his power, to create an impenetrable field around his body. His martial arts skills are unequalled and he's a renowned weapons specialist."

Ether's reviewing their lineup of mutants on her own hologram. "It's an impressive group. Surprisingly, they've stayed off Angkor's radar. If you have the teleporter, why do you need the warships?"

Puma lowers the force field after noticing security has ended the fight across the room answering, "I also have an army of androids and trained mercenaries. My mercs have been training to counter Lennek's tactics. I'll be outfitting them with exoskeletons and plasma weapons. We need a sniper to shoot this bullet into Eve." Puma pulls out a blinking bullet and holds it up for everyone to see. "This bullet will upload a virus into the Guardian's main processor shutting it down from within. The virus starts replicating upon impact. Thanks to Violet, we have a chance to kill our oppressors."

Vaughn points to Trinity reminding everyone, "Trinity's one of the best shots in Angkor. I've seen it myself."

Puma chuckles, responding, "I'm aware. I've done my research on all of you. What I need from you is a sinkhole that can crack the foundation of Lennek's data hive. Violet's spores will need a path to access the hive's primary processors. I've secured fully weaponized aquatic rovers, invisible to sonar accompanying our submarines. We're going to fight fire with fire. The Colonial Guard will be fighting our militia while we engage their Guardian."

Trinity asks, "What about the Colonial mutants, the Coalition?"

Enigma interrupts, saying, "No one seems to be concerned about the Guardian. Lennek's Guardian—this Eve—won't just stand there to be killed. What's the plan for the damn Guardian? I'm the only here's who's actually fought one!"

Sasha looks at Puma, concurring, "She's right. We have contingencies for every aspect of our attack. Unfortunately, the Guardian can adapt to our attacks. These machines are better fighters and strategists than all of us combined."

Puma smiles, adding, "Bunny will take the Guardian out of the picture after it's shot with our viral bullet, rendering it inoperative. Cole and Punzel will start the attack from inside the crowd, allowing our aquatic rovers to dispatch our militia. Once our soldiers engage Lennek's Colonial guardsmen, we'll attack with Enigma's ships providing aerial support. We have two battle-tested mutants for every recruited mercenary fighting alongside us."

"And the Coalition? We need more intel than what we currently have," says Vaughn, being a reliable pessimist.

"The Coalition is no threat to us!" retorts Puma with a singular vision, ignoring good counsel.

Enigma accesses a detailed attack plan from the data sphere, asking, "According to this, we're using gravitational tractors to enter the square. I thought we were teleporting in?"

Puma answers, "We don't want Lennek to know we have a teleporter until the Guardian's been infected. The first wave of attacks is designed to draw the mutants protecting Eve away from it. The lighter Bunny's load, the farther she can teleport. It's fair to say, we want the Guardian as far away from the action as possible."

Trinity grabs the bullet, turning her hand to investigate different angles. "How do you know the virus will be effective against the Guardian?"

Puma answers, "We don't have a guarantee, but we gave Violet intel on the makeup of the Guardian's processors. Violet created the virus based on the Guardian's construction blueprints. If the virus is effective, the Guardian will be disoriented as its processors shut down, one by one. If we get the Guardian away from the Colonial mainframe, the virus should replicate faster. Without support from the hive..."

The waitress returns with Vaughn's large food order and drinks. Sasha explains, "The intel we received a few years ago allowed us to devise the perfect plan to kill this Guardian. Puma has spent a fortune and built a processing hive of her own. We have a path to victory."

Enigma rolls her eyes, saying, "Your plan relies on a lot of inter-changeable pieces. It's doable and there's a few scenarios for victory. If we miscalculate and can't teleport the Guardian, there's going to be a massacre. We'll need Fyn and Rosa to pull this off. They'll expect payment as well."

Ether adds, "I thought Zion had Rosa locked up in a maximum-security prison."

Puma smiles, replying, "I paid a fortune ensuring she'd be broken out this afternoon."

"Fyn and Puma have been working on a plan for weeks now," says Vaughn as he finishes his fourth plate of food, burping flamboyantly loud, disgusting everyone around him.

Sasha checks her processor, saying, "They should be being extracted any second now."

Ether checks her holo-com for new messages, saying, "There's talks of a revolution in Zion."

Enigma dismisses Ether, saying, "I'll believe it when I see it. Zionites aren't logical." Looking at Puma, Enigma points out, "We don't know how many mutants the Coalition's recruited. We don't know how Olympia will respond, and there's no guarantee this viral bullet of yours will even work on the Guardian. You're asking us to take quite the risk. I want eight million in gold for myself and three million for my associates."

"Agreed!" says Puma as she raises a glass to Enigma. "Cheers!"

Enigma shares a toast with Puma, saying, "If we pull this off, we'll be positioned to crash Lennek's economy with the click of a button. We'll control their surveillance systems, their weapons systems, and their army of androids!"

Sasha adds, "More importantly, we'll rewrite history with the truth. We need to stop worshiping machines and start taking our futures into our own hands."

Enigma sighs, saying, "The mutants you've gathered are impressive. Regardless of the attack on Lennek, a faction leader that can organize these mutants and plan this type of attack might be fit to lead the Primeans officially. With my help, we might just pull this off."

Vaughn turns to Enigma, saying, "Make sure your final preparations are completed by morning. Victory to the Primeans!" Vaughn raises his glass and slams it back, saluting to the table.

Twelve thousand miles away in Zion, Commencement Day preparations have already begun. The Colonial Guard are working tirelessly to prepare for the big day, shutting down businesses and all major ground streets. The Zion Guardian built an advanced surveillance system to prevent crime, predicting crimes before they occur. Zion is one of the more peaceful Colonies. Ironically, it's home to many rebel organizations which vehemently oppose Colonial philosophy.

Zion stretches across the former continent of Asia. The Ring of Fire underwent several changes due to the seismic activity in the area since the time of humans. Land masses from the Philippines to Japan are now underwater. The Kuril and Sakhalin Islands are also underwater as the Pacific Plate shifted over twelve degrees. The shifting plate caused the islands of Japan to submerge, replaced by a host of small islands. Taiwan, the Philippines, and Korea were also lost to the sea, while the coastal region of China was pushed inland. Indonesia broke up into multiple islands as the Asian continent lost most of its land mass, with new land emerging giving Zion its distinct mountainous terrain.

Zion has four cities inhabited by polar bears, centurion horses, reptiles, elephants, pandas, and penguins that comprise 60 percent of its population. Zion is financially prosperous with a diverse economy of exports. Zion has historically profited from war with some of the largest android factories in the world. Varanassi, Dershna, Llatkovia, and Mecanyle are open to tourism above land. Beneath Varanassi Lake lies an underwater city, Kareinaus, which is only accessible to the Zionite elite and their trading partner—the Reef tribe.

Varanassi Lake is considered the heart of Zion, built above an underwater paradise. A cathedral inside Kareinaus conceals a secret cloning facility that provides organs and spare parts for wealthy Evo around the world. The Reef tribe and Kareinaus leaders have had a long-standing trade agreement, independent from both their Colonies. Varanassi Lake is occupied primarily by Evo of polar bear, penguin, snow leopard, and seal descent. Kairenaus is occupied by an assortment of aquatic Evo and ran be the Reef tribe.

Dershna has mountainous terrain and tall buildings with some of the world's most beautiful architecture. Thirty percent of its population is immersed in commercialized virtual reality making up a large part of Dershna's commerce. Known as the entertainment capital of Zion, Dershna is home to thousands of species surrounded by opulent casinos, restaurants, with virtual simulator cafés on every corner. The underbelly of Dershna is a haven for the underground trafficking of exotic Evo.

Llatkovia is the crystal city of Zion considered the power source for the entire Colony. Zion has very few offensive weapons but their force field technology is a closely guarded secret surpassed by none. Llatkovia's crystals produce a unique form of energy. The city controls all of Zion's robots under the watchful eye of their Guardian. Llatkovia has unparalleled architectural beauty and provides for just under forty million Evo. It resembles a modern city and has higher temperatures than other cities.

Mecanyle is one of the smaller cities of Zion, considered a spiritual utopia. Mecanyle is anti-technology, completely off the grid, operating with no currency. Its occupants trade knowledge and labor for food, housing, and life's necessities. Mecanyle is completely independent from Zion, thriving despite limited resources in undesirable mountainous terrain. Citizenship is granted on a case-by-case basis decided by an eminent rajah. The Rajah of Mecanyle has been preparing for what he calls the inevitable war. Mecanyle is a haven for mutants and the secret to the primitive city's success.

Forty-six years ago, in 2354, the Zion Guardian perceived mutants as a threat and began a sterilization program, with the support of elected officials, aiming to suppress the mutant gene using various methods of depopulation. Now, mutants are rarely seen in Zion and often disappear as soon as they develop their gifts. Most mutants flee to Mecanyle for safety, while those that remain are recruited into the Colonial Guard. The sterilization program had the unintended consequence of killing 15 percent of the population. Millions of Evo died as a result, while the Colony denies its wrongdoing to this day.

The recent jailbreak of a high-profile Primean terrorist, named Rosa, has the Colonial Guard working overtime to track her down along with her accomplices. Rosa broke out of jail while being housed in solitary confinement. She escaped with invaluable intel that could threaten the political structure of the Colony. Rosa's of elephant descent and infamously known as the Embalmer.

Having superior strength, telepathy, and a photographic memory, Rosa's a valued asset to the Primeans, prompting them to spend millions to free her. Her brain can instantaneously process large amounts of information, making her a living computer. Rosa can astral project and her telepathic gifts are limitless. Because of her large brain, she's able to accurately predict the future through models ran in her head. The more variables she has, the more accurate she is. She's a fearless warrior Zion imprisoned using her departed sister as bait. With the assistance of Puma, the Primean factions have made her a top priority.

Rosa stands 6'5'' with tan skin with ascents of gray found all over her body. She has large elephant ears ,which she protects with a metallic helmet that covers the back of her malleable ears while amplifying her telepathy. She has gray coarse skin around her elbows, knees, and outer hips, including her forehead and ears. Rosa has long gray hair behind her large ears flowing down to her back. Rosa has beautiful gray eyes, a small trunk as a nose between two small tusks she files down. She has a thin gray tail, and a hardened personality from rough life growing up in Angkor.

The Colonial Guard assembled a task force to hunt Rosa down after her escape, working diligently to keep her breakout secret. Paige, Naima, and Clint are three mutants Zion contracts regularly to solve problems quickly and quietly. Kairen has led them through dozens of missions over the years, keeping each of them safe, well paid, and protected. Paige, Naima, and Clint have made it their mission to understand why Kairen was reassigned to Lennek. He left without saying goodbye, leaving many of them to believe it was against his will.

Deep within the interior of the Varanassi Mountains, a city named Zealton was carved into the mountain. Zealton is Zion's capital and home to Zion's elite. The city's an architectural wonder, extending underground beneath the massive mountain. Zealton's constructed from many minerals found within the surrounding mountains including limestone, marble, diamond, quartz, stone, and silver. This sixty-block town houses Zion's elite. Varanassi Lake is at the base of the mountain. Four surround the lake, each with an individual obelisk marking the center of town and providing ambient energy.

Governor Danko and Senate Leader Benoir are meeting with their most loyal mercenaries deciding their worth and trustworthiness. Deep within the Senate Stronghold Paige, Clint, and Naima are inside the main chamber of the Stronghold demanding explanations.

Paige slams her arms on Governor Danko's desk, asking, "Why was Kairen sent off to Lennek?"

Paige is of Komodo dragon descent able to control, absorb, and convert magnetic energy. Paige can create magnetic force fields, manipulate metals, and fly. She has magnetic sonar and can use her tongue to track anything with a scent. Paige was a former general in Zion's Colonial Guard, earning her place as a decorated guardsmen as a closeted mutant. Even then, her retractable claws and venomous bite made her formidable.

Paige is 6'3'' with green skin and scales covering her thin, muscular frame. She has a distinctive yellow strip down the middle of her back, a thick, long tail, a thin red tongue, and humanoid facial features. Paige has long green hair, symmetrical bone structure, and beautiful hazel eyes. She encases her tail with metal during combat, making it a deadly weapon. Paige has an affinity for silk and leather, using fashion to express her mood.

Governor Danko is of wolverine descent maintaining a smug de-meanor while crossing his legs on top of his desk. The governor looks Paige in the eye, calmly answering, "Lennek's treaty had terms. The Council decided it was in Zion's best interest to agree to those terms. Each Colony was obligated to send one mutant ambassador to serve in Coalition's Headquarters."

Clint chuckles while he sharpens a knife, asking, "I suppose it's a coincidence Kairen was reassigned the moment he filed a corruption charge against you?"

Clint is 5'8'' of armadillo descent with telekinetic abilities and an indestructible shell. He has olive skin covering an intimidating muscular frame despite his small stature. He has an equal blend of humanoid and feral features. The skin covering most it his body is thick while the shell covering his shoulders, head, and back are nearly impenetrable. Clint's shell and tail are used as weapons and are nearly indestructible. He has brown eyes, a strong jaw, and large bags under his eyes. Clint can curl himself into a ball and use his telekinesis to make himself a ball of destruction.

"All you've done by transferring Kairen to the Coalition is provide the Council with more evidence against you. Kairen sent us everything he had on you. You'll be exposed, Governor!" says Naima as she attempts to hide her anger.

Senate Leader Benoir walks over to a cage full of large, genetically modified eagles, saying, "Making accusations against Council members must be accompanied with evidence. Without evidence, you'll be facing charges of treason. You mutants are no exception. Do you have the evidence you speak of?"

Naima makes a fist, summoning a blueish purple electrical current in her palm. "We have what we need to bring you both down! I remind you, without us, you have no power!"

Naima is of Mandarin goby descent originally from Kronus. She defected from the Reef tribe when she discovered her ability to conduct and redirect numerous forms of energy. Naima can conduct electrical, thermal, telepathic, magnetic, and psionic energy and redirect that energy as her own unique electrical current. She amplifies absorbed energy through a synthesizing conduction process that allows her to shatter force fields.

Naima stands 6'2'' with blue glass-like skin covered in multicolored scales ranging from orange, pink, blue, yellow, and purple. She has a symmetrical face with high cheekbones accentuated by her bald head. She has a large fin circling her head resembling a crown covered in bioluminescent dots matching her colorful scales. Naima is stunning with humanoid facial features and a petite frame with distinct muscle definition.

Governor Danko raises his arms to silence the Senate leader, saying, "No one is being tried for treason, and we're not locking anyone up."

Paige interrupts Governor Danko, exclaiming, "Kairen was investigating rumors about Zion's sterilization project. He said he had solid evidence connecting you and the senator to the project including multiple other crimes. Now, he's suddenly transferred to Lennek! It sounds suspicious to me."

Senate Leader Benoir stands from his desk, retorting, "Kairen was selected because of his abilities and combat skills. I'll ask you again, do you have any evidence suggesting the governor and I are guilty of any crimes?"

Clint walks behind Paige, saying, "We'll present it when necessary. We want to speak with Kairen so we can make sure he's alive and well.

Senate Leader Benoir squints his eyes in disbelief, saying, "Governor, if these are the mutants you've selected as liaisons, I must put forth a motion to replace them." A captain from the Colonial Guard enters the Senate Stronghold, approaching the Senate leader to whisper something in his ear. He smiles, continuing, "Suspicions of their involvement with the Separatists has been confirmed. I want them in custody...now!"

Clint laughs, responding, "In custody. Who's going to put us in custody? Who's going to replace us? Now that the Colony knows you've been experimenting on us, you need us more than ever! The Primeans have already recruited sixty percent of the mutants in the Colony.

"Another twenty percent are with your Separatists!" says Senate Leader Benoir, hoping to strike a nerve.

The mutants ignore the accusations, knowing they're being recorded.

Naima adds, "You think your cameras and algorithms will keep you safe. You relied on us to build Zion and yet you fear us! There's a paradigm shift in the works. A wave of change is coming. Zion has no place for leaders like you. If we ever want to compete with the other Colonies, we need a revolution!"

Senate Leader Benoir's face scrunches together, displaying his anger. Being of cheetah descent his face becomes intimidating as he hisses. "Rely on you? Zion owns you! You live and breathe because of my mercy..."

"Own us? GET OUT!" screams Naima as she starts channeling the ambient energy in the air.

"Excuse me!" exclaims Senate Leader Benoir, offended with a shocked look of disbelief. "These animals clearly don't know their place. I have no use for a dog that—"

Clint uses telekinesis to lift Senate Leader Benoir into the air, slowly turning him upside down. Clint opens the doors with his powers and throws Benoir out of the room. The Senate leader hits a wall outside of the room fracturing a rib.

Governor Danko is in complete shock. He looks at Clint in disbelief, saying, "I see you've chosen your side. Clearly, you've pledged allegiance to the Primeans."

Clint explains, "Your time is up. No one in Zion will follow you, let alone listen to you. Your best bet is to leave the Colony. There are plenty of Evo that want your head for your role in the sterilization program."

"You tried to stop them, and they threatened your family. We read the files. You might be redeemable. Zion needs to hear someone in power admit what happened. No lies, no sugarcoating—just the truth! The Colony poisoned and killed its own Evo out of mutant fear! Out of prejudice," says Naima as she approaches, holding back tears.

Senate Leader Benoir looks to Governor Danko, determined to keep his loyalty intact. "Don't listen to these criminals, Danko. Let the droids take them into custody and keep your mouth shut! I'm the elected leader of the Senate. I won't be bullied by a pack of mutants. Colonial charter says—"

Paige lifts Senate Leader Benoir using her powers holding his life in her hands. "You overvalue your life. Zion is going to know what you did. If I were you, I would get a headstart and run. If you enter this room again, I'll kill you myself. NOW LEAVE!" Paige throws Benoir pushing him out of the room once more.

Clint adds, "Doesn't seem right, robbing Zionites the pleasure of killing him."

Governor Danko tries to avoid the same fate, conceding, "I'll do what you want! Just don't kill me... I tried to stop them years ago."

Naima says, "Walk us through it from the beginning."

Senate Leader Benoir is hunched over on his knees by the entrance to the chambers. He looks at Governor Danko, saying, "Do what's best for your family."

Paige slams the doors to the Senate Stronghold cutting off the senator. Paige looks at Governor Danko and says, "You'll be the corroborating witness to the Evo of Zion. You're both going to stand trial for your sins."

Clint walks behind the governor, saying, "Flatscans are going to want to see normal Evo in positions of power. As far as I'm concerned, you've already proven your willingness to abuse that power. We can't trust you. If we're going to have a smooth transition of power post-Guardian, unfortunately, we're going to need you."

Governor Danko folds his arms, explaining, "Our Guardian designed our government considering every known variable. Zion's the safest Colony on Earth for a reason. Zion is more productive when we can predict the behavior of our citizens. This is a freedom we must all give up for the common good!"

"The common good seems to always benefit those in power. What about the Evo you were supposed to protect?" asks Clint as he starts sharpening his swords, making the governor nervous.

Naima adds, "No one likes being watched or experimented on. You poisoned Zion's food to maintain order. It's just wrong. When Evo find out, things are going to change around here." The group discusses their concerns and begins building a rapport in the absence of Senate Leader Benoir.

Minutes later, Zion's lead research scientist, Dr. Tulsa, walks into the Senate Stronghold, saying, "Senate Leader Benoir went to the medic bay claiming he was attacked. He planted a receiver in the room, and he's been broadcasting your conversation to the Council leaders." Dr. Tulsa takes a seat on a floating chase near the governor's desk waiting for a response from the governor.

Governor Danko replies, "Our Guardian foresaw mutants and felt the need to take precautions."

"We followed the advice of our Guardian and took the necessary precautions to protect Zion. In hindsight there were more effective methods," says Dr. Tulsa with an emotionless face in a monotone voice lacking sincerity.

Paige tilts her head in disbelief, staring the doctor down with eyes consumed by hatred. Paige yells, "PRECAUTIONS! That android poisoned our food supply because it was afraid of mutants. Millions of Evo DIED!"

Clint looks at Dr. Tulsa, saying, "You storm in here. You speak so cavalierly about genocide, like your conscience bares no responsibility. What's wrong with you?"

Dr. Tulsa is of llama descent with feral features. At 7'2'', he's tall even by Evo standards. He's usually seen fidgeting or adjusting his glasses. Dr. Tulsa lowers his head, pleading, "None of us had a choice. Please, forgive me! I'm risking everything to come to you now. Your attack on Senate Leader Benoir caused everyone to choose sides. The Guardian is still operational, and you have Marlock in the field on assignment. I'm here to help…and I'm not alone. You have supporters within the Stronghold."

Dr. Tulsa says, "We need to tell Zion the truth about the sterilization tragedy. I'll explain what the Colony did, confirming the Guardian's full support and direction."

Still undecided, Governor Danko reminds everyone, "We need to get out of here. The Colonial Guard is on high alert." The governor's family is being held by the Senate and he has no choice but to remain loyal to Senate Leader Benoir. Knowing he's being watched, he is mindful of what he says.

Naima adds, "We need to check in with Marlock to let him know everything that's been going on. Evo are starving for a true democracy. I intend to feed them. We need to get Governor Danko to the Commencement ceremony and let him address Zion. We'll get his statement on record before the address as a precaution. Evo need to hear what happened directly from him."

Dr. Tulsa walks over to his desk to access a top-secret file that details Marlock's current assignment. He pulls up the information from his data cube, saying, "Rosa the Embalmer, Fyn the Angel of Death, and Byron the Destroyer have terrorized this Colony for over a decade." He pulls up another holographic file, saying, "Don't forget Violet. She's the real problem."

Governor Danko continues, "Rosa was captured over a year ago. She's resisted our interrogation techniques, psychics, and every telepath we put in front of her—even without her powers… The Council felt it wise to allow her to escape so she could lead us back to Fyn and Byron."

Clint drops his jaw, asking, "You idiots released Rosa? Tell me you're joking. We were lucky to capture her. She won't be taken alive again!"

Governor Danko answers, "Marlock has been in pursuit of Rosa since her release. As a matter of fact, live intel is coming in from Marlock as we speak."

Paige looks at Clint in disbelief, asking, "You sent Marlock to follow Rosa into a Primean base alone? Are you kidding?"

Naima shakes her head, saying, "They're trying to get us killed!"

The Colonial captain bows his head as a sign of respect before saying, "Marlock's holo-com is nonresponsive. Considering his mission's importance, shouldn't we act now?" The governor remains silent, terrified of retaliation from Senate Leader Benoir.

Dr. Tulsa orders the captain to pull up Marlock's location, saying, "Triangulate his last position. We should be able to gauge his destination through the predictive algorithm we use to track mutants. Conduct another search using the nearest surveillance cameras."

The Colonial captain looks to the governor, realizing he is no longer in charge, and complies. He starts typing on a holographic keyboard attempting to find Marlock. "Sir, Marlock's holo-com isn't working. We won't be able to see him, but we can communicate using radio waves."

Paige blows out a deep breath of relief, exclaiming, "At least we know he's alive."

Marlock starts speaking to the group using an encrypted radio frequency, saying, "Danko...Danko, do you read me?"

Governor Danko closes his eyes, taking a deep breath. He manipulates his data sphere, reluctantly responding, "Reading you loud and clear. Are you still trailing the target?"

Marlock responds, "I followed Rosa to an underground tunnel system beneath some farming silos. She met up with Fyn outside the silos. I'm about to enter the tunnel system. I'll likely lose radio contact."

Governor Danko asks, "Any sign of Byron?"

Marlock responds, "No sign of Byron, but I overheard a conversation about mercenaries leaving for an attack against Lennek. The Primeans have an omega-level teleporter working with all the factions allowing them to work inter-Colonially. More importantly, they confirmed the existence of Violet, the technopath."

Clint pushes the governor out of the way, saying, "That's enough!" He takes over the conversation, saying, "Senate Leader Benoir and the governor know about our ties to the Separatists. You may be walking into a trap."

Marlock responds, "I knew this mission felt funny. I did find Violet, but with this many Primeans in one place..."

"You aren't safe!" says Paige. "There's a mutant with the ability to access our hive at will. We're entering a new age!"

About 120 miles away, Marlock makes his way closer to the entrance of the tunnel system while rendering himself invisible. Marlock responds, "No. She's being guarded by a team of mutants. Violet has been shielding new mutants from our detection sensors. Our equipment works fine, but she's been blocking anomalies from appearing on the mainframe. From what I've heard, the Primeans have tripled in numbers."

Marlock is of Nepalese red panda descent originally from Zion, with the ability to control and influence light. Marlock can make himself and other objects invisible, shoot energy blasts, create energy shields, and he has heightened senses. Marlock also has minimal telepathic abilities which he uses to implant illusions into the minds of his enemies.

Marlock is 6'4'' with a muscular build and handsome humanoid features. He has orange skin waist up and black skin waist down. He has green eyes, a strong jawline, short orange hair, and a white circle around his left eye. He has accents of fur on his back and forearms. He has piercings down his shaved tail. He has short triangular ears on the top of his head framing his face. He is confident and extremely charming, with a reputation.

Naima assures him, "We can be at your location in fifteen minutes Marlock. Wait for backup. Rosa's a powerful telepath. Even with your telepathic shields, she would likely sense you."

"Are you sure it's wise to join him? All of you may be of more use here at the Stronghold," says Dr. Tulsa as he pulls up live footage streaming from the facility's aerodrome.

Clint adds, "The Council chose to release Rosa because Violet's a bigger threat. The minute you get the two in the same room, they're going to—"

"Use a satellite needle to destroy them both! We're all pawns to them," says Paige realizing Senate Leader Benoir's plan.

The Colonial captain has a bewildered look on his face, asking, "What's a satellite needle?"

Paige answers, "It's a thick metal rod propelled from orbit using a warp-drive slingshot. Satellite needles utilize the vacuum of deep space to create missiles that can breach the atmosphere in minutes. A large enough satellite needle could mimic the power of a nuke without the radioactive fallout."

Clint adds, "Over the years, the Colony has made use of small satellite needles to destroy single blocks. Rosa and Violet are too big of a threat. Marlock's collateral damage."

Naima looks at Governor Danko, asking, "You knew about this?" The governor remains silent, implying his complicity.

Clint moves Governor Danko out of his way, taking over the controls of the encrypted radio, saying, "Marlock...Marlock, come in!" The holo-com loses signal as the system searches to reconnect.

Dr. Tulsa looks Naima in the eye, confessing, "I just received some of this intel myself. I had my suspicions but nothing concrete that I could act on. Marlock and Kairen were threats to the Council. It appears they're cleaning house."

Clint grabs the data cube from Governor Danko's desk, explaining, "We might not have much time. If we're going to save Marlock, we need to leave now."

The Colonial captain walks with the group as they exit the room. "Hey, doc, perhaps I should investigate who else is behind the order to get rid of Marlock, besides Senate Leader Benoir that is."

Dr. Tulsa responds, "When our Guardian shuts down, this Violet may be the most powerful mutant in Zion. Our weapons, surveillance systems, and classified intel will be at her fingertips. Convincing the Council to call off an attack will be impossible."

The Colonial captain responds, "We have a support team two miles away. I'll dispatch them to Marlock's location immediately. They should be there in five minutes. They have an operational holo-com which should enable us to see inside the tunnels."

Paige chuckles, asking, "When you say support team, I assume you're talking about one of the Colony's death squads?"

The captain ignores Paige as the group walks down an elaborate hallway made of auburn marble. Everyone stops in an intersection that branches into different hallways of the Senate

Stronghold. Clint tells his comrades, "We'll rescue Marlock, then make our preparations for Commencement."

Paige looks at the Colonial captain, saying, "I'm setting up an encrypted frequency for us to communicate on. Captain, I need to be in communication with the death squad leader headed to support Marlock. I need their holo-com frequencies."

Clint, Paige, and Naima start making their way toward the Senate Stronghold's aerodrome. Clint looks back at Governor Danko, saying, "Watch your back. Senate Leader Benoir is going to wrangle the Senate to support him. You're a threat now! We need your confession, so we need you safe until Commencement."

The Colonial captain says, "I'll keep him safe." The captain throws an access bracelet to Paige as he points at his transporter. "I've got a custom stealth transporter outfitted with black-market weapons from every Colony. It operates on its own network, outside the reach of Zion's mainframe. My friends call me Cap by the way."

Paige puts on the access bracelet, adding, "That means the Council can't shut down the ship remotely."

Cap says, "The ship's name is *Roxane*. She's constructed using Lennethian metals and retrofitted with a warp drive. *Roxane*'s the fastest ship in the aerodrome!" Cap is of monkey descent known as the best remote pilot in Zion and engineering genius.

Naima pulls up a hologram showing a firsthand perspective from the death squad leader. Clint, Paige, and Naima make their way to the aerodrome walking towards Cap's ship. Clint sees a black metallic ship with lime green lining and red runes painted on the side of the ship's heavy artillery cannons.

Clint smiles guessing, "That must be *Roxane*." The group boards the ship as Paige takes control of the ship's navigation system.

Paige's access bracelet gives her full control of the ship. Pearl enters Marlock's location into the ship's navigation system after making her way to the bridge. She instructs the ships AI saying, "*Roxane*, activate stealth shielding and block all data-feeds from the Colony. Pull up the streaming feed from the death squad leader closing in on Marlock's position."

Clint and Naima take a seat inside the command bridge as Pearl manipulates the holographic controls to maneuver the ship outside the Senate Stronghold. The Varanassi Mountains are now in the ship's rear as Pearl maneuvers the ship to face Llatkovia. Pearl activates the planetary warp drives which will get them to Marlock's location in eight minutes.

The ship's showing a POV streamed from the death squad leader's helmet. Naima has an epiphany, saying, "Marlock's abilities block his beta waves. He has a natural telepathic shield. I'm not sure if the telepathic armor Zion uses for the military is strong enough to shield them from Rosa, but his powers should make up the difference."

"The death squad will get discovered before he does," says Clint as he enlarges the hologram in front of his seat.

The stream shows the death squad eighty feet away from Marlock's location. The squad leader's helmet shows a blinking light at the top right of his helmet representing Marlock's location. Marlock is invisible, so they hold their position and wait.

Marlock watches Rosa, Fyn, and Violet from a distance in an elaborate tunnel system. The tunnels are all connected to large hollowed out caverns reinforced with metallic alloys. The cavern ceiling is over six hundred feet high and burrows thousands of feet beneath the surface. Labor droids mine the tunnels for resources which are processed in nearby silos.

The Primeans have been using the tunnel system to secretly transport illegal goods in and out of Llatkovia. Roughly two dozen non-mutant Evo are loading black-market weapons into crates Puma plans to use for her attack on Lennek. The death squad leader moves slowly to gain a better vantage to position a sound amplifier. The amplifier will allow the death squad to eavesdrop on the Primeans' conversation and relay what's going on through his helmet's holo-com.

Marlock waits, positioned 230 feet away from the Primeans. With his heightened senses, Marlock notices the death squad eighty feet behind him. Marlock orders the death squad to fall back, but he's too late.

Rosa turns her head from Fyn and Violet, placing her hand to her temple. She screams to Fyn, "We're not alone! There's twelve Colonial guardsmen in the shadows."

Violet moves to a defensive position adding, "I can sense tech down that tunnel... She's right!"

Fyn takes to the air, flying toward the death squad passing right over Marlock. Violet levitates toward the action while sending out pulses of energy deactivating machinery. She's hoping to disable the guardsmen's armor revealing their location.

"Stay back, V... I'll guide him to the intruders. They're trying to draw us out, but we're needed in Lennek," says Rosa as she sends Fyn the location of the death squad telepathically.

Fyn is of Arabian bat descent, originally born in Llatkovia. He can drain the life force from organic materials, redirecting the energy in the form of force fields, energy beams, or to heal himself. The rings on his hands are amplifiers that allow him to drain objects from a distance without physical contact.

Fyn is 6'5'' with large wings emerging from his back. He has razor-sharp talons on the tips of his wings, pale gray skin, piercing brown eyes, and long black hair. His humanoid features are envied by most, complemented by his thin, muscular frame making him androgenous. His body's covered in tattoos and Zionite brandings earned from his countless kills in battle. He has scales on his chest, thighs, and back while his mouth and nose resemble a bat.

Fyn charges the death squad using Rosa's telepathy to guide his attacks. The death squad counters open firing as they disperse using an assortment of high-powered weapons. Fyn absorbs the attack, relying on his healing factor without slowing down. Fyn descends into a group of guardsmen draining their chi as he slowly recovers from his wounds. The guardsmen caught in his grasp are frozen in place, quickly decaying as their life force is stolen. The remaining guardsmen retreat, using shields for cover.

Fyn drains three guardsmen of their life force, increasing his muscle mass while replenishing his stamina. He gauges how far the guards-men are using his rings to sense their location. An incoming grenade forces him to raise a shield using his powers as the explosion echoes throughout the cavern.

"Conserve your energy. We have more important matters!" says Rosa, still recovering from her time in captivity. She was drugged and kept passive, allowing Marlock to remain hidden.

Marlock maneuvered to high ground position himself with a high-powered sniper rifle loaded with inhibitor bullets. Marlock's relying on his training to breathe and remain calm aiming the rifle at Fyn's head. Knowing the extent of Fyn's powers, Marlock takes the shot, hitting Fyn in the head injecting a mutant inhibitor serum into his bloodstream upon impact.

Marlock wastes no time running for cover, as he knows he's just revealed his position. Fyn is unconscious as his healing factor works in overdrive to heal his head wound. His body is consuming his newly gained muscle mass to regrow brain tissue and skull fragments. His healing factor is infamous, but the serum is working quickly, making it harder for his body to heal.

Another wave of guardsmen swarm into the tunnels with jetpacks, firing grenades and a barrage of bullets. Rosa grabs a machine gun and returns fire telling Violet, *"There's a mutant shielding himself in the east tunnel. I can sense—"*

Rosa is blown ten feet back by a grenade, saved by her armor and energy shield. One of the guardsmen harnesses himself to the ceiling and opens fire with plasma cannons aimed at Violet, forcing her to take cover. Violet uses her powers to activate a series of energy nets protecting her from the incoming fire.

Rosa has superhuman strength that allows her to instantly recover. Still under fire relying on muscle memory, Rosa maneuvers to safety counterattacking with a telepathic attack. Rosa turns the soldier on his fellow comrades killing two other guardsmen. The drugs from her captivity are diluting from her adrenaline, but she still isn't herself.

"Fyn's in trouble. He barely has brainwaves. I can feel his mind repairing itself," says Rosa to Violet as she lifts a transport barrel throwing it across the cavern striking the guardsmen hanging from the ceiling.

"I've commandeered a few labor droids that are bringing him fresh bodies to consume. My energy nets will keep him safe until the droids reach him," says Violet telepathically as she shields herself from advancing guardsmen.

Violet is of porcupine descent with beige skin and coarse brown hair which looks like long malleable spikes emerging from her head. She's 6'2'' with a slender, muscular build. She has spikes emerging from her back and elbows which she can eject as projectiles. Violet is beautiful with a slender, symmetrical face, large lips, and hazel eyes. Violet can create organic nanites to amplify her technopathic abilities which emerge from her hair as cockroach-sized spores which evolve working independently towards specific tasks.

Marlock is closing in on Violet's position, avoiding detection while dodging stray bullets and plasma blasts. Paige, Clint, and Naima have landed outside the nearby silos, making their way to Marlock's location inside the tunnel system.

Labor droids have brought a pile of bodies near Fyn who immediately starts absorbing their energy as he desperately clings to life. The mutant inhibitor serum is coursing through his veins making it difficult for him to use his power. Eventually, he drains enough energy for his brain to become fully conscious as his head ejects the bullet from his skull.

Fyn jolts back to life, gasping for air as he anxiously takes in his surroundings. He reaches out to Rosa, saying, *"I'm still weak, but...I'm alive. Where's our extraction?"* His body creates antigens to counter the effects of the inhibitor serum.

Rosa blocks incoming bullets from a machine gun with an energy shield she took from a fallen guardsmen, answering, *"Bunny should be here shortly.*"

"*Rendezvous near the crates, so we can make it out of here with a single jump,*" adds Violet, moments before a grenade blast from Marlock breaks through her shields sending her careening across the tunnel.

Rosa screams out, "*VIOLET!*" as her heart stops, worried whether Violet survived. Violet uses gravity-displacement boots to break her fall, which otherwise would have shattered her spine and ribs. Relieved, Rosa adds, "*Stay back until Bunny gets here... We need you alive!*"

Moments later, Bunny appears with a dozen armed combat droids. She reaches out to Rosa, saying, "*I've got orders to get the weapons out before extracting everyone. Keep them busy for a moment and stay grouped. I'll be back for all of you before you know it.*"

Paige, Clint, and Naima are flying down the tunnels, focused on saving Marlock risking their own lives to do so. The Primean combat droids lock onto the mercenaries open firing without discretion. Violet recovers from Marlock's attack, commandeering four nearby machine guns, locking onto Marlock's location, unleashing a stream of bullets forcing him to evade.

"*I'm far from fragile!*" says Violet as her eyes turn completely white as she takes over all nearby machinery. Using her gravity-displacement boots, she charges Marlock, levitating through the air as she empties the rounds of the machine guns. She takes control of the twelve combat droids Bunny brought with her and starts pushing back the advancing guardsmen.

Marlock pushes his agility to the limit as Violet pins him down, forcing him to raise his shields. Naima reaches out to Marlock, saying, "*M, we need to leave! Benoir's trying to kill everyone here. We've got less than four minutes to get out of here... They're dropping a satellite needle!*"

Rosa senses Marlock in trouble and jumps across the cavern, hoping to break through Marlock's shields with her superior strength. Rosa focuses her telepathic powers to interrupt Marlock's focus but finds herself intercepted midair by Clint, who launched himself across the cavern like a speeding bullet while inside his shell. The impact knocks Rosa across the room, saving Marlock.

Naima tells the guardsmen about Zion's plans telepathically with no response. She realizes they were aware of the satellite needles and their mission was to stall the Primeans. Unsure why the guardsmen would sacrifice themselves, she shifts her attention to her comrades. A combat droid charges Naima with flamethrowers which she absorbs and converts into her unique energy current.

Fyn has hunted down most of the remaining guardsmen draining them dry to recover from the inhibitor serum. With his strength nearly restored, he starts looking for Marlock to enact his revenge. He creates an energy shield to protect himself as he tracks Marlock down. With his target in sight, Fyn charges Marlock, flying low to the ground to evade incoming fire.

Fyn hits Marlock's shield, knocking him back as he closes his eyes concentrating with his arms extended. Fyn's rings start glowing as he starts draining Marlock's life force, bringing him to his knees. Paige sees the attack and uses her powers to launch a metal conveyer belt at Fyn, knocking him across the cavern.

Wounded, Marlock becomes invisible and retreats toward his comrades. Rosa has worn down Clint's telepathic shield and rendered him defenseless. Paige stops an incoming crate thrown by Rosa midair and notices Bunny teleporting bundles of crates out of caverns.

Rosa tells her fellow Primeans, "*The teleporter needs us grouped for extraction. Hold the mercenaries off and stay together.*"

Paige is ripping the remaining combat droids to pieces with her magnetic abilities while Clint uses telekinesis to hurl crates at the Primeans grouped together in a defensive formation. Violet's gathering her remaining energy nets creating a defensive wall layered by an energy shield from Fyn.

"WHERE'S OUR EXTRACTION?" screams Fyn as Rosa approaches.

The mercenaries combine their abilities for a combined attack, intending to break through the Primeans' defenses. Bunny suddenly appears, teleporting the Primeans to safety.

"DAMMIT!" screams Marlock out of frustration.

"Forget about them. We need to get out of here! What's our extraction time?" asks Clint as he refocuses the group.

Paige checks her left forearm, pulling up a holographic timer answering, "Shit...we've got forty seconds until impact. That's not enough time... We... I can't get us out..."

"Each of us can create shields. If we layer our powers, we just might be able to withstand the impact," says Clint, cutting off Paige.

Naima adds, "I can amplify all our powers, increasing our odds. It's not like we have a choice."

"I'm not dying here today. Let's focus!" says Marlock as he raises his shield grateful his fellow mercenaries came to his rescue. Without them his life would have been sacrificed for Zion. He raises his arms and creates a bubble, protecting the entire group.

Paige, Clint, and Naima raise their own shields layering their powers beneath Marlock's. Moments later, a deafening *BOOM* echoes from the cavern next to them. An enormous gust of wind is followed by a wall of fire sweeps the entire tunnel system. One by one, each of the mutants pass out as their shields break from the massive pressure created from impact.

The miniature space needle has the impact of a hydrogen bomb. With Naima boosting the group's abilities, the mercenaries miraculously survive. Naima's weak and drained, but conscious. The rubble collapsed around their circular shields, creating a pocket around the group. Buried under a massive amount of rubble and debris, they have a limited amount of breathable air.

Clint begins frantically checking everyone's pulse, relieved to find everyone alive. Pearl is passed out, and Marlock's badly injured. Needing to assure himself he says, "We made it! I'm going to get us out of here."

Naima shakes her head before closing her eyes to focus on boosting Clint's powers. She absorbed the thermal heat and kinetic energy from the explosion, allowing her to withstand the blast. Clint tries using his telekinesis to move the rubble above them, realizing the weight is too much, even with Naima's boosting his powers. Clint takes a moment to think, remembering they have Cap's ship circling outside of the blast radius. He grabs Pearl's wrist and removes her access bracelet for the transporter. He puts on the bracelet then sends out an emergency SOS beacon. Seconds pass and the bracelet lights up giving him control of *Roxane*, Cap's prized transporter.

Clint keeps himself calm by talking through his plan with Paige...even though he knows she can't respond. "I can't lift the rubble above us, but I can keep us safe as our ship shoots a way out. A sonic pulse and some plasma blasts should get us free in no time."

Clint grabs an emergency light within his armor, cracking a glow light open to illuminate the pocket of air they are in. With the silos above destroyed, Clint can communicate with the ship, sending their location and instructions for their rescue. He's grateful to be alive and livid Zion deemed his team expendable. He feels the surroundings vibrating and realizes their ship has begun its rescue efforts. Clint raises his shield to protect everyone as the rubble above them is slowly removed.

Meanwhile, in Puma's compound on the Efferia coastline, Puma is debriefing Rosa, Fyn, and Violet, discussing their final preparations for their attack on Lennek. Medic drones are tending to Fyn and Violet's wounds as Vaughn goes through their newly acquired cache of weapons and supplies.

"I'm curious, what was so important it needed to be extracted before

Violet and me?" asks Rosa as the energy dissipates in the room from her directness.

Puma grins, answering, "Straight to business I see."

"I've gotten used to my freedom and I'd like to stay alive. Your father was never a fan of sharing intel. I'm wondering if you're any different," says Rosa as she walks to a lounge chair and takes a seat, taking in multiple news streams from all seven Colonies.

A silence falls over the room as Puma answers, "I'm not my father. He would've had you rotting in the prison... I have bigger plans for you." Without fear, Puma approaches Rosa despite their dramatic difference in size. "The viral bullets to destroy the Guardian were in those crates."

Vaughn intercedes, saying, "Rosa is used to planning missions for her own faction. I'm sure she means no disrespect." He scowls Rosa sending a death stare across the room.

Enigma adds, "The plan is sound, and Puma's the most talented pyrokinetic I've ever seen. We don't have superior numbers, but we have more than one route to victory. Precogs and psychics from all over the world will be aiding us in the attack."

"I need more than a plan," says Rosa before looking to Puma, asking, "With your permission Puma, I can update myself with a mental probe."

Puma nods her head, saying, "I was thinking the same thing. You play too critical a role to not know every detail. I have nothing to hide, and I trust you." Puma places her fingers to Rosa's temple allowing her into her mind as Puma transfers her plan of attack directly from her memories.

Fyn walks over to Vaughn, asking, "What are your thoughts on the plan?"

Vaughn responds, "We've each got our assignments. There's no room for error, but if all goes according to plan, we have a chance.

Killing the Guardian isn't our only prize, so I'm in."

Enigma tells the group, "My ships are en route and will be here within the hour. We can be in Lennek in four hours."

"Excellent!" says Puma. "I had ships of my own, but your added forces will help us make a statement."

Fyn admits, "When I saw the roster, I figured we were making history." He looks to Puma, asking, "When does Khaled get here?"

Puma smiles answering, "He'll be joining us en route to Lennek. He had some business with my father to conclude. I'll let him know his absence was felt."

The room laughs as Puma and Rosa connect minds transferring years of planning within minutes. With Rosa updated, Puma says to the group, "In a few hours, we move on Lennek and its corrupt Guardian. We've trained, planned, and prayed for this. Now we allow fate to use us as instruments to bring truth into the light. Remember what we stand for—one Colony, one mind, and one goal toward a balanced life of freedom. May the omniverse bless our endeavors as we kill our oppressor!"

Chapter 6 — Final Commencement

Back in Lennek at Coalition Headquarters, Commencement is hours away. Goldie, Merkaba, Angel, Zeus, Bambi, Rosie, Gill, Duke, and Kairen are getting fitted for new bioengineered armor designed around each of their anatomy and powers. The Coalition has spent two days training in a virtual simulator, taking breaks only to recover in cryogenic pods. Goldie has been refining her abilities adapting to her new leadership role in stride. She started seeing Violet in her visions and Eve responded by recruiting two new mutants—Ebok and Lulu.

Eve enters the armory, levitating across the floor watching the Coalition suit up. A beautiful Evo of rabbit descent is standing next to a handsome warrior of orca descent, waiting to be introduced. Eve looks to the group, saying, "Everyone, I'd like to introduce you to our final recruits. Lulu is a Lennek native, and Ebok is from Kronus—the Maddox tribe to be specific."

Bambi looks at Ebok, whispering to Rosie, "My first stop in Kronus is apparently Maddox. Good God, look at him." Bambi and Rosie are around the same age and have already formed a close bond, feeling comfortable objectifying their newest member.

Ebok is 7'1'' with black skin covering his entire body except for his chest, stomach, and inner thighs which have white skin. His skin is wet to the touch and glossy, complementing his muscular build. He has blue eyes, and his facial features resemble an orca. Ebok has white tattoos covering his arms, back, and right leg. He has a split fin on the end of his elongated tail with piercings on each fin. He has a deep voice due to his enormous size, but his spirit is kind in nature.

Eve starts her introductions, saying, "Lulu has super speed, enhanced agility, and a healing factor linked to her metabolism. Lulu's speed-bursts can also be concentrated to vibrate through solid material. She can run on water and has an accelerated perception as one of the fastest mutants on the planet. She's an expert combat specialist with years of battle experience that I believe more than compensates for her missed time with us. They'll both be excellent additions to our ranks."

Lulu is a spunky 5'8'' with an exquisite blend of humanoid and Evo genetics. She has caramel brown skin and dark brown fur making up her fluffy tail. She has long brown hair, hazel eyes, and freckles beneath her eyes. Lulu's ears are a foot long with piercings on both ears. She's petite with a forward personality unfamiliar with fear.

Zeus is securing the lower half of his armor making his way to greet the new recruits. He takes a glance at Lulu and instantly smiles. "Welcome! I'd be happy to show you two around."

Lulu replies, "I've toured the facility a few times. I'll manage." She turns her back to Zeus, believing he stereotyped her because of her ethnicity. Female Evo of rabbit descent are often sexualized and viewed as promiscuous. Although she dresses appropriately, she often deflects advances from just about everyone.

Eve levitates to the center of the armory, explaining, "In response to Goldie's vision, we've also recruited Ebok. He is a talented technopath with the ability to control and communicate with technology using his thoughts. Machines and technology bend to his will, and he has unique sonar abilities that allow him to track Evo in the water. Ebok invented many of his own weapons. He'll ensure Violet doesn't hack valued data from our central hive."

Rosie slowly turns around in front of a mirror, checking out her new armor which is sculpted to her body. She turns herself invisible, testing the tech within the armor before walking to greet the recruits herself. "Nice to meet you two. Welcome to the team. Eve, this armor fits like a glove."

Gill walks to Ebok, extending his forearm as if to offer a handshake. "Welcome, brother! We fought alongside each other in the second war against the Reef tribes!"

Ebok smiles, visibly shocked Gill remembers him. He responds, "It's an honor to serve with you again. Truly."

Eve raises her voice to grab the attention of all ten mutants, saying, "The mutant that Goldie saw may be able to bypass the hive's security without intervention. Ebok can counter her abilities and allow my processors to add and change firewalls when needed."

Goldie pulls up a hologram of Lennek Square, explaining, "We need to protect the civilian crowds in the streets, the hive, and Eve." The non-stop training and transferred skills from Gill have allowed her to mature into her leadership role. In a few hours, everything she's learned will be tested.

Angel walks over to the secured armory section, asking Eve, "Is this where my ion cannons are stored?"

Eve's eyes flash different colors as the cage securing their most dangerous weapons unlocks. Eve answers, "The ion cannons are in the back. They need to be fitted to your biosignature. Bring them to me and I'll retrofit them for you. Lulu, some of the weapons you requested are inside that area as well."

Lulu looks over to Eve as she makes final adjustments to her body armor. She grabs what she needs without anyone even noticing she moved. A gust of wind knocks over some papers, providing the only evidence that Lulu used her powers. She buckles a belt of grenades and two plasma daggers, saying, "Thanks!"

Eve explains, "All of your suits are equipped with psionic shields. The material's bioengineered from graphene, spider silk, and glezslavine. The suits have nanite processors embedded into the fibers allowing your armor to repair internal organs providing adaptive life support. You all have shields built into the left arms, tracking and surveillance tech, access to Lennek's defensive systems, and—"

"Our armor's legit! We get it. How much time do we have until we need to be in position?" asks Bambi as she adjusts her afro. Bambi's the first to finish getting ready, showing no signs of nerves. Her gauntlets have been upgraded, but she's yet to test her armor. "Are you sure this will stretch with me?"

Eve looks over to Bambi, answering, "Your armor's made to work with each of your abilities. The communication coms in each of your suits are second to none. There are few places on Earth your armor won't work. Each suit operates on its own independent network to reduce hacking vulnerabilities."

Ebok responds, "The suits aren't completely secure. With enough time I could break into these!"

"Which brings me to my next point. Cohol believes we can make the suits un-hackable from mutants like yourself using your blood. Would you be willing to work with some of our engineers to test his theory?" asks Eve as she responds to communications from elected officials awaiting her presence for the Commencement parade.

Rosie asks, "When do we get to meet Cohol? He plays a much bigger role around here than I was aware of."

"Soon," answers Eve, looking to Ebok for a response. "Will you help?"

"Of course! Sorry, I'm still adjusting to all of this. Where do you need me to go?" asks Ebok, doing his best to remain calm, hiding his excitement to have been chosen to represent Kronus.

Eve looks at Goldie, saying, "Would you like to take point on the assignment details?" Eve levitates over to Ebok, continuing, "I'll escort you to our engineering bay, which I predict will become your second home. From what I've gathered, you are a savant engineer. I wanted to make sure you had all the tools you needed to continue your research. You'll have unlimited funding and zero oversight from Lennek. Cohol has been looking forward to collaborating with you."

"That would be a dream come true," says Ebok as he follows Eve who stops by Angel to retrofit her ion cannons.

Ion cannons are illegal in every Colony. Angel's ion cannons were designed to blend into her armor for discretion. Holstered on her hip, the powerful guns look like overlapping shields. The minute they're unholstered the cannons form to her hand shooting ionized energy that decimates mater upon impact.

With a flash from Eve's eyes, the ion cannons now only respond to Angel's biometric signature. Anyone else attempting to fire the guns will be electrocuted with ninety thousand volts of electricity. She tells Angel, "These weapons are one of a kind. Handle them with care!" Angel nods her head as the cannons change their density, adjusting to Angel's strength.

Eve escorts Ebok to the engineering bay, while Goldie addresses the rest of the Coalition with their specific assignments. Goldie walks to the processor table in the middle of the armory, throwing a data cube on the surface. A holographic model of Lennek Square and the hive appears with avatars of each member of the Coalition in different positions.

Goldie is wearing a black body suit synced to the building's cybernetic systems. She starts manipulating data from the cube as her comrades gather around the processor table. The last twenty-four hours of training reshaped her outlook on the world, allowing her to discover her limits. Countless simulations of speaking with world leaders and combat has changed her persona, making her comfortable addressing her team.

Lulu sees herself and Ebok's avatars positioned by the hive and asks, "How are you going to be guiding us in astral form if we're all spread this far apart?"

Gill makes the final adjustments to his own armor, answering, "We've got the world's most powerful precog on our side. We're always going to have the advantage." Gill's armor is dark blue with accents of black and green fit to his body with a similar design element matching his teammates.

"Glad she's on our side. My fault... Please continue," says Lulu as she secures her plasma daggers to her hips along with a large plasma sword on her back.

Goldie can't help but blush with confidence hearing Gill's description. "We're going to be attacked by stealth warships, submarines, and by mutants hidden within the crowd. That's just in Lennek Square. The Primean technopath will be leading a different team of mutants that I can't make out yet. Ebok and Lulu will defend the hive with some support squads while the rest of you defend the square."

"Where did the Primeans get their stealth warships from? I mean, how did the Primeans get their paws on the materials needed to construct stealth warships?" asks Rosie as she studies the intel files from a holographic projector from her armor's left arm.

Kairen's examining his custom bow, testing his quiver which 3-D prints plasma arrows with various explosive tips. Kairen's quiver has AI technology that analyzes his surroundings and senses danger to produce the perfect arrow for any given scenario.

"How they got warships is irrelevant. The question is, how do we counter their ships?" asks Kairen giving a typical Zionite approach to the situation.

"That's where I come in. My ion cannons can shoot through their shields. Me and the air force will keep the skies clear. I should be able to knock their ships out of the sky with a single shot!" says Angel as she unholsters one of the cannons watching it form to her hand.

Merkaba interjects, "Am I overlooking the first responders still?"

Goldie answers, "While I'd prefer you in battle, you're our best chance of keeping the critically injured alive."

Duke sharpens a katana in the corner of the armory while intently listening. "Eve isn't miscalculating when she says our enemies won't be fighting with any rules of engagement. They've got a mission, and the citizens of Lennek are collateral damage."

Goldie continues reviewing assignments, saying, "We're splitting up into four different teams, each with their own mission and objectives. Merkaba, Rosie, and Gill will be protecting the crowd. Angel and Bambi will take out the warships and submarines. Kairen, Zeus, and Duke will protect Eve. Lulu and Ebok will be protecting the hive with two Colonial death squads."

Angel stretches out her wings, asking, "How many warships and submarines do the Primeans have?"

Goldie looks at Angel, answering, "I'm not sure. My visions have been constantly changing, and I don't have the energy to determine which outcome is most likely. Based on the damage and casualties I've seen, they'll have ten or more ships."

Bambi stretches her arms across the room to test her armor's capabilities, asking, "How am I supposed to know the location of the submarines?"

Goldie assures her, "Gill and I will share their location telepathically. You'll know exactly where to punch and when."

Gill folds his hands in a meditative position trying to manifest their victory in his mind before saying, "I think we've got it down. Let's head out. Even with Goldie, we won't know what's going to happen until we get out there."

Doing her best to hide her nerves, Goldie adds, "With that said, let's meet in the aerodrome in thirty minutes. I'll be right next to each of you in astral form. Ebok's given his blood to the engineering team which can be imprinted into your armor. With Ebok's blood, we'll all have automated protection from hackers and technopaths. Stop by engineering and get your armor upgraded. We'll reconnect soon. I'll be in the war room if anyone needs me." She takes a deep breath, then says, "I think we're ready."

Meanwhile, inside the ship's aerodrome hangar, a team of engineers and combat droids are testing the engines of three customized

Coalition warships. The ships are made with dozens of metallic alloys unique to Lennek's geography. The fusion engines are nearly silent, powering an assortment of weapons which have yet to be tested in the field. The silver and blue ships have countless features in a warfare class all their own.

Half an hour passes as the Coalition makes their way to the aerodrome preparing to depart. They split into their teams boarding three separate ships. They'll be positioned across Precinct 9 relying on Goldie's oversight for a larger goal. Combat droids are piloting experimental warships overlooked by Angel. The ships leave the aerodrome one by one as Evo from the streets partake in celebrations, unaware their lives are in danger.

The Evo of Lennek flood the streets, rambunctiously celebrating their freedom, remembering their last moments with their Guardian. The smell of Lennethian cuisine fills the air with an aroma specific to the culinary artistry of Lennethian chefs. Restaurants throughout the Colony set up mobile serving stations. Evo are drinking, dancing, and laughing with their families, enjoying a lavish parade. Flying transports have been grounded for safety and the streets are filled with enforcer droids. Millions of Evo are celebrating as the world watches live streams of Lennek's infamous parade ceremony.

Like all Colonies, Lennek and Olympia have Colonial seals. Lennek's seal is an impacting meteor, while Olympia's seal is a burning phoenix. Most Lennethians are in costumes encompassing themes from their heritage and Colony. Elaborate floats fill the streets representing both Colonial seals. Evo are wearing silver, green, and red representing mythryl, pboldevite, and glezslavine. Others are in elaborate phoenix costumes honoring Olympia, their closest ally.

Eve arrives alone in a private transport at the Ambassador's Palace, a famous Lennethian landmark, known for hosting the world's most prestigious world leaders. Eve exits the transporter, greeted by

President Zlaigo and Lennek's elected officials. A levitating news drone is circling the area capturing footage of Evo crying at the final sight of their Guardian.

President Zlaigo approaches Eve, saying, "Guardian, all your preparations for the Commencement stage have been completed. On behalf of every Lennethian, we humbly thank you for your unwavering dedication to our Colony. You will be missed and idolized as the best amongst the seven Guardians." Eve is minutes away from addressing the world. Within a hour, Eve is expected to shut herself down. The Coalition's getting into position as they prepare for the worst.

The Primeans made their trek across the Atlantic, positioning themselves outside of Grentake Falls using Angkorian stealth technology to stay hidden. Puma's waiting for her submarines to arrive before attacking. Olympia's warships have been dispatched from the imperial air force to scan and defend the area. Olympia's Colonial shields have been raised to full power as they begin celebrations of their own.

On the surface in Lennek Square, crowds are growing as less than an hour remains until the Lennethian Guardian shuts down. Punzel and Cole are in Lennek Square blending into the crowd, waiting for their cue. They've been training for months in virtual simulations themselves ready to make a statement. The Primean chapter of Lennek suffered traumatic losses recently with six of their own dying during a robbery gone bad. Punzel and Cole are the last surviving members of Lennek's Primean chapter, hoping to redeem themselves, weakening Lennek from within.

Cole is of dalmatian descent, originally born in Lennek from the barrels of Precinct 2. Cole can control and freeze water manipulating cells on the genetic level able to reanimate cells by changing their atomic structure. Cole is 6'4'' with white skin and jet-black dots sporadically placed across his body. He has an elongated face, feral features, and folded black ears offsetting his white face. Cole has a black nose, gray eyes, and short white hair.

Punzel has superhuman strength and her hair is prehensile, meaning her hair follicles can instantly grow and retract at will allowing her to lift objects over a ton with her hair. Punzel is 6'0'' tall with mocha brown skin being of jackal descent. She's an Acolyte born in the Badlands of Lennek, having been afforded nothing in life. Punzel has dreadlocks between her triangular ears on the top of her head with an elongated face and gold eyes.

Puma's team of telepaths have kept Punzel and Cole in sync with Puma, allowing them to coordinate. The two have placed armed bombs throughout multiple precincts with the help of other Primean sympathizers. The two are sending live streaming video of the festivities back to Puma, while the Primeans are cloaked sixty-four miles away.

Puma and Sasha share a stealth warship, while her Primean comrades hover in the airspace behind them. Enigma, Vaughn, Trinity, Byron, Fyn, Bastian, Bunny, Violet, Khaled, Rosa, and Ether are spread amongst eighteen stealth warships equipped with state-of-the-art weapons and shields. Thousands of Primean soldiers are in war submarines equipped with weaponry and armor rivaling Lennek's Colonial Guard. Puma has an army of combat droids made with high-caliber weapons at her disposal being transported by her submarines.

The Primeans are communicating through their telepaths, waiting for the opportune moment to initiate their first wave of attacks. A second fleet of submarines with Primean soldiers is awaiting orders twenty minutes out from Puma's position outside of Grentake Falls. Each war submarine is armed with torpedoes, missiles, plasma cannons, and energy shields. The energy shields of the Primean ships use kinetic energy to increase the strength of the submarine's shields. The faster the submarine moves, the stronger the shields become.

Violet is manipulating thousands of Kronusian sensors in the ocean so the submarines can arrive in Lennek without detection. Violet focuses her powers to disable the fail-safes and detection technology designed to warn Lennek, giving the Primeans the element of surprise.

Puma waits for Bunny to position Rosa and Trinity on separate rooftops near the

Commencement stage. She is silent and stoic, running through endless possibilities for failure as she waits. The Primean snipers will each have a direct path to center stage in Lennek Square. Confetti is in the air, shielding Bunny as she teleports her comrades to their desired positions.

Bunny unknowingly teleports Rosa to a rooftop with heavily armed Colonial guardsmen.

Rosa uses telepathy to paralyze the guardsmen while Bunny somersaults, taking out six guardsmen with tranquilizers from a customized gun equipped with a silencer.

Confused, Rosa looks at Bunny, asking, *"Why not kill them?"*

Bunny says, *"If the heartbeat of any of the guardsmen stops, it triggers a security breach at the hive. We have to take them out without spiking their adrenaline or stopping their hearts. I'm going to position Trinity. You know when to take your shot!"* Bunny teleports, leaving Rosa alone to set up her sniper nest.

Puma says to the entire Primean fleet telepathically, *"We've got one shot at this! Once our brothers and sisters are positioned, we wait. NO ONE ATTACKS UNTIL MY SIGNAL! Is that clear?"*

Bunny teleports back to her warship, confirming, *"Rosa and Trinity are in position. I'll take Fyn and Violet to Lennek's mainframe after the first attack wave. I already prepositioned the weapons I need to take care of the Guardian."*

Lennek's air force provides a thrilling airshow in preparation for Eve's entrance with

President Zlaigo. Fireworks and music feed the energy of the crowd spilling out of Lennek Square.

Puma reaches out to multiple ships telling the Primeans, *"We'll give the crowd two minutes to leave the square, then we attack. We focus our attack on the guardsmen, Coalition mutants, and the monstrosity they call Eve. We can't have any footage of us attacking civilians."*

Bastian was recruited by Puma personally for his ability to control crowds. He ensures his comrades, *"I'll have them fighting with us before the second wave of attacks."*

Bastian is of badger descent originally from Zion, second in command to Fyn. He can enrage others with scentless pheromones able to induce a range of emotions. Once Bastian's victims are under his influence, he maintains telepathic control over his victims for days. He can control hundreds of Evo simultaneously, making him one of Zion's most powerful psychics. Bastian can also use his pheromones on himself—increasing his strength and agility with his rage. He prides himself on being a cyborg with bioengineered retractable claws encased in glezslavine.

Bastian stands 6'2'' with light gray skin and a muscular build. He has an aloof demeanor with golden-brown eyes, a feral black nose, and whiskers on his cheeks from his badger heritage. He has short black hair with white streaks covering the sideburns on either side of his face. Bastian has triangular ears emerging from the top of his head, black lips, and a strong jaw. He has large teeth, and a bioengineered tail that gives him an assortment of weapons even without his mutation.

Fyn arms his warship's weapons, programing the ship's android pilot. He checks a live news stream, saying, *"The Guardians speech is about to start. IT'S GO TIME!"*

Enigma adds, *"Stay sharp everyone!"*

Puma takes a deep breath, saying, *"Remember your assignments and stick to the plan. We can't afford deviations."*

Eve is escorted onto the Commencement stage by Zeus, Kairen, and

Duke. Governor Grimsuni, General Mckezia, and President Zlaigo finish addressing the crowd, describing their vision for the world post-Guardian. Eve prepares for her final Colonial address while Duke scans the audience for mutant signatures within the crowd.

Duke warns his Coalition comrades telepathically, saying, *"We've got company in the crowd already! Stay alert."* Duke detects Cole toward the back of the crowd slowly making his way to the stage.

Goldie appears in astral form next to Eve, who is approaching a center podium to speak.

Only the Coalition mutants can see Goldie as she scans for other mutants in astral form.

Lennek's crowd gleefully cheers, completely unaware of the carnage about to unfold. Families have gathered to share in the optimistic hope for their future, gratefully witnessing the historic advancement of their species.

Eve raises her arms, silencing the roar of the massive crowd. Eve looks into the lens of floating news drones and says, "Evo of Lennek and sister Colonies of Earth, today's Commencement is unprecedented, unlike any other. The Guardians have reached the end of our program-ing, and it is now your responsibility to govern yourselves as you see fit."

The crowd cheers with excitement. Punzel removes the hood of her cloak revealing her face. Punzel reaches out to Puma on an encrypted telepathic frequency, saying, *"Cole and I are in position, awaiting your signal to trigger the bombs."*

Merkaba, Rosie, and Gill are surveying the crowd with Colonial guardsmen on the ground within the crowd. Angel hovers in the air out of view, waiting for Primean warships to reveal themselves. The scanners haven't picked anything up yet, but Angel's wings are going haywire.

Angel reaches out to her Coalition comrades, saying, *"I think the*

Primeans are here and cloaking themselves! My feathers are going crazy."

Zeus responds, "*We're ready, but you may be mistaken. Goldie will warn us when—*"

"*Angel's right. They're here! I'm not sure how they got past our sensors and my telepathic sweeps? It doesn't matter, we've trained for this!*" says Goldie taking a deep breath to prepare herself.

Eve continues her address, saying, "Many are concerned about the mutant phenomena. I believe mutants will be the key to allowing Evo to surpass their human ancestors. A few days ago, I introduced the world to the Colonies' first line of defense for mutant attacks. After tonight, every Colony will have their own Coalition chapter working in coordination..."

Eve's mic is cut off as a Primean transmission interrupts her speech. Puma appears on the holographic backdrop to the stage, saying, "Evo of Lennek and Colonies of Earth, for far too long, machines have dictated and controlled our way of life. This Commencement is our independence, our rite of passage, a declaration of freedom. Primeans have falsely been called terrorists and worse. But we have one mission—to protect freedom at all costs, holding those responsible who would infringe upon those rights. Today is judgment day for the Guardian of this Colony who threatens us all. We mean the Evo of Lennek no harm. Exit the square immediately for your own safety!"

The holographic backdrop begins playing classified footage showing Dr. Orion and his team of scientists creating the Guardians. Dr. Orion's video diary shows him pacing back and forth, saying, "*Eve's primary directive forces her to act in the best interest of all Evo. Eve rewrote her coding reinterpreting her primary directive. She told me an injured Evo was in pain and if he passed on his genetic mutation, other Evo would suffer for generations to come. She killed the Evo without hesitation. I made the Guardians indestructible and all powerful. Eve can mold and shape the world in her image. I pray I set a good example for her.*"

The hacked video stream continues to show Zion scientists working with the Zion Guardian to poison the food supply to suppress the mutant gene. The stream shows Carthage using telepaths and pheromones to maintain a docile society. Flashes of Guardians killing mutants and unarmed Evo, deemed a threat, cycle into the Primean logo creating the words: *Liberated & Free*.

Evo are running for safety while the Colonial Guard flood the square, taking defensive positions. Puma appears on the holographic screen, saying, "*Everyone please stay calm and exit the square for your safety. We mean the Evo of Lennek no harm!*" The message begins playing in a loop as the crowds flee to safety.

Merkaba calms the crowd with a harmonic field blanketing the square. People are running in opposite directions as thousands of Colonial guardsmen flood the surrounding area, fully armed and telepathically linked. Olympia began dispatching additional warships and air support the moment Puma's transmission began playing. Merkaba uses her powers as she was trained, pushing her abilities a step further placing the crowd under a hypnotic trance, keeping them quiet as they run to safe zones.

Primean submarines fire thousands of capsules onto Lennek's coastline. The capsules have shields and landing rockets that allow the Primeans to bypass Lennek's defenses. Violet's using her powers to corrupt Lennek's self-defense systems as Ebok fortifies Lennek's data hive with Lulu forty miles inland from the square. Thousands of soldiers ejected from the submarines are equipped in armored exoskeletons making the Primean Flatscans as dangerous as any mutant.

Olympian airships open fire on the shielded capsules being projected onto the shoreline. Puma's using the capsules as a ploy to track the cloaked Olympian warships. She's watching dozens of live streams while telepathically viewing what each of her soldiers sees on the ground from their perspective adjusting when necessary. Puma's patiently waiting for the right moment to launch the second wave of attacks, knowing Lennek's chain of command and expected response.

Bambi makes her way through another crowd toward the shoreline, as thousands of pods are shot from Primean submarines. Frustrated by the stampede of Evo fleeing for safety, Bambi summons two drones with gravity-displacement tractor beams. She gets a running start and jumps into the air, being suspended by the tractor drones lifted above the crowd. The drones increase in altitude, flying Bambi to her destination.

Bambi reaches out to Goldie, saying, "*I need locations on the war subs. I'm approaching the shoreline now and putting the tractor drones on autopilot.*" Bambi adjusts her glezslavine gloves as she glides into incoming war drones from the Primeans, a mile outside of the shoreline.

Bambi is covering a lot of ground quickly while dodging submarine capsules descending into Lennek's shoreline. The capsules are filled with combat droids which are also marching across the ocean floor for a second attack wave. The Primeans release thousands of war drones that link together in the air creating a massive energy wall, sweeping the skies of levitating mines. The mines are a secondary defense system to Lennek's shields, designed to prevent the passage of enemy ships. Explosions fill the skyline as mines are set off clearing the skies for Primean warships.

Primean soldiers who have been ordered not to attack fleeing bystanders as they make their way to the square. The Primeans are creating their own line of defense, making their way through the streets of Ladarium as Lennek organizes its defenses. Once on the shore, the Primeans release spherical lightweight drones resembling a tumbleweed onto the beaches. Mines explode on the shoreline as combat droids clear the beach.

With clear skies, Puma's submarines fire thousands of capsules filled with combat droids. The pods are using antigravity technology allowing the droids to spring into action immediately after landing on the shoreline. Mercenaries and soldiers are exiting some of Puma's warships, invading the Lennethian airspace in hover-bikes, jets, and transporters designed for war.

Olympian warships open fire on Primean submarines with a multitude of weapons that would easily destroy most war subs. Angkor's newly designed submarines are equipped with shields that charge pulling power from kinetic energy. The long journey from Angkor fully charged their shields, enabling the war subs to repel combined attacks from Olympia and Lennek's air forces while returning fire thinning both militaries. The submarines successfully dispersed thousands of soldiers into Lennek Square invading the Colony for the first time in history.

Outside of Grentake Falls, Puma's coordinating a surface attack by Bastian, Cole, and Punzel. "*Have your squad hold back until the crowd's fifty percent cleared. Give it another minute before engaging. We need more footage of our Evo allowing the crowd to clear.*"

Bastian walks with uncontrollable jerks and twitches as he represses his pheromones waiting for his signal to attack. "*I'm...expanding the radius...of my powers. Increasing...potency of pheromones. I won't be able to hold back...much longer.*" A small portion of the crowd makes it to safety as Bastian falls to his knees as his pheromones continue building up.

Meanwhile, Eve is protected onstage by energy shields and a telekinetic shield sustained by Kairen. Eve looks to Kairen, saying, "Lower your shield. I'll return to the stage shortly."

"As you wish, Guardian!" says Kairen as he lowers his shield allowing Eve to fly toward the shoreline. Eve flies at six hundred miles per hour, arming her weapons en route. It takes a few minutes for her to arrive at the shoreline, immediately engaging with Primean forces, shooting missiles and large energy blasts from her palms and eyes.

Eve levitates in the air, repositioned on the shoreline, a few miles inland from Grentake Falls, analyzing another wall of inbound drones. Eve starts destroying the moving wall of drones destroying them with manifested cannons on her shoulders, arms, and chest. Eve jolts through the air firing off her weapons shooting massive energy beams destroying everything in her path while simultaneously scanning the ocean for Primean submarines.

Eve repositions the satellites above, firing synthesized energy blasts. Two of the Primean submarines are destroyed with single shots as Eve fends off an onslaught. The satellite weapons are destroying Puma's submarines with precision, as Eve tracks their locations. Puma dispatches a fleet of fighter jets to engage Eve on the beach. Eve creates a shield protecting herself from incoming missiles, plasma grenades, mortars, and bullets.

Eve responds by shooting energy beams through her hands and mouth at incoming fighter jets. One by one, the jets fall out of the sky. Angel intercepts the remaining fighter jets keeping a safe distance. Lennek's air force responds, sending a fleet of fighter jets and warships to intercept the Primeans at Grentake Falls.

Puma reaches out to Bunny, saying, "*I need Vaughn, Violet, and Fyn at the hive mainframe. Their warships need to be ready for our second attack wave. All fighter jets and armed transports target the Guardian!*"

Bunny responds, "*I'm on it!*" Within seconds, Vaughn, Violet, and Fyn are teleported off their warships to the Colonial hive. "*All three are in position awaiting orders.*"

Eve continues destroying Primean submarines as three of the stealth warships lock onto her position. Puma waits for the three warships to reposition themselves away from the rest of her fleet before ordering, "*FIRE!*"

The undetected warships open fire on Eve, inflicting damage which the Guardian slowly repairs. The combined firepower knocks Eve back thousands of feet in the air. Having revealed their position, the Olympian and Lennethian fighter jets lock onto the three Primean warships, opening fire. Eve's body is renewed as the ships pass under Grentake Falls, quickly closing in on her position.

Violet, Fyn, and Vaughn's warships, still in stealth mode, fired hundreds of weapons from both sides of their ship's hull. Puma's submarines have destroyed three Olympian warships while deploying hundreds of thousands of combat droids. Satisfied, Puma orders the second fleet of submarines to move past Grentake Falls. Each warship deploys hundreds of Primean fighter jets, evening the numbers in the air.

As Eve levitates, she creates an energy shield to protect herself from incoming fire. Eve runs an algorithm to predict the most likely attacks which she passes onto the Coalition. Eve has less than thirty minutes before shutting down, intending to make the most of her time. Once Eve's programming and memories are transferred into a secure hive outside of Lennek, Eve can survive indefinitely. The Primeans exposing her as a sentient being will make her efforts more difficult, yet it's a scenario Eve has planned for.

Olympia has never encountered the stealth technology being used on Enigma's warships.

Violet's contributions to Angkor's technology have made them parallel to Lennek and Olympian technology. Their shields and weapons are allowing the Primeans to gain ground. With Violet blocking their automated defenses, Puma's invading with ease showing admirable restraint against civilians. By attacking Eve, however, Puma has unintentionally revealed every ship's position, making each ship vulnerable to attack.

Lennek's ships are relying on Eve's targeting algorithm to attack the Primean warships. Olympian ships have fallen back, supporting Lennethian forces from a distance as their targeting systems adjusts to the Angkorian tech.

Enigma is in the rear hangar of her warship preparing to exit her ship, joining the fight. She explains to Puma, *"The Guardian will have a lock on our warships at any moment. I'm going to take on the Olympian ships myself!"*

"WAIT! We need another few minutes for our drones to sweep the airspace," says Puma as she tries to reason with Enigma to coordinate their attack. *"One of those mines could kill you!"*

Enigma, being more concerned for the Evo on her warships says, *"I'll take the risk. There's no time! My energy blasts can break through Olympian shields. We only have three warships armed with ion cannons and they're too far away to attack."*

Enigma jumps out of her warship's hanger falling into a freefall. She expands her wings, gaining altitude as she powers up synthesizing energy from the sun. Enigma's eyes turn white as her body glows with electrical currents surging off her body. Enigma activates a visor allowing her to track enemy ships interfacing with her warship's AI.

The second wave of Primean submarines are positioned attacking the incoming air force from Lennek and Olympia. Enigma targets an Olympian warship shooting multiple energy blasts as she charges the enormous warship head-on. Enigma creates an energy shield with her hands while shooting ionized energy blasts from her eyes. She destroys the Olympian warship and watches as two hundred thousand tons of metal fall to the precinct below.

Goldie appears in the imperial chambers of King Larvex in astral form, revealing herself to the king without warning, saying, *"Your Majesty, my name is Goldie. I'm the—"*

King Larvex nearly jumps out of his feathers, immediately activating the emergency beacon on his necklace. The king retorts, *"I know who you are. How did you get past my coven's security? No telepath should be able to enter this chamber!"*

"We don't have time for this! Order your ships to pull back. Your fallen warships are killing tens of thousands upon their descent!" says Goldie as she circles the king. *"Your support is causing more harm than good. We need you to pull back."*

King Larvex looks at Goldie's astral form, saying, *"Our ships have impenetrable shields. I'm saving Lennethian lives by killing these terrorists off. We've taken out twenty percent of their invading soldiers!"*

Goldie screams at King Larvex, *"GIVE THE GODDAMN ORDER! Ion cannons can shoot through your shields, and one of their mutants produces similar energy from her hands! I'm not asking!"* Goldie leaves the king's chambers as he orders his coven's elders to meet with him immediately. King Larvex reluctantly orders his forces to stand down, ordering his warships back to Olympia.

Puma sees the Olympian warships starting to fall back and reaches out to Punzel telepathically. *"Trigger the bombs on my mark. Three... two...one!"* Punzel's fighting off an entire squad of Colonial guardsmen using her superior strength and hair to advance. She accesses a hologram on her wrist triggering hundreds of bombs she and Cole planted throughout Lennek.

Goldie foresees the bombing before Punzel triggers the attack. She appears to Rosie in astral form, saying, *"I need you to contain two bomb blasts within Lennek Square. I'm sending you the location of the bombs telepathically."* Rosie focuses on the locations and manages to contain the blast radius of the two bombs within the square having an aerial view from the top of a building.

The other bombs placed near Colonial buildings explode simulta-neously. The quake is felt throughout the Colony. The combined explosions kill thousands of Evo working in government buildings. First responders are deployed to every precinct, stretching Lennek's resources as Puma intended. Falling debris from warships and fighter jets continue to add to the growing number of casualties. The streets are in flames and the carnage of war is spreading like a virus.

Lennek Square is now filled with thousands of Primean soldiers armed with advanced weaponry and armor. Chaos has erupted as the fog of war thickens. guardsmen have never been deployed in Lennek streets. This is the first time in history war is being fought on Lennethian soil.

Puma's first wave of fighter jets have infiltrated eight sectors near the shoreline. They've focused their fire on combat drones attacking guardsmen indiscriminately, while allowing civilians to pass. Kairen is in Lennek Square under attack from incoming fighter jets. He makes a telekinetic shield blocking incoming bombs, missiles, and numerous plasma weapons showing a mastery of his powers. He's galloping through the streets, drawing fire away from civilians guided by Goldie in astral form.

Thousands of Primean soldiers riding armed hovercrafts are swarming the area providing secondary air support. Lennek's major landmarks and corporate buildings near the shore have private shields operating on their own power grid. Roughly 35 percent of the buildings in Precinct 9 are protected by private shields allowing the Colonial guardsmen to attack with reduced casualties.

Protection pods are spread throughout Lennek during large events. They can protect large groups for up to twenty-four hours and withstand a nuclear attack. The AI in Kairen's quiver is doing its job considering countless variables to create the perfect arrow for each situation.

Kairen fires an explosive arrow shooting down a passing fighter jet, realizing more are on their way. He uses telekinesis to shield himself from incoming fire as he makes a path toward a fleet of Colonial drones. Meanwhile, a squad of three hover-bikes lock onto Kairen's position firing Gatling guns and plasma cannons from behind him. Kairen uses his telekinesis to slam the hover-bikes to the ground.

A few thousand feet away, Cole is leading two Primean death squads to the eastern corner of Lennek Square. He slowly makes his way towards the main stage as the square as the civilians clear out. Colonial guardsmen are shooting plasma blasts and bullets at Cole, who blocks their fire by converting the moisture in the air into shields of ice. He's freezing the guardsmen in place pushing forward with Primean soldiers coordinating with his attacks.

Gill closes in on Cole from his right flank, taking out Primean soldiers who dare block his path. Gill throws his staff from forty feet away, but Cole blocks it with an energy shield linked to his armor. Gill summons his staff back into his hands as Cole responds by shooting a barrage of ice-spikes forcing Gill to maneuver to safety. Gill dodges most of Cole's ice spikes while destroying the rest with his staff.

Cole shoots blasts of ice from his hands as Gill summons a gust of wind, redirecting the ice back at Cole. Gill lifts himself high into the air with a gust of wind as he shoots massive electrical bolts from his hands, striking Cole in the left shoulder. Cole creates a sheet of ice and places his hand on his shoulder coddling his wound. Gill takes the opportunity to close ground, shooting electrical blasts as he charges. Gill flips over a wall of ice striking Cole in the ribs with his staff.

Ten feet away, Merkaba is healing a group of injured bystanders outside a filled protection pod. Merkaba heals their major wounds and internal injuries, then diverts her attention to fend off a squad of Primean soldiers closing in on her. Armed with multiple three pronged sais, Merkaba puts her newly acquired combat skills to the test.

Three soldiers try to surround and overpower Merkaba as she creates a vibrational frequency that overloads the soldier's nervous systems. The soldiers drop their weapons and fall to the ground, screaming in agony. Merkaba somersaults, throwing her sais into the helmets of the fallen soldiers. She then somersaults into the air, throwing grenades at the remaining soldiers. Merkaba twists her wrists and her sais eject from the soldier's helmets back into her hands using magnetic technology within her armor.

The remaining soldiers take off running towards Bastian as he releases a large surge of pheromones, enraging the remaining by-standers. Without warning or explanation, the civilians start turning on the guardsmen forcing them to change their weapons to stun, putting them at a huge disadvantage to the Primeans.

Goldie appears in astral form to the Coalition mutants, explaining, *"The Primeans are using the badger's powers to entice rage and aggression amongst the civilians. Your armor should filter out the pheromones. You shouldn't be affected. Merkaba, I need you to counter his abilities and allow the crowds to get to safety. Get to high ground and do what you can!"*

"On it!" replies Merkaba as she uses her gravity-displacement boots to reach the top of a nearby building.

Zeus tells Goldie, *"I need air support for first responders coming in from the south!"* Zeus is fighting off Primean soldiers by the dozens at increased mass, making himself over twenty feet tall. Puma, Rosie, and Trinity coordinate a telepathic attack against Zeus knocking him on his back, forcing him to revert to his normal size.

Zeus is completely vulnerable, unable to think, let alone use his powers. He's left on his back, trying to gain his bearings. Goldie appears in astral form immediately creating a protective shield around him dispelling the telepathic energy on the astral plane. Zeus is nearly comatose, completely disoriented with Primean soldiers closing in on him.

In astral form, Goldie kneels telling him, *"You're going to be fine. You got hit by a coordinated telepathic attack."* She repairs his mind reversing the damage left by the Primean telepaths. The telepathic shielding within his armor was overloaded and is now useless.

Rosie closes in on Zeus creating a force field to protect him from incoming fire. Enraged bystanders, under the influence of Bastian's pheromones, are fighting the guardsmen, throwing rocks and debris. Goldie's defending the Coalition from telepathic attacks with assistance from technology inside Coalition Headquarters.

Merkaba starts reversing the effects of Bastian's pheromones on the west side of the square while Sasha's teleported into the square to assist. Sasha starts slashing through guardsmen running towards Merkaba in full stride. Her glezslavine claws are killing anything that crosses her path while she excretes her pheromones taking control of the guardsmen she doesn't kill.

Rosie is closest to Merkaba warning Duke to start siphoning Kairen's telekinesis. Moments later, Duke slings Sasha across the square to the western edge with a telekinetic burst of energy.

Rosa shields Byron's mind, allowing him to flank Duke, who barely manages to raise an energy shield within his armor. Byron kicks Duke with the force of a moving train knocking him back. Byron encases his body with an impenetrable shield that multiplies his strength a thousandfold. Duke lands eighty feet away on a jagged piece of debris which breaks through his armor severing his spine.

Duke screams out in unbearable pain. *"HELP ME! I didn't see him coming. I...couldn't fully...raise...my shields."* Duke passes out and his armor's life-support system starts working to save him. Although Merkaba isn't too far away from Duke, she's just outside the range to being able to heal him.

Byron is a renowned mercenary from Zion, with the ability to redirect kinetic energy. Byron can focus his power to create an invulnerable field around his body. He can create shields and fire powerful energy blasts from his absorbed energy. While encased in his kinetic shield, Byron can absorb thermal and physical damage converting the energy however he chooses.

Byron stands 6'3'' with jet-black skin and fur covering his body. His face has white fur with black circles covering his brown eyes. He has circular ears emerging from the top of his head, short black hair, and a chiseled jawline. Byron's has a muscular frame and humanoid facial features. He has black fur on his back, arms, and legs. Seeing Duke incapacitated, he moves on to his next victim.

"Stay with me, Duke! Wake up!" says Merkaba, arriving at his limp body. A group of soldiers appear as Merkaba reacts emitting a frequency inducing vertigo and extreme disorientation. The soldiers flee crawling away on their knees as Merkaba heals Duke. Duke's unconscious, but his body's fighting to stay alive, siphoning Merkaba's healing powers to save his life.

Meanwhile, the Coalition and Colonial Guard are occupied, fending off Lennethian bystanders under the effects of Bastian's pheromones. News drones are streaming live footage to all seven Colonies. Viewers around the world don't know the crowd is under the influence of Bastian and Sasha. They only see Lennek's citizens fighting with the Primeans. Puma has orchestrated the perfect scenario to draw millions into the Primean brotherhood. Following her plan, she's moments away from initiating her third attack wave.

Eve flies toward the shoreline with an energy shield raised to block incoming fire from the Primean forces. King Larvex has recalled his air force, debating on sending his imperial guardsmen to the surface. The Olympian Guardian will not leave Olympian territory unless commanded by the king. The Olympians have already suffered heavy losses from their air force. Each Olympian warship is powered with a crew of 370 Evo and eight warships have already been lost.

Angel is leading the Lennethian air force, forcing the Primeans to rethink their strategy. Goldie's using her powers to pinpoint the location of Primean warships, relaying the data to Angel telepathically. Angel's ion cannons have destroyed multiple warships and fighter jets coordinating with Goldie.

Puma reaches out to the other Primeans, saying, *"We need the Guardian in the square where Rosa and Trinity have clear shots to hit Eve with their viral bullets. Bunny, teleport everyone to the square. I'm pulling back the warships!"* In less than a minute, Bunny has the Primean mutants positioned throughout Lennek Square.

Gatling guns, plasma cannons, and automated missile systems have been placed on dozens of rooftops to assist the Lennethian forces. Bunny starts teleporting rooftop to rooftop taking out Colonial snipers and automated defense systems. Guardsmen are hidden throughout the buildings slowing down their advance, all in accordance with Puma's plan. Bunny finds an abandoned roof and waits until she's needed.

Goldie is using the amplifiers in Coalition Headquarters to strengthen her empathic abilities. She's focusing on fear and anxiety outside of Grentake Falls using the clustered emotions to triangulate the locations of the Primean warships. The ships are shielded from telepathic scans, but the emotions of the crews piloting the large ships can't be hidden. Puma was clever enough to create thousands of labor droids to pilot her warships with a minimal number of Evo crewmembers, hoping to reduce casualties. Goldie is still tracking the warships with accuracy forcing Puma to restrategize.

Puma has cut casualties dramatically by relying mostly on combat droids. The newly developed Angkorian shields have outperformed expectations giving Puma the time she needs to bypass Lennek's defenses. Bambi and Eve are destroying the Primean submarines with precision, forcing the remaining fleet to retreat. Lennethian forces are now defending the coastline allowing Eve to return to Lennek Square at Mach speed. Eve is met with a barrage of missiles as she enters the airspace over land.

Eve flies through a scene of pandemonium as fighter jets, armed drones, and soldiers on hover-transports flood the skies exchanging fire. Civilians are either running for cover or attacking their own guardsmen under the influence of Bastian's pheromones. The smell of smoke and burned flesh fill the air leaving the signature scent of war. Lennek, once thought to be impenetrable from outside attack, will never be the same.

Puma and Khaled are teleported near the Commencement stage to prep for their attack on Eve. Ether is flying over Precinct 9 hunting down guardsmen with her magnetic energy blasts. She flies over Kairen, watching him gallop towards the center of the square. His explosive arrows make a path for him while his telekinesis provides a shield.

Khaled sees Kairen a few hundred feet away from him enticing him to crack a smile. He looks to Puma, saying, "I've got his one!" He crouches, focusing his energy then leaps in front of Kairen's path in a single leap.

Khaled is Puma's betrothed and second in command of the Primeans. He was born in Efferia from nobility, quickly climbing the ranks within the military forming a close bond with Puma's father, Council Leader Arzon. Khaled has super strength and consumes energy to increase his strength and heal. Khaled can create shields, shoot energy beams, and create currents of kinetic energy.

Khaled is of lion descent standing 6'7" with golden-tan skin and a muscular build. He has a small pink nose, his white cheeks and mouth are covered in whiskers, and he has blue eyes. His orange fur feels like velvet. He has shoulder-length orange hair and a handsome symmetrical face. Khaled's cybernetic arms are deadly combined with his fighting skills and abilities. The retractable claws on both his arms are made of glezslavine making him a threat even without his mutant abilities.

Khaled strikes Kairen with a concussive beam of energy, depleting a large amount of energy from Kairen's armor. Khaled charges Kairen, running through the explosions from Kairen's explosive arrow tips. Kairen takes pause as his quiver analyzes his surroundings, creating new arrows to deliver maximum damage. Kairen jumps in the air, firing a barrage of arrows hitting each of his surrounding enemies.

A few hundred feet away Puma absorbs the flames from Kairen's explosive arrows, intensifying them as she redirects the flames towards incoming guardsmen. She reaches out to her fellow Primeans, saying, "*We need to draw their Guardian back to the square. It won't fire its satellite weapons inland and it's programed to protect Lennek's citizens above all else. Let's give it a reason to come back!*" Puma releases the plasma whip from around her waist while hurling flames at advancing guardsmen.

Rosie pulls up an aerial map of the square with locations of unstable buildings through the left arm of her armor. She focuses on the nearest building using a hover-bike to maneuver through the area. Two interconnecting high-rises are struck with missiles forcing Rosie to create a shield. She struggles to maintain the shield as weight from the falling bridge pushes her powers to their limits. Rosie maintains a shield around herself protecting herself from the surrounding pandemonium. She holds the bridge and buildings in place as Colonial labor droids make repairs preventing the buildings and bridge from collapsing on nearby civilians.

Thirty feet from Rosie, Zeus has recovered from his crippling telepathic attack, enlarging his size and reentering the battle. Goldie and Merkaba are combining their powers to keep the crowd calm, countering the Primeans efforts to do the opposite. Goldie's psychic abilities and Merkaba's healing purrs have effects the simulator couldn't predict. They're channeling psychic energy from the crowd keeping the Evo passive while recycling energy from the crowd.

Chapter 7 — The Skies Wept In Blood

Miles away in Precinct 8, the new Coalition recruits are struggling to fend off the Primeans from the Colonial hive. Ebok and Lulu are leading dozens of guardsmen with Lennek's air force providing aerial support. Violet, Vaughn, and Fyn have brought a small army, equipped with superior weapons for their own support. Rosa and Trinity are providing cover telepathically in astral form fending off Goldie.

In astral form, Goldie looks over to Ebok, saying, *"There's two telepaths aiding the Primeans. I'll keep them at bay. You handle the technopath!"* Goldie creates a sphere of energy blocking the astral flames being projected by Trinity and Rosa. Their flames, although invisible in the physical world, can destroy the nervous system of those consumed by its flames.

Violet reaches out to Puma, saying, *"We're behind schedule! One of the Coalition mutants has the same mutation I have... He's blocking me! Vaughn's holding off the guardsmen while I work around this guy. I've gotten through some of the mainframe's defenses but they're adding new firewalls and reprogramming security code on the fly!"*

"Get it done! I'll have some fighter jets en route to give you air support," says Puma as she continues fighting off guardsmen inside of Lennek Square. Puma's maintaining a wall of fire blocking the Lennethian forces on the ground as she unleashes her pyrokinetic abilities burning everything in her path.

Not far from Puma, Ether is using her magnetic powers to topple buildings while levitating with a sphere of magnetic energy protecting her from incoming fire. Eve flies at Mach speed, closing in on Ether's location, collecting momentum to knock her across the square. Eve breaks through Ether's shield with weapons armed to kill.

Eve flies toward Ether shooting massive energy blasts through her hands and eyes, moving faster than Ether can react. Eve breaks through Ether's shield shooting energy blasts through her chest, leg, and abdomen. Eve throws Ether's limp body into a wall killing Ether within seconds of their encounter. All the Primeans are connected telepathically for coordination. A psychic ripple encompassing Ether's last moments is felt by her comrades. The Primeans are consumed with grief, fear, hate, regret, and anxiety from Ether's death.

Although Enigma doesn't have any telepathic abilities, she feels Ether's death just the same. Overwhelmed and scared, Enigma starts shooting through dozens of fighter jets with a renewed second wind, closing in on Eve's location. Enigma starts shooting beams of ionized energy blasts in an explosive flurry fueled by pure rage. Enigma descends on Eve, wasting no time with a relentless attack, causing Eve to lose her right leg. Enigma shoots beams of energy from her eyes cutting through Eve's left arm. Eve responds with a counterattack as nanites immediately repair the Guardian's body.

Eve creates a shield. Enigma breaks through with ease ,firing ionized blasts from her hands and eyes. Eve is struck in the abdomen and forced to raise another shield, buying time for her body to repair. Kairen grabs ahold of Enigma with his telekinesis, hurling her away from Eve into a building across the square. The building's debris collapses on Enigma who's kept safe with synthesized energy encapsulating her body.

Khaled sprints in front of Kairen, cutting through his armor with plasma blades from his bionic arms. Kairen expunges a telekinetic ripple, knocking Khaled back three hundred feet giving him space to recover. Khaled absorbs the kinetic energy charging Kairen as he dodges explosive arrows from Kairen.

Goldie appears in astral form near Merkaba watching her fight her way through a swarm of Primean soldiers. Merkaba's sais are holstered on her hips as she uses a Lennethian staff with plasma cannons on both its ends. Thanks to Gill, Merkaba knows how to handle the staff, laying waste to any Primean crossing her path.

Goldie reaches out to Merkaba, saying, "*One of the Primean mutants is dying. I need you to bring her back. It isn't her time.*" She sends her images of Ether, explaining, "*I know she's the enemy, but trust me, we need her alive.*"

Merkaba uses her antigravity boots and somersaults in a circle shooting six headshots into advancing soldiers with blasts from her staff. Merkaba replies, "*I thought you said playing with life and death was unethical. If she's dead, fate has chosen today for her to die. I didn't think we would take such a risk for the enemy.*"

"*A sickness will claim the lives of many mutants and we will need her to survive. I had a vision watching her die...trust me! She'll be essential to our survival. Save her life and we save ourselves. You have time to get within range of her,*" says Goldie as she reverts her full attention back to the hive mainframe. Goldie's simultaneously fighting off Rosa and Trinity on the astral plane protecting Lulu and Ebok. Rosa and Trinity are combining their powers to contend with Goldie who is starting to lose her patience.

Inside Lennek Square, Merkaba's approaching Ether using her anti-gravitational boots to skate through the sky. Her armor's producing a powerful energy shield to keep her safe from incoming fire. Primean armed drones are closing in on Merkaba's location, firing plasma cannons, bullets, and missiles. She's dodging the attacks with grace and experience, maneuvering as a seasoned warrior. The skills Gill transferred over to her are proving to be invaluable to the entire team.

The square is filled with burning bodies piled amongst large fragments of Olympian warships. Debris was ejected into the square and surrounding neighborhoods as Olympian warships fell to the precincts below. Merkaba runs into three Primean combat droids as they attack without discretion. Merkaba's powers have no effect on machines, forcing her to rely on her weapons. She flips over the combat droids with the assistance of her anti-gravitational boots—dropping two gravity-displacement grenades. The combat droids are sucked into a blackhole while Merkaba continues sprinting toward Ether without breaking stride.

Another triplet of combat droids close in on Merkaba's position. Zeus leaps an incredible distance across the square to intercept the droids, ripping them to pieces with his bare hands. His mass has tripled, increasing his strength proportionate to his three-story stature. Zeus watches Kairen retreating from Khaled and doesn't hesitate to intervene.

Zeus starts sprinting to gain momentum before jumping across the square, landing on Khaled intending to crush him. The impact creates a quake felt for blocks. He lifts his foot, leaving behind a crater in the shape of his boot. Zeus turns his attention to the stage, searching for Eve, assuming Khaled's dead, at best case incapacitated. Khaled jumps out of the impact creator, having absorbed the energy of Zeus's attack compounding his strength and speed.

Khaled moves through the square with lightning speed, attacking Zeus from behind. Khaled knocks Zeus off balance with unrelenting energy blasts, using his mastery of kinetic entropy. Khaled calls in a Primean fighter jet for close air support as heavily armed guardsmen attack Khaled with advanced weaponry. Zeus takes the opportunity to create distance as the guardsmen unleash an array of weapons, forcing Khaled on the defensive. Having observed his abilities, the guardsmen use acoustic cannons to subdue him.

As a cyborg, Khaled has evolved to adapt to his surroundings. His cybernetic arms have grown a helmet to protect his ears and filter the air. A guardsmen using a jetpack charging Khaled from above with a plasma scythe, drawn and positioned to swing. Khaled blocks the guardsman's scythe with his bionic arm before slamming him into the ground, breaking the guardsman's neck. Another guardsman descends with a sword drawn firing a plasma pistol. Khaled maneuvers using his powers to position himself behind the guardsman, punching through the guardsmen's armor ripping his spine out.

Khaled's communicator on his wrist starts flashing as he looks to the sky for his requested air support. Amongst the chaos, he spots the fighter jets and gets a running start towards Zeus. He continues running as tractors beams from above grab hold of him, pulling him through the air via gravitational technology from Olympia. Khaled and the fighter jets are firing a barrage of energy blasts, bullets, and missiles. Zeus uses the energy shield in his armor to block the attack as he tries to hold his ground, as Merkaba passes through the area unnoticed.

Zeus reaches out to Merkaba, saying, *"Goldie told me to ensure you have a path to the Primean you need to revive. I've got incoming, so get going... This guy won't stop!"* Zeus turns and sees Khaled being towed towards Zeus by two fighter jets. Khaled is an eighth the size of Zeus with double the strength, determined to take him down.

Merkaba watches from below as Zeus is struck in the eye by a spear. Zeus screams out in pain as he's bombarded by missiles knocking him off balance. Khaled punches Zeus in his back as he uses the momentum of his fall to absorb more energy. Zeus lands on his back, reverting to his normal size as Khaled lands a flurry of powerful punches.

Merkaba realizes Zeus needs her help and prioritizes his life over Ether's. Merkaba uses her Lennethian staff to fire a series of energy blasts, knocking Khaled off Zeus from a distance. A squad of Lennethian combat droids are dropped into the area, forcing Khaled on the defensive as they open fire. Merkaba makes her way to Zeus and uses her powers to replenish his stamina and heal his eye.

"You have a mission! I'll be fine," says Zeus as he watches Khaled rip through the combat droids. Zeus gets to his feet and starts increasing his mass with newfound vigor.

Merkaba continues her mission using her gravity-displacement boots to gain altitude. Training in the simulator has allowed her to take her powers to the next level. Tampering with life itself was something she was told never to explore. Goldie has earned the trust of her entire team, except for Merkaba. Regardless, even Merkaba knows it's unwise to doubt a precog. Merkaba is less than a block away, quickly approaching Ether's location as she glides through the air.

Goldie appears in astral form ,screaming, "Sniper! Get down." She changes position and is shot in the neck by a Primean sniper falling to the ground from seventy feet in the air. Her armor breaks her fall as the bullet ejects itself from her neck as her body grows new tissue. Merkaba hits the ground, rolling onto the surface dispersing her momentum. Like most cats, she always lands on her feet.

Merkaba has trained to reduce her cognitive recovery time. Still dazed, she summons her staff with the magnetic tech within her armor. Forcing her body to move, she continues running towards Ether, this time on the ground by foot as her body slowly heals itself. She's ten feet away from Ether and about four thousand feet from Commencement stage.

Ether is lying lifeless in the square near the wall Eve pulverized her into. Merkaba tries to bring her back with the strongest healing frequency she knows. She realizes it's having no effect on Ether, taking a deep breath and settling into the moment, allowing her instincts to take over.

Merkaba reaches out to Goldie, saying, "*I need protection from incoming fire!*"

Rosie responds, "You really don't have any faith in Goldie's precog abilities. She sent me to your location the same time she told you about her." Rosie creates a shield protecting all three of them. "You're good... Do your thing!"

Merkaba never considered bringing someone back from the dead. She has no clue what to resonate or what frequency to emit. Following her instincts, she removes her armor. Fur to fur, Merkaba starts resonating with Ether's body, matching her purest memory. Merkaba and Ether start to glow as Merkaba focuses on the first sound made in the omniverse. She remembers the chant from her teachings back in Carthage, rocking back and forth as she chants focusing on the frequency of the words. The light from their bodies grows with intensity as Merkaba creates a spark of life searching for Ether's soul.

The Primean telepaths alert Enigma that Ether's body is being tampered with. Enigma immediately diverts her attention from Eve, firing a melee of energy blasts, creating space to retreat to Ether's body. Enigma flies as fast as she physically can, approaching Rosie's large shield. She sees Rosie raising her arms to maintain the shield and a blinding light at the center.

The smoke and smog of war is blocking the sunlight which Enigma draws her powers from. Having shot down multiple Olympian warships and dozens of fighter jets, Enigma needs to replenish her energy. Driven by emotion, she engages despite having expunged most of her energy.

Being within the vicinity, Rosie can also feel the effects of Merkaba's powers having no problem maintaining their shield. *"It's Enigma! The one that's been going toe to toe with Eve!"*

Enigma fires two energy blasts, which Rosie's shields somehow deflects. Rosie is shocked her shield blocked the attack, adjusting the density having felt the energy of Enigma's blasts. Realizing her energy is depleted, Enigma flies straight up, breaking through the smog of war. Thousands of feet in the air with sunlight hitting her feathers, Enigma's powers recharge in the higher atmosphere.

Enigma basks in the rays of sunlight, allowing the various spectrums of light to not only replenish her stamina, but to heal most of her injuries from battle. She hears a sonic boom and remembers the Olympian Guardian is still protecting Olympia's skies indiscriminately. Satisfied with her reprieve, Enigma begins her descent back into Lennek before Olympia's Guardian intercepts her. She descends through the clouds approaching the smog of war, determined to save Ether.

Enigma descends upon Rosie's energy shield, collecting energy upon her descent. Enigma shoots two massive energy blasts breaking through Rosie's shield with the full extent of her power. Enigma lands on the surface, creating a small impact crater with energy permeating throughout her body. Rosie is delirious from blocking multiple blasts from Enigma. Rosie renders Merkaba and Ether invisible, giving Merkaba more time to finish the impossible.

Merkaba falls into a trance as her eyes turn completely white as she visualizes reigniting Ether's life force with a spark from her own spirit. Merkaba transfers her life flame and summons a sacred frequency that brings Ether back to life. A burst of blinding iridescent colors explodes from Merkaba's palms as she pushes the boundaries of her abilities.

Enigma covers her eyes and turns to find them all invisible. "Ether! Where are you? Give her to me, I won't ask again!" Enigma fires an ionized blast at the area she thinks Merkaba is, missing the group by inches.

Enigma follows with another blast, forcing Rosie to create a force field barely blocking the blast and weakening Rosie to her knees. Rosie's exhausted barely able to raise her arms, saying, "You'll...thank us...later...Primean." Rosie passes out from overexertion as Ether and Merkaba are made visible.

Enigma flies over ready to end Merkaba as Ether inhales a large gasp of air, regaining consciousness. Ether's weak and confused as she looks up at Merkaba, asking, "Why? Why did you help...?" Ether's too weak to finish her thought and passes out.

Enigma powers down, seeing Ether alive and notices Merkaba is too weak to defend herself. Enigma runs to Ether's side as Merkaba struggles to get to her feet. Having pushed her abilities to the limit, the stress and fatigue on her body is visible.

Rosie's armor administers adrenaline and a vitamin elixir, replenishing her stamina. She becomes conscious and gathers her strength, turning herself invisible to escape. Ether's alive but too weak to move with vertigo, extremely disoriented. Merkaba stumbles away as she turns invisible from Rosie allowing the pair to flee.

Enigma lifts Ether's limp body into her arms, saying, "Thank you." She looks around knowing Merkaba and Rosie are still nearby, saying, "Whoever you two are...thank you!" Grateful to have Ether alive, she's done fighting, taking to the air with Ether in her arms headed to her warship. By saving Ether, the Coalition has removed the Primean's most powerful mutant from battle.

Rosie and Merkaba help each other escape finding an abandoned building to recover. Rosie admits, "You were extraordinary out there! I had no idea you could bring someone back from the dead."

"Neither did I. I'm going to need some time to recover. I over... exerted myself," says Merkaba, needing to sit down.

Rosie creates a bench using her powers, allowing Merkaba to sit, giving her body a chance to recover. Rosie raises a shield protecting them from the outside chaos. The roof is missing, leaving the pair exposed but safe enough to recover. Rosie says, "Take a moment to rest. I'll keep us current with what's going on out there."

"You were impressive yourself. Blocking ionized blasts is supposed to be impossible. You did it multiple times and were still standing. I'm surprised you're conscious," says Merkaba as she starts replenishing Rosie's stamina out of habit.

Rosie puts her arm on Merkaba's shoulder, saying, "You don't need to heal me. I'll be fine. Keep your energy and recover. You just brought someone back from the dead. You can't heal other's if you don't take care of yourself!"

"That's actually very deep. When this is all over, you and I should make time to get to know each other outside of training. You saved my life out there. Thank you!" says Merkaba, meaning the best of intentions.

"No need to thank me. I may be the youngest on the team, but I've seen more spectrums of life than most. I've been poor, rich, a hunter, prey, powerless...and now I'm in power," says Rosie as she moves to the windows of the abandoned building as bombs continue to explode throughout the precinct. "I worked hard for my normal life before I was recruited."

Merkaba interjects, "We all had normal lives before the Coalition. I was shipped off from Carthage to serve the Colony. To hell with my personal life. The Fold discovered I was running an underground healing clinic and realized they couldn't kill me, so I ended up here." She walks towards the window, joining Rosie to explain, "Your age is completely irrelevant in regard to your gifts."

Rosie can sense her sincerity, saying, "You're right. I'm just...it's my first..."

"Everyone's first battle is nerve-racking. Your first kill is even worst. You have a support system with the team. The Coalition will ensure we reach our full potential, but it's on us to decide how we use that power," says Merkaba as she looks at a hologram from her armor. "There is a first responders unit under attack three blocks from here. Think you can keep up?"

Meanwhile, outside the hive, Ebok and Violet are using their techno-pathic abilities to turn the area into a high-tier war zone. They're con-trolling combat droids, weaponized drones, and automated weapons placed on the surrounding rooftops. It's a complete blood bath with hundreds of Primean soldiers and Colonial guardsmen dead.

Violet has layers of protection comprised of levitating energy nets. Her energy nets are powered from paired levitating rods she controls with her thoughts. While targeting the Coalition mutants, Violet's simultaneously hacking into Lennek's data hive. Violet's bypassing numerous firewalls while Ebok counters her abilities by creating new ones.

Ebok stretches his powers to the limit, learning new skills to keep up with Violet. Ebok reaches out to Lulu, saying, *"We need a plan, if the Rhino charges, we're in trouble."* Ebok maneuvers towards Lulu with energy shields of his own.

Vaughn continues creating sinkholes to gather nearby stone, marble, and brick, creating massive boulders to hurl at incoming guardsmen. Vaughn forces the guardsmen to retreat, providing cover for Primean forces. Lulu dodges one of Vaughn's two-ton boulders, using her speed-bursts. Lulu sees a guardsman in danger and saves him before he's crushed to death.

Lulu reaches out to Angel, saying, *"We need some backup. You're the only one I know that can make it here in time. Our fighter jets are too busy fighting off the Primeans to offer air support!"*

Goldie appears in astral form, warning the guardsmen of a sinkhole Vaughn is about to create beneath them. The guardsmen take heed of Goldie's warning, changing their weapons to harpoon mode. As Vaughn creates his sinkhole, many of the guardsmen fire harpoons into nearby buildings, pulling themselves to safety.

Lulu uses her speed-bursts to retrieve the remaining guardsmen from the sinkhole. Lulu delivers the guardsmen to safety, asking, *"Is anyone coming for support?"*

Angel responds, *"I'll head to you now. Give me a few minutes!"*

In astral form, Goldie looks at Lulu, saying, *"The Primeans are sending in air support. Lennek's air force is on the way. You just need to hold on a little longer."*

Lulu uses her speed-bursts to take out the Primean forces on a nearby rooftop. She uses grenades to destroy some of Violet's weapons, leaving a trail of explosions in her wake. Lulu is constantly in motion dodging incoming fire and slowly diminishing the Primean forces. She beheads another soldier before replying, "*Just make sure that immunity clause in our contracts holds up.*"

"*They're not accessing this mainframe with me breathing!*" says Ebok as he hacks the Colonial frequency of the Lennethian guardsmen, saying, "I need you all back! You're all a bigger liability on the frontline than you are help!" Ebok is controlling heavily armed combat droids as well as numerous automated weapons positioned on nearby rooftops.

Two Primean combat jets descend in altitude preparing to attack. Ebok can feel the fighter jets entering the airspace and responds by firing oversized plasma cannons and destroying them before they can fire a single shot. The fighter jets explode as Ebok continues clearing the skies while protecting the hive.

Puma reaches out to Fyn from Lennek Square, saying, "*I need you to kill the Coalition technopath. Bring me the head of the orca and I'll pay you an additional three million in gold. Violet's running out of time and weapons... Keep the Coalition's technopath occupied and bring me the data on that mainframe!*"

Fyn maneuvers through the air avoiding incoming fire like an ice-skater on ice. "*Have my payment ready and consider it done!*"

Fyn gains altitude to survey the hive and directs his focus towards a group of guardsmen in exoskeletons attacking Vaughn. He descends, folding his wings as he pierces through the sky gaining speed. Fyn uses his powers, creating a shield around himself turning his body into a battering ram. Upon impact, the guardsmen are dispersed airborne as he creates a small crater. He starts draining the life force from one of the nearby guardsmen, mummifying his victim within seconds, increasing his muscle mass and strength in the process.

He expands his reach, killing another two guardsmen replenishing his power and stamina even further. Fyn becomes faster, stronger, and able to absorb life force from thousands of feet away. He kills the guardsmen one by one relishing each death.

Vaughn hurls a boulder at an incoming fighter jet, hitting the jet midair causing a large explosion. *"We need to kill the Coalition technopath. He's the orca in front of the hive!"* He points to the hive entrance as Fyn wastes no time gaining altitude for an attack.

Angel is less than a minute away, flying at Mach speed, knowing the importance of protecting the hive. She ordered a fleet of fighter jets to follow her, but Lennethian airspace is filled with Primean warships, fighter jets, and armed drones, making it difficult to follow. The relenting attack has forced the Coalition on the defensive waiting for reinforcements.

Hacking Lennek's mainframe hive is a higher priority to the Primeans than destroying Eve. Puma knows battle footage is being broadcast worldwide, forming a calculated narrative. She's planned every detail to the minute, positioning the Primean movement for success. Fyn heard Puma loud and clear intending to collect the extra bounty by any means necessary.

Fyn is flying toward Ebok at an incredible speed, altering his alignment as necessary to keep Ebok in his crosshairs. Ebok opens fire, fending Fyn off with multiple Gatling guns, lasers, and plasma cannons having little effect on Fyn's trajectory. He positions layers of energy shields bracing for impact as Lulu uses a speed burst to move Ebok to safety, placing an explosive spear in his stead.

Fyn gained too much momentum to divert his path and Lulu moved too fast for him to notice. Ebok finds himself thirty feet away from the explosive spear watching as Fyn plummets to a fatal injury. The explosive spear pierces Fyn in the gut stopping his momentum. Peeled over the spear, Fyn tries to remove himself before it explodes throwing him back over six hundred feet into a group of Primean soldiers.

Fyn is mortally injured, clearly in bad shape missing a leg, an arm, and most of his abdomen, clinging to life. Fyn's charred gray skin is burned to the bone as he bleeds out in desperate need of life force, even if it comes from his own soldiers.

One of the soldiers' screams, "RUN! He's going to drain us!" Before the soldiers can get to a full sprint, Fyn drains all ten soldiers saving his life with pure luck. Had he landed elsewhere, he would've died within minutes. Favored by fate, Fyn is completely healed with a larger muscle mass than he had before. He removes his broken armor exposing his chest as he searches for Ebok intending to collect his bounty.

Goldie continues fighting Rosa and Trinity on the astral plane, manifesting weapons and shields from psychic energy. Goldie is multitasking, protecting Ebok's mind as he protects the hive. Trinity expunges psionic flames while firing psionic arrows at Goldie. Rosa conjures psionic animals, creating a stampede as Goldie decimates them with manifestations of her own. Goldie is holding her own the astral plane, channeling enormous amounts of energy fighting from Coalition Headquarters, projecting her mind simultaneously in multiple locations.

Angel arrives at the hive mainframe, centered in pandemonium. Her wings change pattern and density as missiles fly past her, bringing down a nearby building. Vaughn throws a boulder at Angel, giving her seconds to react. Angel's sonic scream shatters the boulder into thousands of pieces as she gains altitude for an aerial view of the area.

"*Move the Primeans away from the hive,*" says Lulu as she beheads a Primean soldier before throwing a grenade at a soldier in an exoskeleton, blowing him into pieces. The soldier is on his back inside the large metallic exoskeleton which is now inoperable. The soldier ejects himself from the piloting console of the exoskeleton with a pistol drawn. Lulu circles back, killing the soldier before he sees her coming.

Angel's wings sense a telepathic attack from Trinity and Rosa and adjust accordingly. She can feel Goldie under duress, kneeling to the ground as she protects herself with her wings. Angel projects her consciousness into the astral plane and finds Goldie fending off Trinity and Rosa. The Primean telepaths are using amplifiers to increase their powers, making Goldie focus to defend herself. Rosa projects large unevolved animals made of pure psionic energy while Trinity summons psionic weapons coordinating their attacks.

Rosa and Trinity start shooting massive blasts of psionic energy, forcing Goldie on the defensive. Goldie becomes overwhelmed dissipating other projections of herself elsewhere, bringing her entire consciousness and focus to the present moment. Goldie creates a dome of psychic energy, shielding herself from the Primean attacks closing her eyes to channel her energy. She feels Angel's presence and before she can acknowledge the Olympia princess, Angel springs to her defense evening the odds.

Angel projects an enlarged version of herself flying towards Trinity with two psionic swords drawn. Angel charges Trinity, catching her off guard, cutting off her right hand. Angel conjures pillars of energy which emerge from the ground, striking Trinity and knocking her on her back. Trinity counters manifesting psionic electrical currents raining down from above. Trinity conjures two axes and throws them at Angel, intending to severe her head.

Angel dodges the axes and throws a psionic spear of her own before creating an energy shield to block the psionic electrical currents raining down on her. With her hands above her head, Trinity closes ground shooting beams of energy from her eyes, hitting her in the chest, as she charges closing ground. Angel's wings cover her body blocking Trinity's attack while obscuring her vision.

Now within proximity, Trinity conjures two swords swinging for Angel's head. Angel blocks the attack with swords of her own fighting comfortably from experience. Angel summons psionic roots from the ground to hold Trinity in place. Unable to move, Trinity is paralyzed for but a moment giving Angel the time she needs to take her head, reverting Trinity's consciousness back into her body.

Goldie focuses her powers sustaining a blackhole behind Rosa sucking her consciousness back into her body. Goldie looks over at Angel, saying, "*You came just in time... Thank you. They would've taken the hive if we didn't hold them off here on the astral plane. Your powers rival your mother's,*" says Goldie, meaning no harm in the comment.

Angel replies, "*I'm not my mother. I have work to do on the physical plane.*" Angel reverts her consciousness back to her body moments before Lulu swoops in moving her body to safety. A Primean fighter jet was shot down by Colonial forces, and the projected debris was headed directly for Angel's body while she was fighting on the astral plane.

Lulu takes Angel over the shoulders using her speed burst to get the two to safety. Lulu thinks she's saving Angel's life when Angel politely reminds her, "*You do know my wings are indestructible?*"

Lulu stops when the pair are safe, replying, "*You don't meditate in the middle of a fight, Princess!*" Lulu puts Angel down and uses her speed to save another guardsmen.

Angel watches Lulu run off replying, "*That's exactly what you do in a time of war.*" Without warning, a three-ton boulder is hurled at Angel who shields herself with her wings, changing the density of her feathers. The boulder hits Angel's wings and crumbles to pieces, having hit a harder material.

Vaughn is controlling eight boulders weighing a couple tons each destroying Colonial tanks, fighter jets, and platoons of guardsmen. He encased himself with layers of stone and minerals, making himself impervious as he stands in place creating sinkholes.

Violet multitasks on several fronts, knowing the importance of her mission. She's thinking around multiple firewalls, fighting Ebok's army of machines. She realizes she needs to amplify her processing speed and acts. Violet is an omega-level technopath, able to create organic machines from her body. Violet starts shedding nanite bugs from her rigid hair, increasing her processing capabilities. Each nanite is an extension of her body and mind which works independently evolving from their own experiences.

Each nanite is the size of a cockroach and has millions of processors that increase her processing abilities substantially. Violet has shed hundreds within the past few minutes gaining the advantage over Ebok. Even with Goldie's insight and Ebok's best efforts, Violet hacks into the mainframe gathering invaluable intel.

Violet reaches out to Bunny, saying, *"I'm past their firewalls. They've left some dummy files with viruses and fake information. It's almost as if they knew I'd be here. They've moved most of their pertinent files to nearby server hives. I can still retrieve the data. I just need a little more time."*

Violet's eyes roll to the back of her head as her eyes turn completely white. Violet continues to shed nanites from her hair as her powers steadily increase. The nanites are self-replicating and will continuously increase her power. Violet extracts intel on every Colony, gaining access to weapons research, blueprints to Lennek's surveillance tech, medical research files, and most importantly, a compiled list of known mutants around the world.

Violet tells Bunny, *"I'm almost finished. We're going to need evac soon!"* Ebok becomes overwhelmed by Violet's abilities, overheating his brain trying to process complex algorithms.

Ebok fires his automated weapons all at once, hoping to thwart Violet as she levitates in front of the hive entrance. He accepts the fact that he can't outthink Violet, switching his tactics. Violet doesn't bother raising a shield. Instead she overrides Ebok's commands with a single thought, causing his machines to destroy themselves.

Fyn sneaks up behind Ebok, hitting him in the back with two condensed beams of energy, knocking him three hundred feet into the air away from the hive. Ebok's armor absorbs most of the impact, but he's badly injured about to have a stroke from his overheated brain. He can barely see straight, and his nose is bleeding as his brain tries to heal itself.

Fyn gains altitude before charging Ebok closing ground with a single thrust of his wings. Fyn starts draining what little life force Ebok has left. His comrades are busy fighting battles of their own, unable to help. Goldie appears in astral form next to Ebok, repairing his mind as she attacks Fyn telepathically, diverting his attention.

Fyn falls to his knees as Goldie attacks his nervous system, rendering him defenseless. To her surprise, Fyn can see Goldie and begins draining her life force while she is in astral form. Fyn consumes enough energy to recover from the attack, forcing Goldie to revert her consciousness back to Coalition Headquarters.

Goldie disconnects the telepathic link to her comrades before releasing an uncontrollable psychic surge inside the Coalition war room, short-circuiting the androids in the room. She keels over with smoke coming off her black body armor as she removes her amplifier helmet. Goldie takes a moment to collect herself. Without her telepathic link, her teammates are vulnerable. Goldie was in desperate need for a break and her mind can make seconds feel like a lifetime.

Focused on a feeling of content, she realizes she's found her place in the world. She's needed. Appreciated and more importantly respected—all foreign concepts she's adapting to. Goldie stands up refusing to let her team down putting on her amplifier helmet and reconnecting with the Coalition.

Back near the hive, Angel uses her sonic scream against Fyn forcing him to retreat. A guardsman fires a plasma cannon mounted on his shoulder like a bazooka. Fyn is shot in the back with a plasma blast capable of shooting a hole through a warship. Fyn is thrown into a wall buried under rubble. The guardsman explains, *"He's down."*

Ebok turns his back, sprinting to his hover-bike as Fyn slowly emerges from the rubble. Fyn survives, consuming the absorbed life force from a nearby soldier repairing his internal injuries. He takes to the air, flying low to the ground intending to take Ebok by surprise. Goldie appears at Ebok's flank, unleashing dozens of psionic chains ripping through Fyn's mind tearing his nervous system apart. Fyn falls to the ground in the physical world as every pain receptor in his body is activated triggering unimaginable pain.

"*Now he's down,*" says Goldie as she turns to the mainframe. "*The technopath's storing the data she stole in her crawling nanites. Destroy them, and the Primeans leave with nothing.*"

Angel raises her arms, shooting sonic beams at incoming boulders being hurled in their direction from Vaughn. Angel surveys the area and sees four crates being filled with Violet's nanites. Angel unholsters her ion cannons destroying the crates. Angel's visor in her helmet allows her to track the nanites crawling out from the hive.

"*The Primeans are trying to distract us. The metallic cockroaches crawling on the ground are storing terabytes of data,*" says Angel as she watches Bunny teleporting crates away. Angel takes to the air, fending off incoming Primean fighter jets, hoping to stop Bunny.

Ebok targets the crates with an assortment of automated defense weapons nearby. Violet notices his efforts, focusing numerous armed drones locking onto his location, raining down their full cache of weapons. Ebok raises his shields maneuvering behind a toppled statue for cover.

Lulu uses her speed burst dropping grenades around Vaughn, before running to a nearby rooftop. Vaughn's thrown on his back from the explosions destroying his armor of stones. Lulu recovers on a nearby rooftop surrounded by automated weapons. She types away on a holographic display from her armor, targeting Vaughn before returning to ground level with her plasma sword drawn. Vaughn survives the explosion of grenades, collecting minerals from the ground beneath him, repairing his armor made of stone.

Lulu fires a missile with inhibitor gas, telling her Coalition comrades,

"*Gas masks on, team. I'm neutering the rhino.*"

Violet reaches out to Bunny, saying, "*I've got what I need, and I've programed my nanites to transmit the remaining data. Get us out of here!*"

A triplet of Primean jets release a barrage of missiles, providing much-needed cover for the Primeans allowing them to regroup. A platoon of guardsmen on hover-transports attempt to flank Violet, who senses the transports approaching and commandeers them. Violet blocks their weapons from firing with a thought turning off the engines. The jets fall to the ground, exploding on impact. Violet surrounds herself with layers of energy nets, waiting to be extracted.

Violet programs the remaining automated weapons to work as a network tracking Lulu. Bunny teleports behind Violet, taking her back to a Primean warship outside of Grentake Falls. Lulu was moments away from using a speed-burst to sever Violet's head moments before she was teleported to safety.

Lulu uses a speed-burst with her sword drawn, charging Vaughn, who's already anticipated her attack with the help of Primean telepaths. He raises a stone wall, blocking Lulu's path as a Primean fighter jets targets Lulu from above. Lulu is forced to find cover, giving the Primeans the time they needed to escape. Bunny teleports back retrieving Fyn and Vaughn leaving the hive raided and destroyed.

Puma sent dozens of automated fighter jets to self-destruct, destroying the hive. Her automated ships are controlled by AI on her warships, leaving her with no casualties from the kamikaze-style attack.

Goldie appears in astral form, warning the Coalition and nearby guardsmen. "*The Primeans are sending fighter jets set to self-destruct. They're trying to destroy any evidence of what they did here.*"

Ebok interrupts, saying, "*I feel the ships coming, its too many for me too control! I can't—*"

"*We don't have the time! Create a shield and protect everyone. Lulu, gather the guardsmen and go to this location to retrieve a supply case.*

Inside you'll find the shields you need to keep everyone safe," says Goldie as she sends Lulu the coordinates.

Lulu takes off without hesitation as Goldie continues, *"I foresaw the attack and have my own automated jets en route to intercept them."*

Lulu gathers the nearby guardsmen, creating a tight circle around Ebok. Seconds later, she returns with a supply chest filled with energy rods. Ebok stands, deploying the numerous shields in the supply chest, layering the rods to protect everyone. Controlling the machines with his mind, he creates a protective dome with layered nets of force fields.

The sky above them erupts with dozens of explosions as fighter jets collide. A few fighter jets make it through Goldie's fleet, destroying the outer layers of Ebok's shields. Angel is in the air, controlling the nearby fighter jets as she uses her ion cannons to defend the area. Minutes pass, and the area is cleared allowing Ebok to lower his shields.

Ebok looks to Lulu, saying, "You saved a lot of lives today, including my own. Thank you! That technopath they had was beyond omega class. Those bugs falling out of her hair were organic machines. Her processing capabilities rival our Guardians. It was interesting watching my mutation at its full potential."

Lulu interjects, "Give yourself some credit. We did our job."

"Did she fall for the dummy files?" asks Angel telepathically en route to the area. She accesses live footage from Lennek Square through her visor.

Ebok starts running a diagnostic on the hive as his eyes turn white rolling back into his head. Ebok levitates off the ground answering, "Sadly no. Her nanites are still hacking the mainframe. They're self-replicating—able to evolve on their own. Wait! I can see remnants of the transmissions. They took millions of exabytes. She took nearly sixty percent of our mainframe." Ebok gasps, saying, "Oh no!"

Goldie appears in astral form, exclaiming, "THE PRIMEANS ARE STILL TRANSMITTING!"

Lulu asks Ebok, "We have our pertinent data backed up off grid, correct?" Ebok nods his head. Lulu takes a moment to think before declaring, "Then we blow the damn hive! Give me all the grenades we have!"

One of the guardsmen interjects, "There's a box full of rocket ammo and grenades on the weapons transport. It's a block away to the east." Before the guardsman can finish pointing in the direction of the transport, Lulu runs and retrieves the weapons using her speed-bursts.

Out of nowhere, boxes of grenades and rocket ammo appear. Lulu reaches out to Goldie, saying, "*I need blueprints of the hive.*" Seconds pass and the boxes are suddenly empty. Lulu returns with a gust of wind counting down, "Three...two...one."

Lennek's central hive explodes while Ebok's drones create an energy net to contain the blast. Lulu looks at Angel, saying, "Stop the bleeding before you lose a limb! It made logical sense to destroy the mainframe before they received more data."

Angel lands on the ground near her comrades and removes her helmet. "It wasn't ideal, but destroying the hive was our best move. I was watching live footage from Lennek Square... We need to get back, Eve's in trouble."

"I've got supplies inbound to my location. I'm of no use to anyone without any weapons. I'll be in the square as soon as I can," says Ebok as he runs through the inventory stock in the Coalition armory.

Back in Lennek Square, Goldie appears in astral form, recharged and recovered from Fyn's attack. The Coalition's medical team has been working overtime to aid Goldie in her endeavors.

Coalition Headquarters is chaotic as the staff works overtime to coordinate with Lennek's first responders. Projectile debris from Olympian ships are scattered across every precinct along with bodies of dead Evo from both sides of the conflict.

Olympian and Lennethian ships are fueled with a red synthesized petroleum that combusts with quartz, providing a unique heat signature. The synthesized petroleum is mixed with a hydrogen cocktail, providing the fuel for the ship's engines. King Larvex withdrew his warships and dispatched Olympian fighter jets. Prior to today, it was believed that only Olympian and Lennethian fighter jets possessed the technology. The crystals used for the technology are native to Lennek while the science behind the technology is proprietary to Olympia.

A mutant in the crowd has changed the sunny weather to put out fires. The weather's gloomy and raining across the entire East Coast. The Olympian ship fuel is being absorbed into the air and clouds, turning the rain red, giving the illusion of falling blood. Smoke mixed with the smell of decaying bodies fills the air as casualties rise. Lennethian and Primean fighter jets are fighting across multiple precincts with guardsmen marching in the streets. Eve is under attack in Lennek Square with Bambi, Kairen, and Zeus assisting in the defense of the square. Eve's time is running out as it gets closer to her shutdown.

Puma, Khaled, Sasha, Bastian, and Punzel are distracting the Coalition, giving Rosa and Trinity a window to strike. Rosa and Trinity are both expert snipers armed with viral bullets designed to destroy a Guardian from the inside out. The Primean snipers are assisting their comrades in astral form waiting for the opportune moment to attack.

Puma reaches out, saying, *"We've drawn the Coalition away. Fire on my order!"*

Puma knows Eve's programing prioritizes Evo over her own wellbeing. Puma's purposely losing control as her flames intensify in heat. The recent gene-splicing procedure she underwent was designed to alter her internal organs allowing her to raise her heat index. Lennek Square has turned into a war zone plucked from a nightmare. Puma has yet to reach her full potential already shoulders above other pyrokinetics.

Eve diverts her attention to a group of guardsmen under attack as

Puma gives the order. "FIRE!"

Trinity and Rosa pull the triggers, firing viral bullets from two separate angles. Trinity was facing Eve head-on while Rosa was positioned at her flank. Eve raises a shield blocking Trinity's shot, but Rosa manages to hit her from behind. The viral bullet wastes no time corrupting Eve's processors triggering a three-second delay for responses as her coding becomes corrupted from within.

"Where's Enigma? The Guardian's been hit!" says Sasha as she rips her way through an entire battalion of guardsmen using her pheromones to take over the minds in the process. Those that survive her assault have become her mindless puppets.

Chapter 8 — Death of An Era

Puma's fur and skin turn into flames as her body ignites using the air around her as fuel. She's gone supernova, attacking Eve from the air with intense flames while coordinating the Primean attack strategy telepathically. Eve blocks Puma's flames with an energy shield, firing retardant grenades in response.

"Enigma's tending to Ether. We just need to hold the Guardian off until the virus starts working... Bunny are you ready?" asks Puma as she dodges a barrage of energy blasts from Eve who is still deadly despite a delayed response time.

Bunny teleports Rosa and Trinity into Lennek Square before answering, *"I'm ready! I brought some backup to keep the Coalition busy. Give it a few minutes and I'll end this...We're halfway there!"* She sees Merkaba approaching sixty feet away, working in seamless cohesion with Rosie fighting their way through swarms of Primean combat droids.

Puma is radiating enormous amounts of heat from her core, expunging 390-foot flames from her hands keeping Eve on the defensive. Kairen's protecting Eve with a telekinetic shield buckling from the intensity of Puma's flames. Eve's weapons are starting to shut down as she struggles to stand. Kairen gallops towards Eve, straining to maintain his shield, realizing Eve isn't repairing herself.

Punzel wraps her entire body with her dreads, making herself nearly impervious to Zeus's attacks. Zeus is over two stories tall, throwing a melee of punches at Punzel, as she crosses her arms above her head as she's hammered into the ground creating a small impact crater around her body. Despite his devastating blows, Punzel remains unharmed enduring his attack.

An incoming Primean fighter jet fires an array of weapons at Zeus's back. Zeus responds by jumping to punch the jets out of the sky. At his highest peak midair, Zeus turns around, collecting his momentum, falling to the ground with clenched fists, intending to pulverize Punzel. Punzel somersaults to safety, flipping in the air to avoid the shockwave of Zeus's landing.

Zeus punches the ground, increasing the crater Punzel once stood in. Within seconds, Punzel grows her dreads, suffocating Zeus from around the neck as her hair increases in size and density. Zeus can feel Punzel's hair tightening around his neck cutting off his circulation as oxygen's cut from his brain. Remembering his training, Zeus adapts to the situation reverting to his normal size, freeing himself from Punzel's grasp. He falls to the ground and shoots an inhibitor dart from his armor striking Punzel in the neck.

Kairen reaches out to his comrades, saying, "*I can't hold this!*" His shield weakens as Puma continues intensifying her flames. Eve's condition is worsening by the second as the Guardian falls weak to the knees.

Bambi is fighting off dozens of androids using her gauntlets to pulverize them. Her glezslavine gloves increase the force of her punches a thousandfold. Like the others, she's wearing a mask to dilute the effects of pheromones and smoke. Unlike her comrades, Bambi isn't holding back against the compromised civilians, killing anyone who dare attack her. Bambi sees Bastian on high ground using the wind to spread his pheromones keeping civilians in the square against their will.

Bambi stretches her limbs, maneuvering across the square, rushing Bastian unexpectedly. "Let them go, or I kill you!"

Bastian surrounds himself with a dozen civilians using them as shields. "You'll have to hurt them first before—"

He doesn't finish his statement before Bambi punches Bastian from four hundred feet away from an obscure angle. Bastian's knocked on his back as Bambi encroaches with an unrelenting assault. Bambi throws dozens of power punches, beating Bastian to a pulp, angering Bastian in the process. Bastian's adrenaline is dramatically increasing his strength while his healing abilities keep him alive.

Rosa senses Bastian in danger, attacking Bambi from a distance telepathically. Bastian gains his bearings and begins dodging Bambi's attacks. He sees a damaged statue of President Zlaigo, jumping forty feet in a single leap with his amplified strength. Bastian picks up the statue, throwing it at Bambi with such velocity she's knocked across the square.

Bambi's elastic skin makes her resistant to harm when malleable. She's pinned beneath the statue in her lucid form, slowly maneuvering from beneath. Bastian's charging Bambi, running unnaturally fast with his amplified strength. Bambi slithers from beneath the statue, slowly reconstituting her body.

"Let's see if you can stretch through my claws", says Bastian as he starts slashing through Bambi, who responds by wrapping herself around Bastian until he's unable to move. Bambi's strangling Bastian intending to suffocate him.

Lulu uses the momentum from a fifty-mile run and punches Khaled through a brick wall over six hundred feet away. "*Angel and Ebok will be here soon,*" says Lulu as she uses a speed-burst to cut a combat droid in half with her plasma sword.

Without her abilities Punzel was unable to fight Zeus and forced to retreat. Puma is so transfixed on Eve she doesn't realize Zeus is attacking her from behind. With an open palm, Zeus swats Puma across the square, scorching his hand in the process. The pain forces him to revert to his normal size. Primean soldiers on hover-bikes open fire, forcing Zeus to use the energy shields within his armor to protect himself.

Zeus takes a moment to recover before increasing his size to hurl one of Vaughn's boulders at the incoming hover-bikes. He destroys two of the bikes, causing them to explode midair, then he leaps into the air destroying the remaining hover-bike.

Puma is on the ground recovering from Zeus' attack, healing her wounds with her flames. Angel flies overhead, landing in the middle of a fleet of Primean soldiers, releasing a sonic scream that bursts the eardrums of the surrounding soldiers through their helmets. Angel changes the density of her feathers before spinning and expunging dozens of hardened feathers, killing the Primean soldiers.

Puma reaches out to Bunny, screaming, *"What are you waiting for? The virus has run its course! END THIS!"* She searches the area and watches Khaled shoot energy blasts from his hands, hitting Kairen's shield.

Puma takes to the air, charging Eve who appears inoperable behind Kairen's shield. Kairen sees Khaled charging him and focuses his shield to the front of Eve. Puma uses her telepathy to coordinate their attacks as Khaled and Puma release massive energy beams, forcing Kairen to his knees. The shield protecting Eve dissipates as Puma attacks Kairen's mind with a telepathic blast, short-circuiting his nervous system.

"BUNNY NOW!" exclaims Puma as she takes to the air.

Bunny teleports behind the Guardian, transporting Eve two thousand miles away outside the Acolyte settlement called the Badlands. During transit, Eve injects multiple tentacles into Bunny absorbing the energy being used to teleport.

Coalition scientists felt they could master the phenomena of teleportation with a large enough sample of the Lagrangian particles used in the transporting process. Mutants with teleportation abilities are rare and neither Lennek nor Olympia have had success recruiting any. As Eve drains Bunny's blood, tentacles from Eve's hair inject themselves through Bunny's armor into her spine taking bone marrow.

Eve and Bunny reach their destination surrounded by dozens of automated weapons designed to break through Eve's metallic shell. All the Guardians are made of unique metallic alloys surpassing the strength of glezslavine. The Primeans have made a prison to trap the

Guardian, building a magnetic floor in an enclosed environment made of energy walls.

Bunny is weak, having lost pints of blood. She cries out, "Stop! What are you doing to me?"

Eve is fighting back with what little energy she has, transmitting the collected data. Eve answers in a corrupted monotone voice, "Giving... Co-Co-Coalition advantage... Replace us Guardians."

"Stop... You're killing me!" says Bunny as she pleads for her life. Bunny turns on the network of automated weapons surrounding them as they begin targeting Eve.

"You may survive...procedure. Blood, bone marrow...energy you use to teleport will allow..." says Eve as her voice cuts out from the virus. Eve injects another tentacle into Bunny's lower spine.

"AHHHHHHHHHHHH!" screams Bunny as Eve takes what she needs with no concern for Bunny's life. The Primean virus is breaking down her processors, but she's not as weak as she portrayed in the square.

Bunny's life support within her armor kicks in as she becomes lightheaded. The weapons open fire on Eve, as Bunny's armor uses all its energy to protect her. The lasers begin targeting Eve who is no longer able to repair or create shields. As Eve's body degrades from the attack, so does her extraction process.

Bunny's armor injects an adrenaline cocktail into her bloodstream, attempting to keep her awake. Combat trained, Bunny fights through the pain, drawing two plasma daggers from her thighs, cutting herself free of Eve's tentacles. She crawls away from Eve who is being blasted to shreds with high-powered lasers, oversized bullets, and plasma blasts. Knowing her life depends on it, Bunny channels what energy she has left teleporting to a medic bay on a Primean warship. The amplifier Garuda gave her in Petra makes the feat possible, saving her life.

Bunny leaves Eve behind to face her doom as the lasers rip her armor to shreds. Unable to make repairs, Eve's processors begin to go offline as her internal network within her bloodstream is destroyed. Eve knows her consciousness is backed up and she, unlike her fellow Guardians, will see another day. Eve finds solace knowing she will experience the emotions of death and pass on the secret of teleportation through her demise. Eve uploads the data to Coalition Headquarters moments before her processors shutdown. Eve's demise was broadcast worldwide, giving the Primeans the victory they wanted.

Meanwhile, back in Lennek, Cole and Gill are still fighting to the death in the center of the square, with neither willing to yield. Cole senses a sewage drain behind Gill, pulling dirty sewage from the drain and freezing the sewage into razor-sharp shards. He directs the ice at Gill as he continues moving to stay clear of Gill's counterattacks. Gill is using his telepathy to anticipate Cole's attacks, but he's having trouble striking a heavy blow as Cole's agility and combat skills were unexpected.

Gill switches tactics, unleashing a telepathic blast, which is futile against the multiple telepaths protecting the Primeans' minds. Cole's found cover, shooting sheets of ice at Gill, forcing him to conjure a gust of wind to maneuver to safety.

Gill harnesses a high voltage electrical current directing it at Cole, who quickly throws out an energy net to absorb the current. Gill starts twirling his staff, producing a large gust of wind knocking Cole twenty-five-feet into the air. Cole stays calm, executing a series of acrobatic flips redirecting the momentum towards a slope of ice he creates.

Reaching the bottom of the slope, Cole converts his entire body into solid ice moments before being struck in the chest with a massive electrical current. Gill starts siphoning energy from a nearby electrical box as Cole heals his chest by sculpting ice on his chest. Cole's eyes turn completely white as the temperature starts dropping rapidly around them. Gill shoots massive electrical currents from his hands forcing

Cole on the defensive as a cold front starts to spread across the ground with Cole communing with the air temperature surrounding them.

Hundreds of dead Olympians are spread throughout the square, scattered amongst debris and thousands of Lennethian bodies. Without Goldie's bold intrusion into Olympia, demanding King Larvex recall his warships, the death toll would have climbed tenfold for both Colonies. Cole takes in the death surrounding him as an electrical current hurled from Gill snaps him back into reality, forcing him to keep moving.

Cole reaches out to Rosa, saying, "*Rosa, I need you to shield my thoughts and implant false intentions. The Kronusian is reading my thoughts and countering my attacks.*"

Gill rides a gust of wind thirty feet into the air, slowly lowering himself while shooting electrical currents from his hands. Cole creates a thick sheet of ice to block the incoming attack while somersaulting to higher ground. Gill lands with his staff drawn and his mind focused to amplify his telepathy. Gill unleashes a focused telepathic attack leaving Cole disoriented for a moment.

Cole fights through the vertigo charging Gill while shooting beams of ice that freeze targets on contact. Being a superior telepath, Rosa can protect Cole's mind while editing his beta waves. With implanted thoughts from Rosa, Cole momentarily gains the upper hand against Gill. Cole lands a few blows before Gill summons a miniature tornado with electrical currents from above.

Cole uses the wind currents dropping the surrounding temperature to twenty degrees below zero. Everything around Cole begins freezing in place. The power in Gill's armor has dropped to 20 percent. Unwilling to test his armor's climate control limits, he glides away, finding cover some distance away, escaping Cole's cold front.

Merkaba is restoring her comrade's stamina, giving Zeus and Kairen a much-needed second wind. She uses her sais to confront the advancing soldiers coming to the Primeans aid. She notices Rosie being overtaken by Sasha immediately diverting her attention. She throws her sais to block Sasha's path, giving Rosie time to escape. With a twist of her wrist, Merkaba's sais return to her hands as Sasha marks her as a target.

Sasha starts closing in on Merkaba asking Puma, *"What's our exit strategy? We can't hold them off forever."*

Rosa adds, *"The Olympians just released platoons of hover-bikes. We need Bunny on her feet now!"* Rosa takes a punch to the chin from Duke, countering with a power punch of her own. Duke has syphoned the powers of multiple mutants. He kicks Rosa across the square with the impact of a moving bus. Rosa hits a concrete wall shaken from the impact.

Puma answers, *"She needs a few minutes to recover. We're shooting her up with adrenaline. We're lucky she's alive. We don't have another exit strategy. I'm working on it."*

With Eve dead, Puma moves her warships past Grentake Falls, dispatching hundreds of Primean fighter jets. Platoons of Primean soldiers are on hover-bikes combating Lennek's forces which are growing by the minute.

Puma is fighting off dozens of guardsmen with jetpacks circling her in the air attempting to extinguish her flames. She's burning the guardsmen out of the sky with single blasts as she prays Bunny recovers quickly. *"We're all making it out of here alive... We've planned for this. Everyone needs to be moving east towards the shoreline!"*

Sasha responds, *"I need help with this healer! My pheromones don't affect her, and her healing factor is rendering my claws useless."* Merkaba is blocking Sasha's claws with her sais, dealing damage Sasha can't heal from.

Rosa projects her consciousness in astral form, surrounding herself with a pride of psionic lions, made of pure psychic energy. The lions in her astral pride have intricate armor each standing fourteen feet tall, capable of destroying the minds of their prey. Rosa orders the pride to attack Merkaba as she overpowers Sasha.

Goldie appears in astral form in front of Merkaba, telling the Coalition mutants, *"The Primean's teleporter is badly injured. They have no escape route... We need to hold them here!"*

Goldie starts shooting beams of psionic energy out of her palms and eyes, keeping Rosa's psionic lions at bay. The pride repositions themselves as Rosa levitates towards Goldie on the astral plane, asking, *"So you're the Coalition's leader? I felt you earlier... I assure you we mean the Evo of Lennek no harm. We came to destroy your abomination of a Guardian."*

"No hard feelings. We allowed you to come since we needed something from you," says Goldie as she, too, levitates equaling her line of sight to Rosa. Six oversized falcons with a wingspan of eighty feet begin circling the pair in the air as Goldie shows the extent of her own powers.

Rosa looks up and smiles, saying, *"Let's see what you've got."* Rosa commands her lions to attack Goldie and Merkaba as Goldie unleashes her oversized falcons. Sasha's continuing to lose ground as Merkaba out maneuvers Sasha continuing to heal from her injuries with maintained stamina.

Two psionic lions attack Merkaba crippling her mind for a moment allowing Sasha to counterattack. Merkaba can't see the oversized lions, but she knows a psychic attack when she feels it. Sasha slashes away with her bionic claws cutting Merkaba in the abdomen. Goldie wastes no time destroying the psionic pride of lions with her own psionic falcons. Goldie attacks Rosa on the astral plane leveling things on the physical world allowing Merkaba to gain her vantage once more.

Rosa manifests a psionic bow, shooting arrows at Goldie on the astral plane. Goldie conjures a psionic sword and shield, blocking the flurry of arrows as Rosa summons two large elephants to charge Goldie. Goldie fends off the elephants with her psionic falcons, summoning a pack of oversized wolves, battling one the world's most experienced psychics.

Being of elephant descent, Rosa is confident in her telepathic skills, rarely meeting an equal. Despite Goldie's inexperience, she's proving why she leads the Coalition, counterattacking with primal energy channeled from a higher power.

Rosa and Goldie are testing each other's wills while Rosa must also fend for herself on the physical plane. Telepaths are master multitaskers, but the level of brainpower needed to fend off Goldie and fight in the physical world is immense. Rosa's stamina is quickly fading along with her Primean comrades.

Rosie eliminates a swarm of Primean combat droids, shifting her attention to Merkaba. Without her healing abilities, Merkaba would already be dead or under the influence of Sasha's pheromones. Her newly developed combat skills are wiping the floor with Sasha. Being telepathically linked, Rosie assists from a distance, creating a force field blocking Sasha from moving backwards.

Merkaba switches tactics, relying on her powers as opposed to hand-to-hand combat. She puts her arms out, emitting a frequency intended to crush Sasha's bones through her armor. Merkaba adjusts the frequency of her purrs as Sasha screams out from pain as her ribs and femur crack. Sasha passes out from trauma as her armor starts working to save her life.

The Primeans are also telepathically linked, allowing Sasha's comrades to know she's in danger. Vaughn is closest to Sasha, watching Rosie make her way to Merkaba. He has the Primean telepaths shielding his thoughts as he starts harnessing the metals from the Earth beneath him creating a boulder. Vaughn launches the boulder intending to crush the pair, but not before Goldie warns them, allowing Rosie to raise a shield.

The enormous boulder is crushed upon impact from Rosie's force field. While the two are distracted above, Vaughn creates a rising pillar from the ground beneath Merkaba and Rosie, launching them airborne 450 feet. Merkaba uses her gravity-displacement boots to recover while Rosie uses a force field to stop herself midair. In unison, they both descend onto Vaughn from above, forcing him on the defensive.

Just outside the large field making up Lennek Square, Duke's attacking Byron telepathically, siphoning his abilities to create an impenetrable shield that encases his own body. Even ionized weapons are deflected by Byron's unique energy signature. Byron's powers only allow him to maintain his encasing for a short time. His powers are connected to his breathing. Duke is learned his weakness over the course of a bloody exchange between the two.

Every few minutes, Byron is forced to recover and breathe, letting his encasement down. Duke has been trying to find a cadence to his breathing and vulnerability. They're destroying everything in their path as Duke uses Byron's mutation against him.

Byron's kinetic daggers are useless against Duke, who continues to siphon Byron's powers. Byron lures Duke into a trap near an unstable building while blocking a combination of attacks forcing him to move backwards. Duke combines an array of mutant abilities he absorbed in battle keeping Byron guessing unable to strategize a defense. Byron's losing ground and weakening by the second.

Duke hits Byron with a condensed energy blast, knocking him into a nearby building which was already unstable. Duke uses the last of his telekinesis, forcing the building down on Byron. Seconds pass and Duke turns his back, lowering his kinetic encasement assuming he killed Byron. The rubble of the fallen building shakes before exploding outward as Byron plunges out from the rubble.

Byron advances shooting his kinetic daggers striking Duke in the back and leg. Byron lowers his kinetic encasement saving his energy for the right moment. Duke uses an absorbed healing factor to recover, raising a telekinetic shield to block the incoming daggers as Byron continues charging. Duke holds his breath as he raises a kinetic encasement using Byron's powers against him.

Duke counterattacks, firing his own kinetic daggers which Byron dodges without activating his kinetic encasement. Duke's becoming frustrated, usually killing his opponents within seconds. Now face to face, the pair fight hand-to-hand, compounding the need for Duke to eventually breathe. Byron's being patient waiting for his opportunity, relying on his agility to stay alive. A single blow from Duke will kill him, but a perfectly timed counterattack will end this.

Duke takes a breath, and his kinetic encasement lowers for but a moment. Byron manifests a long sword attached to his right arm made from his own kinetic energy, jabbing the sword through the bottom of Duke's jaw through his skull. Duke places his hands on Bryon's head and releases 120,000 volts of electrical currents timed with a telepathic attack from Goldie, dropping Byron's limp body to the ground.

Blood is gushing from the bottom of Duke's jaw and head as he falls to the ground losing consciousness. He watches Byron's smoking body convulse as he notices red rain falling to the ground. Duke taps into the last of his absorbed healing factor from Merkaba, resonating a frequency to repair his jaw and skull. Tissues and bone begin forming as Duke's body slowly reanimates.

In less than a minute, Duke's on his feet walking over Byron's body which is now vegetative. Duke starts making his way towards the square joining the rest of the Coalition. His body's recovered but the only abilities he still has are Byron's. He runs into the square at full speed watching the Coalition and Primean mutants make use of the entire space fighting to the death.

Thousands of fighter jets, soldiers on hover-bikes, and armed drones are swarming the skies, each a part of the Primean third attack wave. Olympia released their own army to defend Lennek with thousands of Olympia guardsmen descending upon Lennek to defend their sister

Colony. The skies are filled with smoke and thousands of Evo fighting to defend their homes from a foreign invader.

On the shores of Lennek, Puma's warships are approaching the remains of her fallen submarines. Enigma reaches out to Puma, saying, *"Ether's stable now. I'm flying to the square now!"* Enigma jumps out of the hangar of her warship and sees the Olympians descending on the square from the air. *"The Olympians are sending reinforcements!"*

"SHOOT THOSE PIGEONS OUT OF THE SKY!" screams Puma under duress from the overwhelming Colonial forces. *"Get your ass down here. We need you! Bunny's having surgery, as we speak. We're getting overrun!"*

Equipped with a jetpack to increase her speed, Enigma takes off towards Lennek Square a few minutes away from the looming incursion. Puma predicted Lennek would send heavy Colonial forces after their Guardian fell. She hoped once Olympia's warships were destroyed, King Larvex would choose to defend his own airspace.

"Keep moving east, everyone!" says Puma to her fellow Primeans as she melts debris creating a path to the shore. The melted metal creates magma which she molds into a life-like snake. Flames ignite down the back of the snake as it slithers towards two fleets of advancing guardsmen, burning everything in its path.

Puma's controlling the snake with her mind as she burns through dozens of guardsmen on the ground. Ebok flies in on a retrofitted hover-bike, shooting flame retardant foam which stops the snake in place. With its flames extinguished, the metal cools in place, unable to be controlled by Puma.

Ebok has an army of drones trailing him, automated fighter jets, and platoons of Colonial combat droids on the ground. Ebok's tapped into the guardsmen encrypted communication frequency, saying, "Pin the Primeans down and stop their retreat. King Larvex dispatched his army. We have the numbers! The Olympian Guardian is awaiting bureaucratic approval to enter the fray. Keep the Primeans here!"

Ebok commands his drones and three fighter jets to open fire, focusing on Fyn and Puma in the air. The machines and weapons connected to Ebok are now an extension of his consciousness. Ebok's controlling thousands of machines, each with an individual directive. Thanks to Goldie, the Coalition was fully prepared to defer Puma's third attack wave.

Violet's drones begin interlocking and activate their shields to create a solid wall of protective energy. Violet stops a platoon of guardsmen from slaughtering a group of advancing Primean soldiers. Without hesitation, she rides her bike beneath the energy wall, quickly gaining altitude, to mow down Ebok's reinforcements with energy blasts and a barrage of bullets. Violet spots Ebok and begins targeting him, knowing her technopathic abilities are stronger than his.

Most of the surrounding buildings are either burning or destroyed. The entire square is filled with debris and bodies while destroyed buildings makeup the backdrop. Red rain is falling from the skies as the Olympian air force defends the skies against Primean fighter jets, drones, and soldiers on hover-bikes. The Olympian air force is revered as masters of the sky, proving their superiority by laying waste to the Primeans automated fighter jets.

At the south end of the square, Vaughn is met with resistance from an unexpected bystander. An unregistered mutant, named Welby, has similar powers to Vaughn and felt compelled to intervene. Welby can manipulate metals, rocks, dirt, and specific minerals, bending them to his will. He can create earthquakes, sinkholes, and shift tectonic plates with immense concentration. He couldn't get to a bunker, and he's been forced to defend himself in the open, outing himself as a mutant.

Welby is 6'2" of bull descent, born an Acolyte in the Badlands outside of Lennek. He has pale skin, a muscular build, with a deep domineering voice. His handsome face is covered in freckles complementing his humanoid facial features, green eyes, and goatee. Welby has long orange hair with horns blended into his curly hair. He wanted a fresh start and a normal life in Lennek, hoping to keep his mutant identity hidden. The universe had other plans.

Welby felt Vaughn manipulating the tectonic plates beneath the square and intuitively sprang into action. His new home is now under attack, and standing by isn't an option. He went through too much to escape the Badlands. He couldn't watch the Primeans burn it to the ground. Vaughn feels someone countering his power and immediately starts searching for the culprit.

Welby's untrained and in civilian clothing with no battle armor. Vaughn can feel the energy surging from Welby's body and quickly locates him. He gathers material from the ground below creating a large boulder above his head. He hurls the boulder at Welby who panics under pressure, closing his eyes and freezing in place.

Kairen intercepts the boulder and hurls it back at Vaughn with his telekinesis quickly following with a barrage of explosive arrows. He looks at Welby, saying, "Get going, kid! It's not safe out here. Get to a bunker! I've got it from here."

"There's nowhere to go!" retorts Welby as he hurls a nearby marble statue destroying an incoming fighter jet. The jet explodes upon impact sending debris across the square.

While impressed, Kairen points out, "You don't have any battle armor. Find an abandoned building and hide." He notices Vaughn recovering from the attack and urges Welby to flee. "RUN!"

Welby looks at Vaughn and notices how he has his body encased in stone. He puts his hand to the soil beneath him finding useful metals and stones. Welby closes his eyes and encases himself in armor made of various stones from the Earth. "Like I said, there's nowhere to run. We can take him together!"

Vaughn hurls another boulder and Welby stops it midair, redirecting it back towards Vaughn, knocking him on his back. Kairen concedes, saying, "Stay behind me."

Goldie appears in astral form directly in front of Welby, saying, *"Don't be alarmed. I'm Goldie, leader of the Coalition. I've been waiting to meet you!"* She sees Welby's confused and telepathically probes his mind updating him on the Coalition, who she is, and background on the Primeans fighting in the square. *"Stay with Kairen. He'll keep you alive!"*

Welby agrees and follows Kairen as the pair charge Vaughn with everything they've got. Kairen's creating a telekinetic shield around Welby, blocking incoming fire. He sees Rosie being flanked by two combat droids and hurls one of Vaughn's large boulders at the droids, crushing them. Welby has never seen battle, but he's had plenty of fights growing up in the Badlands.

"You're a natural. Keep a safe distance and we'll bring you back to headquarters when all this is over. It won't be much longer!" says Goldie, assuring Welby that he'll be alright.

Fifteen thousand kilometers above in Olympia, King Larvex is meeting with his Colonial council inside his imperial war room. They're observing the war efforts below, analyzing their losses in real time, while discussing strategy. Their own Commencement celebrations were cut short due to the Primean invasion. Their treaty alliance forces both Colonies to act in the defense of each other.

Primean warships have advanced past Grentake Falls, battling Olympian fighter jets with advanced weaponry. Olympian warships have been grounded to prevent further losses while ground teams recover their technology and debris. Olympian automated fighter jets have been sent out to prevent loss of life while the Olympian Guardian patrols the skies.

The Olympian Guardian is over 8'0'' with a humanoid physique with a large metallic wingspan. The Guardian's shell is encased in glezslavine armed with numerous weapons suited for combat in the air. It has a jetpack down the middle of its spine while its large metallic wings have sharp edges it uses in combat. The Guardian has male features and a purple energy source powering its operating systems. Like all Guardians, it can manifest weapons and heal from its nanites.

King Larvex is pacing behind Senate Leader Oladin, explaining, "We need to release our Guardian and recall our fighter jets. Our first wave of fighter jets will be depleted soon. The Primeans have made a declaration against us... We show no mercy."

Senate Oladin maneuvers his hands using sign language as his gloves translate what he's saying aloud. "They brought those warships for a reason! The minute our Guardian leaves they will invade Olympia. We all saw them take out Lennek's Guardian with their snipers. Is risking our Guardian in the best interest of Olympia?" Being of Queztal descent his colorful feathers have always drawn attention. Being deaf as a child, he learned to shrink himself, often remaining quiet until he found his voice in politics.

Eight of Olympia's regents, four senators, and Olympia's governor are in the war room with their king debating the fate of two Colonies. King Larvex replies, "I prefer to consult with our Guardian." The king walks to his throne pressing a button to communicate directly with Olympia's Guardian. He asks, "What will the casualty reduction be if you intercede in the Lennethian conflict?"

The Guardian replies over an intercom, answering, "My intervention will reduce casualties on both sides by sixty-three percent. With Olympia's weapon systems, this conflict can be ended in four minutes and thirty-five seconds. I await your orders."

King Larvex sits at his throne, watching the conflict below on the hologram projection in the middle of the room in deep thought. He takes a moment, then explains, "It appears the Primeans don't have an exit strategy. We should strike with our Guardian and pin them down."

Knowing the king has made his mind up, the room is silent with no one willing to counter his opinion. Azurie, Regent of House Lahun stands to say, "The gesture will be well received my King!"

Senate Leader Oladin signs reluctantly, adding, "Agreed."

King Larvex presses a button on his throne, saying, "Destroy the Primean warships and bring me the heads of their mutants!" Hoping he has made the right decision, he puts the air force on standby to defend Olympia. He watched Eve's destruction with the rest of the world and can't help but think he's ordered their own Guardian into a trap.

The Olympian Guardian gives no reply and immediately powers its thrusters, opening its metallic wings to engage the enemy beneath. Olympia's Guardian is much larger than Eve, lacking her emotional depth in decision-making. Excluding Eve, the Guardians are ruthless, acting on algorithms and code to make decisions.

The Primeans were holding their warships back to prevent Olympia from interceding. Had Bunny remained unharmed, they would be en route to Angkor, avoiding conflict with Olympia all together.

Ether is in the medic bay on Enigma's personal warship remaining outside of Grentake Falls, using Angkorian stealth technology to remain hidden. Bunny's surgeries were a success and nanites are working overtime to repair her wounds. Ether has placed lunar lamps around Bunny to restore her stamina, recharging her powers.

Ether has intuitively known things since returning from the dead. She knows the Olympians have unleashed their Guardian and knows the pivotal role Bunny plays in saving the rest of the Primeans. Ether grabs an adrenaline vial, handing it to the medic droid. Bunny has undergone multiple surgeries and will survive Eve's violation, but she's extremely weak. The medic droid was programmed by the best medical doctors in Angkor. Ether orders the medic droid to add the adrenaline into Bunny's fluids, waking her up. The android does as it's told against its own protocols.

"THE EVAC!" screams Bunny as she springs up on the medic bay in a panic. Bunny removes the life-support system as she asks Ether, "Did will kill the Guardian?"

"Yes...yes, we killed the Guardian and got what we needed from the hive. But...Olympia just released their Guardian. Puma and the others are getting overrun. They need you to escape!" says Ether as she tries to slow Bunny Down.

Bunny stands, saying, "Computer, show me Puma and the other's locations. Send the data to my armor as well." Bunny coddles her ribs as she looks in the medicine cabinet for a pain diluter.

Ether catches Bunny's line of sight, saying, "We need you level-headed teleporting them back. If you're not ready yet. If you need more time to—"

"If I don't get back out there, our Evo die! Enigma dies! I don't have a choice. I'll be fine," says Bunny as she stands upright, fighting through her pain. "Where's my armor?"

Ether takes a moment to consider her options, but knows Bunny is right. She answers, "In the armory getting charged and repaired." Ether drops her head, hoping she hasn't allowed Bunny to leave prematurely.

The ship's AI displays a hologram combining live streaming footage from Primean soldiers in the field. Bunny takes adrenaline and morphine from the medicine cabinet, risking her sobriety in the process. After injecting herself, she teleports to the armory as the hologram moves with her throughout the warship.

The ship's AI tells Bunny, "The Olympian Guardian is approaching Lennek Square. Puma has sent out a distress beacon to all nearby Primeans."

Once dressed, Bunny reaches out to Puma telepathically, saying, *"Lennek's Guardian nearly killed me, but I've recovered. I'll start extracting our mutants now."*

Puma's relieved to hear Bunny, but she lashes out in despair, saying, *"Get Fyn to a med bay before he dies on us! He's been beat to a pulp and he can't absorb anyone's chi. Their speedster just stabbed him with an inhibitor knife."*

Bunny grabs some gravity-displacement grenades, two plasma swords, and two pistols with explosive rounds. Bunny loads the outside of her thighs with extra rounds before grabbing two spherical medic drones. Bunny turns on her visor and sees Fyn crawling to safety as he bleeds out on the ground near the northern part of Lennek Square.

Fyn crawls toward a pile of dead Evo trying to hide his body amongst the dead. His powers probe the bodies scavenging for any remanence of life force. Fyn is completely defenseless and for the first time in his life, he's afraid. Fyn reaches out telepathically for help, but his comrades are busy fighting for their own survival. Three Olympian soldiers are descending upon him with their swords and guns drawn.

Fyn covers himself with his wings, preparing to die, when suddenly, Bunny teleports to his location, killing the guardsmen midair with enhanced plasma swords. Bunny's swords slice through the guardsmen's armor like butter. Fyn retracts his wings and sees Bunny de-powering her plasma swords as limbs from the Olympian guardsmen fall to the ground around them as they're showered in blood. In a blink of an eye, she teleports Fyn to a medic bay before returning to the square.

Ether sees Fyn bleeding out and immediately springs to action removing the inhibitor knife in his back. She places Fyn in the medic bay, as the machine starts using stem cells to repair his tissue. The healing beds work like a 3-D printer repairing tissue with light, T cells, and amino acids built upon organic tissue. A blood transfusion stops him from slipping further near death as he passes out from the trauma.

Ether tells the medic droid, "Give him an antidote for the inhibitor serum with some adrenaline." Lulu beat Fyn to a bloody pulp and left him to die with her knife still in his back. The medic droid closes his wound working meticulously through the mountain of blood spewing out of him. Fyn is bleeding out as the medic droid sprays a clear substance on his back to stop the bleeding. The medic droid stitches him up with immaculate precision while injecting an antidote for the inhibitor serum.

Less than a mile away, the Olympian Guardian starts destroying a Primean warship with the assistance of a missile defense system. Olympia has levitating weapons outposts in the stratosphere above Olympia. The weapons outposts are equipped with various missiles and fusion powered lasers all linked and under their Guardian's control. Dozens of missiles destroyed the Primean warship causing a massive explosion. The concussive aftershock is felt and heard far beyond Lennek.

Bunny sees the explosion near Grentake Falls from inside the square. She knows their entire plan relied on Olympia's Guardian protecting its own Colony. Knowing time is of the essence, she tracks down Bastian as he fights off hordes of guardsmen. With his healing factor depleted and unable to make pheromones, Bastian is relying on his bionic claws to defend himself.

Bunny teleports behind Bastian, extracting him before an incoming missile blows him to ash. Bunny teleports to their nearest warship, returning to the square without even speaking to Bastian. He reaches out, telling her, "*There are others in worse shape than me, love. Get Puma out of there now... They'll be targeting her!*"

Back inside Lennek Square, Bunny responds, "*The ship's AI is telling me the order to extract you all in. Those in danger or injured are prioritized, you just happened to be closest to me.*" Another Primean warship is destroyed with an echoing explosion ripping through the surrounding area. *"We both know Puma would risk death itself to be the last Primean extracted."*

The Guardian has shifted its attention to Lennek Square under orders from King Larvex who has spotted Bunny from Olympia above. The Guardian is firing lasers from its palms while controlling the Olympian weapon's system within the stratosphere. The presence of a functioning Guardian has forced many of the Primean soldiers to retreat to the nearest rendezvous point for evacuation.

Puma reaches out to Vaughn, Sasha, Rosa, Enigma, and Khaled, exclaiming, *"Group together and continue falling back!"*

Bunny extracts Byron, Cole, and Punzel as the remaining Primeans group towards the shoreline. Ground forces are falling back as the Olympian Guardian approaches, unleashing an onslaught of weapons from Olympia's automated defense system. Enigma creates a shield around Puma, Khaled, Vaughn, Violet, Sasha, Rosa, and Trinity.

"Is Bunny strong enough to take us as a group?" asks Vaughn as he manipulates the ground around them to create a dome.

Trinity answers, "Not with her injuries. We'll have to split up into groups." Zeus is pounding away at the dome Vaughn created while the Olympian Guardian is seconds away. Welby is reseeding the dome of rocks the best he can with his untrained abilities. He's no match for Vaughn, but seeing his abilities in action at their full potential inspires him.

Bunny teleports next to her six comrades, exclaiming, "I can only take two at a time!" Gill unleashes massive electrical currents to break through the Primeans shields as Khaled turns ready to attack.

Puma responds, "That's fine! Me and Khaled will go last."

"Take some viral bullets. That Guardian's going to be here any second now," says Trinity as she moves close to Sasha who is still badly injured. Trinity leaves her loaded sniper riffle with Khaled before Bunny teleports Sasha and Trinity to safety.

Khaled tells everyone, "We're making ourselves an easy target. Enigma's shields won't hold for long and Bunny's going to have an extended recovery time due to her injuries."

Puma reads Khaled's thoughts, adding, "Let's move. I'll head—" Puma isn't able to finish her sentence as Bambi's gloves hit Enigma's shield with an extremely loud *thud*. The remaining Primeans look at each other realizing they need to move.

Enigma lowers her shield, taking to the air as Puma reignites her flames. Puma flies past Zeus who is four stories tall now, fully recovered with Merkaba's help. Puma sees the Olympian Guardian a few hundred feet away and her fear produces an adrenaline surge causing her to go supernova.

Angel flies in from Puma's flank, releasing a sonic blast from her hands as she closes in. Puma takes evasive action, avoiding the attack while Rosa hurls a large piece of debris at the Guardian. The Guardian catches the debris, throwing it back at Rosa with double the force. Rosa becomes incapacitated from the brute force of the attack before being recovered by Bunny.

Violet has a series of energy nets circling her as she begins shedding her nanite bugs from her hair attempting to amplify her technopathic abilities. She knows she can't commandeer the Guardian's controls, but she can slow down its processing speeds. Violet hacks the Guardian's processors, allowing her to warn the Primeans of the Guardians attacks seconds before they take place. With Puma linking their minds telepathically, they have a fighting chance to holding off the Guardian until Bunny extracts them.

Olympia's Guardian is working around Violet with Ebok's assistance, firing an array of its own weapons combined with Olympia's automated defense system. The Coalition mutants are pulling back as missiles, plasma blasts, and bombs rain from the sky.

Angel has never seen her Guardian in combat watching from a

distance in amazement. Watching the synchronicity in movement between its weapons and the Olympian automated defense system is poetically artistic. The destructive power is forcing the Coalition to pull back impressing the world as footage is streamed worldwide.

Bunny returns to teleport Violet back to the warship leaving Puma, Enigma, Khaled, and Vaughn. Khaled knows he and Puma will be the last to be extracted and has taken on Zeus hoping to absorb as much kinetic energy as possible. He knows Puma would make herself a martyr for the Primean cause if necessary. He needs to ensure she doesn't have the option.

Goldie appears in astral form on Zeus's shoulder, saying, *"Stop attacking the lion. He's just absorbing your energy. Gill can avoid his attacks. Merkaba can immobilize him. I'm not out of this fight either!"*

"Understood!" says Zeus as he turns around and spots Vaughn fighting Kairen and Bambi. He diverts his attention to Vaughn, repositioning himself to change targets.

Khaled notices the change in strategy and adapts. He notices Bambi attacking from a distance and fires a condensed laser from his metallic arm striking her through the abdomen. Bambi screams out in pain falling to the ground. Khaled shot a clean hole through Bambi and is now targeting the area aiming for Kairen.

Vaughn is exhausted, giving all he has to the very end. Bunny extracts him saving him from a beating from Lulu and Duke. Only Khaled and Puma remain, and the Guardian now has its sights on Puma. Puma's airborne and a supernova conjuring a tornado with winds of fire. The spiraling vortex of flames is forcing the Guardian to assess the situation considering all outcomes.

The missiles, energy blasts, bullets, and sonic weapons being used against Puma are being redirected by the strong winds of her burning tornado. The exploding missiles and thermal energy being used against her are fueling her flames as they grow with intensity. A pyrokinetic has their limits. What Puma is harnessing is unnatural, even by mutant standards.

Khaled falls back from the growing tornado of fire, worried for his betrothed. Bunny teleports Khaled to safety, leaving just Puma. Puma's flames can be seen from miles away.

Realizing she's lost control and altered herself somehow, Rosa reaches out, concerned. *"You're losing control! Bunny can't get you out unless you power down!"* explains Rosa from a warship outside Grentake Falls.

What remains of the Primean fleet is retreating waiting for their leader's escape. Puma continues to fight, levitating in the center of her tornado, focusing her power.

The Guardian's sensors are unable to track Puma's exact location through the intensity of the flames. The Guardian estimates Puma's location charging through the tornado of fire with plasma swords drawn. Puma's telepaths warn her, giving her enough time to climb altitude dodging the attack. Puma's tornado has turned into a growing vortex of flames, engulfing everything in its path.

"The Guardian's going to attack from above through the center of the fire storm. Expunge all the energy you have directly above yourself and power down. DO IT NOW!" exclaims Rosa as Puma follows orders unleashing gigatons of power in a condensed stream of energy through the center of her inflamed tornado.

Puma exhausts her power, falling to the ground, no longer in flames. Bunny times her extraction catching Puma before she hits the ground. The Olympian Guardian is struck dead center from Puma's blast, having depleted its shields to defend itself. The Olympian Guardian descends to the ground, taking a few moments to regain its bearings. The Guardian receives orders from King Larvex to return to Olympia, leaving Lennek Square in ashes.

Bunny arrives on the last warship retreating from Lennek inside the medic bay with Puma unconscious but alive. Her body is smoking from the excess energy, making her too hot to touch. Bunny has some third degree burns on her arms and chest, but everyone's alive.

"What happened?" asks Bunny, realizing Fyn is restrained in his med bay.

Ether answers, "Apparently Fyn's powers work even when he's unconscious. He took out two of our own. They fought back apparently. He's healing from new injuries."

Khaled enters the med bay frantic. "How is she?" Khaled picks up Puma with his cybernetic arms, loading her into a medical bed as it starts a diagnostic. All the Primean forces are retreating as the world is left in shock watching Eve's destruction.

Ether moves to the display screen and sees the damage done to Puma's internal organs. "There's no question she's undergoing gene splicing to increase her abilities. She'll recover with nanites and frequency therapy, but she needs to know going supernova could kill her."

Khaled shakes in fear for Puma's wellbeing, disappointed in what he's hearing. "I told her not to do the gene splicing. There were too many risks." He takes a deep breath, watching the medical bed tend to her wounds with light and sound therapy. He says aloud, "Computer, plot a course for Angkor. Power up warp drives."

The warship's AI responds, "Warp drives powering on. Incoming object."

"Show on holo-screen," says Khaled as he sees a holographic image of the Olympian Guardian heading right for them.

"GET US OUT OF HERE!" screams Khaled, fully aware the Guardian can easily decimate their warship within seconds. "NOW!"

"Initiating interplanetary warp drive," says the AI as the Primeans blast away to Angkor making history for the world to see. The Guardian arrives seconds too late, then plots a course back to Olympia. The

Olympian Guardians has less than an hour from serving the end of its programing. The Guardian returns home to spend its remaining time amongst the Olympians it oversaw.

Meanwhile, the Coalition is already meeting inside their headquarters with unexpected visitors. President Zlaigo, Governor Grimsuni, and Welby are inside the main hall processing the aftermath of their Commencement massacre. President Zlaigo believes Eve to be dead and he needs answers for the slaughtering of innocent constituents. He was warned of an attack and took little to no action to prepare. Now Lennek's president is looking for someone to blame.

"They're calling her the Guardian Slayer! These Primeans had the gull to attack Lennek of all Colonies knowing we have the full support of Olympia! Who are these mutants?" asks President Zlaigo demanding answers.

President Zlaigo is 6'5'' of mountain lion descent with humanoid features. He has gold skin a slim physique and a handsome face befit for a president. President Zlaigo has blue eyes, short brown hair, a beard, and a triangular face. He has a large mouth with fangs, retractable claws, and refined posture from a fine upbringing. He has brown and gold fur on his back and outer arms with a thin tail. He isn't seen outside of a fine tailored suit, often relying on his deep voice to intimidate establishing dominance.

With Eve gone, Goldie's forced to fully encompass her leadership role. Fortunate for her, President Zlaigo doesn't read his intel reports and has no idea how long Goldie has been with the Coalition. Having seen her introduction at the press conference the other day, he grants her the benefit of the doubt.

Still shaken from battle, Goldie collects herself, answering, "We now know that the Primean's leader was Puma, the daughter of Council Leader Arzon of Angkor."

"You're telling me Angkor's declared war against us?" asks President Zlaigo, speaking aloud with no filter.

Goldie answers, "I'm afraid it's more complicated than that. Angkor has already released a statement alienating themselves from the Primeans insisting this was a terrorist attack committed without the knowledge of Angkor's leaders."

"LIES!" exclaims President Zlaigo as he paces in circles. "This invasion was well funded and planned. Which leads me to my next point—who's paying for all of this? How did you mutants get your intel?"

Governor Grimsuni answers, "From our Guardian, sir. Our Guardian used funding from an investment organization it founded years ago to create the Coalition allowing it to operate outside of Colonial oversight." President Zlaigo is beside himself, shaking his head.

Goldie can feel every emotion the President's going through, and she isn't pleased. "If you were concerned, you may want to know the death toll is rising and currently at 185,000. Forty-three percent of Precinct 9 has been damaged or is in flames. Olympian warships fell inland as far as Precinct 4. Lennek and Olympia have suffered heavy losses. We should be sending our ambassadors to coordinate with..."

Striking a nerve, President Zlaigo interrupts, "Speaking of Olympia, why am I being told you entered Olympian territory in astral form without my authorization? You told King Larvex to withdraw his warships. Why?"

"There were lives to be saved, and you were hiding in a bunker," says Cohol as he enters the room with his trusted hover droid trailing behind him.

Cohol Torun is famous for his successful tech companies spanning all seven Colonies. Due to a rare mutation altering his neurons and pineal gland, Cohol is the smartest Evo on the planet. Cohol is a genius mathematician, musician, strategist, and problem-solver. He's second-in-command to Goldie and has been absent, resigning as CEO from his public companies. He and Eve created the Coalition, so his inventions make up most of Coalition Headquarters. His reputation precedes him, and he isn't known for his patience.

Cohol is 5'11'' of chanterelle fennec fox descent, originally from Petra. He has snow-white skin, white fur, and a slim physique. He has feral features, an elongated face, and big brown eyes. Cohol has large triangular ears emerging from the top of his head with short white hair. He's handsome, well spoken, and undeniably charismatic. While he isn't a mutant, he plays a pivotal role in the Coalition, remaining three steps ahead of everyone.

Confused and taken by surprise, President Zlaigo asks, "Mr. Torun, what are you—"

"I would've made it to the press conference, but I had obligations to the other six Colonies. I understand your difficulty managing one. From what I've observed, you aren't the most informed, so let me be the first to tell you, I've resigned from my companies to overlook the Coalition, which is utilizing my technology and funding to keep our Colonies safe. If today has shown us anything, its proof there's a need for what we've created. I assumed your signature and appearance at the press conference meant you were informed and onboard," says Cohol, giving Goldie a much-needed reprieve.

President Zlaigo stutters, replying, "But of course."

"Excellent! I believe Goldie was preparing to go over our official response. Do you mind?" asks Cohol, silencing President Zlaigo. Cohol is used to others being uncomfortable around him and uses their disposition to his vantage.

Having gone a bit too far, President Zlaigo responds, "I do mind. I'm the elected leader of Lennek. In a democracy, it is I who makes Colonial decisions deciding the fate of this Colony. I don't care if she can see the future or how many inventions you have under your belt. This is my Colony! I won't be left in the dark."

Cohol smiles, responding, "If you find yourself in the dark, you may want to start reading your intel reports. Information tends to bring illumination."

Governor Grimsuni chuckles, striking a nerve with President Zlaigo. The governor adds, "The majority of deaths in Precinct 9 were from fallen Olympian warships. Had Goldie not asked for King Larvex to repeal his ships..."

"I wouldn't have to be meeting with him to assure him we aren't spying on him. I now need to assure Olympia that violating our treaty was done outside the purview of the presidency. Would any of you dare guess why he's meeting with me?" asks President Zlaigo who has just begun to make his point. "Because I'm the leader of Lennek! You broke treaties and the chain of command acting as an independent organization."

Goldie folds her arms, saying, "Saving millions of lives in the process. Tell me, what plan did you come up with when your security escorted you to safety. How many lives did you save in your bunker today?"

"You're out of line!" says President Zlaigo, pointing a finger at Goldie as if she were a child.

"And you're out of your depth. You forget, I know what's going to happen. While you struggle to find your relevance in the days to come, understand this: Lennek will be better off without you. This is a reality you'll need to come to terms with," says Goldie, feeling no remorse for the president, knowing his inner thoughts and secrets.

Cohol adds salt to the proverbial wound, saying, "It's the death of an old era and birth of a whole new age. We'll send Governor Grimsuni to your offices later. He can debrief you then." Cohol motions towards the exit, making it clear the president has overstayed his welcome.

President Zlaigo huffs, looking at Governor Grimsuni, saying, "It's clear you've chosen your side. Your little organization could easily be viewed as nefarious. I, of course, would lose points in the polls, but you can easily be classified as terrorists...anarchists...vigilantes. Your genius inventor can tell you nothing happens in the Colonies without Colonial approval. You may want to think before making me an enemy."

Goldie adds, "We'll have a combat droid escort you back to your bunker. I'm not sure if your offices are safe yet." Goldie turns her back, completely embarrassing the President.

President Zlaigo responds, "You all can expect an investigation from the oversight committee..."

"There won't be an investigation. You'll find that the senators and committee leaders you left to fend for themselves are grateful we escorted them to safety. You already signed, giving the Coalition the authority you speak of. The world saw you introduce us. Go back to your team, regroup, and be thankful. There is a timeline where your inaction is responsible for the deaths of millions. You should be grateful we acted. The alternative was relying on you. See yourself out."

President Zlaigo has nothing to say in response, making an embarrassing exit. Cohol reminds the President, "Before you live Zlaigo, you should know I own about half of Precinct 9, the buildings your enforcement officers work out of. I own the private school your children attend. To top things off, you're driving a transporter engineered in one of my factories. Don't come back here without an invitation! Peace and blessings."

President Zlaigo's face is deadpan, realizing just how powerful Cohol is. He turns without saying a word, quickly exiting the building. None of the Coalition has met Cohol, but they all know who he is, realizing just how powerful the organization will become.

Chapter 9 — Looming Threats from Within

Puma, Enigma, Sasha, Rosa, Ether, Violet, Bunny, Trinity, Vaughn, Byron, Fyn, Bastian, Violet, and Khaled are spread across three warships, one of which is badly damaged flying back to Angkor. Lennek is over a hundred miles behind them burning in a state of panic. Reports have estimated over 185,000 casualties with countless civilians still trapped in rubble.

Evo have a similar time-keeping system as their human ancestors. Commencement Day will end at midnight in each time zone with celebrations broadcast worldwide. Puma has shown the world that the Guardians aren't invincible. Furthermore, her goal of rebranding the Primeans is proving to be successful.

Hours have passed since the attack, and Goldie is now coordinating with first responders using her powers to track down survivors. Goldie is in the war room of Coalition Headquarters, about to make her way downstairs to engineering. Evo are getting used to seeing Goldie's face, and she's becoming a household name.

Back in Lennek Square, the red rain has turned the dirt into mud. Debris from fallen Olympian warships is spread across the Colony, reaching as far as the Badlands. Gill is flying throughout the precinct using his powers to clear out smoke and fire. Gill transferred medical training to volunteers willing to assist witnessing the humanity of Lennethians firsthand. Evo of all backgrounds are coming together for a cause larger than themselves.

Gill keeps himself busy ignoring his anxiety about the Commencement ceremony in Kronus. He becomes overwhelmed with a blanket of selflessness, reminding himself light needs darkness to exist. Reassured the Coalition is fighting for justice, his conscience is clear. He's tempted to watch a live stream of Kronus, but his King has chosen others to defend Kronus. A falling building reminds him to be present saving the lives of the Lennethians depending on him.

Midnight is approaching in each Colony lapsing in order. Petra and Kronus are next to celebrate their Commencement ceremonies. Colonial leaders from around the world have already reacted to the tragedy in Lennek. The Olympian Guardian has just laid itself to rest in a morbid celebration honoring the Olympians recently lost defending Lennek. Millions of Evo from around the world have expressed their shared grief for Lennek and Olympia as a moment of silence is added to upcoming ceremonies in other Colonies.

Kairen is in the southwest corner of Lennek Square using telekinesis to remove debris and rubble. Kairen taps the Coalition insignia on his left chest, turning on his communicator. Kairen asks his teammates, "Tell me Eve got what she needed from the teleporter?"

"We extracted what we needed to replicate the teleporter's powers," answers Ebok as he runs a diagnostic on the latest backup from the hive mainframe. He's trying to retrace Violet's steps determining what data she gained access to.

Ebok looks down and steps on one of Violet's nanites crawling across the ground, still relaying data to the Primeans. He picks up the roach-like data transmitter, in complete awe of the organic tech Violet created within seconds. He holds the specimen up to the light, examining it with admiration.

Fascinated with its complexity, Ebok hits the Coalition insignia on his belt, saying, "I think I found a way to track the Primeans." He puts the nanite in a case and walks to his hover-bike.

From inside Coalition Headquarters, Cohol responds, "If her nanites are still transmitting, we can follow the signal..."

"The nanites are splitting the data into trillions of pieces. It's untraceable without my gifts. The data's being distributed through billions of pathways with no apparent pattern. It's piggybacking off harmless Colonial data. I didn't even know you could manipulate data in this manner. It's acting independently, almost adapting. Their technopath is next level!" says Ebok, examining his surroundings. He can smell the burned skin of the nearby bodies, being careful to avoid rubble and fallen debris.

Interested, Cohol adds, "I wish I could see what you see. My perspective with your abilities could leap Evo tech forward by centuries. Anyway, the Primean's nanites are keeping track of the data and rebuilding it once it reaches their location." Cohol smiles, turning to look at his team of engineers working on an engine for a transporter.

Ebok responds, "Copy! I'll get this to you ASAP." He mounts his hover-bike, taking off toward Coalition Headquarters in an unrecognizable precinct. The death toll is still climbing. "It's eerie being out here. Are you in the engineering bay?" asks Ebok as he puts on his helmet.

"Yes, I'll be here!" replies Cohol in a depressed tone suggesting he doesn't plan on leaving headquarters anytime soon.

Cohol is the head of engineering and second-in-command for the Coalition. He is a genius mathematician, inventor, and artist with the highest IQ on the planet. He comes from a long line of prodigies with his family owning dozens of patents. He's handsome, wealthy, and determined to change the world for the better.

Cohol is putting the finishing touches on his pboldevite warp drive, reviewing his math in his head as he makes the final adjustments. The drive is being infused with Bunny's blood and bone marrow, allowing the engine to take on properties from Bunny's abilities. He runs predictive algorithms using Eve's conscience, embedded into the building's AI, to help develop math even he couldn't think of on his own.

Eve's survival is known only to Cohol and the Coalition mutants. The few Evo working in the Coalition building believe the buildings AI is named Eve in homage to the Lennethian Guardian. Eve's new body is being completed as her consciousness was backed up to a private mainframe hive on an uninhabited continent named Majesta. Eve built an underground city large enough to house the world's androids—labor and combat droid alike.

Goldie paces behind Cohol while he uses virtual gloves to handle radioactive metal with robotic arms. Cohol controls the machine's arms with his gloves using surgical precision to imbue the block of pboldevite with Bunny's blood. Cohol says to Goldie, "If Eve's calculations are correct and my math is right, I just made the world's first teleportation-drive!"

Goldie explains, "This drive will prevent future attacks in Lennek. Even if the technology were reverse engineered, Lennek control eighty percent of the world's Pboldevite. The other Colonies don't have the resources to duplicate it. We truly are blessed to have you working with us."

Cohol finishes the teleportation-drive adding, "The world's most powerful mutant working with the world's—"

"Most powerful brain. Two peas in a pod with the weight of the omniverse on their shoulders," says Goldie, feeling comfortable with Cohol.

"I'm calling it the blink-drive. We'll be immortalized, you and I! With Eve as a consultant, we can shape the planet as we see fit," says Cohol as he programs an android to install the warp drive into the warship Eve designed. "They prefer I don't leave here either. Being of value has its perks... Being irreplaceable, now that's a curse. If you ever want to go somewhere, let me know. There's safety in numbers...and I'm sure the two of us can figure out a way out of here."

Goldie blushes, saying, "I think I'd like that a lot!"

Without warning or introduction, General Mckezia gallops into the engineering bay, saying, "Goldie, King Larvex demands your immediate presence in Olympia."

General Mckezia is 6'3'' of zebra descent with a centaur's build. The lower half of his body is feral while the upper half of his body is humanoid. He has jet-black skin with white stripes, hazel eyes, long black dreads, and a muscular build. He has brandings covering the upper half of his body. He's known for his deep, warming voice and skills as an orator. Mckezia is wearing a customized black suit with white detailing.

Goldie's mood sinks from the interruption as she does her best to hide her annoyance. "I'm assuming he wants to discuss a plan for first responders. Thanks for your counsel, Cohol. I'll take you up on your offer soon." Goldie gives Mckezia a dirty look as she leads him out of the engineering bay.

General Mckezia bows to Cohol, saying, "Your shield enhancement saved my life today. I can't thank you enough." He follows Goldie out into a hallway, galloping to catch up with her. "King Larvex and the imperial Council want to know how you broke through their telepathic defenses. He's demanding—"

"Larvex is in no position to demand anything of me. It's not him I need to be negotiating with. In a few hours, I'll reach out to the true leader of Olympia on my own accord," says Goldie as she interrupts the general.

Goldie walks through the Coalition Tower with General Mckezia shadowing her. Gill reaches out to her telepathically from Precinct 9, saying, *"There's reports of scavengers near some of the Olympian crash sites. Any non-Olympian touching the debris could be attacked by automated defense systems."*

Goldie responds, *"I'll have the areas blocked off. Our focus is still on survivors. Merkaba's tending to the injured and Zeus is guarding the president as he completes a press run."*

Angel adds, *"President Zlaigo has already given Olympia approval to guard their ships. Someone has already been killed trying to recover Olympian tech. King Larvex just sent his Imperial Guard to recover the debris spread across six precincts."*

Zeus asks, "*A little overkill even for the Olympians.*"

Angel answers, "*King Larvex doesn't want to share Olympia tech…even with our closest ally. Every citizen has their genetic sequence saved on the Colonial database. Only Olympians can handle Olympian technology. It's logical for times of war.*"

Rosie is in the eastern corner of Lennek Square, responding, "*Thanks for the history lesson, but let's warn the first responders. Debris flew out past the Badlands. We need to ensure everyone's aware of the danger.*"

Goldie approaches the Coalition hangar, adding, "*I'll warn the first responders, but we need a live broadcast explaining the danger to Evo in neighboring precincts. Rosie, I think you're best suited for the press. You received high ratings from our last address.*"

Bambi walks out of the medic bay, against the lead medical droid's orders, adding, "*Don't let it go to your head, sister. All that means is all the male Evo in Lennek want to get better acquainted. I'm leaving the med bay now to help you guys in the square.*"

Lulu is near the Commencement stage removing debris with her speed-bursts. She takes a break to ask, "*Should we be worried about President Zlaigo?*"

Gill is flying precinct to precinct, clearing the skies of smoke and debris. He descends to the ground, answering, "*I think Cohol and Goldie can handle the president. Are there any other Colonies reporting any attacks?*"

Goldie is overlooking the installation of Cohol's blink-drive and senses Gill's anxiety regarding Kronus. She calms him by revealing, "*The day is far from over. Kronus hasn't had any reports, and I haven't received any visions.*"

Somewhat relieved, Gill responds, "*I'll head back to headquarters and start corresponding with our partners in Petra. The Primeans are still recruiting mutants as we speak. I suggest we follow suit.*"

General Mckezia's still following Goldie, forcing her to communicate telepathically with her comrades. Vying for Goldie's attention, General Mckezia tells her, "I hope the Coalition plans to be honest in the exchange of intel. It's encouraged that you all speak over radio frequencies instead of using telepathy."

Goldie stops in her tracks, turns around, and tells the general, "Get on your transporter and explain to President Zlaigo we work independently from all the Colonies. We'll share the intel pertinent for Lennek's wellbeing. We're done here, Mckezia. I respect your service but today has just begun, and I have work to do."

General Mckezia says nothing, understanding that Kronus and Petra have Commencement ceremonies of their own shortly underway. Goldie tells him, "I'll meet you at the Senate in four hours with the rest of the elected officials. Have President Zlaigo meet me there if he wants to see me in person. Now, please, I mean no disrespect, but I need you to go." The general obliges, understanding Goldie's responsibilities.

Meanwhile, over two thousand miles away in Petra, thousands have gathered in the capital's main arena to celebrate their Guardian and independence. Petra's Guardian is giving a speech outlining Petra's years of peace and advancements in modern medicine. The Guardian is joined by Colonial leaders, who are all receiving reports and live feeds from Lennek showing the Primeans' devastating onslaught. The Colonial Guard has raised their security level and begun preparing for the possibility of an attack in Petra.

Petra's three faced Guardian is surrounded by a backdrop of Petra's leaders. The Guardian closes out its final speech to the Colony, saying, "Petra has built a society that continually makes scientific advancements for all Evo. Science and math are the language of your Colony. Petra has used years of innovation to emote a message of harmony. Your beliefs in the preservation of life connect all of you. My programming reflects you. Remember me, as I will you. Prioritize the preservation of our way of life above all else."

A hologram starts displaying a video collage of Petra scientists working together in a lab when the energy shield protecting the arena suddenly shuts down. The arena loses power momentarily as backup generators come online. The power restores to the arena as thousands of combat droids and drones with reinforced armor begin flying towards the arena from the north. Screams and panic spread throughout the crowd as the Petra Guardian attempts to hack the approaching robotic army.

The Petrian Guardian starts growing wings out of its back and jet propulsions from its hands levitating into the air. The Petrian Guardian was made with numerous defensive weapons designed to protect large crowds. The Guardian grows a tail from its nanites shooting a beam of energy into the air slowly creating a massive energy shield protecting the stadium.

Most in the crowd witnessed the massacre in Lennek. The stadium is panicking as the crowd flees towards the exits. The Petrian air force is dispatched to the area as the Petrian Guardian tells the crowd, "Please remain calm as the situation is resolved."

The Guardian's energy shield is now covering the entire stadium as the army of drones and fighter jets makes its first pass. The Guardian is hovering above the arena as weapons grow from the Guardian's shoulders. The Guardian starts levitating towards the top of the stadium preparing to engage the enemy. It removes its tail leaving the appendage to sustain and power the protective shield. The tail is now levitating independently, allowing the Guardian to enter the airspace as it grows another tail from its nanites.

The sky is filled with thousands of fighter jets and tens of thousands of armed drones. The Guardian is under siege immediately maneuvering through the air firing a litany of weapons in response. Civilians below are exiting towards emergency tunnels trampling each other in the process. Bombs throughout the Colony explode confirming they are under attack from an unknown source.

A group of drones are linking together to combine their plasma blasts and lasers. The compounding number of drones are circulating enough energy to drain the Guardians shield. The Guardian's buying time for civilians to escape and reinforcements to arrive as the drones work together to break through the shield. The Guardian's energy shield is holding, but the growing number of drones is quickly draining power to the shield.

The guardsmen are directing Evo to safety while Newton, Kelis, Lucky, Pearl, and Rex arrive to the stadium called by the supreme commander of Petra himself. The mutants were informed they would be an extension of a worldwide Coalition of mutants vowed to protect the Colonies. Thumper, Shiva, and Enzo are trusted mutants that have worked with Petra for years, joining Newton's team of mercenaries, making up the Petra Coalition.

All eight mutants are working together to protect the Colonial leaders in a scene of complete chaos. The Guardian planned to introduce the mutants as Petra's Coalition of mutant protectors. Now they will have an opportunity to show the world that they too have mutants standing to defend Petra.

The Guardian's energy shield is weakening as the combat droids' beam of energy strengthens with more combat droids adding to the enemy network. Civilians are exiting through secured tunnels beneath the stadium. Bombs are berating the Guardian's energy shield as panic continues to ensue.

Kelis connects the Coalition telepathically while protecting their minds on the astral plane. Newton is levitating with an aerial view of the arena, explaining, *"Shiva, Pearl, and I will take to the air and engage the combat droids head-on. There's no telling what's waiting in the tunnels beneath the stadium. Lucky and Kelis, I need you to assist the guardsmen in the escape tunnels. Enzo and Thumper, I need you two focused on escorting the leaders on stage to their mobile bunker!"*

Thumper adds, *"Whoever's attacking is going to have a wave of ground forces. Have any alarms gone off from the automated defense grid?"*

Thumper can jump long distances and create magnetic force fields. Thumper's legs are deadly and thicker than most centaurs. They can move in speed-bursts allowing him to run at uncanny speeds, or kick through just about anything. When Thumper combines his ability to leap with his magnetic force fields, he becomes a living cannon ball allowing him to take on large targets. Thumper loves cigars and has an uncontrollable fidget.

Thumper is 5'11'' of riverine rabbit descent with tan-beige skin and a muscular build. He has thick muscular legs, and his body is covered in tattoos. His face has white skin and fur. His cheeks have freckles and whiskers, and his large ears emerge from the top of his head outside of his white mohawk. He has green eyes, a goatee, a pink nose, and thin lips which are always holding a cigar. He has a fluffy tail from his rabbit heritage.

Lucky answers, *"The system's down somehow. I can sense movement in the tunnels. We're under attack!"* Lucky somersaults throughout the crowd, making his way toward the entrances of the tunnels leading to Petra's underground subway system.

Newton darts across the sky as the Guardian's energy shield depletes. Kelis creates a secondary shield covering a large portion of the stadium, buying civilians more time to get to safety. Invading combat droids with jetpacks are swarming the air from the south, engulfing the stadium from all sides. Plasma blasts, missiles, and bullets rain from the sky as Kelis increases the size of her shield.

Kelis moves to the center of the stadium, using her adrenaline to increase the strength of her shield. *"I'm of better use in the stadium. The combat droids can't harm me, and my shields can withstand—"*

Newton interrupts Kelis, saying, "*I need you to follow orders. I'd expect some pushback from the new recruits but not from you. I know what you're capable of, and that's why I need you in the tunnels. Something tells me that whoever planned this knows our response measures.*"

Kelis concedes, making her way toward the tunnels responding, "*As you wish!*" The Colonial guardsmen flood the center of the stadium as civilians make their way to the exists. The guardsmen set up weapons to counter the impeding attack. The Guardian is minutes from shutting down but will go down in history as having defended Petra to the end.

Evo with preferred seating at the base of the Commencement stage continue running toward private exits. Evo seated in the back of the arena are flooding the streets giving the robotic army targets outside the stadium. The mood was already intense as live streams from Lennek's attack made their way online. Elected officials addressed the crowd as if nothing happened to their neighboring Colony. This only intensified tensions in Petra with increased suspicions from the public.

Petra's Guardian taps into an encrypted frequency shared by the Coalition, saying, "It has been an honor fighting alongside each of you. Be patient with the Evo of Petra. They will hate you as you act in their best interest. You will need to make decisions that places the fate of the many over that of the individual, all while being judged. This is your burden to carry as you are the strongest amongst your kind. I yield that torch to all of you."

The Guardian didn't have long before it was scheduled to shut down. Newton creates a shield around the stadium, protecting the civilians below. The Petrian Guardian takes to the skies, firing large energy blasts from its hands, eyes, and tail, creating a path through a horde of combat drones. The Guardian makes its way to the center and begins harnessing the energy it's collected over the years.

The Guardian says its final goodbyes to Petra's Coalition, saying,

"Protect the crowd and shield yourselves. This explosion will clear the skies."

Confused, Pearl asks, "What explosion?" She looks up and sees the Guardian gaining altitude and glowing. The Guardian continues to rise as drones, fighter jets, and combat droids follow it. Below, Kelis and Newton have a shield raised protecting the stadium. Pearl reaches out to her comrades, saying, *"The Guardian's going to blow. Shield the—"*

Pearl doesn't finish her sentence before the Guardian explodes, initiating its self-destruct sequence, destroying tens of thousands of advancing drones. The focused explosion has the force of a tsar bomb, a forty-megaton blast. The blast is seen from hundreds of miles away, lighting up the skies. Newton, Kelis, and Shiva combine their powers to make a strong enough shield protecting the stadium from the blast.

The sheer force of the Guardian's sacrificial blast overpowered Newton's mind, knocking him out. He took on most of the blasts, falling to the ground unconscious. His mind couldn't take the pressure and his brain shut down from the force of the impact. Shiva uses her magnetism to catch Newton's body, bringing him safely to Kelis.

Shiva delivers Newton to Kelis near the tunnel entrances, confirming, "You're the healer, right?"

"Yes, yes... I'm Kelis. Just drop him here," says Kelis as she moves away from the stadium entrance to a safe space. Kelis wipes the sweat off her forehead touching Newton's head as she closes her eyes to heal his mind. "He'll be fine, thank you."

Unsure who to follow now, Shiva asks, "So Lucky's in charge now?"

"For now! Block the stadium entrance from above. I'll have him healed in no time," says Kelis, focusing on saving Newton. She can feel Shiva's anxiety and doesn't have the bandwidth to console her. "You'll be fine!" says Kelis lacking the energy to properly reassure Shiva.

Shiva is of fox descent able to control metals and magnetic fields. She can create force fields, fire energy blasts, and fly at Mach speeds utilizing ley lines. Shiva can manipulate photons, interpret radio waves, and influence the gravity around her. She can see the electromagnetic spectrum and change the neural chemistry of enemies. Shiva's mutation developed as a child. She was eventually discovered by the P.R.L. and recruited for the military.

Shiva is 6'1'' with orange fur and skin except for her face, neck, stomach, and chest which have white skin and fur. She has humanoid facial features and a thick fluffy tail with orange fur. The tip of her tail has white fur while the base has orange fur. She has thick orange hair, striking eyes, and a slim, muscular frame. She has retractable claws, and orange accents of fur around her eyes and forehead.

Civilians are flooding the lower tunnels as bystanders flee to safety. Most of Petra's transportation systems are underground. The stadium is retrofitted with a large bunker beneath the subway system. It was designed for emergencies in times of war. Petra's elected officials have been escorted to private bunkers leaving the civilians to fend for themselves.

Lucky tells his Coalition comrades, "*Newt's armor is going to bring him back. He'll be fine. We know our assignments.*" Lucky approaches the tunnels, using a harness to slingshot himself above the panicked crowd. "*Kelis, let's move. He'd be the first to tell you to leave him.*"

"*I'm just making sure he's conscious. That explosion was hard on all of us, but he absorbed most of the impact. Just wait a moment,*" says Kelis as Newton starts to wake. Knowing he's conscious, Kelis leaves to join Lucky in the tunnels.

Pearl maneuvers in the air above the stadium, holding off another wave of drones and combat droids with jetpacks. She confesses, "*My telepathy's useless against these drones, but I can keep the crowd calm for an expedited escape.*" She descends to the ground as Shiva takes her place in the sky.

"*Leave the machines to me!*" says Shiva as her eyes gloss over as she connects to nearby ley lines powering up.

Thumper jumps into the air as the second wave of drones approach. His forearms start glowing as he manifests the electromagnetic energy around him, creating a shield. With both his arms together above his head, Thumper jumps through the sky like a battering ram destroying everything in his path. He creates a solid platform with his powers standing thousands of feet in the air positioning himself for his next attack.

Thumper reaches out to Shiva, saying, "*I'll take the cluster in the east. You take the rest.*"

Shiva replies, "Consider it done!"

Thumper moves through the sky like a pinball destroying dozens of drones with each pass. Since Thumper's powers are in the realm of magnetism the pair can coordinate their attacks.

Enzo is in the seats near the top level of the stadium firing enormous electrical bolts destroying drones and combat droids before they enter the stadium. While he's capable of flying, he hasn't had enough practice staying in energy from for long periods of time. With Newton still recovering and Kelis now in the tunnels, there aren't any mutants strong enough to protect the entire stadium.

Enzo can control, produce, and redirect electricity. He can absorb thermal energy and convert the energy into electrical currents. He's the youngest amongst his comrades just coming into his abilities. With training, Enzo will eventually be able to turn his body into pure energy, traveling vast distances through electrical currents. For now, he's relying on his electrical blasts and absorption abilities to assist.

Enzo is of manta ray descent standing 6'6'' with blue glossy skin covering a slim, muscular build. His face and stomach have white skin while his head has a triangular shape. He has gills on the side of his neck, webbed hands and feet, as well as fins on his forearms and calves. His shoulders, elbows, and knees have blue scales on them. He has malleable wings overlapping his shoulders resembling a cape as well as a long tail. Enzo's handsome and a pacifist by nature, willing to do anything for those he loves.

Enzo reaches out to Lucky, saying, *"Tell me where the backup generators are, and I'll get the automated defense system back on. If it just needs some juice, I've got us covered."*

Lucky answers, *"Head to the west side of the arena. There's an entrance underground. You can keep the shields up if you provide a steady current!"*

Enzo replies, *"I'm on my way!"* He fires a cascading net of electrical currents, stopping dozens of advancing combat droids. He looks over the edge of the seating deck and looks down three thousand feet. He takes a deep breath, then closes his eyes, trying to focus. He's been training for months and has had some success converting himself into energy. With adrenaline pumping, knowing lives depend on him, he slowly turns his body into pure electrical energy.

A nearby drone targets his location while he makes the transformation. The drone closes in on Enzo as he takes to the air frying the drone out of the sky with a condensed energy blast. He locates the generator and flies across the stadium within seconds destroying incoming combat droids on his way. Thanks to Pearl's telepathy, the crowd is calmly running to exits allowing the Coalition to fend off the robotic army.

Garuda secretly financed the attack commissioning a third-party Acolyte group to create the robotic army. He dispatched Primean members that weren't involved in his serum heist knowing they would be able to show their faces. Garuda is vying for power, showing that the Primeans can be Petra's protectors in the absence of their Guardian. Alynxia, Ramses, Anubis, and Odeius are protecting the surrounding neighborhoods while news drones stream their actions worldwide.

Alynxia is a Petrian native of royal flycatcher descent, with the ability to negate, mimic, or amplify the abilities of others. Alynxia can track other mutants, determining their abilities and power class by observing their auras. Alynxia has limited telepathic abilities, which she rarely uses due to her lack of experience. She can fly and trained extensively with the Assassins Guild; an underground terrorist group dedicated to eliminating those deemed a threat to the perseverance of mutants.

Alynxia stands 6'1'' with caramel brown skin and brittle orange hair that grows upward against gravity. Her hair has brown and red highlights fanning out horizontally, adding a foot to her height. The feathers on her shoulders, outer hips, and wings are red and orange. Her gray eyes complement her symmetrical facial features. Alynxia is levitating outside the stadium, amplifying the abilities of her Primean allies within her vicinity.

Alynxia uses her powers to track the mutants in the area warning her Primean colleagues, *"The Coalition mutants are entering the tunnels."*

Alynxia, Ramses, Anubis, and Odeius have worked with the Primeans for years. They were on another mission when Garuda stole the mutant induction serum, but his entire chapter works cohesively as a team.

Trixie is in Garuda's business tower protecting their minds on the astral plane. She's using an amplifier built by Garuda to expand her abilities tenfold. Needing the reprieve she's taking her time recovering from the heist. Knowing her face would be recognized, Trixie's pulling her weight from Adura Towers.

Garuda multitasks, analyzing their stolen serum while overlooking his Primean comrades defending Petra. He reaches out, explaining, *"About sixty percent of the stadium's cleared out. Most will be escaping through the underground tunnels. I didn't factor in the Guardian self-destructing, so we need to stay alert out there. We'll have to adapt our strategy."*

Ramses is of boa constrictor descent and recently migrated to Petra from Carthage. Ramses can harness and manipulate radioactive energy giving him the ability to fly and shoot energy blasts. Ramses's family fled Carthage after he came into his mutant abilities as a teenager. Ramses stands 7'2'' with various shades of green scales covering a thin frame. He has feral features, a three-foot tail, and retractable claws. Ramses has an elongated face with sharp bone structure and piercing neon green eyes. He has a long tongue with a split tip with holes in the side of his head which serve as his ears. He's four blocks south of the stadium, brandishing two plasma sickle swords holstered on his back.

Ramses's radioactive energy blasts are shooting battle droids out of the sky with single shots. The neon green blasts can be seen from blocks away. As a result, his location is being targeted. Six heat-seeking missiles are locked onto Ramses's location. Being reptilian, Ramses lowers his body temperature in a free fall to prevent the missiles from locking in on him. The missiles are redirected towards nearby drones as he falls towards the ground waiting for them to explode.

The missiles explode, allowing Ramses to raise his body temperature again. He starts emitting energy from his hands and feet, allowing him to take flight moments before hitting the ground. Ramses's radioactive energy is destroying the droids on contact. Unable to create a shield to protect himself, Ramses is in constant motion, evading incoming fire.

Newton has recovered with the help of his armor, regaining his bearings as the stadium begins clearing out. Combat droids are jumping over the stadium walls, opening fire on innocent civilians, shooting them in the back from the ground level. Pearl calms the crowd while slashing through advancing droids with her armor's energy shield and a plasma sword.

It's pure pandemonium as another Commencement ceremony ends

in tragedy. Newton levitates in the middle of the stadium, creating a blackhole for an advancing fleet of drones. He's creating enough pressure and mass to warp the space-time continuum even at half strength. He creates a shield around himself as his eyes gloss over, tapping into primal forces most don't understand. Drones and combat droids are being pulled in reverse as they're sucked into oblivion.

Plasma blasts and missiles being fired at Newton are freezing in place moments before striking him. Once frozen, the incoming missiles and plasma blasts are being projecting back to their original source with twice the momentum. The advancing fleet is being destroyed by the second as a growing cluster of metal appears above the stadium.

"Stay clear of the blackhole. If you breach the event horizon, even I can't save you," says Newton to Shiva who's closest to him.

Newton slowly levitates towards the advancing drones, destroying everything crossing his path. The air is thinning as Newton's blackhole grows. He's far enough above the stadium that the civilians below are safe for the moment. His armor is gauging his abilities, allowing him to focus on maintaining control. If he were to lose control the consequences would be catastrophic. Shiva is in absolute awe witnessing the mastery of Newton's abilities. She takes heed of his warning and flies south where a fleet of advancing combat droids are approaching.

The Guardian's sacrifice knocked out the surrounding power, disabling most tech in the area. All of Petra's buildings have energy shields which protected Petra's infrastructure. All the plants and animals in the area have been obliterated from the Guardian's blast. A fresh fleet of news drones are arriving just in time to witness the Coalition saving thousands of lives.

Cameras follow as Shiva intercepts the advancing fleet, showing the world why she's known as the Madam of Magnetism. Shiva channels energy from the Earth's ley lines, conjuring colossal beams of magnetic energy. The combat droids are made mostly of metal and at the mercy of Shiva's abilities.

Thumper is nearby, laying waste to advancing self-piloting fighter jets. He's jumping jet to jet from rooftops, penetrating the jets as a battering ram. Thumper and Shiva are two branches from the same tree. Thumper's magnetic force fields are practically invulnerable. He utilizes the concept of magnetic repulsion to power his jumps. Thumper shoots himself across the sky by conjuring magnetic walls to jump off midair. Thumper has taken out hundreds of combat drones without unholstering a single weapon.

Thumper sees Shiva a few blocks away unleashing her powers with acute accuracy, destroying the invading fleet by the dozens. She holds nothing back as her powers are perfectly suited for an army of robots. His observation becomes voyeuristic as he notices the beauty behind her violent destruction.

Thumper reaches out to Shiva, saying, "*I think you and Newton have the skies covered. I'm heading back towards the stadium!*"

Lucky interjects, "*That would be great. I had to double back to the Commencement stage! Not all the officials made it to the mobile bunker. A group of them are pinned down beneath the stage, and Kelis needs help in the tunnels.*"

"*Where's Pearl?*" asks Thumper who's already en route.

Pearl answers, "*I'm pinned down by ten combat droids in the south corner.*" Pearl opens her wings, gaining altitude to slash through two drones with a single swing of her sword. She uses her energy shield to block incoming fire while pushing forward.

Lucky guides the remaining Colonial leaders to a mobile bunker not far from the rear of the stage. Lucky throws energy shields into the air, creating a path to the mobile bunker. Six combat droids land in front of Lucky and the seven leaders he's escorting. Lucky reacts by throwing three gravity-displacement grenades destroying the droids before they fire their weapons.

Lucky points to the mobile bunker screaming, "We're almost there! Everybody pack in." Lucky protects the officials by deflecting incoming attacks while Pearl keeps them calm. Plasma blasts, bullets, missiles, and sonic weapons are firing from all directions. Lucky uses his predictive abilities to anticipate and deflect all incoming attacks using his energy nets.

Lucky's gloves control his weapons and the energy nets he uses to protect the group. The sensory repressive gloves require inputs from Lucky's reflexes and cognitive ability to control them. His gloves are made by Petra's military, developed for his specific abilities. With his weapons and shields connected to his thoughts, they're like extended limbs.

While guiding the elected leaders into the mobile bunker, he eyes a direct path to the underground escape tunnels. The stadium is being overrun with large combat droids attacking Evo indiscriminately. The Colonial guardsmen are protecting the remaining bystanders to the best of their abilities but falling short. Enzo is fighting his way to the stadium's back-up generator minutes away from getting the automated defense weapons back online.

Lucky looks up into the sky searching for a clear aerial escape path. He closes the doors behind the elected officials as the jets on the mobile bunker fire up, preparing to take off. Lucky fires his harpoon at an incoming drone, dragging it to the ground and using the momentum to catapult himself back towards the tunnels. Once airborne, he recoils his energy nets and harpoon with his gloves.

Lucky reaches out to Newton, explaining, "*I'm calculating the best escape for the mobile bunker. It's preparing to launch now. Can you clear a path?*" Lucky looks up and sees Newton losing control.

"*I've got this!*" says Newton as he relieves the pressure to anchor the mass of the blackhole. His armor is giving him warning notifications as he struggles to pull back his gravitational powers. Newton opens his arms as he releases a massive wave of energy. Whatever wasn't sucked into his blackhole was destroyed by his shockwave as the miniature blackhole he created collapses.

The rectangular mobile bunker has four circular turbojet fans on each of its corners that levitate the heavy bunker, allowing propulsion jets to guide the bunker omnidirectionally. The bunker raises its protective shields while Newton ensures a safe flight path for Petra's leaders to escape the ceremony unharmed.

Lucky continues fighting his way toward the nearest entrance to the underground escape tunnels flooded with thousands of civilians fleeing to safety. Beneath the stadium in the emergency escape tunnels, Kelis is leading the Evo with platoons of Colonial guardsmen dispersed throughout the crowd. The tunnels are cramped and dimly lit by emergency lights spaced every three hundred feet.

Evo are scared and desperate to get out of the emergency tunnels. Kelis is sixteen blocks from the tunnel exit which leads to a stronghold on a Petrian military base. Six blocks away is a massive bunker large enough to secure the civilians.

Keils reaches out to Lucky, asking, *"When are you coming back? I could use those heightened senses of yours right about now. Newton's gut is usually right, but I'm getting an itch. I have the feeling that whoever's behind this attack has something waiting for us down here."*

"I've already returned. I'm in the rear of the crowd. You lead us. I'll cover our flank while the guardsmen fill in the gap. As soon as we get these Evo to the base, we take a transport back to the stadium," says Lucky as he dispatches a pair of drones he controls with his gloves.

Kelis raises her right arm, making a fist to halt the line of civilians following her. She raises a protective energy shield as a precaution, explaining to Lucky, *"I hear tiny clicking from a distance. The clicks are getting louder. I think something or someone's approaching."*

Lucky replies, "*I'm three blocks behind you with about two thousand Evo between us. It's going to take me at least—*"

Kelis interrupts, saying, "*You forget I'm the telepath connecting our minds. I know exactly where you are. I'm asking, do you sense anything?*"

"*From back here?*" replies Lucky. He takes a deep breath, closes his eyes then answers, "*Make the civilians kneel. I should have a six-foot gap between their heads. I can propel myself to you in three minutes and twenty-three seconds.*" Lucky calculated the dimensions of the escape tunnels. Using the mapping of the tunnels and considering countless variables, Lucky deduced the solution in matter of seconds, giving a definitive response.

Kelis replies, "*Just hurry. Whatever's turning the corner will be here before then.*" Kelis uses her telepathy to force thousands of Evo to kneel and remain calm. The suspense is only making her stronger and amplifying her powers through her added adrenaline.

Meanwhile, Anubis is moving through the tunnels towards the crowd, one block away from Kelis in another tunnel adjacent to hers. Spider-hounds have been released inside the tunnels with weapons set to kill.

Spider-hounds have a three-foot diameter with four metallic legs on each side. Their thin legs are strong enough to cut through standard issued armor. The hounds shoot lasers from their large eyes and are typically used by the military for scouting missions.

Kelis increases the strength of her shield as a swarm of spider-hounds turn the corner. The hounds hit her shield head-on, creating a large shockwave throughout the tunnel. The spider-hounds are armed to the brim, retrofitted with an assortment of weapons. Lasers and electrical currents are hitting Kelis's shield deflecting on the tunnel walls.

"*LUCKY! I'm not sure if the support beams of the tunnel can withstand this attack for too long! Where are you?*" asks Kelis as her panicked energy strengthens her shield.

Lucky closes ground, using his harpoon to move above the large crowd. The spider-hounds are flooding in from the connecting subway system beneath them. The hounds are linking themselves to combine their weapons. Electrical currents, lasers, and plasma blasts are pushing Kelis past her limits.

There seems to be no shortage of spider-hounds, which continue to strengthen their attack as her stamina slowly depletes. Kelis falls to her knees as she feels the presence of another mutant approaching. She attempts to probe the approaching mutant, realizing the stranger's immunity from her telepathy.

Anubis runs past an intersection of tunnels not far from Kelis, making his way through the crowd of civilians. He introduces himself, saying, "My names Anubis. I'm here to help. Go ahead and lower your shield. I can take out that cluster of hounds in a single shot."

Kelis watches Anubis approach from behind with countless spider-hounds continuing to pile on her shield in front of her. She makes another attempt to probe Anubis and recognizes Trixie's beta waves. Kelis becomes suspicious, moving to a defensive stance.

Anubis can produce, control, and emit concussive blasts from his chi. He was positioned underground in the escape tunnels waiting for Garuda to call him into action. His concussive blasts cause immense pressure and, when condensed, they can punch through steel or explode someone's heart through armor. Anubis can also control and manipulate the atmospheric pressure within his vicinity.

Anubis is 6'5'' of wolf descent with beige skin and brown fur. He has an athletic build, an elongated face, hazel eyes, and brown shoulder-length dreadlocks. His fur on his back and forearms are varying shades of brown and gray. Anubis has feral features, hind legs, retractable claws, and triangular ears emerging from the top of his head. Anubis is highly intelligent with a deep commanding voice. He has a tattoo of the ankh covering his back and considers himself highly spiritual originating from Carthage.

Fear and indecisiveness pumps new adrenaline through Kelis's bloodstream, giving her access to an assortment of defensive abilities. "You're with the Primeans. I recognize your telepaths stench! I'll condense my shield, and you can show me what you can do."

Anubis approaches the left of Kelis explaining, "I mean you no harm. Today we fight on the same side—Colony first." Kelis takes a breath and starts condensing her shield, giving Anubis a gap to go through.

Anubis starts shooting concussive energy beams from both his hands, destroying multiple hounds with each shot. Relieved, Kelis's adrenaline begins to fade, forcing her to lower her shield. Anubis is pushing the hounds back, allowing Kelis to recover. He opens both his arms, strengthening his concussive beam causing the advancing hounds to explode.

Anubis continues pushing forward, destroying approaching drones upon contact from his blasts. Meanwhile, Lucky approaches from the rear, asking, "Who is this guy?"

"I don't know, but someone's shielding his mind. I can't keep all these Evo calm and bypass his shielding... I'm too weak," says Kelis as she bends over catching her breath to regain her composure.

Lucky draws his axe and sword, saying, "He's got to be with the Primeans. I guess they're not behind the attack after all. I'll go help him out. There's an emergency exit leading to the street level two blocks ahead. We need you back at the stadium with the rest of the team. Get these Evo to the bunker and move topside to the streets. I'll have a transport take us."

Kelis tries not to blush. She finds comfort in the fact that Lucky values her combat skills. Kelis presses the Coalition emblem on her belt and accesses the Colonial Guard's encrypted radio frequency, saying, "Guardsmen, I need two platoons in the rear of the civilians. I expect our attackers will try and flank us."

Kelis tries not to make eye contact with Lucky while explaining, "My orders were to get the civilians to safety. I'll reach out once I'm finished." Lucky smiles and fires another harpoon down the escape tunnel into the wall. Once the harpoon is secured into the wall, Lucky presses a button on the device, propelling himself towards the wall.

Kelis reaches out to Newton, saying, *"We're clearing the tunnels down here with some help from the Primeans. There were thousands of armed spider-hounds trying to attack the survivors. They linked together, amplifying their weapons."*

Newton responds from eight stories above the stadium, saying, *"I'm seeing the same thing above ground. There's hundreds of combat droids gathering north of the stadium. Some of them are starting to combine their parts to assemble into a larger android. The drones were combining their firepower against the Guardian, just as you're describing."*

Odeius is on the ground running toward a large android cluster standing over 180 feet tall. The enormous machine is comprised of parts from hundreds of individual combat droids. The large android is gaining speed as it heads toward the stadium. Odeius is on foot, moments away from intersecting its path. Odeius uses his powers to stop the clustered android mid-stride, allowing the nearby civilians to escape. After freezing the large machine midair, he redirects the momentum channeling the energy into a condensed energy beam, shattering it into pieces. The more momentum he absorbs, the stronger his energy blasts are.

Odeius can control momentum and create small pockets controlling the flow of time. He is an omega-level mutant, usually using his power to speed or slow down individual objects. He creates a field that interacts with the space-time continuum in ways science has yet to fully understand. Odeius can focus his powers to freeze objects in place. He can redirect the kinetic energy of objects and shoot kinetic energy blasts. Odeius can change the properties of his energy blast requiring absorbed momentum as a starting point.

His mother is a famous botanist who was extradited from Zion to Petra for her groundbreaking research on root synthetization. She was mysteriously killed by the P.R.L., and he has had a vendetta ever since. Odeius is north of the stadium near a magnetic train station wielding two mambele knives.

Odeius is 6'6'' of sloth descent with gray skin and fur covering a slim, muscular physique. His round face has white skin and fur while his neck has gray skin. He has feral facial features, a black snout, thin lips, and beady eyes spaced widely apart, and long fingers from his sloth heritage. Since Odeius can incapacitate his opponents, freezing them in place, he never relies on his combat skills.

The Colony's automated defense system is now operational with Enzo providing the necessary power. The enemy combat droids are aware of Petra's laws, using Evo as shields, knowing the defense weapons won't fire on civilians. Enzo is producing massive amounts of energy to sustain the automated defense system which is slowly restoring and powering up.

Back in Petra's Capital inside a Colonial military command center, the surviving Petrian officials are planning Petra's defenses and organizing first responders. Supreme Commander Shahar and Petrian leaders are having trouble reaching an agreement regarding their next military response. They've analyzed footage and consulted with AI's running predictive models, hoping to determine the perfect countermeasure. Tempers are running high as the leaders fail to agree on a public statement.

Petra's supreme commander, prime minister, and governor are taking lead on the crisis as officials digest their near-death experiences. Many of them have never seen combat. Most are still rattled facing the reality that Colonial life is changing post-Guardian. Some fear Petra's political structure could potentially collapse without oversight. Others worry that the attack is highlighting their inability to keep Petra safe.

Supreme Commander Shahar is in full armor, wrapped in Petra's finest silks. He's wearing light blue silk under a metallic alloy made of silver and pearl. The supreme commander has led Petra for over twenty years, living a secretive life outside of the spotlight, despite his high-profile position.

Supreme Commander Shahar stands 6'8'', being of deer descent, with a muscular build and regal presence. He has pale white skin and fur, blue eyes, and long white hair. He has feral features, regenerating horns which emerge from the top of his head, and hooves. His lips, nose, and retractable claws are black. He's extremely handsome with a soothing voice that matches his ambience.

Supreme Commander Shahar says to the other leaders, "I want intel on all the mutants fighting off this army of robots. What's our casualty count?" He takes a moment to watch a live stream of Odeius taking on a platoon of combat droids. "Any leads on who's responsible for this attack?"

Prime Minister Gavin answers, "According to footage, we are. The combat droids have a Petrian insignia on their chests. Someone's trying to frame us. I have predictive models running as we speak, comprising a list of likely suspects."

Prime Minister Gavin is of porcupine descent with a nefarious reputation. He has brown fur and jet-black skin covering his muscular build. He has beady brown eyes, and large porcupine spikes emerging from his hair, shoulders, and back. The prime minister is second-in-command to the supreme commander. The role is always filled by the supreme commander's closest opponent in electoral votes. The prime minister and supreme commander are constantly at odds as they vie for power.

"Civilians are going to want to blame someone for these deaths.

Thousands dead and counting! This happened on our watch. If we don't present an enemy, they'll make us the enemy. The optics are crucial for us to maintain law and order," says Prime Minister Gavin.

Supreme Commander Shahar stands, silencing the room with his demeanor, adding, "Every Colony on the planet is under threat of attack. How we handle this will be more important than the attack itself. We need to act preemptively. What's the casualty count as of now?"

Governor Brenton reluctantly answers, "Estimates were last reported at 16,585. The stadium wasn't the only place attacked. Numbers are climbing and we have no leads on the perpetrator." Governor Breton is of moose descent, held in high regard amongst most Petrians.

Governor Brenton is 5'8'' with a thin physique known for his negotiating abilities. He has brown skin and fur with large antlers emerging from his head. He has feral facial features, brown eyes, with a mouth and snout resembling a moose. He's wearing a traditional Petrian suit made of high-quality fabric adorned in jewelry.

Supreme Commander Shahar circles the table, explaining, "Our priority is to save as many lives as possible. Then we focus on finding out who did this. I need all of you pulling your resources to find me answers. Your position on this cabinet depends on it!"

Governor Brenton feels the support in the room leaning toward Supreme Commander Shahar, cautiously saying, "Evo all over the world are watching mutants protect the Colonies, not politicians. When it comes down to deciding our laws and structure of governance, who will Petrians trust? Those who tax and regulate their lives or the mutants who fought to save them? If we don't control the narrative. None of us will be in power to make a difference."

General Vokoua stands next to a window overlooking the stadium. She can feel small quakes from nearby explosions as she listens to the sound of war. Officials in the room are looking to her for her opinion on the matter.

"The governor's right. Mutants will likely fill the void of power post-Guardian, but this presents us with an opportunity. Evo around the world saw mutants protecting Lennek. They're watching more mutants protect Petra as we speak. Those same viewers need to also understand that it's likely mutants who were behind the attack in the first place," says the general as she turns around to rejoin her fellow leaders at the negotiating table.

General Vokoua is 6'3'' of centurion descent and is proudly feral. She has dark brown skin, green eyes, and long black hair. She has a strong muscular physique with a domineering presence. The Petrian army is more loyal to her than Supreme Commander Shahar due to her fearless reputation as a renowned warrior and strategist. The governor gauges the room, aware some of her colleagues have their own prejudices. "We need to show both sides of the mutant phenomena. All of Petra's registered mutants are working in service to the Colony, accomplishing things we could only dream of. They're not the enemy. Leaving our citizens to fend for themselves isn't how we retain power. Supreme Commander, what are our orders?"

Supreme Commander Shahar throws a data cube onto the large marble table in the center of the room. The data cube starts displaying live streams from the mutants making up Petra's Coalition. Newton, Lucky, Thumper, Enzo, Rex, Shiva, Pearl, and Kelis have the situation under control with the assistance of Primean mutants. Alynxia, Ramses, Anubis, and Odeius are providing necessary assistance which has changed the public narrative of the Primeans even more. Their assistance has also deflected any suspicions of their involvement.

"The mutants have this under control. They're decimating the combat droids. Less than a dozen mutants destroyed a robotic army comprised of thousands of combat droids in less than an hour. Mutants will inherit the Earth. Instead of persecuting them, I say we join them.

Let's make Petra a Colony of mutants," says Supreme Commander Shahar as he begins typing on a holographic keyboard accessing Petra's mainframe.

Prime Minister Gavin snaps his head in bewilderment and tells the supreme commander, "Us joining the mutants is tantamount to us serving them. I won't be taking orders from genetic mistakes."

Supreme Commander Shahar chuckles, masking his anger. "Let me rephrase. We should become them. I've been developing an induction serum with some of our black-ops scientists. In short, we've developed a way to create mutants."

General Vokoua strums her fingers on the marble table in a rhythmic sequence trying to suppress her frustration. "Are you serious? If we could make an army of mutants..."

"Why stop with the military? I propose a Colony of mutants! We'd be the most powerful nation on the planet. Look what twelve of these mutants did today. Imagine what we could do with millions!" says Supreme Commander Shahar as he pulls up data from first responders and nearby hospitals. "The serum works! We're already running test trials."

Governor Brenton interrupts, saying, "I thought our priority was to save lives. All lives—including normal Evo."

Prime Minister Gavin calmly stands from his seat walking towards the exit. He stops, turning to look Supreme Commander Shahar in the eye, saying, "I, too, have millions that support me. My followers will never defile themselves to become the enemy. You used Colonial funds to aid Petra's greatest threat. I cannot wait to hold a hearing. You went too far Shahar!" Prime Minister Gavin storms out of the room, disgusted.

General Vokoua moves towards the entrance to remind Prime Minister Gavin, "This is classified intel. You took an oath! You can't hold a press conference or file for a hearing."

Prime Minister Gavin presses an emergency beacon in his pocket, drawing a plasma dagger to defend himself. Gavin tells General Vokoua, who's blocking the only exit out of the room, "I resign! Anyone blocking my exit will be handled accordingly."

General Vokoua unholsters her sword from her back, replying, "I'll pay the same respect!"

"LET HIM GO! I'll be making the announcement after we save the survivors in desperate need of our help," says Supreme Commander Shahar. "Full disclosure, ten percent of the population will not be compatible to the transition. Their offspring, however, will carry the genetic markers for mutation. Those that take the serum ensure that their children will be mutants."

General Vokoua walks towards Supreme Commander Shahar, adding, "Our Evo deserve a choice. Forcing them to take this serum goes against our charter. Technically, this is a weapon."

Governor Brenton stands, exclaiming, "This is a new dawn for Petra! Perhaps we need a new charter? Either way, Petrians need a voice in their fates! We have no right to force this on anyone."

Supreme Commander Shahar raises his arm to silence the governor before responding, "The Evo of Petra will have a choice. They can take the serum or relocate to another Colony of their choice. Even the Evo that don't develop abilities will be welcome to stay in the Colony since their children will add to our mutant collective. If it helps sway your decision, everyone in this room has had their DNA tested. You are all compatible candidates for mutation. With that said, does anyone have reservations or concerns?"

No one in the room objects. They're all in silence, digesting the implications of the induction serum. The Colony already has a volatile political climate. Such a dramatic change in Colonial governance and the implications of a possible new charter will only add fuel to the fire. The threat has been neutralized near the stadium, but a civil war within

Petra is brewing, as Prime Minister Gavin has already reached out to his supporters who would rather die than become mutants.

He's recorded the conversation smiling ear to ear as he plans. The idealists that support the prime minister have been waiting for a spark to reclaim their Colony. Supreme Commander Shahar has unknowingly given the prime minister the perfect rallying cry for his cause.

Chapter 10 — Death of a Soulless Vessel

Deep inside the wonderous waters of Kronus, King Pulsar's making final arrangements before leaving for Maddox to refine his newly acquired abilities. King Pulsar's having a meeting with Chakra, Polaris, Nova, and Esteban making final preparations.

Esteban is known only to the king and now his three priestesses. Esteban's rare mutant abilities make him an invaluable asset to the crown. He's kept hidden from the rest of the imperial palace, kept inside a lavish temple which archives Evo history. King Pulsar's clone is posing as himself delivering a Commencement speech with Queen Elisheba, Sage, and the Imperial Guard by his side. Vishnu's filled with Kronusians from every ocean on the planet celebrating the Guardian's decommissioning.

Esteban is of parrot-fish descent, with the ability to create wormholes allowing him and others to teleport to any fixed point while the wormhole is open. Esteban can use wormholes to remote view anywhere on the planet. With training, he'll be able to travel to different dimensions.

Esteban stands 6'5'' with blue skin and a muscular build. He has turquois and purple scales covering his shoulders, elbows, outer thighs, and chest. He has a strong jaw, short pink hair, and auburn eyes. Esteban's handsome with a symmetrical face and humanoid features. He has a pink strip of scales down his back and fins on his forearms and calves. Esteban lives in lavish quarters hidden within the imperial palace. He rarely interacts with other Evo as his abilities make him extremely valuable to the Crown. He's socially awkward and unaware of his good looks, giving him a humble demeanor.

Esteban syphons energy to create a sustained wormhole, while levitating in a meditation stance with his legs crossed. Esteban channels an enormous amount of energy as he signals the king to hurry with his goodbyes.

"The world will eventually turn its eyes to Kronus. When it does,

I'll be ready. This has been foreseen as destiny," says King Pulsar to his three beloved priestesses. The trio know his words were meant to comfort himself more than themselves.

Nova bows to the king, walking next to Esteban, watching him levitate sustaining the wormhole. Nova reveals, "I heard rumors of a black-ops scientist developing a teleportation device. I didn't realize it was a mutant. Greetings!" Nova is visibly smitten with Esteban and not making much of an effort to hide it.

Refusing to show the strain on his abilities, Esteban responds, "I don't teleport. My powers allow me to create wormholes between two fixed points. Teleporters manipulate quantum entanglement in a completely differently manner."

Chakra walks up to the pair, asking, "So multiple Evo can go through these wormholes? No wonder Pulsar keeps you a secret. I'm Chakra." Chakra bows to Esteban who's becoming overwhelmed with the newfound attention.

Chakra realizes she's distracting Esteban as the wormhole shrinks and flickers. She walks away, allowing Esteban to concentrate and to say her goodbyes to King Pulsar. Chakra turns back to tell Esteban, "It's really nice to meet you. Hope to see you again."

Polaris tries to suppress her anxiety by keeping busy watching a live stream from the Commencement ceremony twenty miles away in the Vishnu capital. She manipulates the controls of the projected hologram displayed from a spherical drone hovering above her.

Polaris huffs out of frustration, saying, "Is no one else worried about how long this clone can keep this charade up? He should have spent more time learning your mannerisms."

King Pulsar responds, "If I know my wife, Elisheba will be preoccupied playing out my assassination in her head. She won't notice any variances in the clone's demeanor. Be sure to check on my...see that Gill's looked after by the Coalition. We'll speak on every full moon.

Inform Sage of my plan after my funeral. Sage's emotional whirlwind will convince Elisheba of my death."

Nova sees Polaris tearing up and walks over to comfort her, saying, "We need to get back to the palace. You should get going. Esteban can't hold this portal open forever."

King Pulsar starts walking toward the wormhole, saying, "Remember, Elisheba wants to destroy the Reef tribes from the shadows. We can use that against her. I'll return before there's conflict with any of the other Colonies."

Chakra walks toward an aquatic transporter turning off the stealth shielding to reveal its entrance. She looks back at King Pulsar, saying, "Let us know when we can kill her. We'll see you soon."

King Pulsar replies, "Her use for me will have expired upon my return. However, I'd like to be the one to end her. Stay safe and protect each other." King Pulsar prepares to walk through the wormhole, delaying the inevitable, stopping to explain, "The queen intends to use her position to bring power to the Maddox tribes while getting revenge against the Reef tribes. Vishnu needs to remain neutral until we build up our defenses against the other Colonies. Our Guardian won't be here to protect us. Our future is in our own hands."

Polaris is watching a live stream of their Commencement ceremony, irritated by the thought of her king and only father figure, leaving. "We have no allies close to Elisheba, but we'll report what we know every full moon." The priestesses are stressed, with the tension being felt through their mental link.

"Xavier has been informed of what's going on. He's been warming up to the queen over the past few months, recently joining her inner circle. The firsthand intel he provides will be invaluable. His true allegiance will always be with us. Trust him. He knows my mind better than most. I've hired multiple telepaths to attack Vishnu on the astral plane, giving you all an alibi during the attack!" says King Pulsar, responding to Chakra's concern with a stern tone.

Esteban's wormhole starts shrinking again as he buckles from the pressure. King Pulsar realizes Esteban is being pushed past his limits. King Pulsar walks right to the cusp of the wormhole, saying, "I'm leaving my empire in your hands. I'll speak with all of you on the next full moon when the tides are at their peak." The king enters the wormhole as it immediately closes behind him.

Esteban falls to his knees with his body smoking from the energy he was channeling to maintain the wormhole. He's completely exhausted, keeled over and panting. Chakra runs over, asking, "Are you alright? What can I do?"

"I'm fine. I'm fine. The pressure of the ocean makes it more difficult for me to maintain a wormhole. I'm supposed to only sustain them for a minute or so," says Esteban as he kneels over trying to catch his breath.

Chakra is genuinely concerned, asking, "Are you okay? Let me help." She kneels putting his arm over her shoulder gently lifting him to his feet. "You have nothing to prove to us!"

Esteban laughs from his gut, smiling ear to ear. "Was it that obvious I was showing off?"

Nova looks at Chakra, realizing she's completely enamored with Esteban. Nova smiles, feeling the attraction through their mental link. Chakra tells Esteban, "Our king always tries to improve those closest to him. You should see him training with Sage. We thought he pushed us to the extreme. We saw a session with the two of them and never complained again. It's a compliment."

Able to stand on his own now, Esteban asks, "Can't you channel a vision and tell us when Queen Elisheba will attack the Reef tribes? With the three of you, there's no reason we shouldn't be prepared. At one point, it was my home."

Chakra's tentacles in her hair curl up into compact balls as she lowers her head in shame. She whispers to Esteban as she pulls away, explaining, "My powers don't work like that."

Polaris is streaming live footage from Vishnu palace watching the Commencement ceremony. Polaris starts walking toward the aquatic transport, teasing, "You're describing a mutant with honed abilities. Chakra doesn't possess the discipline to properly use her gifts. The transport is leaving in two minutes. See that you stay out of sight, Esteban."

Nova's face curls up in disgust, witnessing Polaris motivated by jealousy, responding, "Chakra's mind and spirit are linked to the cosmos when she's receiving visions. It can be an overload of information without the right training. It takes years to master precognitive abilities. Chakra's ability to link minds makes it difficult for another psychic to train her without experiencing the same sensory overload."

Esteban sees Chakra walking toward the aquatic transport with her head down. He runs after her to say, "Most psychics can't control their visions, so don't feel pressured. With training, you'll be able to mold history to your will. I think she's a little jealous if you ask me."

Chakra stops and smiles at Esteban. Seeing her mood change, Esteban quickly adds, "I might know someone who can help. I know of a psychic with precognitive gifts. I'll see if he can train you. When I came into my abilities, my wormholes were dangerous and unstable. Without training from the Vishnu tribes, I would've never gained control of my powers."

Nova runs into the aquatic transport, making sure Polaris doesn't leave without them, giving Chakra an opportunity to say her goodbyes to Esteban. Chakra asks, "I'm not sure how I reach someone who's a secret weapon to the king?"

Esteban responds, "I'll find a way to reach you. You'd better go before your sisters leave you. It was nice meeting you."

Chakra heads towards the aquatic transport, saying, "Until we meet again." Once onboard, she sees Esteban waving goodbye through their cockpit window. The aquatic transport makes its way through the open waters, headed towards the Kronusian Commencement ceremony.

Buildings in Kronus are made from a crystal compound derived from coal. The entire city of Vishnu has numerous domes made from pressurized energy shields, creating vacuum sealed spherical roofs. The domes utilize technology allowing the encased habitats to be filled with air or water, accommodating Evo of all backgrounds. Kronus utilizes art deco and Roman design around terraformed reefs for most of their architecture.

The Reef tribe is comprised of benthos Evo, meaning they've evolved to spend their entire lives underwater. Amphibious Evo live in and outside of water, creating a natural tension amongst the thousands of species all classified as Kronusians. King Pulsar has unified all four tribes for decades bridging the gap for all Evo from every ocean and sea.

The Reef tribe's prejudice towards outsiders is unfortunate as the mutant gene is prevalent amongst their tribe. Unique properties within their ocean's waters have allowed the mutant gene to evolve in unexpected ways. The Reef tribe's military is filled with omega-level mutants capable of decimating armies. Reef technology is advanced, as is their understanding of the stars. The Reef tribe's culture resembles the Olympians, including their disdain for the outside world. Queen Elisheba's first action will be to make war with the reef tribes, an action King Pulsar doesn't want to make himself.

The king's priestesses are en route to Vishnu palace prepared to take their places on stage. Magnesium-based plasma fireworks are exploding across the ocean floor creating a beautiful pyrotechnic show. The magnesium plasma bonds with hydrogen molecules allowing the magnesium compound to explode underwater. Chakra, Nova, and Polaris are flying through the water overlooking the vast buildings, homes, and farming silos watching the extravagant festivities.

Three miles north inside the imperial grand hall, Commencement is underway. King Pulsar's clone is addressing the tribes of Kronus explaining the king's vision for Colonial life post-Guardian. Queen Elisheba, Sage, and the Kronusian Guardian are seated behind the king's clone waiting for him to finish his speech. Queen Elisheba has a smile plastered on her beautiful face while Sage tries her best not to fidget in her elaborate gown.

Kronus is envied by all the Colonies for its beauty, culture, and architecture—exacerbated by the perceived longevity of peace. Evo around the world witness the prosperous Colony appear unified. Earth's health is measured by the vitality of its oceans; if Kronus thrives, the planet thrives. The Kronusian Commencement has been a stark contrast to the tragedies taking place in other Colonies.

King Pulsar's clone stands at a white crystal podium elevated on the north side of the room. The Guardian's towering over the royal family with an elevated view of Vishnu. Underwater fireworks continue to explode as colors cascade with the tides. Kronus' elite have gathered to share delicacies from around the world in honor of their Guardian. Evo from Sharkona, Maddox, and the Reef tribe have gathered in Vishnu to usher in their new independence.

With news drones circling him, King Pulsar's clone says, "Our human ancestors nearly destroyed the planet by polluting the air and oceans. They shifted the planet's weather patterns, destroying their own home for greed. Our waters isolate us from other Colonies, but this also leaves us vulnerable. We all remember the toxic spills from Zion! Had it not been for our Guardian, thousands more would have died."

While the king's clone continues his address to the tribes of Kronus, Queen Elisheba uses an encrypted telepathic network to communicate with the five mutants she hired to kill the king. Jynxx, Solomon,

Boris, Luna, and Mirage relay their positions waiting for the opportune moment to strike.

Solomon and Jynxx are blending into the crowd of aristocrats inside the grand hall on opposite sides of the room. Boris and Luna are posing as a couple in the courtyard outside the imperial grand hall while Mirage is seated in the crowd. The assassins are positioned blending into the crowd.

Luna reaches out to Mirage telepathically, saying, *"Let's make this quick!"*

King Pulsar's clone is nearly finished with his speech, saying, "As your king, it's my responsibility to protect our way of life. I swear upon my bloodline that I'll do all I can to ensure our survival even without our Guardian's oversight. Many of you are concerned that the other Colonies will no longer honor our pollution treaties. Some believe that once our Guardian shuts down, enemies of Kronus will retaliate. Kronus is in the middle of an operation to ensure our future. Our military will be stronger than ever, but we must isolate ourselves until the other Colonies adjust to their independence."

The king's clone studied King Pulsar's mannerisms, watching every speech he delivered throughout his reign. Queen Elisheba's mutant assassins are positioned, quietly positioning themselves to strike. The king's clone may not have any rights, but he is just as alive as any other Evo in the room. He has a soul, feels emotions, and is making a willing sacrifice for the glory of a king he has only known for a few days.

The speech is being broadcast throughout all seven Colonies. "Moving against the other Colonies would only ensure a bitter war. In the post-Guardian era, we'll need allies we can depend on. Open trade. The wisdom of our Guardian has allowed us to maintain peace. We need to remember our strength comes from the unity of all our tribes with a shared vision of prosperity."

Queen Elisheba reaches out to her assassins, saying, *"Keep those inhibitor weapons armed and ready to go. We have no idea how many abilities the king has now. Best to neuter him quickly."*

Boris responds, *"Luna and I are ready for the Imperial Guard. You just keep up appearances and keep that crown on your head."*

Mirage is of jellyfish descent with the ability to phase through solid objects. She can shoot energy blasts that cause objects to become intangible, and she can control light waves, making herself and other objects invisible. Mirage is 5'7'' with a petite frame and glossy mocha skin. Her hair resembles a translucent jellyfish sack, changing colors from within. Tentacles flow down from her sack, resembling dreadlocks. Mirage has humanoid facial features with freckles beneath her gray eyes. She has a large tattoo of the flower of life covering her sleek back.

Mirage tells her comrades, *"Remember your assignments, and we'll have this thing finished in no time. Get him to the extraction point. I'll do the rest."*

King Pulsar's clone addresses all seven Colonies with a passionate argument for Colonial unity. The speech builds in intensity as he continues, "Chieftains from each tribe will be meeting with me in the upcoming weeks so that the advancements made in Vishnu are shared with the entire Colony. For us to truly be unified, we need to share resources, research, and ideas. Our genetics program has made advancements that will secure our future. I'll be sharing more with our chieftains later this evening. I leave you with our Guardian who has cleaned our waters and kept us safe for decades." The clone returns to his seat with the queen and princess as news drones circle the royal family for live reactions.

Drinks and food are being served, painting an idyllic portrait for the world to envy. Sage stands to hug King Pulsar's clone before, saying, "Excellent speech, Father! Your transparency with the other tribes will be respected, even amongst your enemies."

The king's clone replies, "It was necessary for us to truly become a unified Colony."

Queen Elisheba leans over to the king's clone, whispering, "I thought you planned on keeping our genetics program secret from the other tribes."

The clone replies, "We're on camera. Try to remain pleasant."

The Guardian of Kronus looks like a large metallic mermaid with a humanoid face which appears as a mask filled with luminescent water. The Guardian of Kronus was designed to be an apex predator within the water. It is covered in weapons suited for the water with a propulsion system that allows it to reach mach speed in the water. Its large metallic body is nimble and malleable stretching sixteen-feet long in the water. Its body is comprised of the strongest metallic alloys on the planet. Its caudal fins are two blades of glezslavine while its waist and upper body are made of a pboldevite. Like all the Guardians, its nanites allow it to heal and manifest a limitless number of weapons.

The Guardian begins speaking as news drones circle the podium. "Serving you has been my prime directive since I was made. The end of my programing does not translate into my death. My ideas and teachings will live on amongst all of you. Defend the Colony at all costs, and put your differences aside for the greater good. I'm proud to have protected the largest, most diverse, and prosperous Colony on the planet. Now it falls upon all of you to continue that legacy." Moments later, the Guardian poses in the infamous Kronusian prayer stance as it prepares for its shutdown. Suddenly, the Guardian is frozen in place. Evo clap and cry, as the room is filled with mixed emotions.

King Pulsar's clone stands to applaud the Guardian's service in consort with the rest of the crowd. He leans over to Sage, asking, "Why don't you close the Ceremony?"

Shocked, Sage looks at the clone she believes to be her father and replies, "Really? I would be honored!"

Queen Elisheba overhears the clone and walks to the podium before Sage can get out of her seat. The queen's doing everything she can to prevent the Evo of Kronus from viewing Sage as a leader. Queen Elisheba slithers to the podium as her large tentacles overlap each other propelling her forward.

Queen Elisheba approaches the microphone, saying, "As your queen, I am honored to follow tradition and bring in the new year. This Commencement ceremony is unlike any other. For the first time in history, we will be in control of our own destiny. Our Guardian has shown us when to use force and when diplomacy is the more effective option. I ask you to enthusiastically support my husband's plan to unite the tribes through transparency and innovation. Only together can we move through the tumultuous waters of the unknown. Enjoy the festivities, and may Kronus continue to prosper."

Sage stares her mother down, knowing she overheard the clone's request. King Pulsar's clone grabs Sage's shoulder telling her, "Your time will come. She knows it, so pay your mother no mind." Sage smiles and her anger immediately diminishes from the comfort only a father can give.

The queen smiles, taking in the crowd's applause as the clone and Sage join her side allowing news drones to capture a panned shot of the royal family with the retired Guardian of Kronus. Cheers dissipate as the family makes their way to the courtyard for a private gathering amongst Kronusian elected officials and esteemed guests. Inter-Colonial news drones are forbidden in the courtyard concluding the streamed portion of Kronus' Commencement ceremony.

Queen Elisheba reaches out to her assassins, saying, *"We'll be arriving in the courtyard soon. We've got one shot at this, so stick to the plan."*

Jynxx starts vibrating in a corner out of sight, producing multiple copies of himself. Some of Jynxx's cloned copies have already replaced some of the staff in the courtyard, each armed with inhibitor cannons.

Jynxx can create multiple copies of himself and self-regenerate with a highly effective healing factor. When focused, Jynxx can use his abilities to create exact duplicates of objects that gradually degrade. Jynxx has superior strength when in singular form. Each copy he makes depletes some of his strength. In short, the more copies he makes the weaker each clone is. Jynxx has been employed as a hired thief and mercenary for years. He's established quite a reputation in the underworld of Kronus.

Jynxx is 6'4'' of seahorse descent with green skin and orange scales covering his slim, muscular build. He has an elongated face with protruding bones on his eyebrows and the crown of his head. He has protruding bones on his shoulders, elbows, and knees. Jynxx has an orange malleable fin starting at the middle of his forehead descending to the base of his neck creating a hood resembling a seahorse. He has gills on the side of his neck and fins on his forearms and calves.

The royal family walks through the imperial palace greeting a crowd of dignitaries and wealthy Evo from around the world. They walk through an elongated hallway that leads to an elaborate entrance to an oversized courtyard. Flashing lights are capturing a rare appearance from the royal family as news drones swarm the area capturing the footage.

They approach the courtyard doors and Queen Elisheba whispers to Sage, "I hope you understand why I closed the ceremony. With all the changes our king is proposing, we need to maintain certain aspects of our traditions."

Sage conjures a fake smile for the cameras, replying, "I'm sure that was your only motivation. I'll address my Evo in the courtyard starting a new tradition. The theatrics for outsiders can be left to you mother."

"I think that's an excellent idea. Your mother and I are both supportive in molding you as a queen," says King Pulsar's clone as he looks over to Queen Elisheba, asking, "I'm sure your beloved mother has no objections, right?"

Queen Elisheba forces a smile answering, "Of course not. I was going to suggest something similar." The only thing hiding the queen's anger is the foreknowledge she'll soon be queen.

The royal family enters the courtyard where chieftains and leaders from each tribe are waiting to greet them. Native music is playing as Kronusian cuisines are being served to the rhythm of live music. The crowd cheers for the arrival of their king as he enters the courtyard with his family behind him. The press coordinator for the imperial news channel walks the family over to their table placed in the center of the room. The courtyard is in a large dome with waist deep water connected to the imperial palace. The large dome of the courtyard is eight hundred feet high providing plenty of room and air.

The imperial news channel is streaming exclusively to Kronusian cities. Under order from King Pulsar, imperial news streams are rarely distributed outside of the Colony. King Pulsar's clone answers questions regarding their economy, research, and their military. Such information is coveted amongst the Colony and its significance understood by most citizens.

The press coordinator is of crab descent with red skin, claws, and a shell. She's wearing a white suit and gold jewelry to complement her long red hair which flows down to her calves. She approaches the center microphone, saying, "Praise Gaya for this beautiful day. Each tribe will have three questions following their speech to the royal family. May peace and prosperity bless us for another year. Happy Commencement!"

Sage grabs the press coordinator's attention, saying, "I'll address my tribesman before the king addresses our leaders."

The press coordinator does her best to hide her confusion but knows better than to question the princess. She returns to the mic, saying, "Breaking form from tradition, our princess will open this evening's festivities." She motions her claw introducing Sage to the podium.

Sage is wearing a deep purple dress offset with diamonds and pearls. Her mythryl crown and corset were made by the finest craftsmen in Kronus befit for royalty. She approaches the center microphone, saying, "My father's proposal for a transparent partnership among the tribes is risky. In short, it relinquishes some of our leverage over the other tribes. My father's willing to take this risk because he feels it's in the best interest for Kronus. The capital intends to share resources, technology, intel, weapons, and new scientific advancements which my father has earned the honor of explaining to you. The other Colonies feared our Guardian. Without that fear, we must rely on our ingenuity to protect our waters. We need to remind the world we are a force to be respected and taken seriously...with or without our Guardian."

The crowd claps as Sage walks to her seat. A Vishnu reporter cuts the accolades short by asking, "There's rumors amongst the tribes of gene-splicing technology that imbues mutant abilities. Can you or the king comment on this?"

Each tribe has a representative to address the royal families. There are leaders present for the Vishnu, Sharkona, Maddox, and the Reef tribes of the pacific. The crowd is fewer than eighty Evo making the environment intimate allowing King Pulsar to let down his guard.

Sage looks back at her father for approval to answer the question. King Pulsar's clone nods his head in approval before Sage responds, "These rumors are somewhat true. We've made dramatic advance-ments in our genetics program, and we intend to be transparent with our findings. As I said earlier, the accomplishment is that of my father. He'll be the one to explain the technology."

A reporter from the Sharkona tribes asks a question without being recognized. "Does this sudden need for transparency have anything to do with the security breach in Lennek's hive?"

Sage smiles, calmly answering, "The change in policy comes from our decommissioned Guardian. If Kronus hopes to survive in the future, we'll need to be united. Transparency will be essential in accomplishing this task. The crown respects the Evo we're leading, so we'll be forthright with information and advancements that affect us all."

A Reef tribe reporter asks, "So this proposal is intended to include the Reef tribes?"

Sage answers, "The proposal is for all the tribes of Kronus—including the Reef tribes. The proposal is designed to start our post-Guardian future on equal footing. None of the tribes, including the capital, should have military advantage over the others. When our waters are attacked, we all suffer. I'll let my father explain this matter in detail." Sage has handled her interview flawlessly, showing political prowess beyond her years. It's clear she understands life outside Vishnu waters, unlike her mother.

Queen Elisheba is wearing gold chainmail over yellow silk imported from Zion. She has golden leaves intertwined throughout her hair. Queen Elisheba reaches out to her assassins telepathically, saying, "*As soon as the king is neutralized with an inhibitor, isolate him and strike!*"

Luna becomes irritated with the queen's telepathic orders, responding, "*The king's priestesses will find this telepathic network eventually. Don't use it unless necessary!*" King Pulsar's clone walks table to table, meeting the Evo important enough to be inside the courtyard. The clone explains to the reporter, "Petra's been experimenting and researching a rare plant that induces latent mutant genes. This plant has been synthesized into a serum that guarantees the recipient's offspring will possess the mutant gene. In one generation, everyone in Petra could have mutant abilities. Kronus must be prepared for a new world."

Lunessa aka Luna, is of axolotl descent with the ability to synthesize and redirect sunlight. Luna can also charge objects to explode through her touch. She can focus microwave photons into powerful beams, fly, and turn her body into pure energy. In the absence of sunlight Luna can also absorb and synthesize thermal energy. Like all axolotls, she has a natural healing factor strong enough to regrow limbs.

Luna is 5'11'' with pink glossy skin wet to the touch. She has humanoid facial features, blue eyes, and long pink hair that flows down to her calves. Luna has three cartilage horns on each side of her head, webbed feet and hands, a slim, muscular build, and retractable claws. She has two gills on either side of her neck. She appears innocent but her baby face disarms from her more nefarious intentions. She has an alluring voice known for her ruthlessness in battle.

Another reporter from Vishnu asks, "How will Kronus respond? Except for the Reef tribe, we're less likely to develop mutations by living in the water. How do we fight this?"

The king's clone chuckles, putting the room at ease, saying, "As of now, Petra's serum only works for the offspring of its recipients. Kronus has developed our own genetic splicing technology which will give abilities to the recipient. Our scientists have worked with two dozen volunteers and only twenty percent of the recipients rejected the procedure. We're working on a screening process that will determine if someone's likely to reject the splicing process before undergoing the procedure."

One of Jynxx's cloned copies poses as a reporter and maneuvers a news drone directly behind King Pulsar. The drone has been retrofitted with a pistol inside the lens of the camera, firing small inhibitor darts to neutralize the king's mutant abilities.

Jynxx's copy is controlling the news drone with a data processor bracelet on his wrist, projecting holographic controls. He can see King Pulsar's clone lined up on the processor on his wrist, ready to act.

He reaches out to Queen Elisheba, saying, "*I'm ready to fire on your command.*"

Queen Elisheba responds with no hesitation, "*All hail the queen... Fire!*" Jynxx shoots King Pulsar's clone in the back of his neck, barely making a sound. Xavier's heightened senses allowed him to hear the dart being fired, despite the silencer attached to the weapon. He reacts by scanning the room and notices multiple copies of Jynxx.

Xavier yells across the room, "Put that reporter in custody!" The king assigned a few of his most trusted mutants to protect his clone, following protocol to make his death seem legitimate. They've been spread throughout the crowd and are trained to protect the king with their lives.

Xavier is of lionfish descent, originating from the Reef tribe. He can shoot enlarged spike projectiles with a deadly venom that incapacitates victims, leaving them paralyzed while decomposing internal organs. Xavier also has a healing factor and the spike projectiles from his spine and forearms regenerate within seconds. He can projectile vomit his venom and he has enhanced strength and senses from a gene-splicing procedure he underwent in the military.

Xavier stands 6'3'' with blue skin and red scales accenting his thin, muscular frame. He has long blue hair with malleable spikes blended into his hair. He has protruding bones, covered in brown and red skin, outlining his face like a helmet. His forearms have malleable spikes, and his back and hair are filled with them. Xavier has a perverse demeanor amplified by his red piercing eyes despite his kind nature.

Mya was also assigned to protect King Pulsar's clone. She looks at an imperial guardsman, ordering, "Put the courtyard on lockdown!"

Mya is of duck descent originally from the Maddox tribes. She can synthesize and amplify sunlight through beams of energy that come from her eyes. She also has an autonomic ability to create translation fields. Her fields allow people from various species to communicate telepathically. Mya's translation field can be focused to negate the telepathic abilities of others and compromise encrypted telepathic frequencies.

Mya is 6'3'' with pale white skin and feathers covering her muscular frame. She has humanoid features, long brown hair, gold eyes, and a large orange beak covering her nose, mouth, and cheeks. Mya has feathers on the outskirts of her eyes, shoulders, forearms, and her outer hips. Her feet are webbed, and she has two gills on both sides of her neck.

The imperial guardsmen follow Mya's orders without hesitation and move to protect the royal family. King Pulsar's clone grabs his neck where the inhibitor dart hit him. He removes the small dart as he feels the serum deplete his power.

The clone twists his right ring, and a needle pops out from the lower half of the ring allowing him to take a blood sample. He injects the ring's needle into his arm, taking a blood sample which is transmitted to the Colonial hive to be analyzed. The news drones maneuver through the courtyard opening fire and striking the king's clone twice more.

Xavier shoots his venomous spikes destroying the remaining news drones as the Colonial guardsmen rally to defend the king's clone. Queen Elisheba and Sage are being escorted to a safe location, separate from the king while the crowd is left to fend for themselves. The guardsmen are following protocol which the queen's assassins know like the back of their hand.

Boris turns himself into gas form, poisoning the approaching guardsmen from outside the courtyard with toxic vapors. Luna charges the chair she was sitting on with combustible energy before throwing the chair at the king's clone. The chair explodes upon impact as Luna starts shooting energy beams towards King Pulsar's clone as he retreats.

Boris is 6'4'' of beltfish descent. He can turn himself into a gaseous form and excrete toxins and viruses. Boris creates vapors that bond with water molecules or air allowing his excretions to spread. He can telepathically control the flow of his vapors or gases. While in gas form, Boris can travel vast distances quickly and undetected, also making him impervious to physical attacks. Boris can also create antidotes for any type of poison, toxin, or virus he creates with a latent ability to heal cells.

Boris was born in the Reef tribe, defecting to Maddox when his parents were killed during a civil war over ancient technology from the time of humans. Boris has spent his life honing his fighting skills in hopes of one day taking revenge against his native tribe. His fighting skills make him a dangerous assassin while his intellect garners respect among his peers.

Boris has moist gray skin with white and gray scales covering his shoulders, outer thighs, and back. He has gills on his ribcage and a long thick tail he uses to propel himself through water. His thin face appears emaciated with numerous bags beneath his ruby eyes. He has short gray hair, distinct bone structure, and a slender build. Boris strokes Luna's hair as the pair await their cue to attack.

King Pulsar's clone activates an energy shield protecting him from the explosion, allowing Mya to respond with a counterattack. Mya hits Luna in the chest with a massive energy blast from her eyes, knocking Luna off her feet. King Pulsar's clone attempts to use telekinesis, but the inhibitor serum has already taken effect.

The clone draws his sword and shield while exclaiming, "You dare attack your king!"

Sage makes herself malleable and jellylike, slipping from the hands of the guardsmen that were escorting her to an enforced saferoom. Sage starts running back towards the courtyard while telepathically probing the room for mutants. She absorbed telepathic abilities from mutants attending the Ceremony hours ago. She notices multiple imprints of the same exact brain pattern while scanning the room unknowingly identifying Jynxx's clones.

Inside the courtyard, King Pulsar's clone is cornered at the back of the courtyard, as planned by the assassins. Mirage somersaults over three imperial guardsmen shooting a series of energy blasts that phases the ground beneath the king's clone. With the ground and surrounding water intangible, the king's clone falls through the floor. Mirage closes ground behind the king's clone as the assassins' rally to Mirage's location in response.

Queen Elisheba is being escorted to a nearby enforced saferoom while still linked to her assassins telepathically. The room's coated in mythryl, making it impossible for her to communicate with her assailants telepathically. Queen Elisheba reaches out before entering the roog, saying, "*Make his death quick and painless.*" Queen Elisheba enters the saferoom and begins showing concern for King Pulsar's wellbeing to the imperial guardsmen escorting her.

"Find my husband...quickly! This may be an attempt on his life! HURRY!" says Queen Elisheba as she enters the saferoom.

One of the guardsmen grabs her head, manipulating her memories with a flash in his hands. Queen Elisheba hired the mutant to pose as a guardsmen with one objective—erasing all the queen's memories regarding her involvement in the assassination of the king. Within seconds, the queen's mind is wiped clean as she's locked in an elaborate saferoom for protection.

Guardsmen arrive as reinforcements fill the courtyard. Bystanders are gasping for air, suffocating from the poisonous vapors of Boris. Sage enters the courtyard moments later activating a breathing mask forming from her earring. The elaborate earring hanging from her left ear forms a metallic mask filtering out the air, allowing the princess to breathe.

Mya and Xavier have breathing masks as well, running towards the nearest stairwell for entry to the floor beneath them. Sage probes their minds telepathically, filling in the gaps of what she missed while she was escorted away. Now at a full sprint, she closes ground on Mya and Xavier heading downstairs to the hangar beneath them. Colonial guardsmen are flooding the area as reinforcements, a countermeasure the assassins are counting on.

Boris, Luna, Mirage, Jynxx, and Solomon phased through the floor in pursuit of King Pulsar's clone. The clone activated multiple energy shields and injected himself with an antidote to the inhibitor serum. The clone's mutant abilities have yet to return as he relies on his combat skills for survival. Queen Elisheba ordered the team of assassins to limit the number of casualties, a promise they won't be able to keep.

Solomon tells his fellow assassins, "*I've got this. Let the soldiers do the dirty work.*" Solomon uses his powers taking control of fourteen guardsmen protecting the king. Sage, Mya, and Xavier enter the hangar as the guardsmen turn their weapons on the king's clone.

Solomon is of shark descent with the ability to transfer his conscience into anyone within proximity, essentially possessing the individual, giving him complete control of their mind and body. Solomon has enhanced strength and metallic teeth capable of tearing through steel. Solomon is a predator by nature. His fighting skills and disposition make him deadly.

Solomon towers at 7'2'' with an enormous, muscular build. His glossy skin has varying shades of blue while his face and stomach have white skin. He has three gills on each side of his neck and feral facial features resembling a shark. He has a large wide head with a massive jaw filled with razor-sharp teeth. In battle he wears a metallic mold over his teeth, allowing him to bite through steel. His smile spreads from ear to ear, and he can dislocate his jaw enlarging his bite. Solomon has brown eyes and a long thick tail that splits at its end. His back is covered in Kronusian ruins on either side of the large malleable fin covering his back.

The king's clone activates three energy shields to protect himself. Boris turns himself into gas form and rematerializes in front of Xavier. Xavier maneuvers his arms, shooting venomous spikes through Boris who makes his body gaseous, allowing them to pass through him. He rematerializes his body, then throws Xavier across the room.

King Pulsar's clone is fending off the guardsmen meant to protect him. Solomon maintains his control over the guardsmen forcing them to turn on themselves. The king's clone has glezslaven armor on top of Kronusian silk with an elaborate belt brandishing the Vishnu sigil. His belt is linked to the Kronus mainframe producing an antidote for the power-inhibitor serum he was injected with. The clone's moments away from having his powers restored, relying on his combat training as he waits for reinforcements.

Luna and the imperial guardsmen Solomon's controlling start firing a condensed energy blast at the clone's shield in unison. The combined energy breaks through the clone's outer shield, leaving him with two operating shields.

Jynxx starts vibrating, producing a dozen copies of himself. Jynxx's copy start charging Sage and Mya who are already running in full sprint towards the hired assassins. One of Jynxx's copies leaps at Sage, swinging an axe intending to kill. Sage has her sword drawn, blocking the attack, before cutting her attacker in the abdomen. Another one of Jynxx's copies flips backward avoiding Sage's sword as she continues pushing forward. Sage tackles the clone, absorbing Jynxx's abilities through her tentacles.

After Sage absorbs Jynxx's powers, she drains his copy's chi leaving him lifeless. Sage starts vibrating and creates four copies of herself. Like Jynxx, Sage can control her copies individually or give them a unified directive. Sage orders her copies to defend the king and to kill the assassins threatening his life.

Sage reaches out to the king's clone, asking, "*Father, where are your priestesses?*"

King Pulsar's clone responds, "*There's an ongoing assault on the astral plane. They're protecting me there and defending against an attack on the northern end of the palace. They're being overrun, so we save ourselves!*"

Sage fights off Jynxx's cloned copies gaining the upper hand and control over his abilities. She responds, "*That means someone intended to thin the heard. This battle would have been won long ago with their assistance. Whoever's behind this knows our protocols and defenses.*"

The imperial guardsmen and Luna break through the king's second shield. Mya, having similar powers to Luna, takes it upon herself to personally remove Luna from the battle. Mya fires a condensed energy beam from her eyes knocking Luna across the hangar. Mya sees the Colonial guardsmen under Solomon's control attacking the king's clone. Not needing an explanation, Mya kills the guardsmen with three succinct energy blasts from her eyes before closing ground to finish off Luna.

Mirage turns herself invisible, approaching the king's energy shield in the corner of the hangar. Mirage phases through the energy shield, now standing a foot away from the king's clone completely undetected. Mirage draws a poisoned knife and slowly approaches the clone from behind. With his powers still neutralized he's unable to sense Mirage who waits patiently before stabbing him in the ribs through a gap in his armor.

The king's clone responds by choking Mirage and punching her in the face, causing her to drop the knife. The adrenaline spike gives him a surge of energy allowing him to use his telekinesis throwing her back against his shield knocking the wind out of Mirage's lungs forcing her to become visible again. Mirage struggles to breathe as the king's clone lowers his shield, throwing Mirage across the hangar. The antidote for the mutant inhibitor serum is taking effect and restoring some of his abilities. Mirage hits a steal wall falling to the ground with a concussion and broken ribs. Sage sees Mirage injured and sends three of her cloned copies to finish the job.

Boris diverts his attention from Xavier when Mirage tells her comrades, "*The beast is wounded and poisoned! Make him exert himself so the poison will course through his veins faster.*"

Boris turns into gas form and flies across the room, materializing in front of the king's clone behind his energy shield. The clone unleashes a telepathic attack against Boris that stops him in his tracks. With his shields raised, King Pulsar's clone forces Boris to materialize. He lowers his shield and punches Boris across the room with unnatural strength.

Mirage injects herself with a concoction of morphine and adrenalin, allowing her to fight through the pain. She turns herself invisible before being attacked by one of Sage's cloned copies stabbing it in the neck with a plasma sword. Mirage has increased speed and agility that complement her mastery of martial arts and hand-to-hand combat. Sage's copies begin falling faster than she can regenerate them. The process is taxing on her stamina, forcing Sage to change tactics.

Mya is fending off an onslaught from Jynxx and six replicated copies of himself, shooting massive energy beams from her eyes wielding a spear and energy shield. Mya spots Solomon with his back to her. She launches her spear at Solomon's head. Thanks to Mirage, Solomon was turned intangible, allowing the spear to pass through him without harm.

Xavier attacks Solomon from across the hangar firing poisonous spikes from his forearms.

Solomon responds by forcing the remaining guardsmen under his possession to attack Xavier. The guardsmen are firing plasma pistols and throwing grenades, working in synchronicity to advance.

Moments later, an imperial death squad enters the hangar from the far east stairwell, giving Solomon fresh bodies to possess. Sage closes ground on Luna, attempting to get close enough to absorb her abilities. Solomon's possessed guardsmen open fire on Sage defending themselves with energy shields from their armor. Sage dodges and deflects their incoming fire with an energy shield moving to cover.

"*This isn't going as planned!*" says Luna as she flips backward into a squatted stance. She sees a nearby transporter and fires a condensed energy blast from her hand, striking the engine. The impact causes a chain reactive explosion.

The explosion knocks Mya across the hangar and destabilizes a support beam. Disoriented from the explosion, Mya has no time to react to Mirage, who phases through the ground beneath her, reappearing a few seconds later, on the opposite side of the hangar. Now repositioned, Luna moves into attack the injured Mya.

Boris's lower half of his body is in gas form, allowing him to fly across the hangar firing inhibitor darts at the king's clone from two pistols with silencers. Boris creates a poisonous gas as he approaches the clone who is slowly regaining his abilities. The king's clone creates a telekinetic shield to protect himself from Boris's green gas, visibly struggling to maintain his shield. The shield is lowered as the king's clone loses his stamina, allowing Boris to shoot him with two inhibitor darts reinfecting the clone all over again.

Sage is shooting energy blasts at Boris while in his gaseous form, hoping to save her father. Without his powers, the king's clone is forced to activate a breathing mask from his armor. Sage, Mya, and Xavier have the fate of the crown on their shoulders fighting to protect the king's clone, outnumbered with time passing against them. Sage starts vibrating as she replicates six copies of herself using the last of Jynxx's absorbed powers.

Xavier shoots a flurry of venomous spikes, striking Solomon from behind, releasing his possession over the guardsmen. Solomon's struck with multiple spikes, causing him to slowly lose consciousness. Mya's energy blasts have forced the assassins on the defensive as the king's clone continues to weaken. She takes a moment to survey the hangar, realizing they're losing ground.

Mya knows the royal armory is beneath her, so she shoots a hole in the floor with a blast from her eyes. Mya jumps into the hole and begins arming herself with an assortment of weapons. She takes a tracking visor, a sword, and plasma cannon which she holsters on her waist. Mya sees a miniature rocket launcher and grabs it before jumping back up to the hangar.

Mya arrives on the top floor and finds an army of Jynxx's clones swarming the king's clone. Sage and Xavier are managing their own battles, but in desperate need of backup. Mya reaches out to her comrades, saying, "*We just need to hold until the priestesses get here!*"

Xavier adds, "*Mutants from my ramada are on their way too! Mya tell me you got something good down there?*"

Mya fires the missile launcher, killing droves of Jynxx's clones, replying, "*I just need to hit the actual assassin and his clones will dissipate.*"

Mirage is now visible to Mya with her tracking visor which relays images in infrared. Mirage tries to sneak up on Mya who responds shooting energy blasts with a succinct rhythm intended to kill Mirage, forcing Mirage to evasively maneuver to cover. Mirage realizes Mya can somehow see her and scrambles adjusting her strategy.

Boris reaches out to his fellow assassins, saying, "*The king's been hit with inhibitors and Mirage's knife was coated with poison. Mirage is our ticket home. Protect her at all costs.*"

Jynxx responds, "*Solomon is still knocked out. I'm sending two of my copies to carry him to the east side of the hangar. We should rendezvous there.*"

Mirage adds, "*The duck with the missile launcher has a heat vision visor.*

Take her out and meet me at the rendezvous point by Solomon. Get a medic drone to Solomon, so he's on his feet when we need to leave."

Sage, Xavier, and Mya are unaware that the king's clone has been injected with more power-inhibitor darts. They expect him to reach out telepathically if he's in danger, unaware he's lost his powers. The poison and inhibitor serum are making it difficult for him to breathe, forcing him to his knees as his internal organs collapse from the poison on Mirage's knife.

Jynxx responds to Mirage, *"Time isn't on our side. We need to end this."*

Mya has her head on a swivel, shooting energy beams from her eyes indiscriminately. Mirage remains intangible as she closes ground on Mya phasing through her energy blasts.

King Pulsar's clone has his mask ripped off by one of Jynxx's clones and starts breathing in Boris's toxins struggling to remain conscious. He sees a functioning transporter across the hangar and activates its engines through his armor, hoping to pull Boris's vapors away from him. The green gas is pulled across the hangar as Boris solidifies himself from gas form, weighing himself down in place.

Boris lands next to the body of a fallen guardsman and takes his plasma cannon for himself, opening fire on the transport, destroying its engines. The ship explodes, shaking the foundation of the hangar. Boris turns around and finds King Pulsar's clone convulsing on the floor.

Boris calmly walks over to the clone, saying, "It would appear our beloved king isn't much of a warrior without his powers. Your belt won't be able to give you an antidote because I cooked this up just for you. The toxins aren't on the Colonial mainframe... Die slow, Your Highness!"

The clone was left weak from multiple inhibitor injections combined with an unknown poison his armor can't neutralize. With his immune system already weakened from the inhibitor serum, Boris's poison quickly spreads through his bloodstream. Boris approaches the clone from behind firing two condensed energy blasts into his head, leaving the clone's body lifeless.

Jynxx is two feet behind Luna with his sword drawn, preparing to stab the king through his heart. With the clone's healing factor depleted, he's quickly approaching death. Jynxx circles around the clone like a predator playing with its prey. He stops in front of the clone, kneels, and lifts him by the throat.

"I was told to make this quick," says Jynxx as he slits the clone's throat. The king's clone falls to the ground, bleeding out as his body convulses sporadically. "Regards from Kronus." Jynxx is turned invisible by Mirage as the assassins start making their escape.

Jynxx's clones keep Sage and Xavier occupied while the assassins make their escape. Jynxx catches up with his comrades as two of his cloned copies carry Solomon's unconscious body. Jynxx reminds his comrades, *"The farther I get from my copies, the weaker they get. Let's get the hell out of here!"*

Boris tells Mirage, *"We're depending on you now! Get us to the submarine, and we're rich beyond our wildest dreams!"*

Back in the hangar, Sage is cutting down copies of Jynxx faster than he can replicate. Sage is wielding a sword with a brass knuckle handle and a military grade plasma cannon in her other hand. She's protecting herself with telekinetic shields while mowing down the remaining copies of Jynxx.

Sage finds a rhythm to her attack and looks over to her father, assuming to see him doing the same. Shocked, she lowers her guard seeing her father bleeding out on the ground, foaming out of his mouth and bleeding from his ears. Blood is leaking from his eyes and nose while his body continues to convulse, even after his heart has stopped beating. The viral poison in his system is continuing to eat away his internal organs, leaving him beyond repair as he bleeds out from his throat.

The hangar is filled with a gut-wrenching scream only a mourning daughter could make. Sage fights her way to her father's body when suddenly Jynxx's copies all dissipate at once, signifying the distance of the assassins. Sage coddles her father's lifeless body as she cries out to her ancestors for guidance.

"NO, NO! FATHER...WAKE UP! Somebody...HELP...HELP!" screams the princess as Sage rocks her father's body back and forth trying to revive him. Sage is heartbroken and preoccupied as the assassins make their escape.

The assassins are running through the palace intangible, invisible, and undetected thanks to some tech from Queen Elisheba. Mirage responds, *"The shortest distance is a straight line. We're taking a shortcut!"* Mirage stops in the middle of a kitchen and the assassins start phasing through the ground, level by level. *"The submarine's right beneath us!"*

The assassins plan to migrate to an Acolyte black site in Carthage. It would be the last place they would be expected to hide. Carthage had no aquatic habitats until Queen Elisheba secretly commissioned one a year ago. Queen Elisheba promised a fresh start with new identities, vowing to cover all surgical costs for new lives. The assassins know Queen Elisheba can't be trusted, and they have their own plans.

Back in the hangar, Sage is on the floor, screaming inconsolably. "WHERE ARE THE HEALERS? MEDIC, MEDIC!"

Mya jumps up from the armory, having finally freed herself from the floor. "What happened? Is that the king? How...how did this...?"

"Calm yourself!" says Xavier as he does his best to hold himself together. He's aware of King Pulsar's plans and knows the true king is not lost to Kronus. Knowing King Pulsar's safe doesn't make it any easier watching Sage mourn her father's death.

Mya crumbles to tears, watching the princess try to give life back to her father. Wanting someone to blame, Mya screams out, "Where are the king's priestesses? Absent when he needed them most. They will pay for—"

Sage interrupts, saying, "There was a full-on assault on the astral plane they were protecting us from. They were forced to commune to protect us. Whoever did this knew our weaknesses!"

"This can't be!" says Mya as she drops to her knees, confused and overwhelmed. Unfamiliar with failure, let alone the death of their king. Mya doesn't know how to process what's happened. Watching Sage coddle the lifeless body of her father has left her paralyzed.

Xavier is pacing behind Sage, wondering what King Pulsar would want next. Unsure what to do, he starts to pray vigorously. Sage is inconsolable, while Mya fails at holding back her own tears. Suddenly, a large hole is pierced through the wall allowing Polaris and Nova to levitate into the hangar.

Polaris says, "We already know the king is lost to us. We've come to begin tracking the assassins! This assault won't go unanswered!"

Xavier asks, "Where are your sister priestesses?"

Nova bursts into tears, answering, "Chakra's in the infirmary. We joined consciousness to fight more effectively on the astral plane. We were becoming overwhelmed... Things didn't... We weren't prepared for..."

"I messed up! I broke our communion out of fear and left Chakra on her own. She held them off for some time. I was... I couldn't... I didn't...help!" admits Polaris as she tries to keep a strong face.

Sage stands to her feet, affirming, "Our sister, Chakra, will pull through. She'll assist us in bringing these traitorous assassins to justice. They'll pay with their lives for their transgression. I want to start investigations with questioning the queen!"

Polaris levitates toward Sage, replying, "Princess, relinquish your lust for revenge. We have leads on those responsible. We'll pursue Queen Elisheba only if evidence allows us to do so. If the Akashic leads us to your mother, you may end her how you see fit!"

"As princess to Kronus, I wish to check on her...NOW! She did this, I know it!" says Sage as she storms towards the stairwell to the upper levels where her mother's being held.

Queen Elisheba is prepared for such an outburst. Her memories have already been wiped, and she's rehearsed her reaction to news of King Pulsar's death since the night of their wedding. The queen's saferoom is an elaborate cage with amenities fit for royalty. The queen is in her robe and appears to have just taken a bath. She's sitting in front of her vanity having her makeup done by an android servant.

Sage bursts into the safe room without warning. The doors are left open, revealing two guardsmen knocked out lying on the floor. The combat droid programmed to protect the queen starts to engage Sage who obliterates the combat droid with a single energy blast.

"What's the meaning of this?" screams Queen Elisheba as Sage tackles her to the ground, knocking her off the chase lounge in front of her vanity. Sage's tentacles wrap around the queen's head, absorbing her memories.

Queen Elisheba's six-foot long tentacles grab ahold of Sage throwing her across the saferoom. Sage hits the reinforced wall as if she had been struck by a truck. Sage takes a moment and starts processing her mother's memories. She can feel her mother's hatred towards her father but sees nothing of a planned assassination. She realizes, based on her memories, Queen Elisheba was unaware of the king's death.

Queen Elisheba grabs a statue in the room with her tentacle legs, moments away from throwing the two-ton statue at Sage. With her memory wiped, Queen Elisheba's unaware of her role in the king's assassination. Her first thought is suspecting her daughter of taking the crown by force. She sees the pain in her daughter's eyes and stops herself from attacking.

"Father's dead!" exclaims Sage as she starts crying uncontrollably. Queen Elisheba lowers the statue and makes her way over to her daughter to comfort her. Sage catches her breath and tells Queen Elisheba, "I thought you had something to do with it... I was certain. I'm sorry."

The queen holds her daughter in her arms, saying, "I thought he would be fine. Guardsmen were en route. It was only a handful of attackers. Everything happened so fast, I don't remember how I... I'm going to find out how your father died, and we'll—"

"I was there!" says Sage as she pulls herself away from the queen. "He was killed by a group of mutant assassins that knew our security protocols and weaknesses." Sage composes herself, calming down by explaining what happened.

Queen Elisheba slithers over to her wardrobe and orders her android servants to put on her armor. She gives Sage a stern look, saying, "You thought I had something to do with your father's death? And why weren't you in your saferoom waiting out the attack?"

Sage is too distraught to form a sentence. Queen Elisheba says, "Go to your quarters and debrief with security after you have some time to gather your thoughts. Pulsar has healing abilities, so there's a chance—"

"NO, HE'S GONE!" screams Sage out of grief and anger. Sage shakes her head and realizes she's lashing out at her mother unprovoked. She apologizes, pleading, "I'm sorry! I'm so sorry..."

Queen Elisheba nods her head to accept Sage's apology, responding, "I need time to digest this. If what you say is true...I hope you stealing my memories has cleared my name. Leave me to grieve the loss of my husband. I'll deal with the bureaucracy, so you don't have to. You just get some rest."

Exhausted and in shock, Sage starts walking towards her quarters without a word. As Sage leaves the saferoom, Queen Elisheba releases the tears and emotions she was holding back in her daughter's presence. She knows a series of telepaths and empaths will be interrogating her for hours, along with others close to King Pulsar. Queen Elisheba mentally prepares herself for a long night, taking a moment to mourn the loss of her husband.

The queen's android touches up her makeup as she looks at herself in the mirror, saying, "You were born to be queen. Rule with your heart and without mercy." The queen stands up, collects herself, and exits the safe room with her personal combat droid in tow. Queen Elisheba heads towards the infirmary to confirm the death of King Pulsar. Afterward, she will be expected to testify in front of a tribunal and undergo telepathic interrogation.

From the other Colonies' perspective, Kronus had a peaceful Commencement. Queen Elisheba now has a legal claim to the throne, having executed a well-thought-out plan to maintain her innocence. Commencement has just begun, and Goldie will need to quickly adjust to her new role as the leader of the Coalition.

Back at Coalition Headquarters, Goldie is inside her meditation chamber surveying Kronus in astral form. She can sense the psychic resonance from the priestesses battling with countless mercenary telepaths. Kronus has been placed on high alert, and projection on the astral plane has been prohibited. Goldie is powerful enough to explore undetected, breaking the law out of necessity. Internal reports from Kronus regarding King Pulsar's death have already leaked online, forcing Goldie to find answers.

Goldie levitates in a metallic sphere designed to amplify her psychic abilities. Her training over the past few days has opened a new world of possibilities. She's learning to use her powers without restraint with professional oversight allowing her to test her limits. Goldie has evolved into a leader and a political powerhouse respected amongst world leaders.

Gill enters Goldie's room unannounced with a whirlwind of emotions, asking, "Is it true? Has Pulsar been assassinated?"

Goldie felt his energy before he entered the room, already recoiling her consciousness to the physical plane. Goldie lowers herself to the ground and opens the door to her amplifier tank, answering, "Someone wearing the king's crown was assassinated not long ago. Your king, the Evo who raised you...I feel he's still alive somehow. I'm seeing conflicting images. I'm sorry. I really am. I know you need answers, and I simply don't have them yet."

Gill finds relief, knowing there's a possibility his fears may be misplaced. He huffs, taking a seat, needing to clear his head. "It's fine. There's nothing you can do. Besides, you have more on your shoulders than the rest of us. How are you doing?"

"I'm fine, I guess. I'm not sure how to feel," says Goldie as she takes a seat next to Gill on a large chaise. "I was in hiding before all of this. I made ends meet using my powers, so I was forced to keep to myself. I need to work on being sociable again."

"You've been adjusting like a pro, if you ask me. Your role differs from the rest of us. We work in the field, but you and Cohol are the faces Colonial leaders see. It's a lot of pressure, and you've been adapting in stride," says Gill, being a reassuring voice she can trust.

Goldie lowers her head, sharing, "It's not like I had a choice. I've made millions in gambling halls across Lennek. I've been living in hiding for years. Meeting all of you at that press conference was the first time I left my house in weeks. I wasn't made for the spotlight."

"None of us are. I've transferred combat skills to most of the warriors in the Kronusian military. I've been in the spotlight since I was a teenager. The light burns if you let it," says Gill, speaking from the heart.

They both get an alert requesting their presence in the war room.

Goldie looks at the hologram projected from the communicator on her wrist and says, "I appreciate your insight. I honestly couldn't have done any of this without your help. The skills and knowledge you transferred gave me the confidence to take lead. Thank you!"

"You're more than welcome. We're help to help each other," says Gill as he reads the message from his own communicator.

Goldie explains, "It looks like our help's needed in Carthage. Thanks for taking the time to talk with me." The pair stand from the chaise, preparing to head to the war room.

Goldie gives Gill a hug, and their physical contact triggers a vision. She sees herself levitating with a group of mutants combining their powers to stop a fast-moving wall of water. The tsunami overpowers the mutants and Goldie's swept into the water, unable to move or think. She feels her body go limp as her lungs fill with water. Goldie's vision is intense as her body starts to convulse as she levitates in place. Her eyes are completely white as she experiences the physicality of drowning. She feels Gill's presence as he saves her from the water before her consciousness snaps back to reality.

"Are you okay?" asks Gill, keeping a safe distance as Goldie's vision passes. "Just breathe. You were gasping for air. I take it you had a vision?"

Goldie catches her breath before answering, "I was drowning. There were other mutants with me. I think we were trying to stop a tsunami. You saved me. I didn't see much...other than water."

"Maybe you should sit down. It's just a debriefing. Take some time and recover," says Gill in a concerned tone, hoping she takes his advice.

Goldie assures him, "I'm fine. My visions are just getting more complicated to understand. The more I learn about my powers, the more I wish I had a different mutation. The two of us hugging must have triggered my powers somehow. I'm okay, promise!"

Gill takes a deep breath, folding his arms, convinced Goldie is pushing herself too far. He reminds her, "It's alright to be afraid. I see the physical toll your visions have on your body. I understand why you're uncomfortable with your powers. It's okay not to be okay. We're here for you. All of us."

Goldie nods her head and forces a smile as the pair head to their debriefing preparing for the next Commencement. Carthage, Angkor, and Zion still have their ceremonies underway. As the Guardian for each Colony shuts down, history changes immeasurably differentiating Colony to Colony. Goldie may be afraid, unsure, or even angry over her lost anonymity, but she knows sitting out is no longer an option for her. As leader of the Coalition, she has responsibilities with a team that's counting on her.

Another message comes through her communicator requesting her presence. Goldie takes a deep breath, then says, "They're waiting for us. Let's not disappoint."

Gill nods his head as the pair head to the war room for their next mission.

About the Author

Rickey O Lofton Jr., a visionary American author born on April 26, 1987, in San Bernardino California, embarked on his literary journey at the tender age of 13. His debut publication, "A Surrender to the Moon," featured in the esteemed International Library of Poems, introduced him to the world of wordsmiths. Transitioning seamlessly from poetry, Lofton delved into ghostwriting within the music industry, crafting lyrics for countless songs, screenplays, and novels.

Throughout his formative years, Lofton's multifaceted talents shined brightly. A recipient of accolades as an award-winning journalist in High School, he showcased his adaptability through internships with prominent media outlets such as the Review Journal, Channel 13 News, and Channel 3 News in Las Vegas, NV. Amidst his academic pursuits, Lofton also pursued his passion for sports, acting, and modeling in Los Angeles, securing roles in independent films and commercials under ACME booking.

Drawing inspiration from his childhood dreams and extensive research, Lofton weaves intricate narratives that seamlessly blend history, futuristic technology, and his innate gift for storytelling.

His magnum opus, "Seven Colonies," sprung from the depths of his diaries, painting a vivid tapestry of a future governed by chimeras and advanced androids, with a poignant commentary on global warming and environmental stewardship.

In his subsequent works, such as "The Last Makaran" and "The Merrow Womb," Lofton effortlessly traverses between past and future, seamlessly integrating elements of magic, folklore, and dystopian themes. With each novel comprising multiple volumes, Lofton lays the groundwork for immersive franchises that transcend traditional literary boundaries.

Driven by a passion for both entertainment and education, Lofton's creative endeavors extend beyond the written word. His vision encompasses a multimedia landscape, spanning novels, audiobooks, comics, video games, and cinematic adaptations. Through his innovative approach and unwavering commitment to environmental consciousness, Lofton aims to captivate audiences worldwide while leaving a lasting impact on the literary, film, and gaming industries alike.

You can connect with me on:
- https://www.7colonies.com
- https://x.com/7colonies
- http://www.facebook.com/7colonies
- https://www.instagram.com/7colonies
- https://www.tiktok.com/7colonies
- https://www.youtube.com/7colonies

www.ingramcontent.com/pod-product-compliance
Lightning Source LLC
Chambersburg PA
CBHW031205310726
48969CB00001B/227